About the Author

For those out there who are curious, he's Nicholas. He turned eighteen in June but he's been writing since the dark ages (primary school). He lived in a town called Hemel Hempstead up until he moved to university. He doesn't have many friends, that's why he had time to write a book. But he couldn't have done it if it wasn't for his friend Ellie showing him creepy lyrics from a musical song. She knows which one. He's definitely experienced an up and down life, but who hasn't these days? Now excuse him whilst I wait 2 years for therapy.

The O.S Project

Nicholas Armitt

The O.S Project

Olympia Publishers
London

www.olympiapublishers.com
OLYMPIA PAPERBACK EDITION

A CIP catalogue record for this title is
available from the British Library.

ISBN: 978-1-80074-892-7

This is a work of fiction.
Names, characters, places and incidents originate from the writer's imagination.
Any resemblance to actual persons, living or dead, is purely coincidental.

First Published in 2023

Olympia Publishers
Tallis House
2 Tallis Street
London
EC4Y 0AB

Printed in Great Britain

Dedication

To Ellie. We've come a long way since Year ten science.

Acknowledgements

Thank you to each and every person who has helped me reach this far, thank you to my mum for not thinking I'm a lunatic after writing this, and especially thank you to my old school teachers for having lessons so boring that I thought up this entire book instead of revising.

Chapter 1

My Name's Noah

Well... Isn't this strange? I, um... How am I meant to start this? Um, my name's Noah. Coleman. That's right. My name is Noah Coleman. That's one of the few things I was able to remember. Right now, I'm sat in a room at the Ocean Cliff Psychiatric Hospital. I don't know why I'm here, and don't know how either, but I know I'm not allowed to leave. The staff all use the same excuse on me. 'It's for your own good.' So I just listen to what people have to say and follow the rules. The rules and the regime. I haven't got the entire list of the rules at hand, but I do have my own personal timetable. It tells me this:

Room locked: 7p.m. – 8a.m.

Breakfast: 8a.m. – 9a.m.

Room locked: 9a.m. – 12p.m.

Free Period: 12p.m. – 1p.m.

Lunch: 1p.m. – 2p.m.

Free Period: 2 p.m. – 5 p.m.

Dinner: 5 p.m. – 6 p.m.

Free Period: 6 p.m. – 7 p.m.

Lights Out: 11 p.m. – 7 a.m.

Medication given at 9.15 a.m. each day.

Psych review every week at 11.30 a.m. in Office 16. Each weekday.

Psych Test: 1 and 15 of every month at 10.15a.m. in Test Office 4.

My psych review is actually the best part of my week. I'm allowed to be in contact with someone who isn't regarded insane. I'd say crazy, but you don't use that word around here, it's degrading. Insane isn't much better, but it doesn't affect people as much when its used. Mostly because that part is actually true. We aren't sane, but we're not crazy either.

The people here are okay, I guess. About eighty-five per cent of the patients are so hyped up on meds that they don't do much else other than stare into space or talk to themselves. The rest of us just shuffle from one room to the next, watching the world go by.

When I get bored, the most common thing I do is read. Not books, more of just what's around me. Wherever you go, there's a poster hanging on the wall. They say things like 'Need someone to talk to? We're here to Help,' and 'Reform is Around the Corner.' I guess the staff think it spreads positivity and makes them feel like they're trying, but all it really does is act as another layer of wallpaper.

The thing I've read the most out of everything is my I.D. band. I pretty much have it memorised by now.

Patient Name: Noah Coleman. Sex: Male. Patient #1975. Date of Birth: 19/11/1999. Date of Admission: 17/02/2022. Sector 3.

Oh, right. I haven't actually written why I'm doing this yet. Like I said, I don't know why I'm here. I don't remember much about my life. I've been told I have amnesia – Retrograde Amnesia if we're talking professional terms, and possible Anterograde. My memory is dangerously and unpredictably fragile. I've got no idea about who I was, who my friends were, or even who my family is.

I do have a general idea of what my life was though. I *did* have one. I think that's the thing that drives me round the bend the most. I know that I had a life before all this, I know I didn't just randomly appear in the world. I can feel I have a past, I just don't know what it is. The majority of my memories feel like they've been lost in a fog, or that they didn't really happen, like they happened in a dream. Of course other memories are just gone forever, there's no trace of those. But there's no point in me worrying about what I can't remember from the past, it's forgetting what's left that's the main concern. That's why I'm writing this. I'm taking any chance I can to stop me from forgetting what's left.

Especially people. Especially the ones I can't see every day. Actually, it's more like the *one* person that I can't see every day. My literal partner in crime – Aaron. I'd say boyfriend in crime, but that doesn't really have the same ring to it. I don't know what caused me to only remember him – nobody really does – but it's something that keeps me hopeful. What a magical romance! The amnesiac and the gem collector! A true love story!

Anyway, I've had memories come back to me before and it's mostly from when I've seen him in visitation. He's allowed to see me every now and then. He can't come all the time, he has to catch the train to come here, and he does have his life to attend to, but when he comes, he tells me stories about things that are happening in that outside world, and I tell him stories that go on in here, which isn't much. Mostly small, pointless things that no normal person would probably find conversation in. I'll probably write the same kind of thing in here. Small, pointless things.

Like the scar on my neck. A small, pointless mark that definitely hasn't always been there. That's another one of those foggy memories, I know something happened, but I couldn't tell you a thing of where it came from. The scar's not massive, just like a scratch. You can't see it because I'm so pale, but you can feel it. The outfits they make us wear doesn't help with my skin either, I basically fade away. If it weren't for my hair, I probably would.

Pastel blue, that's the colour of my sector's outfits. It's one of the only things to bring us some colour around here. Everywhere else is completely white. The tiles in the corridor, the paint on the walls, all of it. The only time when there isn't the piercing emptiness around me is in the offices, probably because the staff get sick of it too.

My room used to be white, it technically still is, but I got to cover it with my own stuff. Paintings, drawings, magazine pages, posters, and whatever else I can get my hands on. It gives me something else to look at instead of blank concrete. I will confess that I did steal one of the posters that they had hung up outside, but hey, it was nice. It had a picture of the ocean on it. I like the ocean. This place may be named after one, but you can't see it through any of the patient windows.

My window's by my desk, just at the right position for me to sit on it and imagine that mystery of a sea. Whether it's like the one on my poster – smooth and blue – or like the one I saw on the TV in the common room – rough and grey. The best place for me to think is looking through that window, the glass may be two-inches thick with bars on the outside, but when I fall into a daydream, it's almost like there's nothing there. I sometimes end up falling asleep up there, even though I have a perfectly good bed, I sleep better on the table. Of course, when the doctors notice me they force me to get back into my bed, even though they all know I'm better by the window.

I asked if I could have my bed moved to the window once, but that suggestion was denied. I tried to move it myself, but then I jammed the wheel at the end and now the bed can't go anywhere. I blame the fact that

13

they hadn't replaced the furniture in years. It's *definitely* not my fault.

Then, whilst writing, I was sat on my bed and heard a sudden knock at my room door, and I flinched. I looked up and watched as the light above the frame flashed green with a buzz and a woman stepped through. She was short and plump with dark tan skin and black hair tied up in a bun, her white doctor's coat swinging around her knees as she turned to face me.

She smiled as she approached me. "Afternoon, Noah. Feeling okay today?"

I lowered my journal and brought my knees to my chest and held them tightly, gripping at the blue material. "M-hm."

She stopped beside my bed and gestured towards the space at the end. "Is it alright if I sit down?"

"Yeah… sure."

She sat by my feet. "Okay." She touched my journal and moved it to the side.

I watched her movements intently as she placed it down on the sheet.

"I'm sorry. Was it okay that I touched your book?"

I pulled my legs in tighter then gave a timid nod. "Yeah, yeah. It's fine."

"Good," she replied with a relieved smile. "Let's get you your medicine then, shall we?"

I glanced at the clock on the wall then nodded and we both slid off of my bed, the woman watching me closely as I stepped across my room and approached my door. I stopped by the black painted line on the floor that stretched across from one wall to another, forbidding me to get too close to the exit. The doctor gave a thumbs up at the one-way glass and the door buzzed once more. She stepped through to the other side and I waited for her permission to step through too. The door closed again, leaving me stood waiting. I tapped my foot on the carpet rhythmically as I counted the seconds.

When you live in such a systematic place, you learn all types of things. From which staff members are working at which stations to how long my medicine takes to kick in. After five counts I heard another door slide open and close then watched as my door unlocked again. It slid up and I stepped into the airlock room and waited on another line, this time a yellow one. As one door shut, another opened. The door that faced the corridor had a slot below the window, which was meant to be used for you to place your wrists on so that the staff can restrain you. I had to do that for my first five months, it killed my hands, but after they realised I wasn't as threatening as they originally thought, they stopped and just let me walk straight out. As I stepped out to the corridor, I met with the woman and a man, who was also dressed in a doctor's coat.

The woman smiled as I caught eyes with her. "Alright, let's go."

We headed down the corridor, passing airlocks to the other rooms in my sector. When I first got here, I was registered to stay in Sector 1 – AKA Dark Down. So called because it's where the most dangerous patients are kept. The wing's underground and the outfits are this coal black colour. If you get taken to Sector 1, you're labelled as 'going dark down'. The people down there are the ones that have done some seriously dark stuff, which is another reason I worry so much about my own crime. I really do fear it sometimes.

It was all a bit of a blur down there for me, but a few weeks later I was transferred up to here, Sector 3 – AKA Riptide. Everyone here is calm. But that's why it's scary. It's too calm. The patients who are kept here rarely break the rules. We just get shuffled from one place to the next without any drama. But if you take a wrong move – if you break the system – if you say a syllable in the wrong dialect – you can get dragged into rough waters. Just like a riptide. Never underestimate the power of a riptide, just like you should never underestimate the power of someone in Sector 3.

We reached a door to an office off the side of the medical ward. This unit is a pretty small place, considering this is meant to be a hospital. The walls are pieced together by large, white-painted bricks, whereas the rest of Riptide is just concrete and metal with a weird, cushioned lining across the bottom half. The waiting benches are made out of some kind of wood, but I don't think it's real – it's too smooth. Then I get taken to a bed and have a blood test.

That's only for my physicals, though, this is just medicine. I get taken out to take my medicine just in case I choke or have anything else happen to me when I take the pills. There is a lot that I have to take so it makes sense. I have to take four in total. One for every part of me that's broken. I get given a cup of water to do each one with and whilst I take them I look like I'm trying to do shots down the club. That's what one doctor described it as. I laughed after the others did, even though I didn't know why we were laughing. My medication is given to me as quick as possible to keep me from getting too adrenalized and bolting down the corridor.

15

As the doctor's led me into the room, that's what they immediately did. They checked my name, they checked my dose, then passed me the paper cup of coloured tablets. Ten seconds later they were all gone, and I was marched back to my room again.

I felt their effects pretty quickly. My entire system became drained, my energy flushing from me and leaving me in the dazed state the rest of the patients were usually in. My escort lightly grabbed my limp arms and directed me home. With each step I became heavier and heavier, almost like my canvas shoes were magnetised to the floor. My pupils dilated and my eyelids drooped as my head bobbed up and down. My heart rate slowed, and my hands tingled, the blood in my body feeling like it had reached its end.

Before I knew it, I was face down on my busted bed with my head buried into the puffed-up pillows. The woman I was with tutted and rolled me onto my side to stop me from suffocating myself. She slipped my shoes off and placed them by my cabinet then moved my journal onto my drawers. I tried to lift my arm to stop her, but the weight on me was so strong that I barely raised my little finger.

With one last look at me, she sighed. "Get some sleep, Coleman."

Her words echoed around me as I watched through closing eyes as she left my room.

I didn't get any sleep. The thing was, I was too tired to sleep. I don't know how that's possible. Instead, I just laid there staring at the mirror on the wall. I couldn't move. I couldn't really do anything. That's the joys of drugs, and these were only the mild kind. Other people get given a lot worse than I do. I don't think I want to know why they get so dosed up.

After a while, I started to regain my movements again. I pushed myself up from my bed and swung my legs over the side then fell onto my back. I groaned in annoyance. This is always the worst part. Every time, after about an hour, the real effects kick in – as do the side effects.

I hoisted myself onto my feet then fell against the drawers, trying desperately to grip at it with my nails. I took slow and seemingly exaggerated steps towards the sofa underneath the mirror until my left knee buckled and I fell onto the arm. I grunted as I tried to push myself up again, but the door alarm distracted me, and when I looked up, a man entered.

He grabbed my arms and directed me back onto my bed. "Noah, you know you've got to stay in bed for at least two hours after your medication."

16

I laid back down, my head crashing against the pillow again. "I can't…
I'm not… tired."

The man shook my blanket out. "You need to, Noah. It's too risky for
you to be up and about when your body isn't ready yet."

I closed my eyes then rolled onto my other side to face the bathroom
door.

"If you move from the bed again I'm gonna chain you to it for the rest
of the day, understand?"

I pulled the blanket over me and trembled at the thought.

"Good," he replied, understanding my gesture. "Now sleep." His
footsteps distanced and he disappeared into the air lock.

I made my body go limp and tried to fall back into my original state. I
shuffled around for a while, but I still couldn't manage to fall asleep. I never
can. Sleep is terrifying. Your unconscious body left alone for anyone to
sneak in and do what they like to you.

Another hour passed. I heard the sound of the doors unlocking half an
hour before, but I couldn't bring myself to move. It was only lunch. Nobody
ever shows up on time, we're all too high to realise that we're hungry. The
canteen's not that great either. It's just this vast space with a few rows of
plastic tables and chairs lined up together, all boxed in by bright painted
yellow lines on the floor. The food hatch only opens during mealtimes
otherwise they risk the chance of patients reaching the kitchen. The
downside is that if you don't make it to the meals on time, you won't get a
chance to eat until the next allocated period, or you can starve yourself until
you go into shock and get fed through a tube. The doctors do try to urge the
patients to go to meals even if the patient says otherwise. It's in the rules to
eat, so we've got to stick to that.

This is why I try my hardest to make it to the meals, but I never feel
well enough to eat the food, that's why I'm so underweight. The medication
makes me nauseous and lethargic, so I hardly manage to gain enough
energy to lift my spoon into my mouth, and then from the few mouthfuls of
food I do swallow, I only end up bringing back up again later. The doctors
have tried to find me a medicine that doesn't give me this reaction, but
there's yet to be a drug that one: keeps me from relapsing, two: doesn't
make me ill, and three: doesn't react with my other medication. So that's
why I just follow the system. You step in. You follow the lines. You wait.
You sit. You eat. You wait. You leave. Like clockwork.

17

So, that's why I ended up trudging down the hallway of the hospital with sunken grey eyes and my hoodie covering my ears. I joined the almost empty queue of dazed men and approached the counter. The worker on the other side carelessly passed the trays over to each of us, every so often stopping to give over the specially made trays for those who needed them. I was not one of these chosen few. I got what was on the commoners menu. A buttered roll, a pile of shrivelled vegetables, and a pot of strawberry jelly.

At least I don't have to eat alone. I've got Kyle. He's one of my very few friends. We actually look quite similar, except he has a blonde, curly quiff, with freckles across his nose, and his eyes are this sharp green colour, whereas mine are a more washed out blue. I can see why people would get us confused if they didn't know us closely though. We're similar heights, we've similar accents, and we both enjoy staring out of windows for no particular reason.

He sat down opposite me with his matching food and stared across the table at me. "You okay, mate?"

I stared back carelessly as I tried to keep my head up.

"I'll take that as a 'no'."

I drifted me eyes down to my tray and poked a piece of spinach.

"Not hungry?" he asked.

"Starving," I replied, my lack of energy making it come across sarcastic.

Kyle scoffed then scampered his fingers across the table. He leant in closely to his tray then lifted his right arm that was cast out across the surface and reached in for his spoon. He kept his elbow raised just above the table as he stabbed each grain of food.

I laid my spoon back down on my tray and placed my hands in my pockets. I looked around, skipping from patient to patient as I watched each of them conduct their movements. Everyone had their own way around the canteen. Some ate fast, some ate slow, and some were like me and didn't eat at all. There were people who had to tap the table three times before picking up their cutlery, and there were others who had to eat underneath the table on the floor. As entertaining as it was, I had to move again. I felt the corner of bread that I ate rising up my throat.

"I'll be right back," I muttered and shot up from the table, rushing over to the door on the far wall.

I stepped into another glistening white tiled room and ran into one of

18

the bathroom stalls. I fell onto my knees and gagged. I sat there for several minutes trying to stop the room from spinning then clambered against the side of the stall and pulled the chain, although nothing came up. I stumbled over to the rows of untouched sinks that sat only a few feet from the toilets, but they felt much further. I ran the tap and slid down the boxed-in basin, crouching with my forehead against the porcelain and my fingers drooping under the gushing water.

"Oh… God…" I groaned as my body was overrun with a shivering warmth, and a shooting pain that pierced across the side of my skull.

I knew it wouldn't last forever, it never does, but each time it does happen makes me feel like ripping my skin off and bursting into tears. From the stage I was at now, I knew there wasn't long left of the cycle. By the time that this phase passes, I'll be back in a trance then by the time I get back to my room I'll be back to normal. Never in my life would I enjoy this feeling, but it saves me from the dangers of myself. If I want to keep going through the days then I have to sacrifice a few hours of them each time.

I took in a sharp inhale and pulled myself back up to my feet. I splashed my face with the freezing water then turned off the tap. I closed my eyes and ran my hands through my hair, the hood on my jacket slipping off the back. I scratched violently at my neck, the tingling and shivering feeling worst around my scar. I took in a few more breaths then opened my drowsy eyes again.

As I managed to recover, one of the staff members joined me in the bathroom. I glanced at her, and she stared back in concern.

"What are you doing in here?" she questioned.

"I… I, uh…" I panted and gripped at the side of the sink.

"You know you can't come in here without permission from a doctor."

I shakily stepped towards her. "I know… it's just… I really didn't feel well, and…"

Her eyes became fiery. "Have you been throwing your food away?"

"N-No…"

She quickly darted into each open stall, checking the inside of them before she returned to me. "Alright, show me your tray and I'll let you off after you've finished everything. I know you've only just come in here, so I know you haven't finished yet."

I nodded sheepishly then shuffled back over to my table with the woman following me. I sat back down and gently lifted the tray to show her the untouched food.

"Fine." She placed her hands in her pockets. "I'll be checking again. I know you're a funny one with food, Coleman, and I don't want you starving yourself." She then turned away and headed for another table of patients.

I let out a breath and looked back up at Kyle. He gave me an awkward smile before continuing to rapidly rip apart his roll. I stared back down at my tray, the sight of the food drawing back the queasy sensation. I powered through it, though. I ate the lot. From then, I presented the woman my achievement and she agreed to release me.

I then proceeded to dump my tray on the trolley, wave goodbye to Kyle, and march back into the hallway, keeping focus on the wall ahead. I flicked my hood back over my head and zipped up my cardigan. I placed my hands in my pocket as I started to drift to the side. My head grew heavy, and my gaze tilted to the scuffed lines that weaved from corner to corner. I followed it, trying to stay in line with it to keep from collapsing. I felt like I was in a maze. Switching directions with every few steps I made.

I passed many other Riptide patients on my journey, occasionally catching eyes with some of them and the both of us freezing for a few seconds before carrying on. It's kind of like a respect thing. Some people might smile or give a wave, but here we just stare at each other on the spot to demonstrate we're of no harm, we're just making our way through. I don't think anyone was ever told to do this, it just sort of happened. Just like the nicknames for each Sector.

I know I wrote about Riptide and Sector 1 before, but there's others too. There's eight in total, only five are used for patients. As the numbers increase, the danger declines. Unless you've been to one of them, you can only guess what happens on the levels above or below.

Sometimes at night I wake to shrieking coming from underneath me, quickly followed by the crackling of electricity. It goes on for about two minutes then stops for the rest of the night. It never happens at the same time, but it always sounds the same.

I've never actually heard anything from above me. Sometimes I wonder whether there's anything up there at all. Not once has a sound come from Sector 4. Maybe because the Sector 2 boys are too busy raving with their night terrors for me to hear anything else.

Then there's Sector 5. Sector 5 is for the people who had a choice in coming here, unlike the rest of us. We all have our own reasons for being at

Ocean Cliff, they just brought themselves here. Whether they make it through or not, though, is a game of chance. That's why it's called Freefall.

When you freefall, you live off of chance. Not only are you going to fall hundreds of feet to the ground, there's everything else happening around you. From the height you fall, you'll have no oxygen. You wouldn't be able to breathe. You'd be suffocating in the air and there's nothing you can do about it. There's also temperature. You might freeze before you suffocate. I can't decide which I would prefer. You'd be unconscious either way before you hit the ground, so would it matter? Still. It's chance. The height you fall. The weather outside. If you're equipped at all for this situation. You could live, but it's more likely you won't. Just like freefalling in Sector 5.

Kyle was from Freefall. He brought himself here because there was no one left to help him at home. He knew something wasn't quite right with him, but nobody took him seriously. Even here. By the time the doctors actually found a match to his conditions, he had already left. They tried to contact him, but they couldn't find him. Not until he was arrested for attacking his niece.

Turns out he doesn't see the world like a lot of people. His senses can change, and the things around him can move away. He can feel smaller or bigger than he really is, which is one of the reasons his niece didn't take his real size. He felt smaller than her when in reality he was six stone more and three foot taller. I don't know exactly what the condition's called, but it's something about Wonderland. Match that with bipolar and that's how he ended up three rooms away from me.

I've been told I have several conditions since I've been admitted. Amnesia is obviously one of them, another is delirium, and my third one is schizoaffective disorder, quite a few problems link off that last one. They found out I had them since my stay in Dark Down. Whether it was caused from being down there or not, it didn't matter. The doctors say it's more likely that it was caused from trauma in the past, which developed into me having quite jumpy reactions to things. They're trying to test me for PTSD, but because I have no memory, there's barely any evidence, aside from my running habit.

When I feel threatened or in danger, I run. I don't know why. It's my instinct. If something isn't right with me, I run. Most of the time I don't get very far – the place is locked at every door – but once I did manage to get

21

from the cafeteria to the stairway. I was caught before I could make it any further, though, which was probably for the best. This hasn't happened for a while. The doctors found a way to stop me from panicking too much now. They move slow and force me to keep my attention on one person. It may scare me sometimes, but it works.

I think it was Dr Olsen who figured it out. He's good at what he does. It's probably why he was made the head doctor of Riptide. He's a very likeable man. Very charismatic. The first day I met him, I knew he was kind. You can see it in his eyes. I think he comes from London, I'm not sure though. I'm not good at accents, I just take a guess, as well as listen to other people's conversations. London's up north, right? Or is it south? I know it's west of me. This place is in Maldon or something?

I haven't seen a real map since I've been here, but I do have a train one, Dr Olsen actually gave it to me. It was part of an experiment they did to test my memory. They wanted to see whether colours had any effect on improving my condition. It turns out he was right once again. They were the only part of the map I could remember. All of the stations and line names just blurred together. The coloured lines are all that I can make of it. I keep it Blu-Tacked on my wall by my desk. I swear, I ended up dreaming about those coloured lines for about a week.

There's really not much else to do when you're locked in a room. That's why you try your best to make something out of anything. Before I knew that you could request for items, I used to try and unscrew bolts from my chair and roll them across the floor, each time trying to get them closer to each other. It may not sound fun, but it was one of my favourite things to do. That was until the staff caught me walking around with a screw in my hand in the hallway. They let me get away with unscrewing my stuff because they knew I was only doing it to play a game, and they knew I'd put it back once I was done, but when I had a relapse with the screw, they banned me from doing it again. I still want to know what I was planning on doing with that screw and how I managed to get so far from my room with it, but I guess that can go on the list of things that everyone is asking. There's a lot on that list.

Like I said, you can ask for items and activities for you to do. It can take a while, though. First you have to fill in a form for what it is you want, then give it to your counsellor or one of the guards watching from their room on the other side of the mirror if they're there. They look into what you want, then examine whether it could be used dangerously towards yourself or others. If you pass their test, you can say hello to your new pass time within the next week. If you fail, your request goes in the shredder and the leftover paper is given to the guinea pigs in the courtyard.

That's right, we have guinea pigs. Last time I checked, there were six. Cookie, Cleo, Ginger, Blossom, Bluebell, and Nemo. I think my counsellor's daughter named them when they dropped them off here together. They're kept in this fenced off section by the far wall with a big wooden hut and grass across the bottom which has mostly been gnawed to the roots. They're pretty cute. My favourite's Cookie. She's this light brown colour with dark speckles all across her back. She likes to climb up my chest and fall asleep on my shoulder, and if that's not good enough for her, she keeps scaling me until she nestles in my hair.

You have to get special permission to be allowed near the guinea pigs, this place does have quite an array of people with… certain attributes, so the staff have to make sure that you're safe to work with animals. They use the guinea pigs for a lot of reasons. Therapy. Behaviour tests. Emotional consideration. Or just as a reward. Mine was the latter. If I've shown an improvement or just simply behave, I get to sit with them for an hour. I may have to sit in a cage, but it's worth it. My counsellor usually sits outside on one of the benches and watches me, sometimes even sitting in there with me.

She's a young woman, I think she's about thirty-four. Her name's Dr Maddens, but she lets me call her by her first name. Jaiden. She's the one who does my psych review. She has hazel eyes with thick matching hair that flows just past her shoulders.

Jaiden's another one of the rare, nice people around here. She actually lets you talk to her about normal things or what you want to do, and she does try to help you. We chat often about her life, probably because I'll forget everything the next day. I know she has two kids, both girls, and her husband's called Tom. I'm not sure what he does, apparently he works a lot. Jaiden's also the one who came up with this journal idea. She gave it to me as a present for my birthday, but I didn't find a use for it until now. We're both hoping for it to work. I'm hoping that I start feeling better than I do now.

If I'm honest, I've been feeling kind of down lately. I think I've only just come to realise that I'm not going to see the outside for a long time.

Your thoughts wander at this time of night. I fell asleep after dinner. I woke up again at about 01:00 AM. Wide awake. I tossed back and forth on my bed then after ten minutes I gave in and sat up. I slipped off the sheets then stepped over to the window, which casted the only bit of light. I checked my clock which hung on the wall just above the one-way mirror. I sighed as I saw the time then picked up my hoodie that was folded up on the table in front of me. I slipped it on over my head then hoisted myself up onto the surface. I shuffled towards the wall, brought my knees to my chest, then leant my head against the glass.

As I stared through the bars at the horizon, I felt a slow phantom-like weight crawling up my back and the growing feeling of guilt pressing down on my shoulders. The guilt of too many things. It sneaks up on me when I least expect it to. When I feel my best, I can count on it to bring me back down. Guilt is an elusive and devilish emotion, working off your other feelings to empower itself. Guilt is a manipulator. It's dangerous. To end the stream, you've got to find the source.

Chapter 2

Twist in the Path

Last night I had a bit of a rough sleep, followed quickly by a rougher morning. About fifteen minutes after I took a seat on my desk, the bed check officer came around and shone his flashlight into my room, spotting my absent bed. By now I had started to drift off a bit, but the pounding on my metal door shot me back to my wide-eyed state. When I jolted forward in shock, I almost forgot how to breathe. I swallowed and felt my chest tense as I stared at the silhouette through the glass. He pounded again.

"Get into bed. Now!"

I scrambled to the ground and stumbled across in the darkness towards my bed. The night guard kept his torch fixed on me as I dived underneath the blankets and laid my head on my pillow. I kept my eyes firmly shut and panted heavily as I waited for the light to disappear. He remained for quite some time but must have left when he got bored. His keys jangled and the airlock door facing the corridor opened and closed in sequence.

From then, he checked in on my room every hour. Usually, bed check happens at the beginning of the night and towards the morning. The guards never have the energy to keep up with the required checks that it says on the policy, so they just check at the start and the end then fall asleep at their station. I only know this because Jaiden told me a story about when she stayed late one night and saw Officer Kingston asleep with his head on the desk, his mug in one hand and his flashlight in the other. I'm guessing it wasn't him who was on watch last night, he wouldn't have been bothered to keep unlocking the airlock each time. Because of this repeated cycle of light, I became too anxious to sleep. Every time I started to maybe drift off, the flashlight would come along again to freak me back awake. In total I think I got about 3 hours' worth of sleep.

When I knew we were allowed to get moving again at seven, I pulled myself to my feet and shuffled into the bathroom. I pulled the door towards me, hooking my fingers inside the gap that replaced the door handle – they get taken out for safety reasons, the insides are replaced with a soft Velcro lining. I stopped by the sink and turned the knob on the sink and splashed my face with whatever water could seep out from the tap. I pulled my almost cardboard towel towards me and dabbed away the excess water. I hung it back then sluggishly stepped back out to my room.

I shuffled over to my calendar that was hung on my wall by the desk and lifted the marker that was rested in my pen pot. I crossed off yesterday, flipped the calendar to the next month then sighed as I read the date. December 1st. The worst dates are on the first. And the 15th. They're the dates I have my psych tests. They're something I can't predict. They're never the same. You get taken by a doctor through to a small box room and get told what to do through the window. The first one I had in Riptide, I was terrified. I was terrified for three straight months after I was moved from Dark Down. The psychologist gave me an audio tape and I had to repeat back each word to her. Then they gave me a wheel with four coloured buttons on that illuminated in sequence. My job was to watch them as the colour lit up and press the button to match it. Each time another colour added, and if I pressed one incorrectly it would buzz and start again from the beginning. The noises it made scared me too much for me to focus on the actual task. I was so scared that I ended up dropping it and cowering in the corner away from it. It sounds silly to me now, but with all that happened underground I was on the edge of snapping. Because of this, I've yet to enjoy a psych test.

Thankfully, I have from breakfast to prepare for it, until 10:15, that's when it starts. Speaking of breakfast, I was more than ready to eat. Breakfast is how I gain energy to make it through the day, since I can't eat at lunch and barely make it to dinner. The menu for today was orange juice, burnt toast, egg, and the drabs of bacon left over from the staff meals. I took my tray from the man behind the counter and joined with Kyle at the table, along with another patient, Shawn.

Kyle's not my only friend in this place. I've met with quite a few people here in Riptide, whether or not they like me is a different story, but I know Shawn does. He's tall – a lot taller than me – but not quite as scrawny. He also has this swirling blend of hazel and emerald in his eyes, one a lot greener than the other. They're always locking some kind of suspicion behind them, it's why people call him Shifty Shawn. I don't tend to like it though. He's the least shifty guy here. You know what he's doing when you're around. He's looking for a friend.

We met when I was working with Jaiden once. My job is to help make sure that her and Dr Olsen's files are in order – not the patient files, just staff lists, deliveries. I'm not allowed to read them (I'm technically not even meant to be allowed near them), but they trust me enough to touch them and move them into the correct place on their shelves. Alphabetical. A to Z. Although I don't think I've seen half of the alphabet on Jaiden's shelf. They're always the same letters. I hope that someone asks for a xylophone just so that I can cross the letter X off.

That's how me and Shawn bonded. Yes. Our bonding started with a letter. Like with me and Kyle, Jaiden's his counsellor too. One day I was stood by the back of her office, tidying up as I usually do, when Shawn stepped in. Then stepped out. Then stepped in again. And then stepped out again. I tilted my head in confusion as I watched his repeated movements over and over until about the sixth time he stayed inside with me. He tapped across Jaiden's desk rhythmically then tapped his foot on the ground and stopped. That was when he caught eyes with me.

"Oh, uh. Oh, uh. I'm sorry. I didn't, I didn't know someone was in here."

"It's okay. I'm not really meant to be in here anyway. Jaiden, I mean, Dr Maddens lets me help out in here sometimes."

"Oh, okay," he said with a positive grin which quickly followed by a zip of his hoodie four times. "What's your name?"

"Noah," I said as I turned back to the shelf. "Yours?"

He walked over to me, clicking his heels on the ground when he stopped. "It's Shawn."

"You having a good day, Shawn?"

"I guess. I guess."

"Good." I crouched down and shuffled the folders along, Shawn following.

"Watcha doing?" he asked.

"Oh, I work in here. Y'know, just sorting out things, making sure they're positioned right."

We both rose again.

"Like how people think of me?"

"What?" I questioned as I scanned him up and down.

27

"OCD? You know how people think that… You know how people think that it's all about positioning and stuff?"

I shook my head. I can quite easily say that I didn't know that. I had no clue what he was talking about. "I'm sorry man, I don't know what you're trying to say."

"Obsessive Compulsive Disorder?"

I felt my head drift down, the feeling like I had insulted him pushing it more. "I don't know…" I replied shyly.

That was when we heard Jaiden enter the room. She smiled up at the two of us. "You okay, boys?"

We both remained silent as we stared at her.

"Fellas?" she continued with concern as she approached.

"Nothing, Dr Maddens," Shawn replied with another few zips of his hoodie.

She scowled at us in a humorous way. "Hmm. I'll trust you."

Shawn smiled then circled the sofa before sitting down.

Jaiden rubbed my shoulder. "Thank you for your help, Noah. You've been really great at organising this lot. I could barely look at it before." She chuckled.

"Thank you." I lifted one of the files from the pile and shook it in my hand. "You know, nobody in Riptide has asked for anything beginning with the letters V and X. There's this big jump and it's annoying me!"

"That annoys me too," Shawn added.

"So, I'm not just being weird, right? It's annoying int it?"

We caught eyes and laughed weakly at one another.

I placed the file back down then headed towards the door. "Bye," I said quietly to Jaiden. "Bye, Shawn."

"Bye, Noah!" he replied with a grin on his face.

I stepped into the hallway and lightly closed the door.

From then we couldn't stop seeing each other. Everywhere I went I ended up finding him tapping across a windowsill or zipping up something. Shawn told me all about his OCD and why he was so eccentric. He says that keeping in a high mood keeps him from turning to other things. He tells himself that if he's happy, then he believes he will be. I don't know if it works or not. He doesn't like to talk about what he's done to himself or others as a result of what goes on in his head, but for the most part I know he just lies in his room on the floor, staring up at the marks on the ceiling with a veil of emptiness disconnecting him from the rest of the world. Well… That's what he used to do. I don't know about anymore. He doesn't talk about it now. He acts like there was nothing there in the first place.

You never know whether he'll be feeling high or low, but all he really wants is someone to be around him, so I sat down opposite Shawn at the table and flashed him a quick smile. He gave one back then continued running the edge of his spoon back and forth across his tray before tapping it and placing it back down. Since our misunderstanding from our first conversation, he knows about my unstable memory, and I feel that he worries I'll forget him. I worry about that too, but there's not much I can do to stop that from happening. That's why I make the most of when the three of us are together.

"Do you ever wonder if the universe will come to an end?" Kyle began, holding his toast in hand.

Shawn and I glanced at him in intrigue.

"Like, the universe is always expanding, yeah? But, what if it expanded so far that it met with the other side and then it stops?"

Shawn shrugged. "If it did, would it be a bubble?"

"A bubble?" Kyle questioned.

"Well, if it wrapped all the way around, wouldn't it make a sphere? The rest of the planets and stars are spheres, so wouldn't the universe be? Then if it met, would it keep trying to grow and then, like, explode?"

Kyle froze and stared off into the distance. "Oh." He darted his head friskily back and forth across the room with a fearful look on his face.

I bit my lip to keep from laughing at his humorous actions. Kyle does make me smile. I don't like to show it too often, just in case he's having an episode in Wonderland, but I do tell him when I know he's firmly on Earth.

I yawned and drew both their attention's away from their existential queries.

"Are you okay, Noah?" Shawn asked in concern.

"Huh?"

"Are you okay?"

I nodded and rubbed my puffy, grey eyes. "Yeah… I'm just… tired. I didn't get any sleep last night."

Shawn ran his finger around the edges of the orange carton. "You didn't look so good at dinner either. Did something bad happen?"

I shook my head. "No, I felt really drowsy from my pills and fell asleep through till the middle of the night then couldn't get back down again. Then the night guard saw me awake and wouldn't leave me alone for the rest of his rounds."

Shawn sighed, seeming relieved. "Yeah, they, uh, they annoy me too," he took a sip of his drink. "What's the plan for today then?" he asked with a smile.

I shrugged. "I dunno... I got my tests today, so I'll probably be trying to recover from that trauma."

"I had mine last week," replied Kyle. "They made me do some weird drawing task. They told me a word and I had to draw how I imagined it. I thought I was allowed to draw how I liked and add things to it, but then they scolded me for not following instructions and now I have it on my record that I failed the task. I didn't know that it had to be accurate!" He jabbed at his toast in anger.

Shawn gripped at his spoon, finally being able to start eating, then tried his hardest to break up the burnt bacon. "I swear they make them tasks purposely more difficult than they need to be."

He was right. The tests are near to impossible. The thing is, they're easy tasks. Anyone should be able to do them, but the doctors, they put you off. You focus so much on trying to prove that you're normal to them that you just end up screwing yourself over and ending up worse. Then it goes on your record as a downgrade. That's what happened to me today.

After breakfast, I was given my pills, and laid in my room for an hour to recover before several staff arrived and escorted me back towards the medical unit, where I was placed in a small box room. I stepped in and the metal door sealed shut behind me, barely waiting until I was clear from the mechanisms before sealing. I scanned around the pewter painted room, my body still adapting to the sedative. The only furniture with me was a metal table with a matching chair. Atop the table were a stack of red plastic cups and a light purple ball resting next to them to the left, a stack of pictures in the middle, and a notepad and pencil on the right. On the wall above it all was a thick, tinted window. It was barely transparent enough for me to see through it, it looked as though a crystal sheet had frozen over it. But as I continued to inspect the area, a voice came through the speaker on the wall, she sounded blunt.

"Mr Coleman?"

I faced the window and noticed a blurred figure in a white coat.

"Please, sit down."

I hesitantly pulled the chair out and sat at the table. I held my hands in my lap as the woman continued speaking.

"We've set out some activities for you to do today."

I reached out for a cup and inspected it as she explained to me my instructions.

"All of your tasks are specially designed for your psychological level. Your first involves the red cups and ball. It's a simple recall task. Place the ball under a cup and move them then find the ball again. I will be monitoring your actions and responses."

This was proved to be easier said than done. I pulled the stack of cups towards me and pulled each one out. In total there were five. I rolled the ball towards me and caught it in one of the cups before it fell to the floor.

"You can use any number of cups you desire," said the woman.

I stared at each one until I decided on using three. I moved the remaining two to the floor then slowly scraped each one around on the table. I focussed on the one I knew I placed the ball in then lifted the cup to reveal it. I grinned from my success and looked up at the window.

"Very good."

I covered the ball again, repeating the motion. I lifted the cup to reveal it once more and felt pride grow inside me.

"Keep going. You're doing well."

I continued, over and over picking the right cup. Each time I felt more happiness within myself. Until I lifted the cup once more. It was empty. And there were no longer only three cups, there were four. My pride fell. I lowered the one in my hand back onto the table and tried another one. It was also empty. I leant back in my chair and sadly placed it down.

"Don't worry. Try again."

I lifted up each of the cups until I found the ball. I inhaled deeply as I focussed as best I could on it, but that didn't seem to help. I still got it wrong. I never let the cup leave my sight and I still got it wrong. I pushed them to the side but kept the ball in my hand. I rested my head in my arms as I leant against the table.

"It's okay. Just move to the next task."

"What do I have to do?"

"Do you not remember what I told you?"

I looked up at the glass in confusion. "You didn't tell me anything."

31

"I told you twice and you confirmed your understanding. Do you not remember this?"

I swallowed and shook my head before burying it again.

"I see." I heard the scratching of her pen against the paper. "Please take the pile of pictures in front of you."

My panic started to settle in its usual place, making me slightly twitchy. I reached forward and dragged them towards my face. I kept my head on the desk as she explained.

"I want you to look at the pictures on each card and place them to the side. If you see a picture you think you've seen before then place it in a separate pile. Do you understand that?"

I nodded and sat up again. I tapped the pile against the table to straighten the edges then held them in my hands as I analysed the pictures. The cards were all white with a singular cartoon image in the middle, all in an array of colours. The first was of a dog. It was bent down in a playing position with its tongue dangling out of its mouth. I placed it to my left and turned to the next card. This time the image was of a grey kitten sat with its head tilted. I placed it on top of the dog and continued happily with the task for the next few minutes until I found a card that I thought had repeated. I looked up at the doctor as I placed the card to the right.

"Am I doing okay?"

"Just keep going until you've reached the end. I'll tell you the results after all three of the tests."

I lowered my head, afraid that I had done something wrong. My hands trembled slightly as my anxiety grew.

If I was okay she would have told me, right? Why wouldn't she tell me if I was passing?

As I became increasingly nervous, I knew my memory was starting to flicker. Each time I went to place an image down, I would hold my hand hesitantly above the pile, doubting myself that I was correct. I let out a small whimper as I became overwhelmed with my own thoughts and overlapping memories – whether they were true or not was what was driving me towards the edge. I had a lump grow in my throat and my knees bounced up and down.

"Mr Coleman? Are you feeling okay?" asked the woman.

I twitched my head back and forth between the two piles as I reached the final card. "I, um… I don't… I don't know."

She sighed and scribbled more on her paperwork. "Alright, we'll finish that task there."

I placed the final card down between the two piles and pulled at my sleeves.

"Please place the two piles into the slot beside the window in their separate piles."

I nodded and rose from my seat. I grabbed both of the stacks and lightly placed them beside one another before the slot sealed. I jumped back then returned to the chair. I failed. I hadn't even finished the whole test yet and I already knew I failed. I've failed the past three months, what makes a fourth? I heard the doctors shuffling on the other side of the wall as they examined the piles.

Between the two voices I heard, they made small comments to each other.

"That one's a repeat."

"He can't distinguish the animals and their colours."

"About half, I'd say."

"That's in the other pile."

I picked at my nails and hung my head shamefully. I couldn't hear everything they said, the walls muffled their voices too much for me to understand.

The main examiner pressed on the microphone button again and a slight feedback echoed through the speakers, making me cringe. "Mr Coleman."

I looked up sorrowfully.

"Would you like me to repeat the final task?"

I bit my lip and nodded.

"Okay. I am going to say a string of words, and after I would like you to write down each that you remember – it doesn't matter how you spell them. Do you understand?"

"Yes…"

"Please, repeat the task."

"I have to write down all the words I remember you saying…Spelling don't matter."

"Very good. Now…"

I inhaled deeply and sat up straight as she spoke, concentrating the best I could on what she was saying.

"Blue."

"Wire."

"Car."

"School."

"Boy."

"Apple."

"Pencil."

She continued, saying each word in the same tone. I tried to preserve each one in my mind as she said them. It felt one hell of a long time before I was allowed to pick up the pencil. By now though, I had given up. There was no point in me trying to finish a task when I knew I had already failed.

"Okay. You may now write your answers."

I quickly picked up the pencil and scribbled across the lines, desperately writing whatever was still in my mind. I got down the few she began with but froze up once I got to my last memory. I sighed then slowly laid the pencil down in defeat, my head dropping with it.

"Done…" I muttered, then chucked the notepad onto the shelf below the slot. I heard the metal slide up and down then let a tear seep out onto the table.

"Thank you, Mr Coleman," the doctor said with a mix of disappointment and carelessness. "Please stay where you are as we unlock the door."

I remained still as a stream of beeps and thuds fought against each other until the door opened. I pushed myself up, using the table for support, as an officer approached and held me by my arms. He assisted me to the door, and we stepped back out to the corridor together. I shuffled along, my feet trudging along the tiles as we approached a door to a new room. I was pulled to a stop and waited in position for a doctor to take me inside.

The lock clicked and a man directed for me to step through. The officer remained outside as the doctor closed the door. I pulled at my sleeves as I watched the two nurses in the room move back and forth collecting different materials from secured cabinets. I kept my sight on them as I heard the man speak behind me.

"Mr Coleman? Please take a seat on the bed over here."

I turned around and stepped over to a small medical bed with a sheet of paper rolled across it. I hoisted myself onto it, my legs swinging back and forth as I waited for what was to come.

After the psych test comes the vitals test, which means needles. Several needles. I wouldn't say that I have a total fear of them, but more of the things they do. I'm fine with the doctors and nurses using them on me because I know they're trained in using them, so it's unlikely that anything will go wrong. The reason I don't like them is because I can feel everything that they're doing to me. I can feel as my blood gets drawn out and sucked from my veins. It just makes me so uncomfortable. I usually close my eyes when it happens, but once I saw the process when there was crashing outside that made me flinch. I saw the different vials of my blood sticking out of a tray and I freaked out. I shot up from the bed frantically which caused the needle and tubes to get ripped out of my arm. My body had an internal shivering feeling all over as it happened then I passed out from fear. I woke up with a bandage around my arm and back in my room. Ever since then, I refuse to open my eyes during a blood test.

Before my blood does get stolen from me, the doctor checks the rest of me. You know? Breathing. Reflexes. Make sure I'm still alive.

As the doctor prepared for today's check, he read over my file. "Alright." He brought over a green plastic case and placed it beside me. "How have you been feeling recently, Noah? Not feeling off or anything like that?" He clipped a pulse metre to my finger on my right hand and twiddled with different knobs on the machine beside the bed.

I shrugged. "Felt pretty normal. Got sick from my meds again."

He sighed as he adjusted his stethoscope around his neck. "We're doing the best we can to find you something. Lift up your top for me."

I followed his request and rolled up my two layers. He placed the stethoscope buds in his ears and ran the freezing drum across my chest.

"Breathe in." He listened carefully. "Breathe out." He repeated the two commands as he moved the drum to different positions, then did the same across my back. "Okay." He took the stethoscope away and rested it back around his neck. "All seems good there." He jotted down his information on a clipboard then lifted the blood pressure cuff. "Arm, please."

I lowered my top then rolled up my sleeve.

The doctor wrapped the cuff around my arm. "You're gonna feel a slight tension. Don't worry." He squeezed the pump, the cuff tightening around me and causing a tingling down to my fingertips. He glanced at the metre and nodded. "That's all good." He rose from his seat and stepped over to the nurse, whispering in her ear.

35

Oh, God. Oh, God. Oh, God. What's the problem? No, wait! He said it was all fine. Of course, he could be lying. They all lie, that's what they do. They lie.

My paranoia started to weasel its way into my head, and I began to tremble. I still had the cuff around my arm, and I caught a glimpse of the device attached to the end with its numbers rapidly climbing and falling. I faced the pulse metre and watched as my pulse jumped up and down at an increasing speed. I shuffled on the spot as the doctor noticed the unsteady beeping. He rushed back over and rubbed his hand on my shoulder.

"Hey, hey, calm down. It's alright." He ripped the blood pressure cuff off of my arm and placed it back in his case. "Sorry, Noah. I didn't mean for you to work yourself up like that."

I took in a few deep breaths as the tension around my arm ceased and the pounding in my chest started to calm. "S-sorry," I stuttered in embarrassment.

"No, no, don't be! It's fine. I know how you can get. It's my fault." He reached into his box and pulled out a small stick with a funnel on the end and a flashlight on top of it. "I'm just going to check your ears now, okay?"

I nodded and gripped at my I.D. band as he stuck the funnel into my left ear.

"Okay, good," he said softly as he moved around to my right.

My eyes twitched as I saw the flashlight flicker in my peripheral.

He removed the device and returned to his original place. "You're all good." He then reached into his case for a final time and pulled out the needle and tubes for the blood test. He caught a glance of my fear-filled eyes. "It'll be over in a flash. It always is, isn't it?"

I shrugged and kept a hold of my arm defensively. It's always over quickly, but that doesn't mean it doesn't hurt. No matter how fast or slow something happens, pain will still happen – nothing around that. The only thing you can do is pray that the pain doesn't linger, and it goes and gets on with its life. I inhaled and presented my arm to the doctor, holding my breath as he prepared to pierce my skin with the needle. I clenched my eyes shut and turned my head away as the familiar scratchy feeling occurred.

"You're alright," the doctor said as I felt the blood gush out of my arm.

I tried to smile, but only let out a whimper.

"It's almost done."

I bit my lip and nodded until the moment passed.

"There," he said with a smile as he taped a cotton bud to the injection site. "You can take that off in an hour."

I hadn't even realised that he'd taken the needle out until I looked. My arm felt heavy and lifeless, so I wiggled it about with my other hand to try and regain its life – almost like an arm resuscitation, I guess. Nothing happened, but I seemed to entertain the others in the room since they all gave a chuckle as I flopped it from side to side.

"You're all good here, Mr Coleman," the doctor said as he passed the case of my blood to the blonde nurse.

I lowered my arm. "What about my other stuff? You haven't even measured me yet."

"We've got a new doctor to do those things now."

I shuffled anxiously on my seat. I've never been good with new people, especially doctors. New patients I can handle because they aren't in control of what I do. New doctors, however, I can't do. Who knows where they've come from or where they go or who they tell their stories too. At least when you tell a patient a story the furthest it can get is a few rooms down – and that's counting if they listen to the story at all. The staff? They leave at the end of their shift to go home and see their families and tell them whatever strange stories they've heard from work that day.

"I like it when you do it…" I said.

He gave a chuckle. "Noah, I've been here long enough to know when you're lying."

I hung my head down shamefully.

"Hey." He tapped my knee. "If she does it wrong, it's not on you. You're the patient, remember?"

I nodded and he helped me down from the table.

"But what if she does get it wrong? How am I gonna tell anyone?"

"She won't get it wrong," he replied as he walked me over to the door. "Trust me. She's come up from another hospital, so she's done this all before."

I was given back to the guard and directed towards the next stop. The whole of the medical unit had the exact same doors with the exact same space between them. It felt like I was in some kind of time loop hall. It wasn't a time loop though as we did eventually reach the required door, and we stepped through together to enter a newly refurbished room. Of course, it looked the same as any other place in the hospital, just shinier and not riddled with decorations (or vandalism as some of the staff like to call it).

As we entered, a bright-faced nurse approached me. "Hello, Noah. You doing okay, love?"

"Is it bad if I say 'no'?" I replied.

"It's perfectly fine to not be okay. That's what the psych meetings are for." She separated me from the guard and sat me on a bench in the waiting area. "Dr Wilks will see you in a minute, okay?"

I nodded and watched as she disappeared into the next room. The guard had also left me, and so I was left alone with one other patient opposite me. We both acknowledged each other with a quick stare, but we remained in silence. Occasionally, we would glance back at one another then look away as we'd get caught. On about the fourth look, I noticed that he had a rather worried manner. I wasn't sure if he was worried because of me, or because he also didn't feel his best around new people. Either way, I guess I was making him uncomfortable since we had never met before.

I don't think.

Around ten minutes passed until I was finally collected. A woman – very young in appearance – stepped out from behind the wall and called for my name.

"Noah Coleman?" Her voice was rough and made both me and the other patient tremble slightly.

"Th-that's me," I stuttered as I rose from the bench and began to approach her.

"Stay there. Show me your I.D. band," she ordered.

"Um, okay..." I returned as I shakily lifted my arm to present the plastic around my wrist.

She analysed it carefully. "Alright. Follow me."

She swiftly turned back around and marched into the room she had emerged from. I exchanged one last glance at the patient before heading into the next room. I checked the place out before moving on.

It was bare, just like the waiting area, with the only things on the shelf being a mixed stack of files. Opposite that was a desk with two chairs on either side and a computer facing the window behind it.

"Close the door. Come here," Dr Wilks said bluntly.

I nodded and gently let the door go then slowly shuffled towards the desk, Dr Wilks sticking her arm out and pointing at the plastic chair as I reached her.

"Sit there."

I immediately followed her command and sat down, fearing to make contact with her.

She laid my file out in front of her. "Noah James Coleman." She typed onto her keyboard.

The file was only a few inches away from me and I took a chance at reading it. I edged forwards slightly as Dr Wilks' head was turned and began to read over it.

'PATIENT NAME: Noah James Coleman.

D.O.B.: 19/11/1999

SEX: Male

D.O.A.: 17/02/2022

DIAGNOSIS/CONDITIONS:

Retrograde Amnesia

Delirium

Schizoaffective Disorder (Bipolar Type)

SUSPECTED CONDITIONS:

Anterograde Amnesia

PTSD

REASON FOR ADMISSION:

Coleman was—

Then before I could read further, Dr Wilks snatched the report away from me and snapped it close.

"What do you think you're doing?"

I sat back. "I wasn't doing anything… I was just looking…"

"You know that you've been told to not read your file. Don't think that they didn't tell me."

"I-I'm sorry," I stammered.

"And so you should be." She turned away and continued to read my information away from my sight.

I felt rather teary, but given the way she'd spoken so far, I didn't want to risk crying in front of her. She probably wouldn't approve of it. I had a chance, and I couldn't even take it. Everything I read, I already knew. If she didn't want me to read it then why put it out for me to see?

I kept my head hung as she turned back. "Right." She clicked her pen. "Have you had any of the following: blurred vision?"

"No…"

She scribbled on the page. "Nausea and/or vomiting?"

"Yeah."

"Restlessness?"

I nodded.

"Dry mouth?"

I had to think about that one. I wasn't quite sure how to answer, I didn't know what classed as Dry Mouth, but apparently I needed to know quickly as Dr Wilks repeated the question in a firmer tone.

"Yes or no, have you experienced dry mouth in the last two weeks?"

I quickly shook my head.

"Have you had any dizzying sensations?"

"Yes."

She turned away again, and I let out a sigh of relief. I felt like I was taking a quiz that I didn't know the answers to. How is that even possible when the answers are of my own accord? I moved my hands underneath my thighs and listened to Dr Wilks as she questioned me about each of the side effects of my medication. That is one long quiz.

Once it was over, Dr Wilks read over the data and muttered to herself. "Well, that doesn't add up."

"What doesn't?" I asked sheepishly.

She groaned. "That's none of your concern. Go and wait on the bench outside until I say otherwise."

I quickly scampered off of the chair and returned to the waiting room. I sat back in my original place and rocked back and forth as I tried to hold myself together. I looked around for the other patient, but he had vanished. He had probably gone through the same fate that I had.

I waited patiently for Wilks' return; it wasn't for another fifteen minutes that she came to get me. I was taken back to the room and forced to stand on a scale. I had to take off my shoes and my overtop to reduce any unneeded weight, but it didn't make much of a difference. I was still the same as last time.

Dr Wilks scribbled on her clipboard. "Do you skip meals, Coleman?"

She didn't even use my first name. I'm only called Coleman on two occasions. Either because the person wants to keep their professional stance or because I'm *really* in trouble.

I shrugged. "Sometimes I forget and sometimes I can't eat because I feel too ill, but Dr Olsen or Lloyd usually comes and finds me."

40

"Aside from those times, do you still eat?"

"Well, um… I don't really know. It depends."

"It depends?"

I pulled at my sleeves. "Y-yeah. Sometimes I'm not in the mood."

She scribbled on the clipboard and spoke maliciously. "I see."

I stepped off the scales and approached the height board, but Dr Wilks called me back.

"Coleman, do you realise that the medication you take usually promotes weight gain not weight loss?"

I did know that. That's something the doctors here took a while to understand, but that's because I lied to them about feeling ill. I was too scared to tell them the truth, plus they know that I can barely eat and take that into consideration.

"I've been told," I replied bluntly, slowly becoming agitated by her pressing queries.

"Do you understand the fact that your irregular meals could be contributing to your current state?"

I looked away. "I don't know…"

She scoffed then forced me under the height board, pushing the scale down harshly so that it clipped my head before she stopped it.

She gave a smirk upon seeing the number then jotted it down on the paper. "Five foot six."

Yes, I know. I'm not average height.

I pulled my top back over me and slipped my shoes back on, gaining my one centimetre of size back. "Am I done?"

"Yes, at last," she replied as she stepped back over to her desk. "You can leave now."

With a final deep breath, I exited the exam room and knocked on the window for the nurse to unlock the door for me. She stepped out and freed me, giving me a few moments until I was collectively scooped up by a herd of other patients and the guards. I clocked the time when I was leaving, and I knew I only had a few minutes until my meeting, so I stayed with the group until I reached the door outside. I took a seat on the bench outside and drummed my fingers on the plastic, eventually leading them to pick at the stuffing that was peeking through the wall pad.

After a while, I heard the door unlock and Jaiden said her goodbyes to another patient who swiftly disappeared around the corner. She sighed then caught sight of me on the bench.

"Oh, hello, Noah. You ready for your meeting?" Her voice was so refreshing after the Wilks ordeal that I could finally let my front drop.

I smiled up at her. "Yeah, I'm ready."

She grinned back and reached her hand out for me. "Good. Come on."

I lightly held her hand as I rose from the bench, and then followed her into the office. Jaiden settled into her position on the sofa, preparing her items around her, whilst clearing the one's from the previous patient. I hesitated by the door, unsure of where to go as I struggled to recover from the numerous amounts of tests I had undergone throughout the day.

Jaiden looked over at me. "You alright, Noah? You're looking a little frazzled."

I shook my head to break from my dazed state. "Yeah... I'm fine." I shuffled over to the sofa opposite and balanced on the edge of the cushion.

"So, do you want a drink or anything before we start? I can find you something nicer than water if you'd like?"

I flashed her a smile and shook my head. "No, thanks..." I then lowered it again and picked at my nails.

Jaiden noticed my mannerisms and instantly flicked into her psych mode. "Noah, is something bothering you?"

I shook my head and laid back, the pitch in my voice increasing as I spoke. "No. No, I'm fine."

She lifted her notepad and clicked her pen. "Don't you lie to me, mister," she said jokingly. "Tell me what's the matter and you'll feel better."

My attention began to drift. "Today's just been... a lot."

"I know. What was it you've had today? Was it two..."

"I had three separate medical routines. This is my fourth one."

"Wow. How did they go?"

I kept quiet, hoping that she would understand that I wasn't in the mood to share.

"It's alright." She placed her paper back on the table. "I'll tell you what."

I glanced back at her.

"Why don't we make a deal that if you answer me the questions on my form then we can find something more fun to do? That sound alright to you?"

"Okay..."

"Alright." She smiled and reached for the clipboard. "So, on a scale of one to ten, how would you rate your current emotional state?"

I raised my eyebrow, and she gave a chuckle. "I'd say about three."

"What's your reason for this?"

I shrugged. "Today hasn't been the nicest."

She continued to ask the questions from her sheet, and I continued to give my vague answers. The first page is usually just generalised stuff, they get given to all of the patients, then the second page is more direct.

"When was your last schizoaffective attack?"

I cast my mind back a few weeks, barely even being able to tell if it actually happened or not. "Um… Two weeks – no – three weeks back. I had a pretty wild mix going on after I got a bit upset over the movie night."

"Yes, I remember that. It wasn't your fault though."

"It felt like it."

"I know, Noah." She tapped her pen on the side of the sofa arm. "Now, have you had any feelings of paranoia?"

My voice shook. "Um, maybe…"

"There isn't a wrong answer. It's just an overview of what's been going on with you."

"I get them a lot, and it's not like when the narratives start. They come all at once in a few seconds and then go again."

My paranoia is a main part of my schizoaffective, but it differs from hallucinations. With my paranoia, I tell myself things just to mess with myself and most of the time it only comes when it's triggered, whereas my schizoaffective comes with hallucinations of flashes and colours with, what I call, narratives. I get voices in my head that just tell me exactly what I'm doing and how I'm doing them, and unlike my paranoia, it comes at random times but is more likely to come when I'm panicking or stressed. Then if I'm *really* lucky, I'll get both at the same time, and that's one hell of a ride.

Jaiden continued to mark off each of the questions, and as she did, I became more and more restless. I started to pull at the stitching on the sofa, causing the lining to fray. Then with a final sigh of relief, Jaiden lowered the clipboard and tucked her pen away.

"There. All done."

I exhaled and closed my eyes, thankful that the ordeal of the day was over.

"So, what would you like to do, Noah?"

My mind was in a blur of exhaustion whilst my body was ready to run. "I don't know."

She glanced down at my legs as I repeatedly switched them over each other. "Why don't we go on a walk? Come on." She pushed off of the sofa and approached the door. She looked back at me. "You coming?"

I nodded then shuffled past her to the corridor. I yanked down on my sleeves as she joined me, only for them to fling back up again. We began our journey down the left, moving further and further away from the medical unit. As we ambled along, Jaiden and I talked. She told me about Tom and her kids, and how they're planning to go on a holiday somewhere together. She seemed hesitant to tell me that part, seeing as we both know I can't leave, I guess it makes her feel as though she's rubbing her freedom in my face, but I don't feel that way at all. I know I can't leave, it's not a secret. I don't want other people to avoid having fun in their lives because they know that other people have it worse. In a way, that will just make more people miserable. I'm sure others would disagree, though. Anyway, I like hearing about Jaiden's life, it makes me happy to know that she is, because she deserves it.

We fell quiet for a few moments and within the fallen silence, I worked up the courage to ask her what I was so desperate to know.

"Jaiden?"

She smiled at me. "M-hm?"

We came to a stop. "Why am I here?"

Her expression dropped and she shook her head with a breath. "Noah. You can't know. At least, not yet."

"People keep telling me that, but that doesn't make a difference to what I want to know!" My voice rose and caused a seemingly shocked manner through Jaiden, as she stepped back slightly and tilted her head. "I'm sorry. I didn't mean to yell…"

"It's okay." She moved her scarf around her as we continued walking. "I can understand why you would feel like that, I would too if someone was keeping something from me that I didn't know. But the thing is, Noah, the reason we don't tell you is because we believe it's the reason for your amnesia. Whatever it was that happened must have been too much for you, and your mind covered it up so that it won't hurt you anymore. That's what the brain does."

I stopped her again. "But can't you tell me one thing?" I fiddled with

44

my I.D. band. "Did I hurt someone?"

Her eyes remained focussed on mine as she bit her lip. "Every patient here has either hurt themselves or someone else, but in no way wanted to. That's why you're here in Riptide. You don't want to hurt people, do you?"

I shook my head.

"Good, because otherwise we'd be going straight back to that office," she said with a giggle.

We continued further, until after a while, we met with the man himself. Dr Olsen. He was stood outside his office with another patient who was sat on the sofa with a folded piece of paper. I just about recognised him from passing in the corridor on the way to Jaiden's meetings. He was the one leaving. His meeting finishes just before mine. His name's Justin.

That's one of his names anyway.

He's also Tim, Ollie, Jazz, and Ryce. They have DID. I know very little about DID, but Justin and his alters don't seem dangerous. I've talked to them once or twice, but they switched to Ryce halfway through and she doesn't like me very much. Justin always apologises for what she says to me, but I don't care much for what she does. She's one against four for liking me, which is a win in my book.

According to the doctors, I've had plenty of conversations with them, but when an amnesiac tries to talk to someone with amnesia walls, it's easy to say we don't progress very far with our relationship. Well, from what I do remember about them is that they all seem quite nice – aside from Ryce. She tends to be the grumpiest of them all.

Tim's very timid. I've only seen him twice and only spoke to him once. That's because Ryce came back and defended him from me. That's why she doesn't like me, she always thinks I'm gonna hurt her alters and so fronts to scare me off. It makes sense though – Tim's only seven. As for Jazz, she's quite the opposite of Tim. She's eccentric and sensual. She tried to hit on me once, but I had to explain to her that I had a boyfriend and she seemed rather betrayed. She obviously knows that she looks like a man and has a man's body so the fact I'm gay to begin with was probably a win for her, but then the boyfriend line ruined her dreams of love. Sorry, Jazz.

As for Ollie, he's the most relaxed out of the system. He hasn't the energy to cause trouble nor even fight to keep his place in the body. He retreats whenever someone else wants to appear, probably because there's nothing much for him to do.

45

In all fairness, I'm probably more dangerous than them. They've never been to a below sector. I'm more scared of what I'll do to them than what they'll do to me. I've heard what everyone says about me when I'm not around. Well, they *think* I'm not around, but I move in silence for the most part. People rarely know when I'm near them. That's how I learn things. The lines that are said about me.

'When he gets scared he gets violent.'

'Who's to know what the guy will do if a patient scares him.'

'He's not the brightest.'

'He's practically a child.'

'He barely knows what's real or fake.'

The thing is what they say is all true. I do get violent when I'm scared, I'm not smart, I never know whether what I'm living is real, and I do feel like a child – I certainly get treated like one.

I shuffled on the spot, as Jaiden came to a stop beside the duo. I picked at my nails uncomfortably as she spoke.

"Hello, doctor."

"Dr Maddens," he replied with a smile.

"What are we doing here then?" she asked.

"Justin's just teaching me how to make origami."

"Have you learnt anything?"

He pulled a crumpled piece of paper out from his pocket and presented it to her. "Not really."

The three of them chuckled.

Justin balanced his creation on the wooden arm of the sofa. "It wasn't exactly how it was meant to turn out."

"May I?" Jaiden asked, gesturing towards the paper.

Justin nodded with a smile and Jaiden picked it up. She fumbled with it in her hands then turned to show me.

"What do you think, Noah?"

I stared at it, trying to figure out what it was without asking. It looked like a flower, the folds reaching up around the sides like the petals of a lily. I got lost in awe at it and almost forgot to reply. I stuttered and tried to gather my words. "I like it."

Justin gave me a weak grin and I nodded back.

Jaiden placed the origami back on the arm. "It's very good work, Justin."

46

"Thanks." He took the paper back and held it in his hands.

Jaiden turned to Dr Olsen. "Doctor, is it okay if I speak with you a minute?"

"Sure."

"Thanks." She turned back to me. "We'll keep on our walk soon, Noah. Just wait there."

They stepped aside and spoke quietly to each other.

I shuffled over to the wall and leant against it. I glanced over at Justin who was seeming to try his best to stay conscious. His blinking became sluggish. He stood up and spoke the best he could at me.

"Bye, Noah."

"Bye," I replied as I watched him amble back towards the rooms.

I know he doesn't like people to see when he dissociates like that because he doesn't want to scare people. If he can tell it's going to happen he leaves whenever he can, but I tell him there's nothing to worry about. Seeing a guy stare into space is the least scary thing around here.

As he trotted back to his room, I began heading on a walk myself. I headed down the way I came. Very slowly. My head drifted to the floor, and I kept my eyes on the lines. Like usual, I didn't know where I was going – I wasn't looking. I just followed my feet. I was apparently walking rather quickly since I had already made it back to Jaiden's office, and that was quite a way from where we were. But, then I slowed right down again, returning to the pace I was at originally.

I scuffed my shoes along the tiles, accidently tripping on one of them and falling against the wall pad. That's why they're there, you see? For idiots like me when we fall over ourselves. I gripped against it tightly as I tried to steady myself and get back on my feet. Once I had, I continued on my way much more carefully. I reached the door to the examination room again and came to a stop. I caught sight through the closing crack and spotted another patient in incredible distress. They were being scolded by Dr Wilks and the nurses, whilst he sat whimpering on a bench. He made eye contact with me, seeming to try to call for help through the ever-so-desperate look in his waterlogged eyes. The door was then locked, and I tore my head away. I don't want to be biased or anything, but I don't think he did anything wrong, and I don't think he deserved what he was getting.

I persisted on my walk, heading down the splitting corridors. By now, I began to realise where I was heading too. When you start to reach an area

47

that's close to a staff area, the halls separate, the doors become more frequent. They all overlap each other, creating a maze that the patients can't understand. It was a clever design choice. No one ever knows where they're going so whichever way they take they'll find themselves back where they started. Sided with this, the floor lines begin to merge too, so my plans on following them became aborted.

I lifted my head and scanned around me. The walls were completely bare, not even a single poster hanging from them. I checked behind me to see an endless strip of hallway that broke off in two more directions at separate intervals – the entire thing porcelain white. I looked back down at the floor to find the line, but it had vanished. I had successfully managed to lose myself in the maze.

I was alone, the only sound being my footsteps echoing as I tried to find my way to civilisation. I was wandering for a good ten minutes, just lost in the glow of light that was bouncing off each surface from the window in the horizon. I scampered over to it, the glare of the sun passing me and revealing the staircase that led you towards the other sectors. Beside it was a metallic, whirring lift that I took on my journey up from Dark Down. In all honesty, I had no idea how I managed to get here. I must have passed at least two doors to even get through to this part of the hospital. All I could think to do was turn back and investigate, but as the thought came, I turned to see a frantic, panting Dr Olsen a few feet away from me.

He exhaled deeply, as he approached. "Oh, thank God. We've been looking for you." He lifted his radio and spoke into it. "I've found Coleman, I'll bring him back." He placed his hand lightly on my shoulder. "What are you doing down here?"

I looked back and forth between him and the staircase. "Um, I don't really know. I was just walking. I don't know how I got this far, though."

He began walking me back towards the patient wing. "Did you go through the admin door?"

I shrugged. "Probably."

"Ah, we've been having issues with that one, it doesn't lock properly. Been trying to get it fixed, but no contractor wants to come here."

"I don't blame them."

We both chuckled.

He pointed the tip of his radio at me. "Hey, if anyone asks, I didn't tell you that, okay?"

"Okay," I said with a grin.

We reached a door that wasn't too far from where I was, and Dr Olsen scanned his key card. The reader flashed green, and the door slid up. We stepped through and appeared around the back side of the storage rooms. We followed the corridor around and met with the main area again.

"I feel like I walked a lot further than that," I said to him as we calmly passed each airlock.

"That's what I say every time I exercise."

We continued to bounce remarks off of each other until we reached Jaiden who was waiting rather flustered outside her office. She had relief come over her as she saw me.

"Oh, Noah. You shouldn't run off like that, alright?"

I tilted my head down. "I know."

She smiled and rubbed my arms. "You scared me there. Look, I don't have enough time left for you today, but I'll see you again another time, okay?"

I was really quite saddened by that. I mean, it was my fault that I wandered off in the first place, but I really wanted to spend more time with her. She relaxes me and she doesn't judge me on what I say.

"No, no. It's fine," I lied. "There's always gonna be another day, right?"

She tapped my nose and I giggled. "Exactly."

Dr Olsen edged me away from her office as another patient arrived. "Come on, Noah. Let's get you back to your room."

I agreed and waved goodbye to Jaiden. I was then kept close by the doctor as we headed over to my room, his hand hovering around my arm. Before he unlocked it, however, he stopped me.

"Noah. I'm not sure if you've been told…"

My fear spiked.

"There's going to be a new doctor starting."

My frustration returned. "I know."

He looked surprised. "Oh. You do?"

I nodded. "Yes."

He shuffled then pulled out his key card again. "Ah, well, I guess that covers all I really needed to say to you. Nobody told me you were aware of the change, but here you are." He scanned the reader.

I stepped into the airlock and faced him. "Why do we need someone new? Everything worked fine before."

"I know that it's bound to cause some disruptions around here, but trust me, it'll help in the long run." He lifted his hand for a short wave. "Get some rest, mate. The rooms should unlock for free period soon. See you later."

I was then sealed into the airlock and entered my room. With everything that was racing around my mind, I needed some down time, even if it was only for twenty minutes. I kicked my shoes to the edge of my bed and shuffled around collecting materials before dumping them on the carpet and beginning a sketch.

Chapter 3

The Start of a Long Storm

About a week has passed since that draining day. Besides from the irritation that Wilks ensues on the patients, not much has changed – except this – it snowed. Not a lot, just a slight dusting. I didn't know it was snow when I saw it since I've never actually experienced it before, and when clumps of white started falling from the sky, let's just say that paranoia engaged. I tried to explain to Dr Olsen that the clouds were peeling away and that soon they were going to land on us, but then he cleared it up for me that, in fact, it wasn't the end of the world.

My routine hasn't changed. I still get up, sit in my room, wander the hospital, get given my pills, then pass out on my bed. Nothing happened to be reported. I mean, I did see Kyle in Wonderland talking to a guy who thought he was an imposter – so that was an interesting watch. They were both separated and sedated, so I didn't see Kyle for two days because he was still recovering from his episode, but he came back seeming totally normal. I haven't seen the other patient for a while though so who knows if he's coming back.

The only reason I came back to write was because of a chat I had with Jaiden. She told me she was leaving. Not only that, but something else too. I was sat with her in her office, just finishing off the usual stuff, when I noticed her demeanor become somewhat down. I was still smiling along at the time of the conversation until she spoke.

"Listen, Noah…" Her fingers interlocked. "I'm not going to be here for a few months."

"What?"

"I'm not sure of the exact date, but I won't be able to stay much longer around here. I received some news at home, and I need to be there to deal with it."

"Right…" My mind began to wander.

I don't want her to leave. Not now. Not with that woman around. Without her, my system will be damaged. It already is. What if I do something bad? What if I hurt someone and don't even want to? She won't be here to stop me from going down under again. I'll be back in Sector 1. Where I've been told I'm meant to be.

It was then that I realised I hadn't heard another word she'd been saying to me. We were suddenly by the door, and I was systematically nodding my head, agreeing to something I didn't know.

I stuttered then shook my head to re-shift my focus. "S-Sorry… W-What are we doing?"

Jaiden sighed. "Are you forgetting things I've said already?"

I couldn't quite work out the tone in her voice. It was a mixture of concern, annoyance, and worry. Whatever she was feeling, I didn't want to make her feel worse, so I shrugged and tried to act like I was trying to remember. This was the first time I've ever had to actually fake forgetting something.

"This is what I'm worried about, Noah. If you can't even remember what I'm saying to you now, then I'm worried that you'll forget other things. People: me, Aaron. Even day-to-day tasks."

I dragged my gaze to the floor.

"Look. If you have a relapse and I'm not here, then I'm afraid you might have to move to a new Sector."

I shot back up. "No! Please, don't send me back to Dark Down! I can't go down there again!"

"I know. I don't want you to go back down there. I've seen the effects it had on you. Sending you dark down again is our very last resort. It's for when all of our other options fail." She placed her hand on my cheek. "I will not let you get taken down there."

I nodded. "I'm gonna miss you…"

She sighed. "I'm gonna miss you too. But, hey! I'm not going right this instant. I'll be around for a few more weeks for sure." She reached for the doorhandle.

"But who am I s'posed to talk to when you're not here?" I questioned with a wave of my arms.

She retracted her hand and sighed. "Noah, have you been told about the new doctor?"

"Yeah, Dr Wilks. She's my new person who does the thingies," I replied, my mind going blank as I tried to speak.

Her voice became very mellow. "No, no. The new counsellor?"

My throat went dry, and I backed away, shaking my head. "No. I-I don't think… so…"

She reached her hand out towards me. "Noah, it's okay. Don't panic. He's nice. I've met him."

"H-he?" I trembled.

"Yes. I've spoken to him several times, he's been trained in all of the procedures here, and he says he's going to do his best to help everyone he sees. His name's Caleb."

I shook my head back and forth faster, pushing myself against the corner of the wall. "No, no, please. Please, I can't—I don't…"

She stepped over to me and held my hands in hers, shooshing me quietly. "It's okay, Noah. He's not starting until next week, and even then, I'll still be here whilst he adjusts. I won't let him send you downstairs."

I swallowed and nodded friskily. "Okay…"

"Okay." She edged me away from the wall. "Let's get you out of here, huh?"

"M-hm." I followed her out of her office and retreated to my room, the thoughts in my head spinning around with worry and paranoia.

She kept a hold of my arm as we walked. "I'm so sorry, Noah. It's just… I thought you knew."

I shook my head friskily. "No, no. I didn't."

"Dr Olsen told me that when he went to tell you, you said you already knew. I was confused when he told me since it was decided that only me or him were to give the news to you."

I stopped in place, the realisation hitting me. He was talking about the counsellor. A counsellor. First the medical monster, and now some replacement Jaiden. Two new people starting within a week from each other will not end well, not just for me, but for everyone.

I tugged at Jaiden's sleeve. "Why can't I just have one of the others that are already here? At least I know them."

"We thought about that too, Noah. We looked over a lot of things about it, but we couldn't move you to another counsellor because they're a part of the other patients' systems, and we didn't want to risk messing up two groups so instead we brought Caleb in."

She was making sense, but I was being too selfish and scared to hear her. I was refusing to believe it. "No, no. You can't leave. Please, you can't leave me here with them."

"I'm sorry, Noah, but I have to."

I was locked into my room once again and slid against the wall as I tried to process the changes that were to come. I haven't told anyone about the way Wilks treated me, I'm too scared to; what if it gets back to her that I'm the one who told on her? She'll probably have me slaughtered. Or just blame it on the fact that I'm 'the confused, delusional patient', and then she'll be here to serve another day. That's why I don't have the strength to speak up, I have no position of power to change anything, and now Jaiden's leaving I'll have even less.

I haven't dared question the other patients about it either, I don't want to trigger any of them by making them relive the moment – I'm even getting the shakes by writing this now. It seems silly. She was only doing her job. It's probably my fault anyway.

Just before my visit with Jaiden, I was taken to the medication area and given the paper cup. I took the pills then began the march back to my room. The hours of exhaustion and nausea followed, and I did the routine of laying in my bed face down to try and stop the room from taking off. It was a struggle when the time came for my meeting, but I managed to arrive in one piece. That meeting blurred past, and I was soon returned to my original position – lying motionless on my bed, my eyes watering and my body trembling as a cold cloak cast over me.

Later, the doors unlocked for free period. As they did, I nuzzled my head further into my pillow. My chest repeatedly jerked forwards as I fought to keep my tears locked up. I was doing well until my nose became clogged and I was forced to exhale sharply out of my mouth. That was when I let out the brief sob. It scratched up my throat as punishment and I continued to rock back and forth in regret.

Then came the grind of metal from behind and footsteps rushed over to me. I refused to look up at them, my restrained cries still building up. They sat on the edge of my bed and stroked my back gently.

"Oh, Noah," she said softly. "I'm so sorry. I really wish I could stay, but I can't."

"It's my fault," I muttered. "It's my fault you're going!" I sniffled and lightly pushed her hand away.

"It's not in any way your fault, Noah, how could it be?"

54

I shrugged. "I don't know... I get in the way of everything... I'm selfish!"

She leant forwards and gripped at my shoulders, attempting to roll me over. "No, Noah. Don't think that. That's not true."

I shook her off and reached for my blanket that was folded below my feet. I yanked it over my body and hid from her. "Leave me alone!"

"Hey, hey," Jaiden said as she lifted the corner of the blanket. "It's okay to feel angry, Noah. We get angry for a reason – that's why it exists."

I shuffled onto my side and stared through the gap at her.

She smiled in a comforting way. "Are you gonna come out?"

I chuckled weakly. "Is that a gay joke?"

We both gave a laugh and I burrowed back out from my nest.

"There you are," she said upon seeing my puffy face.

I adjusted my fringe then glanced up at her before I wrapped my arms around her. "I'm sorry, Jaiden! I'm really sorry!"

She rocked me from side to side. "Shh, it's okay. It's not your fault."

I nuzzled against her shoulder. "How long are you going for?"

She sighed. "I don't know, but when I find out, I'll do my best to tell you."

We separated.

"Okay," I replied with a sniffle. "I hope everything's okay at your house."

"It's fine. It's just family stuff, Noah. Thanks for asking, though."

I smiled. "That's okay."

She smiled back and glanced at her watch then quickly slid off of my bed. "Oh, gosh. I've gotta go. I've got another meeting to get to." She stepped over to the door. "You'll be okay, right?"

"M-hm."

She grinned. "Good boy."

I waved her goodbye as she vanished into the airlock. Then by the time lunch was called, I hobbled over to the canteen and joined the food line, the sedatives giving me another surge of drowsiness. Whilst I was queuing, I noticed paper cut-outs of trees stuck to the window. A doctor was stood beside it with a patient, who was holding the same paper trees in his hand. He stuck the final few onto the glass, positioning them carefully until he was satisfied.

This wasn't the only time when I saw this happening, the next week in the common room, a group of patients were sat on the floor rifling through a cardboard box of felt decorations. That was when I realised. It was December. I didn't quite understand the excitement that some of the other patients were showing, but I've yet to have had Christmas in my mind.

The first holiday I experienced around here was Easter. We were allowed to make our own ornaments out of different soft materials and take them back to our rooms. We were only allowed three each, however, because it was feared that one of us would use them in some way to hurt ourselves. That was the same reason as to why they were all taken away after the holiday ceased. My guess is that the same will happen for the Christmas decorations. By now, the time had almost come for the big day and I'm still waiting on the excitement.

It was likely that my excitement was being held back by the fact I knew another week had passed, and that meant one thing. The counsellor was starting. Whilst I was waiting for his inevitable arrival, I stepped over to the window. I glanced at the guard by the wall who seemed to be busy picking at the peeling bookshelf wood. I turned back and stared through the glass. The bars on the outside made it hard to see through – as did the frost on the window – but I still managed to catch the sight of a car in the horizon as it swerved down the road that ran towards the hospital. It disappeared behind the outer wall, and I drew closer to the glass. A sleek model in a shining silver paint job. It looked familiar. But it couldn't be. I couldn't have seen it before. It's probably just a popular car. It skidded into the car park, splashing the puddles of slush as it turned.

I heard shuffling beside me and faced it to see Kyle. "Hey," I said as I turned back to the window.

"Hey," he replied. "Watcha… Watcha doin'?"

"Watching."

Kyle followed my gaze out of the window. "Watcha watching?"

I shook my head and moved away. "Nothing." I stepped over to the sofa and fell back on it, pulling my legs up and kicking my shoes off.

Kyle shuffled along behind me and sat at the other end. He pulled a battered book out from his trouser band and opened it to the marked page.

As he sat there reading silently, I looked around the room at the others. There were a few characters dotted around. Some were staring at the walls. Some were busy sculpting towers out of clay at the craft table. There was a group watching an obviously intense game of draughts in the corner. Then there were men just watching the world go by.

Everything seemed fine. But it certainly didn't feel it. Something in my gut told me that the guy arriving wasn't going to be how the doctors have described him to me. My leg began to twitch up and down and I quickly grabbed it, holding it with the other to stop it from moving.

I leant against the arm of the sofa and bit at my nails, scraping the underneath with my teeth. I swung my legs back onto the floor and sat up again.

"I'm gonna... do something," I said to Kyle.

"Have fun," he said nonchalantly, not taking his eyes off of his book.

I pushed forwards onto the floor again and shuffled around the room. I checked in at the bookshelf, then at the games table, then at the craft table. I pulled open one of the plastic drawers and took out a piece of squared paper. I sat down beside another patient and picked up a pencil. I sketched across it lightly, marking an outline of an image. I spent the entire hour getting lost in the drawing. Colouring, shading, outlining, it ended up being one of my best pictures in the end.

Making things is actually a type of therapy for me since it helps me move my focus from panicking towards something fun instead. My sketches are also used for the doctors to investigate mine and others' memory loss. Since I wasn't taught how to draw here, it's theorised that my mind recognised the process from before the incident I had and continued as if nothing happened.

As I added the last few strokes of the chalk piece, a man cleared his throat behind me, and I very nearly shot my hand across the sheet as I flinched. Thankfully, my hand was just far enough away from the paper that I missed it. I turned to face who made the noise, and met with a tall, slender man with little hair and very dark skin.

"Mr Coleman," he said sternly.

"Hello," I replied, lowering the chalk.

He glanced over my shoulder at the picture. "That's very good."

I turned the page over to the blank side in embarrassment. "Thanks."

"Would you care to come with me back to your room?"

I swallowed anxiously then rose from the table, holding the picture in my hands. "Sure."

We shuffled around the craft area together until the man stopped me again.

"Coleman, why aren't you wearing any shoes?"

I looked down at my feet to see that all I had on was my black and grey socks. I hadn't even noticed that my shoes weren't on my feet. In a startle, I scurried back over to the sofa where I'd left them, relieved that they were still there.

"Here they are." I hooked them up with my fingers.

"You shouldn't take your shoes off outside of your room. You could lose them."

"Sorry," I said, wobbling from side to side as I tried to put them back on.

"Never mind," he replied with a fold of his arms. "Let's go."

He kept me close by him as we returned to my room. Waiting by the door were two more doctors, both women, speaking to each other. With them was a wheelchair with a straitjacket laying over the back. One was the lady who sees me to take me to my pills – Dr Phillipson – and the other was the doctor who handles patient transfers around Riptide. She's the first doctor I met in Riptide.

She turned to me with a calming smile. "Hello, Noah. It's good to see you again."

I nodded back to her, gripping at the picture in my hands and creasing the corners. "Hi."

"Are you feeling okay?"

My voice remained in a calm tone. "Yeah…"

I glanced at the wheelchair, the doctor catching me and quickly moving me into my room. I started to fall into a lost daze as my thoughts raced around, trying to connect the theories in my head as to why they'd need such restraints for me if it was just a meeting. Maybe they're worried what I'll do to him after the changes over the month.

I placed my drawing on my desk, not realising that I was staring at it in my head race. The woman cleared her throat, and I faced her again, the man waiting just behind her.

She stepped towards me cautiously. "We're going to get you into the straitjacket, okay?"

"Uh-huh." I continued to drift my eyes around my room.

"Okay." She lightly touched my arm before directing it into the jacket.

I think I was so lost in confusion that I didn't even notice what they were doing to me, until I snapped back to reality. As I did, my head and shoulders shook forwards, causing the other two to flinch.

I glanced between the two of them. "I'm sorry. I didn't mean to—Sorry."

"It's alright," the man replied as he hoisted my arm into the other hole.

As they both moved to the back straps, I began to mess around with the ones hanging off of my arms. I swung them back and forth, sometimes getting them caught in the other, causing the buckles to entwine together. I felt as the doctors continued to pull at my back, grunting every time it fell forwards again.

"Noah, sweetie?" the woman began.

"Yeah?"

"Do you mind holding still for us?"

"Oh, sorry…"

"It's okay," she replied before yanking the back tightly and fixing the straps in place.

I felt my skin get dragged along with the layers of fabric I was wearing, and it caused my body to shudder. With each strap, they constricted my movements further. They hadn't even tied my arms down yet and I was still losing my ability to move.

"I must be having someone special here to see me if I'm getting dressed up like this," I said, trying to make light of the situation.

"Very funny, Coleman," the man replied as he reached for my arms.

Together, they forced them across my body, wrapping them around so strongly that I was almost able to shake hands with myself. At this point, I was struggling to breathe. The buckles on my back were digging into my spine, my arms were at the brink of snapping, but they still weren't satisfied. They continued to pull at the straps, groaning that they couldn't go further than what they had.

The man let out a breath and stepped back. "There. Done."

As the woman kept a hold of my side, I felt my right hand start to cramp and I twisted back and forth, trying to find a better position.

The doctor checked his watch then pulled out the wheelchair. "Right, it's time we got moving."

He tapped the back of the chair and I wobbled over to it before falling back into the leather material and shuffling into position. They pulled one last strap across my stomach for good measure then waited for the door to buzz.

I don't mind being in the straitjacket so much anymore. I was wearing one when I was preparing to get on the bus to take me to this place. When Aaron hugged me goodbye, all I wanted to do was hug him back, but I couldn't. That was the first day of my new life, and the first memory that was formed since my past faded. There was a lot of shouting when I left, whoever it came from, they sounded desperate. I didn't get the chance to think about it because I was sedated during the travel.

I was wheeled through the corridors of Riptide and out to the mazes. They took me through the door that Dr Olsen told me about and weaved in and out of the walls, stopping by the lift. My chest started to flutter, causing my shoulders to jerk as my heart skipped. I whipped my head from one doctor to another as the man pushed the button on the panel.

"W-Where are we going?" I stuttered.

"Upstairs," the man replied as the metal doors opened.

Whilst waiting in the lift, I looked up at the increasing numbers. Four. Five. Six. You don't pass any further than Sector 6 unless you're really needed. Levels seven and eight are only for administration. I felt my hysteria start to rise and I became twitchy. My leg began to bounce up and down. I tried to fight my urge to run as the elevator door slid across, exposing a brightly lit corridor that was lined with floor-to-ceiling windows on each side.

The doctors pushed me towards the double doors at the end. As they did, I stared through some of the only glass that wasn't blocked by bars. I managed to see over the entire hospital, and even got to see the ocean that named the place, even if it was a hundred feet away. It destroyed some of my hope of the outside, it wasn't as blue as I'd hope it was. It was grey. Just like the TV said.

We came to a stop, and I flicked my head back then braced myself for what may have been waiting for me. The woman pulled the door handle down and revealed an incredible circular office with more of the same windows wrapping around it. Ahead was a long dark coloured desk with a single lamp and a leather chair behind it. Just in front of that were two long sofas and a coffee table. I glanced back at the door and saw two towering shelves either side of it. I turned back as I felt the wheelchair slow. Sat on one of the sofas was Jaiden and a man.

He didn't don a white coat, so it was clear he was a counsellor. Instead, he was wearing a light blue shirt and a dark shaded tie with matching grey trousers and blazer. His hair was silver and was slicked back tightly into a short ponytail with the underneath shaved. He didn't seem too old, but not too young either. He seemed as though he'd experienced enough from life to know where he stood. He turned to me and lifted his head, fitting an authoritative manner.

To my right, hidden by the woman beside me was the main man himself. Dr Mathew Hawthorn. He's the one who rules the roost. If you're lucky, you might see him on one of his rare visits downstairs. There's nothing of interest for him down with us. Dr Hawthorn's a tall guy, always wearing a long kind of coat that swings past his knees when he walks, as well as military style boots so that you can always hear him coming (if he ever does come, of course). He's much older than most of the other staff with the greying hair and beard to prove it. If he didn't scare what's left of the daylight out of me, I'm sure I would have forgotten him.

He faced me and forced a smile. "Hello, Coleman. I'm glad you could take the time to join us today." He chuckled cunningly.

I remained silent and turned my head away.

He ambled across his office. "You should feel pretty honoured to be up here, ay? It's not often your sort are allowed in High Town."

I gritted my teeth as I watched him stroll back over to me. He crouched down to my level, and we locked eyes with each other. I refused to let my gaze wander as he ran his hand across my neck.

"How's the scar?" he asked, not a single shred of empathy in his voice. "Still trying to figure out what you did to yourself?"

"Mathew!" I heard Jaiden call.

He rose back to his normal position and glanced back at her over his shoulder.

"I don't think Noah's in the mood."

He faced me again and smirked. "If you say so." He walked over to the sofas. "I've brought you here to meet someone... *Noah*..." he continued, spitting out my name worthlessly. "I'll let Dr Maddens explain further."

I glanced up at Jaiden as she pushed off the edge of the sofa to stand. She stepped over to me and grabbed the handles on my wheelchair. "Come on," she said quietly, and she wheeled me over to the sofas, keeping me away from the counsellor. She crouched down beside me. "This is Dr Caleb Hudson. He's going to be your temporary counsellor whilst I'm gone, okay?"

I stared over at him, and he flashed me a smile and a wave. "Hello," he said.

"Hello," I muttered back.

Jaiden rubbed my shoulder. "You can tell him anything you would usually tell me. He's very nice."

I shook my head and closed my eyes. "No."

"Come on, Noah," she replied softly. "He's gonna be here for a while, so it's best to get used to it."

Caleb edged off his seat. "May I?"

Jaiden moved to the side and Caleb approached me, taking her spot in front of me. I kept my head down.

"Noah?" he said, his voice calm and sincere.

I shifted my eyes up to his.

"How do you feel about me?"

I didn't know how to respond. I liked him. He was kind, sensitive, and yet still had authority, but I couldn't bring myself to break the front I made, so silent I remained.

"Noah..." He cleared his throat. "I'm here to help you. I'm here to make sure you stay safe and don't get yourself into trouble. Now, you don't have to like me, that's fair enough, but I just want you to be able to talk to me like you do with Dr Maddens."

I met with his eyes. They were trusting, and thoughtful, but that's how they get you. With their trust. You put all your trust into one person, and they have all power over you. Of course, if you let them think that they have control, they'll feel empowered, and they start to trust you. Overall, trust and control come hand in hand.

I stuttered. "Okay..."

He grinned. "Yeah?"

"Yeah..."

Jaiden stroked my shoulder. "Good boy."

Hawthorn joined my side. "Yes, well done." He pushed me towards his table. "Now, there's one other thing that I brought you up here to talk about." He took a seat behind the desk and dropped a file in front of me. "Your behaviour."

I edged closer and watched as Hawthorn removed a page from the cover.

"Over the past month you've had a fair few incidents, starting with what happened on the movie night."

"I didn't mean to do it…"

"Then how did patient Dray end up with a crayon lodged in his throat?"

I shrugged.

He scowled at me. "Either way, you broke the rules, and we need to make sure you understand that."

I turned away and muttered. "I understand the rules…"

"Well, from the looks of things you haven't been playing by them. Dr Wilks, Olsen, and Phillipson have had to write out reports on you multiple times since then."

I tensed my jaw and kept my focus on the window in the distance. Hawthorn continued to throw words at me – not one processing in my brain. Instead, I stared at the tip of the ocean's horizon. It was just visible over the edge of the cliff. My focus sharpened on the fragments of waves for several moments until it was diverted to a small, orange blur that shot past the glass and didn't return. I gave a rapid blink to readjust my eyes – assuring myself of which reality my mind was in.

"Noah?" called a voice from behind.

I twitched my head to face them.

It was Jaiden. "Are you okay?"

I stuttered. "Um, y-yeah. Yeah, I'm fine." I turned back to Hawthorn. "S-Sorry."

"Hm." He scowled as he returned to my file. "This is a final warning, Coleman. One more major incident then we'll be sending you to the Isolation room."

I nodded shortly.

"Good." He closed the file. "Get him back."

After my agreement, I was returned to Riptide. I was freed from the straitjacket and left in my room with Jaiden. I sat down on the side of my bed and kicked my feet back and forth as Jaiden settled beside me.

"Are you sure you're okay with this, Noah? You're not presenting to me as if you are."

I shrugged and shook my head. "If I wasn't, would you put everything the way it was in November?"

She sighed. "I wish I could."

I stood up and wandered over to my sketch pads and slid my back down the wall. I reached for the pencils that were scattered across the carpet and harshly scribbled over it.

Jaiden joined me at the wall before departing. "I'll leave you be." She glanced at the picture on my desk. "You're getting good at those."

I ignored her and continued to dot my pencil across the paper. She then headed back out to the corridor, a fact I only knew after the air lock seal sounded. I lowered the sketch book and held the pencil tightly before launching it across the room in frustration. I rested my head in my hands before being interrupted by a short tapping coming from the other side of the mirror. The guard in the office had obviously seen that short tantrum and was ready for it to become a storm.

Speaking of storms, the next day, after I had started to settle around the fact Caleb was now here, I was listening to the weather report on the TV. I wasn't watching it, I was too busy sticking sequins to a piece of card, but the reporter spoke of the snow to become heavier and the wind to become stronger, because there was in fact a long length of storms that were on their way to the UK from the west coast. From where the hospital stands, we'd be the last to get hit, but it's not like we'll be out in it anyway.

I knew that the hospital was going to be much harder for the coming weeks, but I didn't expect all the other patients to be so calm about it. Something wasn't right with them, any of them. They were all too calm. Calmer than any Riptide patient had ever been. Even when Christmas eventually came, the energy had dissipated. I never got to see the result of the overwhelming holiday, and I was even getting somewhat excited myself just so that I had something to look forward to, but then… nothing. Even Kyle was acting different. He was no longer twitching about the place looking for something to inspect. He became wispy and barely spoke to me when we met. He kept getting lost in a fog and ended up staring into space. Each day I'd notice another patient turn to this state, almost like they'd been hypnotised.

Every patient who was getting transferred from Jaiden to Caleb was taken to meet him, but I was the only one to be taken to High Town. Amidst this calm chaos, I took my chance to use the usually busy phone area. When I received permission to use them a few months ago, the doctor's wrote me Aaron's number on a post-it note and stuck it to my wall. I took it with me and tapped the numbers onto the wall keypad. The line rang out several times before he picked up.

"Hello?"

"H-Hey. It's, uh, it's me."

"Noah!" he said excitedly. "How are you?"

"Yeah, you know, insane. What about you?"

"I'm good. I, uh, I just got back from the shops. I bought this weird pastry thing that I probably won't like and a, um... a hammer. I don't know what I'm building but at least I'll be prepared."

I chuckled. "That's always good."

"Yeah, heh." I could tell he was smiling through his tone. "I also bought a tent. It was only twenty pounds – not many people go campin' in the height of Winter, you see, so I got it at quite the discount."

I smiled. "Where you gonna go?"

"I'm not sure. Maybe I'll go see my sister – hide out in the woods or something."

"Take a friend with you, maybe. You could go fishing together on a highjacked boat."

"Hah, that sounds fun, but my friends seem to have made themselves quite scarce recently. They're probably laying low or something. I'd've heard it on the chain if they were in prison. Although, I haven't heard much from the connects either so maybe there's something big going down. If so, I'm glad I'm being left out of it."

"I'm glad too. You're not allowed to get involved."

"Don't worry, I won't." I heard him rustling through his bags. "Anyway, how's hospital life?"

I sighed. "Yeah, well... you know... it's hard... and boring."

His voice became softer. "I can visit if you want. I'll bring my tent and wait for the doctors to let me in."

I grinned happily at his gesture. "It's okay. I don't want you to get blown away in the storm."

"Heh, thanks. Are you sure you don't want me to come?"

"I don't mind. I don't really know what's going on around here at the minute, though, so maybe call the place first."

"Right... I miss you."

"I miss you too." The phone gave a beep and a message appeared on the small screen in front of me. "The call's nearly out of time. I'm gonna have to go."

"Alright. I'll see you when I see you, then."

"Yeah… I love you."

"I love you too. Stay out of trouble."

I chuckled. "You too."

"Hah, I will."

"Bye."

"Bye."

I gently hung up the phone and stepped away.

By the time the New Year came, everyone was still acting as they were. Nothing special happened for us on the New Year, in fact, it was probably a lot more dangerous. The amount of fireworks that got shot into the sky at random scared people, which is why we were all given an extra dose of sedation with our pills. The halls of the ward were completely empty, not one patient set foot outside their rooms that night – not even me. None of us could make it far enough to even reach our doors. We each had to have food brought to us whilst the guards watched us extra closely. I couldn't eat a thing, though, I couldn't even lift the spoon.

The day I'm writing this, is the day I actually ended up staying nights outside my room. The day after the sedation just so happened to be another turn for the psych tests. You'd think that on the first day of the new year they'd give it a pass. I was given a selection of tests – this time involving numbers and maths – and attempted them with the little energy I had. I think I was so exhausted at the time that I didn't really care what I was doing. I was then marched through to do the blood tests then over to Dr Wilks. This was another one of the many encounters I had with her since our first meeting. Our relationship has only worsened. She treated me the same way she treated every patient because she was above us.

I followed the doctor through the usual routine. Stand up. Sit down. Extend your arm. Stand here. Stand there. I did it without thinking. I returned to the table as Dr Wilks fumbled around with my file by the counter behind her desk. At least I thought it was mine. It had my name sticking out the side, but the cover was blue. It's never been blue before and that's something I just know. It's meant to be orange, of course others argue it could be yellow, but since I've been here it's never been blue.

I shuffled around on my wobbling chair trying to get a better look at what was actually in the doctor's hands, but she kept blocking my view. I had a feeling she knew what I was trying to do, so repeatedly turned back and forth. Suddenly she slammed the file down on the table with a sigh.

"Right," she said as she headed over to the cabinet, sliding the file across the counter as she walked. "We've received your new pills, Mr Coleman."

I swallowed anxiously and tried to scrape back on my chair. "I-I didn't get told about getting anything new."

She unlocked the glass doors and pulled out a pill box. "Well, that's what I've got on here," she replied bluntly.

"I-I always get told when I'm g-getting something changed," I stuttered out.

She swung around and approached me with the pills in a paper cup in her hand. "Well, maybe they did tell you and you just forgot."

My shoulders tensed and I lowered my head. I knew that I hadn't been told. I knew that whatever was about to happen wouldn't end well, but I couldn't do anything about it. I couldn't react. If I reacted, I'd be written up, then I'll be down in the isolation room. Wilks grabbed my right hand and wrapped my fingers around the cup. She pushed it towards me and stood with her arms crossed watching me.

"Well, go on, then. The sooner you take them, the sooner you'll feel better."

I stared down at the two multi-coloured capsules rolling around the edge of the cup. My hands were trembling and my urge to run was growing but I forced myself to stop. I inhaled then swung my head back to swallow the pills. I had never taken medication without water before, but I was too scared to ask Dr Wilks, from the way our past visits had been going I had the growing feeling that she didn't like me. I certainly didn't like her. I felt my throat contract. I couldn't breathe and I let out several desperate coughs.

I was okay, I was just on the edge of choking. I crunched up the paper and threw it in the bin.

"Am I done?" I said croakily.

"Yes." She kept her eyes away from me and just stared at the papers in front of her on her desk.

I nodded and headed back around through the door. I knocked on the window of the staff waiting area and a nurse stepped out. I gestured towards the door, and she unlocked it. I headed down the corridor towards Jaiden's office. I was still trying to recover from the near choking incident, but otherwise I was okay. I was fine for the beginning of my meeting too, until my head started to tense up and my chest tightened. I tried to hide it from Jaiden, I couldn't cause any more of a ruckus, so I acted the best I could to keep a normal appearance. I obviously wasn't very good at hiding it, though. Jaiden brought me on another walk, keeping a close watch on me as we took each step.

"Noah, are you okay?"

She kept repeating that question, but I didn't know the answer. My movements began to slow and with each breath I took came a wheeze. Following this came an overwhelming itchiness across my skin. I lifted my sleeve to look at my arm, only to see it turn completely red with spots.

Jaiden then gripped at my side and inspected my body. "Oh, my God. Noah, what's wrong? How long have you had that?"

My eyes drooped. "I don't... I don't know."

She continued to inspect me, speaking as she did, but her words just faded. All I made out was 'Dr Olsen' and 'return to medical'. I then glanced to my right and saw the man beside me. I didn't even notice him until he also started inspecting me. As this happened, my breathing stopped. My throat clenched shut in what felt like seconds. I flailed my arms at the two doctors, trying to signal what was happening. They both stared at me in concern before I fell backwards onto the tiles and gasped desperately, gripping at my shirt as if that would help me. Jaiden and Dr Olsen dropped beside me, frantically trying to save me. They repeated my name over and over. It was the last thing I heard before I blacked out.

Later that night, I was woken abruptly with a jab in my thigh and my body lying in a bed in the emergency wing. According to the nurses I'd had an allergic reaction, and I'm only allergic to one thing. Penicillin. I wasn't convinced when I was told about having an allergy as I wasn't the one who gave the information to the doctors, Aaron was. I couldn't tell them a thing to save my life, so in this case I guess I would have died if Aaron didn't tell them.

The doctors ordered for me to stay in the wing until my symptoms were under control enough for me to return to my room. I didn't have the best time in the medical unit since I was questioned for a solid three days about why I didn't speak up when Dr Wilks gave me pills I knew I wasn't supposed to take, but then I bounced the statement back at them that my vitals doctor tells me.

"I'm the patient. It's not my fault."

I think I was getting a bit antsy having to stay in bed, so I took it out on the staff through passive aggressive comments, until they'd had enough and left me alone. I was kept out of the loop for most of the investigation that followed, but I do know this, I wasn't the only one with wrong medication, most of the patients were. That's why everyone was acting so strange. As well as this, I was also given the blame for not speaking up. I don't know why or even how the staff twisted it to become that. I guess they'd had enough of my sarcasm, so this was their revenge.

I was written up for it – like I knew I would be – but I wasn't sent anywhere else. They thought it would be too risky for me to be segregated in the state I was in, so instead, they took my job from me. I'm no longer allowed to help with anything. I have to sit, and do what I'm told, and learn to speak up when someone takes my voice.

The day after I was told this, I was let out of the wing. The doctors kept a closer watch on me just to make sure I didn't have another reaction, but it was really quite off-putting. They'd watch me from afar, which is worse than when they watch you one-on-one, because then you can actually see when they're watching you. From afar, you can't.

This happened in the common room. I was sat on the floor, in front of the movie projector, busy pushing sequins onto a sticky mat. An advantage of my height came in handy by the fact that the projector shone over my head, so no aggro came from the other patients (even though they were all probably still coming down from the sedatives). I wasn't really paying attention to the movie because I had that constant, whelming sensation that the staff's eyes were on me. I kept checking around to see who was there, only to be surprised when the room remained the same.

One person did enter at one point, though. It was Caleb. I clenched my teeth as he caught eyes with me, and I pushed the sequins on harder out of panic. He flashed a quick smile at me, and I turned my head back to the picture. I heard his footsteps approach me and I felt my inside tighten out of hope he would walk on and bug somebody else, but he didn't. He knelt down beside me and glanced over my shoulder at the picture that was slowly becoming a fox.

"Hey, buddy. What're you making?"

I ignored him the best I could, watching his actions through the corner of my eye.

He nodded. "I get it. It's okay. I'm some stranger that's come in and now has to analyse everything you do, I wouldn't want to talk to me either."

I shuffled around on the spot and gave him a quick nod.

"I just wanted to know if you were doing okay from the whole fiasco the other day."

I nodded again.

"That's good then."

I turned away out of shyness.

"I was worried how you'd be after losing your job."

"I'm okay," I said quickly.

"Are you sure? You can talk to me if you need to."

I stopped reaching for the sequins and listened to him carefully.

"It's what I'm here for – to help you."

I sighed and returned to my artwork (if that's what you could call it). "I'm okay…" I grabbed the picture from the floor and carried the pot of materials back to the craft area. Caleb followed me, stopping me in my tracks as I tried to escape to the hallway.

"Noah, look at me," he mellowed his tone. "It *is* alright to not be okay about something. It's strong to accept when you're feeling down."

I looked up at him and he smiled. I didn't smile back, or even speak. I glanced at the picture in my hands then gave it to him.

He looked down at it, his smile growing. "Thanks."

I reached for the slanted handle and headed into the corridor to find a new place to hide, Caleb staying behind in the common room as I disappeared. I didn't want to go back to my room, I had only just got out of there, so instead I just continuously walked in circles around the halls. I passed a few characters along the way – all of whom were in a daze, staring at the ground. I kept thinking that they were avoiding me because any time I got near one of them they would shuffle away. If they *were* doing it because of me, I didn't want to make them uncomfortable, so I just scampered in the direction that was empty. I did about four rounds of Riptide before the free period came to an end.

Then it was dinner, and this time I could actually eat. Why? Well… I'm taking a risk writing this in here, but I didn't take my medication today. I was too scared to swallow them after the penicillin incident. I was under heavy watch as I had the different cups, but they didn't notice that I hadn't actually swallowed them, I just hid them behind my teeth. My pills are small anyway, so they were easy to hide when the doctor quickly flashed a torch around my mouth. Let's just say I held my breath when they checked, and once I was returned to my room, I forced them down the drain. I was expecting the worse from the missed dose, but nothing happened. For the whole day, nothing happened. I had nerves the whole time I was in that common room with Caleb about whether I was gonna do something to him because I wasn't under whatever was keeping me down before, but nothing did happen.

I didn't want to draw attention to myself at dinner so I ate my food the slowest way I could, forcing myself to lower my spoon after every few bites, but it was great to finally be able to eat something normally. I then bussed my tray at the table and headed back to my room in a bliss state. I tried it again the next day and still nothing happened until the third day when I felt a tingling sensation running through my arms and across my chest. That made me even more nervous and self-conscious about what I was doing and what I was thinking with the paranoia joining forces with it so that I questioned every move I made, but I still hadn't had anything happen.

I went on for almost a week and a half without them, and the height of the delirium that followed was an episode of shooting pains down my back and increasing scattered thoughts. They jumped from one to the other, some colliding and disorientating my thought path – the path now had about eight different ones branching off of it, some meeting again with another whilst some shot out in a sharpened bolt of lightning, with others curving around everything to connect with itself at the beginning. If I were to read a sign to tell me how to follow this path, the sign would say 'turn left to go up, turn back to go right, and turn down to go forwards.'

I was at the peak of this when once again something new was found in the dreary waters of Riptide. Another meeting had come around again, and I was waiting on the same bench I always wait at for Jaiden to open her door to let me in. I was rehearsing with myself on how to act with her because the whirring in my head was altering my actions. I started to react at a delay, and I knew that I'd need my best head on whilst in that meeting since Caleb was scheduled to take over today. Jaiden was still gonna be there, but Caleb would be asking the questions. That's how changes are usually made in Riptide – not with a sudden spring. But as I was waiting, I experienced a hell of a shift.

There was a noise, but I was alone. That was the first sign, both doctors and patients were nowhere to be seen. Then I heard it again. The scampering of feet walking down the hallway with a trembling pant. I rose from my seat, panicking, then closed my eyes and faced the wall. I clenched my hands against my ears.

It's not real. It's not real. You're spiralling. Come on, get back to the surface.

I hesitantly opened my eyes and lowered my hands. With my forehead resting against the wall, I sighed.

"You're losing it, Noah..." I whispered softly.

"Why are you talking to yourself?" came a small girl's voice.

I swallowed anxiously then slowly lifted my head from the wall to face where her voice came from. "I, uh..."

Stood about seven feet away from me was a tiny black-haired girl in a pink frilly dress and black leggings. She stared up at me with her shining blue eyes waiting for my response.

"Um... I... How did you get in here?"

"I went through the door over there." She pointed to behind her then swung her head back around, her two plats swishing along with her.

"W-Was it not locked?"

She shook her head.

I took a step back from her and tried to understand how this child was in front of me. I cleared my throat and rubbed my eyes. I pounded my hands together behind my back, out of the view of the girl, as I fought to stay calm. "O... kay, um. What's your name?"

"Olivia."

"Olivia? That's a nice name."

"Thank you!" she said gleefully. "What's your name, mistah?"

I crouched down to her level. "I'm, I'm Noah."

She picked at the teddy in her hands. "Why are you talking to yourself, mistah Noah?"

"I, um... I do that sometimes to help me hear what I'm thinking."

"Do you not think in your head?"

I rested my knees on the tiles and sat back. "I can, but... sometimes it's a bit too loud in my brain to think. I end up playing tricks on myself."

"That's a bit of a silly thing to do."

I chuckled. "It is, isn't it?"

She shuffled towards me and pointed at my I.D. band. "What's that?"

I twisted it around. "It's my patient band. It lets other people know who I am and how they can find me."

"Like if you got lost playing hide and seek?"

Her voice was so innocent that it made me smile. "Yes," I replied.

She shuffled even closer then sat down on her knees, mimicking how I was.

"So, heh... What are you doing here, Olivia?"

She bounced her toy up and down across the floor. "I came here with mummy."

I flicked through my memory, trying to remember who would have a daughter this age. "Olivia?"

"M-hm?"

"Is your last name Maddens?"

"M-hm!"

"Do you know if mummy's around here?"

She kept playing with the bear. "She was talking to a man in a white coat, and we followed him into a lift. Then I got out of the lift and followed the yellow lines over here and they led me to you." She looked up at me and grinned.

"I can see that," I said with a smile.

"Why are you wearing pyjamas?"

I let out a stifled laugh then bit my lip. "They're not pyjamas."

"They look like pyjamas."

I looked down at my clothes and nodded. "Yeah, I guess they do." I mean, she wasn't wrong. I did look like I just crawled out of bed.

"Why are you wearing not-pyjamas?"

"So that I don't hurt myself."

"How could you hurt yourself wearing clothes?"

I shrugged. "The doctors' rules, not mine. They're a lot smarter than me, so I don't like to question them."

"Mummy's a doctor."

I smiled at her. "I know she is."

Her eyes widened in intrigue. "How do you know that?"

"She's one of my doctors."

"Are you sick?" she asked worryingly.

"Well, not exact—"

"When I'm sick, mummy lets me stay home from school and brings

73

me spag-a-hatti hoops and lets me watch whatever I want on the big TV!"

"Spag-a-hatti? I don't think I've ever had that."

"Yeah, spag-a-hatti! It always, *always* makes me feel better." She rolled across the floor beside me. "And then I bundle up in my blankets and sit with my teddies!" She giggled as she star-fished out on the tiles.

"I see."

She jumped up and scampered back over to me. She patted me on the head. "I hope you feel better, mistah Noah!"

"Thank you, Olivia."

She wrapped her arms around me and nuzzled her head into my shoulder. "I like you, mistah Noah."

I felt a lump grow in my throat. "I like you too… Olivia."

I hesitantly placed my hand on her back and was overwhelmed with the feelings inside of me. Not once have I been allowed to be hugged like this, let alone by a child. She was so small, my arms could have wrapped twice around her, and I'm the one that's usually tiny. She seemed so careless about me. No fear. No distress. She just liked me.

I saw a documentary on the TV about how different the world would be if we all kept the mind of a child. They don't care for the differences in people, it's the adults who corrupt them, but if Olivia has Jaiden as her mum then I doubt she'll be corrupted. Of course, I fall between the two – being an adult and a child. I've been told a thousand times that my mind reverted back to its child-like ways, but sometimes, something clicks, and the innocence vanishes. So in a sense, I guess I corrupt myself.

Then before Olivia let go, there was the thunder of stampeding footsteps coming from the other side of the door. Before I could take my hands back, I saw the door slide up and several guards and doctors pour in. They all shouted over each other, and I scrambled back on the floor, Olivia watching my actions in confusion. I saw past her as Dr Olsen pushed through the crowd with Jaiden by his side.

"Olivia!" she cried in desperation, tears dripping down her cheeks.

"Mummy!" she called as she went to break into a run.

"No! Stay there!" she screamed back.

Olivia immediately stopped and swished her head back and forth between me and the group.

Dr Olsen cautiously approached the two of us with his hands raised. "Noah. We're not gonna hurt you. As long as you stay calm."

74

I stumbled to my feet. "I didn't hurt her. Please, I wouldn't."

He kept walking. "Okay. Just stay there."

I overheard the group muttering to each other, the guards all reaching for tools on their belts.

Dr Olsen took another step forward. "Noah. Keep your eyes on me. Don't look at them."

I drifted my eyes back to him.

"That's it," he said softly. "Keep looking at me."

I shook my head and scrunched my eyes shut.

"Hey! Look at me!" he ordered.

I started to tremble as the voices around me grew louder.

"Noah," Jaiden called over, her voice broken. "Please, do what he says."

I opened my eyes again and guiltily kept contact with Olsen.

"Okay, good," Jaiden continued. "Olivia, honey. Come towards me slowly."

I couldn't see what was going on beside me, but from the sound of Olivia's footsteps, I could tell she was moving. Jaiden kept beckoning her over and the footsteps got faster.

I went to take a step, but Dr Olsen forbid me.

"Don't move, Noah. Stay where you are. I'm going to come to you, okay?"

I nodded anxiously, picking at my nails as Olsen approached with his hands remaining raised.

"See? It's all okay. It's all good." He reached me and held my head in his hands. "Close your eyes."

I shook my head in worry. "No, no. They'll hurt me."

"No, they won't. I'm not going to let them touch you." He wiped the tears from my cheeks. "Close your eyes for me."

I bit my lip and followed the order, my fear and anxiety growing as I listened carefully to what was around me. I heard Dr Olsen whisper and he removed one of his hands from me. I gripped mine towards him and held his thin coat.

"It's alright. It's alright. You're okay."

I heard footsteps in the direction of the group fading down the hallway. I shuffled as it happened, wanting to give anything to let myself run from it but I stood my ground. It wasn't until I heard a door creak that Dr Olsen spoke to me again.

"Alright, open your eyes."

I opened them again and looked around frantically. The hallway was empty once again.

"W-where did they go?" I stammered, gripping harder at his coat.

"I sent them away so that they didn't come near you. They're gone now."

"A-are they gonna come back?"

"No." He placed his hands on mine and removed them from his coat. I can't blame him, I was probably strangling the poor guy. "Where do you wanna go?"

"I-I-I don't know," I replied shakily.

"Do you wanna go to the common area? Or your room? Anywhere."

"M-my room."

"Okay," he said with a smile. "Let's go."

He stepped around me, keeping a hold of my hands as he directed me down the corridor. I darted my head around me as we took a few steps until I changed my mind.

I stopped in place as I spoke. "No. I d-don't want to go back there."

He turned to me. "Okay, that's fine," he replied calmly. "Where do you *want* to go?"

To be honest, I didn't know. I felt so embarrassed. I just wanted to sit somewhere alone and cry it out, but there was nowhere to do that without someone watching me, whether it's in person or behind a screen.

I pulled my hands back and looked around. "Um… Can I go outside?"

"Outside? Sure. It's a bit cold, though. Are you sure?"

I nodded. "Can I see the guinea pigs?"

"Yeah, sure." He smiled at me, and we headed back in the opposite direction.

Dr Olsen unlocked the cage and opened the door for me. I stepped in and he closed it behind me then proceeded to move back to the bench that sat opposite. I reached my foot over the small divider that stopped the animals from tunnelling out then carefully tiptoed across the grass, being mindful of the little creatures that were poking around and slid down the fence into my usual spot. I laid my legs out and watched as the guinea pigs scampered over to me, hooking their tiny toes onto the loose bits of cotton that were

76

undoing from my trousers. I chuckled and gave a smile at them as Blossom and Ginger clawed themselves onto me and trotted along to my stomach. They both twirled around in circles chasing after one another before jumping back onto the grass and burrowing back into the hay. I felt a familiar nibble by my fingertips and looked down to see Cookie.

"Hey," I said as I reached my hand down and scooped her up. I brought her to my eye line. "What d'you think you're doing?"

She darted her head up at the sky and sneezed then rubbed her nose against my hand.

"Bless you."

Cookie wiggled her way out of my grip and climbed across my arm and sat down on my shoulder.

"Can I help you?"

She twisted herself around and hooked onto my hair, holding onto it as she tossed her head from side to side.

I sat in the cage for about thirty minutes. Dr Olsen was right, it was freezing, but I didn't mind. If giant hamsters can handle it then I can too. As I continued playing with them, my feelings began to level. I didn't feel so scared, and I began to smile.

That was until I heard movement from the other side of the fence. I shot my head up as I heard footsteps crunching in the thin layer of frost outside the gate. It was Caleb. He stopped beside Dr Olsen and whispered to him before approaching the cage.

He looked down at me with a smile. "They told me you'd be out here," he said, his breath swirling in the air.

I turned away. "I thought they'd be cold. I wanted to warm them up."

Caleb smiled. "That's very thoughtful of you."

I felt Cookie let go of my hair and slip down my chest. I saved her from falling and held her in my hands. "Am I in trouble?"

"Of course not. There's no reason for you to be in trouble."

I nodded. "I just... I was scared. I didn't want to hurt her."

"I know. But you didn't though, did you?"

I looked back up at him. "But what if I did? I could never forgive myself if I hurt a kid."

He glanced away and sighed then tapped on the fence. "Come on. We better get you back inside."

"Okay," I replied sorrowfully, placing Cookie on the pile of hay and paper.

I stepped over the barrier again and he opened the gate to the courtyard. I stepped through the gap, keeping my head down shamefully. Caleb placed his fingers on my chin and tilted my head up to meet his eyeline.

"Hey," he said softly. "You won't be like this forever, alright?"

I smiled weakly at him then noticed as Dr Olsen rose from the bench.

"You okay, mate?" he asked.

I nodded.

Caleb placed his hand on my shoulder, and we began to walk. "Come on."

He turned inside first, making sure the area was safe as I was escorted back inside. I heard Dr Olsen's muffled shivering beside me, and I glanced at him to see his awfully pale face – he was paler than me – and his lips were a tint of blue.

I picked at my nails as I shivered along with him. "Are you okay, doctor?"

He nodded friskily. "Yeah. I'm fine."

"You look... cold."

"It's a bit nippy out there, I will say."

"Do you need a blanket?"

He chuckled and smiled at me. "I'll be okay."

"I have a blanket – Aaron made it. It's not very warm, though."

He rubbed my back. "Thanks, mate, but I'll be fine."

"I think you could both do with a blanket," Caleb added.

We reached Dr Olsen's office and we sat down together. Caleb didn't stay for very long, he had to return to the Olivia situation – apparently Jaiden was quite shaken. He said that the reason the kid was here was because her dad was called up on work last minute and they couldn't find anybody to look after her, so Jaiden had to bring her with her. She hadn't planned on keeping her here long, she was just checking in and was going to leave her at reception, but she got away.

Before he stepped outside, Dr Olsen asked him a final question quietly by the doorway. I'm guessing that he didn't want me to hear, but I managed to anyway. "Do you know what her husband was called up for?"

"Apparently the school said they needed another teacher to go on the French trip, so he had to go." He then swiftly closed the door, and his footsteps were heard seemingly sprinting down the corridor.

Something about his answer lingered with me. It made me think. It was like the jumble in my brain was actually trying to tell me something for once, and then a path finally brought me somewhere.

"I used to work at a school," I said calmly, not even realising what I was saying was far more important than it sounded.

Dr Olsen swung so fast back around to face me that you could have missed it if you blinked. He just stared, seeming in complete awe and wonder about what I just muttered. "What did you say, Noah?"

I looked up at him, still not realising. "I worked at a school."

He returned to the sofa and climbed over the arm of it in fascination. He raised his hands, and his tone became articulated and serious. "Noah. Think about what you just said to me. Are you just saying that, or do you remember something?"

I shrugged as I repeated the sentence over and over in my mind. It took me a while, but then I was finally able to read what was formed. "I worked at a school." I clenched my jaw. "I remember it, I do! I used to work there. It was called Layset."

Dr Olsen gave a smile and tears seemed to be welling up in his eyes, as were mine, but I think for a different reason. Whilst his were of pride, mine were of trauma. I did indeed work at a school. I wasn't a teacher or anything, I was like the librarian, but more of just an intern. All I did was sort out books, organise them – maybe that's why I managed to keep on track with it here. It was always the quietest place, none of the students were very much into reading when they could just go on their phones, or the computers, or talk to their friends. Sometimes, the regular few kids would come in and they'd sit with me and talk – sometimes they never left me alone. Then other times I'd be alone all week. I had no reason to complain. It was the only job I could get. Nobody wanted to take me.

Although I had this memory back, it was patchy. Parts were missing. The puzzle was still very much incomplete, but there was one large piece that was the reason my tears were falling. There was a wire. There was me. There was a boy. The wire was wrapped tightly around my fingers and was being pressed just as hard against the skin of the boy's neck. He was still alive, but he was bleeding. His blood had covered the entire of the metal strand and was running down my fingers. Around me was half of the school. They were all watching as the wire dug deeper into him until I had the sudden urge to stop. He ran to the care of his friends as I was taken to the ground.

My breath was shaky, and my cheeks had two streams running down them. This was when Dr Olsen must have realised because his smile turned.

"Ryan…" I said through the state. "His name was Ryan."

Dr Olsen took my hand and held it tightly as his name flashed through my brain. "You remember Ryan?"

"I tried… to… kill him." I turned to the doctor. "I tried to kill him."

I fell into a state and Dr Olsen tried his best to comfort me. For once, I don't think he knew quite what to say. He couldn't tell me it was all right because it wasn't. I tried to kill a sixteen-year-old kid. That's not all right.

"Is that why I'm here?" I asked. "Because I hurt him?"

He sighed. "That's the gist of it, yeah."

Well, I guess I got the answer I was looking for. Now, I know why they kept it from me, because even I hate myself for it. I dread to imagine what the world thought of me, and it led me to question why anyone would want to stay in my life when they knew what I'd done. I wouldn't be friends with me, that's for sure. Maybe that's why nobody knows here.

Breaking free from the tides of thoughts, I looked back at Dr Olsen who now had his notebook in his hand and was frantically scribbling down the information I had told him. He did it in seconds, and once he finished he slung the notepad in his jacket pocket and reached for my hands.

"Noah, what you've just said is really important, okay? I'm going to have to share it with the other doctors. I can't keep this information hidden, I'm afraid."

I shook my head. "No, no, you can't. What if they think that I've just been lying to them this whole time? None of them believe what I say!"

"I believe you, Noah, and I will assure them that you have well and truly remembered this on your own."

I closed my tearful eyes and begged him not to, but he kept telling me that he was required to share the information with the required staff. I didn't want them to know. Too many things have changed. I just want to go back to three months ago. When Sector 3 was Sector 3. The same routine, the same doctors, the same feelings. I should be happy that my memory has come back to me, but I wish it didn't. Jaiden was right – they all were – I shouldn't have known what I did. Even now the truth is out, it's still not complete. Huge patches were missing, voids in my mind that had taken the rest of the moment, and I'm thankful for that for once.

Dr Olsen continued with his persuasions until I finally ran out of energy to deny him. He didn't ask me anything else, he knew that this was enough for me that day. He held me close as he returned me home. We had to stop along the way, occasionally taking a seat on one of the benches to catch my breath as the scene played over and over again – disconnecting me from what was really around me. I kept going back to the school. The people. The noise. The blood. Dr Olsen forever stayed by my side through it, talking me out and getting me back to the hallway.

He had warned over the radio to get something to calm me down after my third attack, and when someone tells you that they're getting something to 'calm you down', it will *knock* you down. But I was in so much emotional pain that I didn't care. When we reached my room, Dr Olsen joined me inside with another man. I followed everything they said to me, trying to seem as gentle as possible. As the man prepared the needle, Dr Olsen kept a hold of my hand, gently rubbing it as the other doctor injected the sedative into my lower back. They both tried to distract me by talking and directing my attention to different things around my room. I started to become lethargic and rolled onto my side. I tried to stay conscious, but they gave me the strong stuff. I was out for the whole day and night. It's likely that they refilled me at some point, but I had no clue. Let's just say that I woke up feeling pretty good in the morning.

The withdrawals from my pills had worn off and I felt relieved to not have that racing track of thoughts going on upstairs. I was in and out of it the whole day. Caleb came in to check on me at one point when I was awake with what looked like a bowl with whizzed up chicken inside it. He asked me if I was hungry, and I slowly nodded my head.

"Do you wanna sit up?"

I nodded again and Caleb gently lifted me up so that my back was against my propped up pillows. He passed me the bowl then took a water bottle from his pocket and placed it on my bedside cabinet.

"Thank you," I said groggily.

"My pleasure," he said with a smile.

He went to leave but I called for him back. "Um, Dr Hudson?"

He leant against the edge of my bed. "You don't have to call me that. You can call me Caleb, or any other name you like. Although, I may not reply."

I gave a very tired chuckle. "Can I ask you something?"

"What's that?"

I swirled the spoon around in my bowl. "Am I a bad person?"

He shrugged and tapped his fingers on the mattress. "I don't think I'm the person to ask. If you were to ask anyone that, it would be to the person you know you've hurt."

"How am I supposed to do that? I doubt that Ryan would be willing to come here to see me."

"It's not likely, no. But that doesn't mean you are a bad person. People just sometimes do things that others might not understand. Your reasoning for doing what you did won't get through to people, but that doesn't mean you're bad."

"But I did something bad. I know it was bad, nothing's gonna change it to be good."

"Well… sometimes realising that what you did was wrong can be just enough help for you to understand how to make it right."

"How do I make it right?"

He paused as he worked through his thoughts. "Just try. Try as much as you can to make something around you better."

So that's what I did. Once I regained enough strength to make it around the hospital, I did everything I could to help, which in the end didn't feel like much. I tidied what I could in the common room without changing it around too much to avoid confusion, but I straightened the books on the bookshelf, I stopped the craft table from wobbling, I cleaned the DVDs to stop them breaking, I coloured in the chess board with a black marker so that you could actually tell the difference between the two squares – I tried everything, and it did sort of help.

I proved to the staff that I could be useful, and they praised me for it. Dr Olsen even let me clean the top of his desk – and that was scary. He had a lot of junk, but I got some of it! He gave me a foam ball that I found inside his pen pot – don't ask me how it fit in there – and he said I could have it for being helpful. I didn't have much to do with it, I just squeezed it and threw it in the air. It didn't bounce. I dropped it on the floor to see how high it would go but it didn't even come back up.

One day I was playing with it in the common room. I was rolling it back and forth along the windowsill as I watched the rain pouring outside. Once again I was listening to the TV that was on in the background. Two patients were sat watching it. It was a report about butterflies. It was saying how a rare species was found in the lower region of England and how unusual it was for them to be down here. They said they're called 'monarchs'. I have no idea what they look like since I wasn't watching the screen, but I like to imagine them as red and white with a crown on its head. The report was kind of interesting, but whilst I was listening to it, I had a strange sensation cast over me after they spoke.

'The whole event is peculiar, really. It's strange to see them in the UK in such large numbers, and in such a large size, but what's stranger is that these monarchs fly in the rain.'

I wasn't sure what it was, but it was weird. I didn't feel ill, but I didn't feel well. I quickly grabbed the ball and shuffled anxiously out of the room. I thought that it was the withdrawals coming back, annoyed that the sedative didn't stop them. Then my vision started to deter. The place that was void of colour had sudden vibrant strobes of green and blue. My shuffle became a slightly faster jog as I felt random jolts run up my back and into my neck. That's when the green and blue strobes were replaced with an overcast of crimson. My speed faltered and I came to a brief stop by the medical wing. I had no idea who to go to for help, especially after I was witness to a rather angered patient being taken from Dr Wilks's room.

"I'm gonna kill her! I'm gonna kill her!" He kept screaming before he was detained by the guards.

Me and the rest of the patients in the hall were backed away from the scene but I was desperate and tried to explain myself to the doctor, but my words came out as a mixture of sounds that weren't heard over the frantic yelling behind us. We were taken down a corridor, but I couldn't tell which. It wasn't until I got a brief clip of sensation back that I noticed that I was suddenly alone. I fell back against the wall and gripped at my hair as echoes ran around my head of what the patient was declaring. It was almost like the words themselves were sharp and were slicing away at my membrane. I then slid to the tiles, just crumpled up in a ball wishing to be found. I even tried praying to the foam that Dr Olsen had given, as if that would signal for him to come, but he didn't. Then I went blank. The red tint of the area around me strengthening just as I retreated amongst the corners of my mind.

Chapter 4

Crimson Overcast

I was so dreary, my mind feeling almost blocked by a fog wall, separating me from reality. It felt like I was watching from above as my body was being controlled by phantom strings that dragged me towards my destination. Then the fog began to disappear, and my vision became clear again. All I could see was the crimson haze, but as it faded I was still seeing red.

I was in my bathroom. The light shining down and reflecting brightly off the white walls, making me disorientated. I lifted my hand to rub my face but flinched as I felt a liquid run onto my cheek. I looked down at my hand and fell breathless, my eyes suddenly fixated on my red-covered hands. I flicked my head to my other hand that was gripping tightly to the sink side, water gushing from the cold tap and splashing up at my fingertips. Blood consumed the sides of the bowl and I watched fearfully as it was swallowed by the drain.

I broke free from my trance and moved rapidly to rid the red from my skin. I violently rubbed my hands together under the jet of water, desperately trying to clean myself. I was panicking. No. I wasn't panicking. I was feeling like I was about to implode. Just get sucked from existence in a snap. My heart was going too fast for my lungs to get air. I couldn't feel myself breathing. Adrenaline stormed me, causing my limbs to buzz and tremble. I couldn't stop. I kept rubbing my hands. Rubbing and rubbing and rubbing until I let out a short shout of fear and I fell against my shower wall. Tears flooded down my face, twisting with the drying scarlet that was staining my cheeks.

I snatched the towel from the shelf and wrapped it around my soaked hands. I buried my head into the fabric and sobbed. I leant my head back again, trying to breathe the best I could. I shut my eyes tightly, hoping that what I was seeing wasn't real. But it was. It was seared into what was left of my memory. I was terrified. Terrified of myself. Terrified of what I was capable of. Terrified of what was going to happen to me. I couldn't keep my thoughts on track, everything inside me was racing.

I threw the towel at the wall as if it would help my situation, then shot back up to my feet, shaking. I took in several more breaths as I gripped at the tiles and rested my head against it. I looked down at my jumper and noticed the patches of red splattered across the cotton. I jumped back then ripped it over my head and held in my hands. I closed my eyes, keeping them clenched as I tried to calm myself down.

I turned on my shower and held the jumper underneath the slight trickle that was permitted to fall. I felt an overwhelming nausea as the floor became covered in a thick carpet. There was so much. It just kept pouring from the inside of my clothes. I had to leave it. I couldn't look at it any longer. I let the water run as I fled from the bathroom, standing frozen by the door.

I darted my eyes across my room, focusing on Aaron's blanket that was dangling off the edge of my bed. I quickly yanked it off and ran to my desk. I tossed it over the gap then crawled underneath. Hiding was the only option I had. Maybe it wasn't real. Maybe that was just another flashback or a hallucination. A very, very vivid hallucination. I refused to move from under the blanket. I gripped tightly at my knees, just crying. I sat, barely breathing, for what felt like an eternity until I heard the sound of my door. There were footsteps. Footsteps of one person. They were slow, but they were light. They came close to my cave, eventually stopping and reaching their hand down to lift it up. The light blinded me, and I turned my body to face the wall.

"Noah? It's Jaiden." She spoke ever so softly. "Can I talk to you?"

I gripped my nails at the bricks, unable to even respond.

"Noah, sweetie, look at me."

I pried my head from the wall and looked up at her figure with swollen and desperate eyes.

"What are you doing under here?"

"I… I… think I did something… really… really bad," I trembled, my whole body jerking as I used up what little oxygen I had in me.

She knelt down and I noticed a radio strapped to her belt. "What is it that you think you did?"

I shook my head. "I don't know… I was in the common room… then I… was here and…"

She nodded. "Noah... something has happened in the wing today that's... really quite... impactful on everyone here."

"What?"

"Would you say you don't remember what happened earlier?"

My shaking worsened. "When I came back, I was... I was..." I broke into a further spurt of tears and fell onto Jaiden's lap.

She rubbed my shoulder, caringly wiping whatever mess was left on my face. "Shh, it's okay." She pulled the radio from her belt and spoke into it. "I've got him. He's pretty worked up, but he doesn't seem of any danger."

I gripped at her scarf. "What's going on?"

She sighed. "It's Dr Wilks."

"W-What about her?"

She struggled to get her words out. "She's... she was... she died, Noah."

It instantly clicked in my head, and I bawled more. More staff had now entered the room and I quickly crawled back to the corner, huddling there as they spread out across my room. Then the blanket lifted again. This time it was Olsen. He crouched down and gave his best attempt at a smile.

"Hey."

"Hey," Jaiden replied.

"How are we doing under here?"

"I'm not too sure," she whispered. "I think he's either had a break or in the midst of one."

"Okay." He scratched on the carpet to get my attention. "Hey, mate. D'you wanna go somewhere we can have a talk?"

I shook my head, terrified that if I left the spot the scene would come back to me. They glanced at each other, and Dr Olsen shuffled closer, resting on his knees.

"Noah, mate. Do you feel comfortable talking with us?"

"Y-Yeah."

"Alright. Why don't you want to come with us?"

I nodded at the crowd that was searching the room. "They're gonna hurt me..."

He glanced back at them. "No, they won't, Noah. They won't touch you. Only me and Dr Maddens will be with you."

I turned back to the wall.

"Come on. We'll go to my office. It'll be quiet and we can just sit and have a chat. That okay?"

I nodded slowly and heard him sigh in relief.

"Alright. Let's get you out of here shall we?"

He reached his hand out and he pulled me out from the camp. He held me tightly as we hobbled over to the opened door together. Jaiden muttered to one of the staff and they nodded in understanding and headed into the halls. I was still trembling and jolting back and forth as I tried to breathe, both Olsen and Jaiden were holding me up as we headed for Olsen's office. They kept me between them, edging me away from any type of escape route that they assumed I would take. Jaiden opened the door to the office and Dr Olsen sat me down on his sofa. He reached for a cloth that was folded in one of his many supply boxes and dabbed the blood from my face, continuing to talk to me as he did.

"It's alright, mate. You're gonna be safe in here."

"W-What's gonna happen to me?" I stuttered.

Jaiden rubbed my shoulder. "We don't know yet."

"Did I do it? Did I kill her?"

She glanced at Dr Olsen, wishing for him to tell the story instead.

He took the rag away. "We have a recording of you…" He cleared his throat. "It was of you doing what you did to Ryan to Dr Wilks. The rest of the staff noticed you when you were stumbling back to your room with blood all over you."

I burst into tears and fell onto Olsen's lap. "Oh, my God."

He stroked my back. "I know, mate."

"Doctor, can I speak with you outside?" asked Jaiden.

"Sure." He lifted my head then the two of them stood up. "Just lay here, Noah. I'll be back in a minute."

I nodded and laid back down, bringing my legs up onto the sofa. They both headed outside, leaving the door slightly ajar as to keep track of my movements, but they spoke very quietly.

"What are we gonna do with him?" Jaiden asked.

"I don't know."

"What do you suggest, Joel? We can't send him back to his room, and we can't leave him with the other staff. We both saw him on that video, he wasn't acting right – he was in a fugue. We need to test him."

"Okay, but what about Wilks? She had a family, they'll want him to… be punished. And he killed her. You know legally he'll have to be charged?"

"I know…"

Dr Olsen sighed. "You should go home. I'll look after him."

"I'm fine."

"Go home, you need rest too."

"So do you."

"I'm pretty much nocturnal these days. I'll stay."

"You'll take care of him, right?"

"You know I will."

They stepped back in, and Jaiden knelt beside me, brushing my fringe out of the way. "Noah?"

"Yeah?"

"I'm gonna leave you here with Dr Olsen, okay? I'll be back in the morning."

I closed my eyes. "Okay…"

"Bye, Noah." I heard her step away and the creak of the door as it shut. She whispered to Olsen. "Thank you."

"No problem."

Jaiden disappeared and Dr Olsen sat beside me, gently nudging my legs for him to sit. "Hey, mate."

"I'm in a lot of trouble, huh?" I said with a self-depreciating chuckle.

"Unfortunately, yeah."

I sat up. "I didn't mean to hurt anyone. I just… I was scared after… what happened to me, so I stopped taking them."

"What?"

"My pills. I didn't think they'd make all this happen, I was just too scared. I'm so sorry."

He lifted his head in concern. "How long have you been skipping them?"

"I don't remember… It was after I had that allergic reaction."

"Noah, that was weeks ago. Did you not feel any different?"

I sighed and picked at the cotton on my trouser leg. "I did. I couldn't think straight – it was all really loud, and I kept getting aches over my body and some tingling feelings."

"Alright." He stood up. "Noah, do you understand that I'm gonna have to put you in the isolation room?"

I swallowed. "I know."

Well, I guess now they had a reason to send me away. The isolation

88

room is the most secure room in Riptide. I've been there an odd few times. It has a single bed attached to the wall and a toilet on the other side. From top to bottom it's protected by the cushioned pads to stop any chance of you hurting yourself or the staff, because you could throw yourself at any force and it would take the damage instead. That's it. That's all there is in there. It's also silenced. The walls around it are so thick that you can't hear a thing through them either way. The only way a doctor can see you his through the rounded camera that's fixed to the ceiling.

I was as calm as I could be as a hoard of doctors surrounded me to take me there. They all seemed on edge and forced me to stay in the middle of them with my hands restrained and cuffed to two of the doctors who were willing enough to be so close to me. One was Olsen. He was quite happy to keep me with him. The other guy wasn't so keen. He kept pulling his hand away which, in turn, brought my arm along with it. We entered the cell, the chain of doors to get to it halving the amount of people that were around us each time until there were only three. They laid me down on the bed and moved the handcuffs from the doctors' wrists to the rail along the side of the bed. I started to panic – the sensation flashing me back to how they treated me in Sector 1 – I tossed my head from side to side to ignore it.

Dr Olsen held my arm in place. "Keep still, Noah. Keep very still."

"No, no. I changed my mind! I don't wanna be in here. I'll stay in my room! I won't go anywhere, you can watch me!"

"Noah, that's why we've brought you in here. We can make sure that you're safe from through the camera without having to pull up the screen each time."

I shook my head as the doctor beside him lifted my sleeve. "No." I jerked my arm the best I could. "No!"

Dr Olsen continued in his calm and caring manner as he settled me down. They did the same procedure that they had done with me when I was having flashbacks, but this time they didn't just give me sedative, they gave me my medication through the tube instead of me swallowing it. It turns out that my memory meds *do* help in stopping me forgetting things, but they also stop me from remembering. The reason this chain of events started was because I remembered the school, and because the memory was broken, my paranoia kept taunting me with the scene over and over so much to a point that I acted it out on someone else.

That was the conclusion they came to. Because I couldn't remember what happened, they had to theorise with me from the CCTV video. I didn't make a sound in the video, just how I didn't make a sound when I tried to kill Ryan. I had taken a wire, similar to before, and wrapped it around Wilks's neck, and the fact I continued until she was lifeless on the floor was because no one was there to stop me. I could barely watch the video when they showed me – Jaiden was against the idea to begin with, but the staff wanted answers from me and were then annoyed when I had none.

A few days passed and I was still stuck in the isolation room when two out of town detectives showed up at the hospital. I was taken to an investigation room where I was put in a straitjacket and chained to the floor as the two of them asked me questions. I didn't give them any answers either. They both seemed rather uncomfortable, and I was just the same. I kept getting asked if 'I knew what I did wrong', and I kept replying with yes, which confused them more on how to deal with the charges. They couldn't do much else with the information so agreed to come back at a later date.

As well as this, there was another factor that was being considered. If I could stay in Riptide. I was now the only patient here that had actually killed someone. When a patient is sent to Ocean Cliff with a murder charge they go straight to Dark Down, and they very rarely resurface. I hadn't taken the life of a stranger either. I killed a doctor. So let's just say that the bare minimum of people were left to like me. I got rid of one person who hated me to get about fifteen more. If they did send me back down I wouldn't have blamed them.

In the midst of contemplating my fate, I heard the door behind open. I glanced back and saw Olsen step inside.

"Hey, mate," he said. "You alright?"

"Yeah…" I turned back.

He stepped beside me. "Is it okay if I sit and talk with you for a bit?"

I nodded. "M-hm."

He took a seat next to me on the cushioned floor. "Okay. So, I came here to talk to you about what we're doing tomorrow."

I looked back up again.

"Do you remember when you first got here, we took you to that place with the machines?"

I shook my head. "No…"

"Okay, well… We've set up an appointment at an outside hospital to

90

give you an MRI."

"What?"

"I know that sounds scary, but I'll be with you. The MRI is just to see if we can find out what else could have cause this relapse."

"Oh…"

"It's gonna be fine," he continued reassuringly. "You've managed it before. We'll be gone for a good few hours, but the test should be shorter. We'll be coming to get you in the early morning, so don't be alarmed. We'll secure you then take you to the van. Okay?"

"M-hm."

"Okay." He rose. "Good boy."

He gave me a light pat on the back, and I watched as he disappeared. I hadn't much else to do, so I returned to picking at the stitching on the floor. This was what I had to pass the time. That and sleep. Later, in the very early morning, I was awoken by the doctor, just as he said.

He was sat at the end of my bed, gently shaking my side. "Hey, mate. Morning."

I sat up. "Hi…"

"Feeling okay?" he asked softly.

"I'm tired…"

"Me too," he replied. "But hey, we can nap later." He smiled. "Do you need anything before we go?"

"Um… no."

"Okay. Come on." He reached his arms around me and hoisted my legs over the edge.. "We're gonna put you in the straitjacket and give you a light sedative. Is that okay?"

"M-hm."

He rubbed my back. "Good."

I glanced around at the other staff joining the room. They kept at the far side as they secured each part of the equipment. One doctor stepped over with a small case in hand then passed it to Dr Olsen. He opened the top and revealed the sedative. I brought my knees back onto the bed and held them tightly.

"It's okay, mate." He rubbed my shoulder. "It's okay." He finished adjusting the needle. "Can I have your arm?"

I shakily extended my arm and rolled my sleeve.

"Okay." He tapped around my skin with his finger. "Good boy." He then injected the needle into the muscle. "Good boy."

I winced as he did it, the feeling of the liquid entering my body and the feeling of the needle being removed.

"Well done, mate." Olsen passed the case over to another doctor, transferring it for a straitjacket. "Just this now." He stood up.

I shuffled after him and Olsen slipped the jacket over me. He tightened the buckles quickly then lowered me into the wheelchair. He pulled the final strap over my lap then took the handles.

"Alright, we're good."

The doctors muttered to each other as I was wheeled out of the isolation room and back to the main wing of the hospital. I lopped my head from side to side as I fought to keep my eyes open. I'm not sure whether it was the sedative that was putting me to sleep or the fact I was already dead tired, and maybe even a bit of both.

I stared at the passing walls of Riptide, the emptiness of the halls giving me a sense of unease. It was strange to see the place so still – the only ones about were the group surrounding me. They took me through to the mazes and we stopped opposite the lift. A guard pushed the button and I glanced over at the staircase beside us that wrapped down to the lower sectors. I bounced my legs up and down as we were all sealed in the small space. I watched intently at which floor number was pressed. I couldn't tell. My view was blocked. There were a series of beeps and the electronic voice followed.

"Going down."

The metal shook as we lowered below Riptide, arriving at Sector 2. The doors slid across and revealed the near-identical level. All that was different was the sign and the occurrence of a door to the right, opposite the stairwell. The staff wheeled me over and unlocked it as I read the sign above:

INTAKE/OUTTAKE

I felt a sort of shimmer run through me at the recollection of such a sign – and the first time I saw it wasn't at the hospital. I gave a short giggle to myself as we entered the area.

Dr Olsen gazed over me in confusion. "Are you okay, mate?"

I nodded and went quiet. "M-hm."

He patted me again and I turned my attention to the windows beside me. They were still barred, but I could see the blur of a fence in the distance

92

with a dark stretch of concrete behind it – the outer wall not too far beyond that. There were bright, glowing lights swirling around the corner, and as we drew closer to the exit, I could make out that they were police cars – two to be exact. I didn't panic. I thought I would have, but slowly I was drifting unconscious, my eyelids fluttering with every second.

Eventually, we stopped inside a corner room. I was unclipped from the wheelchair and lifted up by several staff onto a moveable bed. I tried my best to walk myself, but my feet had given up. I doubt I was much help, though. Me trying to flail my noodle legs about probably made it a lot harder to get me on the bed.

Once I was down, Olsen lifted the rails and strapped me back down. "Come on, mate. We're nearly out." He adjusted several of my straps. "Are you comfortable enough?"

"The buckles… are kinda… digging into my back," I said drowsily.

"Not much we can do about that I'm afraid." He snapped the other railing up. "Everything else okay?"

I closed my eyes. "M-hm."

I didn't hear whether he responded or not, I just felt the jolt as we started moving once again. I took in a breath as we reached the final door. The doctor scanned their card, and the seal was broken. The rush of frozen winter air flooded past us, and the staff quickly rushed through the breeze to reach the van. As they did, I stared back at where we came from. The hospital drew further and further back, the sheer size of the place wasn't even viewable. It scaled heights above my tiny form and even trying to see the upper sectors made my head spin. The structure itself seemed pretty grim, you could tell what level they always stopped cleaning at, but even then you could tell it was once the same shade.

We turned past another fence, which snapped my thoughts away from the endless building and towards the car park. They unlocked the final gate and we rumbled across the pavement to meet the rather guarded van that awaited me. I continued to twitch my eyes as they grew heavier and kept them open for just enough time to see the doors swing open and get myself tucked inside. Olsen stepped beside me, along with another doctor and guard as the doors slammed shut.

Through my worn-out state, I muttered to him. "You're… staying… with me… right?"

Olsen flashed a smile. "Yeah."

I inhaled and nodded, just in time for me to get knocked out cold as the rumble of the van began.

It felt like I awoke fairly quickly, but as I opened my eyes expecting to see the van, I was greeted by the ceiling of an unknown place. I struggled to move, I was still restrained tightly. I peered to the side and saw a wall with a bright pink strip painted across it. Just above that were words in the same colour, reading:

Short-Term Stay – Adult Admission Unit

I twisted my head as far as I could, and spotted Dr Olsen stood behind me, staring anxiously ahead at the group across from him. I tried to make my presence known with a movement, but each muscle was so tightly clamped back that all I could do was strain and struggle. This still worked, though, as Olsen was quick to settle me back down.

He spoke in a whisper. "Noah, Noah, Noah, calm down. It's alright."

I stared up at him. "W-Where are we?"

"We're at the place," he replied. "It's very early, though, so try to keep quiet, okay?"

I nodded shyly. "Okay."

They started dragging me through the wing of the hospital, the sound of the squeaking wheels rattling down the corridor. We stopped outside a doorway, and I heard a doctor step away. They muttered quietly to a nurse whilst I looked up at Olsen. He seemed worried, I could see it flickering in his eyes.

"Are you okay?" I asked him.

He smiled and nodded. "I'm fine, mate."

"You look, um…" I trailed off, realising that I wasn't being quiet. "Never mind."

He patted my arm lightly. "Are you okay?"

I nodded the best I could before nestling my head back into the pillow as the doctor returned with the nurse by her side.

"I'm afraid the machine isn't ready yet," the nurse began. "We'll have to keep him aside for a bit."

"Oh," Olsen replied. "Well, if it's no trouble."

"Of course it's not," she said with a smile. "It's my job to make sure the patients are okay." She stepped away.

I gently looked back at Dr Olsen, the panic in him showing more.

"Doctor?"

He didn't respond, the dread in his soul reaching its peak.

"Doctor?" I repeated, this time getting a response.

"Yeah, Noah?"

"What are they gonna do to me?"

"Uh, well, they're gonna put you in the MRI machine, which is going to help us see the inside of your brain."

"Is it gonna hurt?"

He stuttered. "No. It's most likely it won't. As long as you keep to the rules we give you to keep safe."

I settled back down again. "Oh."

The nurse then returned and directed the staff towards a vacant room. I felt my bed tremble as it was pushed along the corridor and hidden away. I strained my head to have a look at my surroundings but was repeatedly lowered for safety. The group spun me around and parked me behind a large curtain that covered my half of the room.

"Unclip him," Olsen ordered.

I felt as the doctors removed each of the restraints and I quickly shimmied upright. Some of them jumped back as I performed my speedy manoeuvre and assured the security of the room as I felt the buckles on the straitjacket loosen. My arms slumped down, and I shook out the cramped muscles the best I could in my drowsy state. I giggled excitedly at my freedom, but it was short-lived as I felt a clamp around my right wrist when I wasn't looking. I turned to it to see Dr Olsen fixing the other end of a pair of handcuffs to his wrist too. I dragged my hand back and brought his with me and I tilted my head in confusion.

"Wherever you go, I'll be going too," he said with a tired smile.

I smiled back and began picking at the cotton sheet as the nurse appeared around the curtain. She kept her distance as she explained what was to come.

"Sorry about this, but the computers were playing up a bit, and without them we wouldn't be able to monitor anything, so we've had to reboot them, and it might take up to thirty minutes to do that. We're not used to doing MRIs this early." She chuckled.

"It's okay," a doctor replied. "Our fault. We just didn't want to risk him running about in the day around the other patients."

"That's perfectly fine," she continued. "I'm happy to help anything like this."

"Thank you," Olsen said as he adjusted the cuff.

She nodded and turned to another staff member.

I laid back on the bed, leaving my arm hanging over the edge. I stared up at the ceiling tiles and sighed deeply. Olsen sat down in the plastic chair beside me and kept his arm pointed up. I turned to face him and gently bounced my wrist up and down to get his attention. He glanced up with his tired eyes.

"Yeah, Noah?" he whispered.

"I'm hungry," I whispered back, almost shamefully.

He sighed and rubbed his face. "I don't think there's anything for us to give you yet. Do you think you can hold on for a bit?"

I nodded and rolled to face away from him, keeping my arm behind me. The time passed slowly. With nothing to do except go over my thoughts, I started falling anxious, slowing time more. I practically leapt off the bed when the nurse returned and called to us. The group surrounded me, and I was led out to the corridor.

I bounced back and forth as they escorted me through. It was strange to see how different the place was to Ocean Cliff. It was so much brighter, the walls were beaming with a pastel lilac – similar to the colour of the Freefall outfits. I always wanted to wear that colour. Fixed to the ceiling were vibrant royal signs, the writing so crisp. I jumped up to try and touch one, only to remember that the other half of me was handcuffed tightly to Olsen. He still held the fearful look in his eyes, joint with a slight annoyance, probably due to the fact that each time I leapt in a new direction, his skin got grinded around his wrist.

He glared at me in this same manner as I fell back down from the sign. "Noah," he said sternly.

He needn't say another word. I understood the look. I tilted my head down shamefully. "Sorry, doctor…"

"It's alright," he replied softly. "Keep walking."

We continued following the group until we came to a stop beside a large door. I glanced between each of the staff members in confusion, trying to understand where we were, but no one spoke. Then a slim, freckled nurse popped out from behind the panel and smiled. She approached Dr Olsen and whispered to him gently.

"We're all ready, he just needs to have his clothes checked before he can get settled."

Olsen nodded. "Okay, thanks."

The nurse stepped back and flashed me another grin before she scampered back inside the room. I intently watched her actions before turning to Dr Olsen as he tugged at my sleeve.

"Alright, Noah. You ready, mate?"

"Um…" I glanced back down the hallway, focussing on the many lockless doors that we passed.

Olsen followed my gaze before he cautiously rested his hand over the handcuffs, locking them slightly tighter. "Noah?"

"I…" I shuffled towards the open stretch, my eyes fixed ahead for several moments before I shot back to the staff in confusion. "What?"

As Olsen took me by my hand, a woman reached for the other, the both of them gently pulling me towards the room.

"Come on, Noah," she said calmly. "It's gonna be fine."

I swallowed anxiously but willingly followed their wishes and stepped through the door. They positioned me in a small side room with two doctors and a guard. Olsen removed the handcuff and spread my arms out wide.

"Keep still, mate."

He ran his hands over my clothes, patting down my body until he reached my feet.

"Take your shoes off quick."

I did as he said and stepped onto the tiles, the cold seeping through my padded socks. I shuffled up and down as I tried to keep off of it as the guard inspected each of my shoe's insides. I expected him to return them to me, but instead he just tucked them under his arm, and I was dragged back out again.

Olsen patted my back. "Okay, Noah. We're gonna lay you down on the machine, alright? Don't panic, I'll be right here."

I nodded friskily as I approached the large, circular machine.

"That's it," he continued softly.

The staff lightly grabbed my shoulders and ushered me to sit down on the long metal strip, lowering me onto my back. I looked up at Olsen as he was passed an item that was blocked from my view, and I shuffled anxiously.

"What's that?" I questioned, jerking my head back slightly.

"It's fine, mate," Olsen replied. "They're just ear defenders. They're to protect your ears from the machine. It can get very noisy, and we don't want it to hurt them."

I jolted upwards but the doctors swiftly lowered me back down as I exclaimed. "It's gonna hurt me? "

"No, no," he returned in a rush. "Not if you have these on."

I loosened my body. "Oh…"

"I'm gonna put them on you now, okay?"

I nodded and he smiled back.

"Good boy."

Olsen gently placed the defenders over my ears. Once he let go, they snapped to my head and all noise ceased. Complete silence. I couldn't even hear the sound of myself. I rapidly tapped my nails at the metal around me, desperately searching for a sign of a noise. But there was nothing. Only a deafening, crisp emptiness. I shook my head back and forth as my chest began to tighten. This was followed by the doctors fixing a device around my head, my instincts causing me to jerk about and scream in silence.

Olsen then took my hand as another doctor lowered a mask onto my face. I tried to avoid it as the contraption grew closer and closer towards my powerless state until it was strapped onto me and stole my right to react. Within those long seconds, my sharp movements became blunt, and my eyelids drooped as I slowly fell into a bliss state.

I gently rocked my head from side to side as I tried to stay awake. My eyelids fluttered open, and my consciousness returned. I gazed over my surroundings, only to notice I was in a completely different place. It definitely wasn't the MRI room – it was just a regular one. I was lying still on a bed. I tried to push myself to sit up, but my body got dragged back down by the two leather restraints that were tightened to both of my ankles. I had my hands free, so I could probably undo them if I tried, but I couldn't bring myself to do it. I just rested back against the crisp and softened pillows, and that's when I noticed how alone I was. There wasn't a guard in sight, and the only doctor with me was Olsen, and he wasn't exactly ready for action. He was sat slumped in a chair to my right with his arms folded, his head drooped forwards, and his eyes firmly shut.

I glanced at him in confusion. "Doctor?"

He shuffled his legs.

"Um… Dr Olsen?"

He didn't respond.

I leant in his directions, reaching over the side bar to nudge him. I strained as the restraints held me down and I scanned around me at what I could use to wake him. I tapped on the table beside me, but he still remained asleep. I tried again, but then slumped back on my bed as the aches in my body grew stronger. I pulled myself forwards and began tugging at my leg cuffs. I wasn't strong enough, though. I fell back as a dizzying sensation cast over me. I rested against the pillow and glanced back at the doctor, panting,

"Doctor?" I said breathlessly.

He rocked his head back and forth.

I inhaled and sat up, flopping against the side of the bed and gripping at the bar as my head rushed.

"Doctor…"

My gaze drifted down, and I spotted a pen laying on the surface beside me, so I picked it up and reached over to Olsen. But as I did, the end door swung inwards, with a clatter of footsteps rushing towards me.

"Coleman!" a man called as both me and Dr Olsen flinched.

Olsen glanced around in confusion. "What?"

The group scrambled over and pinned me back down on the bed, ripping the pen out of my hands and cuffing my left hand onto the rail. I struggled against them in a panic as their weights pushed down on me.

"Don't move, Coleman. Stay down."

Olsen jumped up and fought his way to the bedside. "What's going on?"

"He was reaching towards you. He had the nurse's pen in his hand."

"I was just trying to wake him up!" I cried as they backed off, my hand firmly in place. I tugged at it frantically before Dr Olsen gently held my free arm.

"Noah. It's okay," he said softly. "Stay calm."

I was panting quickly from the shock and covered my embarrassed face with the thin blanket that was laying over me.

The doctor folded it back. "Come on, mate. It's alright."

I hesitantly poked my head out again and tried to sit up, only to slide back down as the leg cuffs stopped me. Olsen must have noticed my discomfort and so unstrapped both ankles, the restraints clattering against the metal sides as they fell.

"What are you doing?" a guard questioned under his breath.

"What?" he replied. "It's not like he's gonna go anywhere. There's five of us in here and he weighs under eight stone – you could carry him with one arm."

The guard scoffed and turned away. Once my legs were free, I sat up and consoled the red, burning skin that the leather had dug away at.

Dr Olsen turned to the staff. "See? He's fine. You just startled him." He stepped away. "He's still the scared kid, he always is." He pulled a woman aside and lowered his voice. "Now, tell me what's going on with the results."

I stared at them as they spoke.

"That's what we came in here to tell you." She glanced at me and whispered. "We should talk somewhere else."

Dr Olsen gave me the same concerned look before he nodded and followed her into a side office. As they left, the same freckled nurse from earlier entered with a small cart with several items across it. She wheeled it over to the guard and he checked the contents. An Ocean Cliff doctor then swung beside me and kept his hand hovering in front of my chest, keeping me from jumping forwards any further.

"I understand the urgency to get him back to where he needs to be, but it is coming up to the usual time that patients have breakfast around here, so I brought a spare tray," the nurse explained.

"Thank you," the man beside me said. "But our patients don't have breakfast for another hour or so, and we wouldn't want to mess up his eating plans – he struggles with food as it is."

"That's fine, I understand. I'll leave it over here for you." She placed it on a far table. "Are you okay with me doing the assessment on him?"

He gazed over me in hesitation before he nodded.

"Lovely." The nurse stepped back over to the cart and collected the equipment.

It was the same as Riptide's – just maybe a bit newer. My limbs shook anxiously as she measured each of my stats, even turning away and clenching my eyes as she taped several red stickers across my chest and wrist. She then clamped the end tab of each and typed across her system.

I did my best to ignore what else she was doing to me, and instead laid back and listened carefully to the conversation that was being muttered on the other side of the wall.

"… so then what happened after?" asked Dr Olsen.

100

"We still managed to get a reading of his brain, which is good, but it seems a little distorted," the woman replied. "We're not sure whether it was the machine or not, but we can still see the basic idea of what activity is going on in his head."

There were muffled sounds of sliding papers.

"So when did you get this?"

"Not too long ago. Like I said, it took a few hours to even get the data sorted out, we haven't even got half of it yet, but they gave us this one to work with. I gave a quick glance over it and spotted that same issue with his hippocampus."

"That's the same injury he had the last time he was scanned, so at least we know he hasn't hurt his brain any more since he got here – even if we still don't know what caused the first incident."

"Yeah, but if we look around his injury and in the parental lobe, he got such a big sensory overload that even the machine couldn't read it."

"How could he even get an overload? He was sedated and had ear defenders on. Even then, you can't break an MRI machine just by being overstimulated."

"That's why me and Toby were talking earlier. We put it down to his schizoaffective disorder, but even then, some points don't add up. Even schizophrenics don't have the power to break technology with their minds – even if they sometimes think they can."

Olsen sighed. "Oh, God. What are we gonna do with him, Paige?"

"I don't know, but I think we both know that this is evidence to give to the police. It's proof that even with his rehabilitation, he's still not fit to go to court. He falls into fugues that we can't get him out of and sending him to a place with so many people, you can bet he'll have an episode of something. He *has* to stay in Sector 3. Not just for this case, but for as long as he can."

"That's not what I'm worried about – I was always gonna keep him in Riptide – I'm worried about *him*. His behaviour's unpredictable, he always gets where he shouldn't be, and he'll switch in a second from being this innocent child to this lost adult. The only time I've ever seen him calm is when he's near someone he trusts, and that's not many people."

The woman's voice softened. "Have you spoke to his family?"

"Yeah…" he replied in a disheartened tone. "They're upset, obviously. Getting told your son just killed someone isn't exactly the easiest thing to hear halfway through work, and the fact they can't do anything about it probably makes it worse."

They fell quiet, the noise of my room becoming highlighted for a brief moment before the conversation continued.

"About this fugue…" Dr Olsen began. "He had it with Ryan, he had it for a few minutes in Sector 1, and now he's had it with Wilks. I know we've been over this theory before, but I think we need to test him for DID again."

"Joel—"

"I know, we've done it countless times, but I can't think of any other possibility right now. We've checked Autism, BPD, the lot."

"Maybe we should just tick 'em all off," she replied jokingly.

"I'm getting to that point, y'know." He gave a yawn.

"Joel, why don't you go home? Your shift ended an hour and a half ago. We can easily manage without you—"

I jolted forwards on the bed, reaching towards the door and it's empty space surrounding it. "NO! Don't leave! I don't want you to go!"

The nurse attending to me jumped back, as did the others, and the man beside me snapped his fingers in front of my face, bringing my attention to him.

"Hey, hey! Look at me. Stay calm. What did you see?" He gripped at my shoulders.

I tried to tug away from him in defiance, desperate to hear what else was happening beyond the bricks.

"We can easily get someone else in to cover for you," Paige continued. "You've done more than enough. We can call Jaiden, she's the next one on the staff list that he likes."

"No, no. I don't want Jaiden to get involved in this, at least not by getting in close contact with him. I'm not trying to say he'll attack her on sight or anything like that, but with Noah, you don't know. Plus, if he does get his hands on her, it's not just her that he'll hurt."

"What d'you mean?"

"It's why she's leaving. She's pregnant. She still wasn't sure for a while, and bless her, she didn't want to leave work unless it was absolutely necessary. I only know 'cause I bumped into her leaving the doctor's surgery, and I told her it's best to go as early as possible – for that same reason I don't want her near Noah. It's dangerous. She didn't want any of the patients knowing just in case something went wrong and didn't want to break their trust with a lie."

I shuddered. "No... she... she..."

The man then forced me onto my back and kept his arm across my chest. "Noah, answer me. What do you see?"

I looked up at him in a tearful confusion. "What?"

"You're looking at something, what do you see?"

I shook my head. "I dunno. I don't see anything."

"Alright," he replied calmly. "You were talking to someone, who was it?"

I pointed over at the empty space. "Dr Olsen and the woman!"

He followed my gaze before he slowly turned back to me. "They're in the other room, Noah."

"I know they are, but I can hear them!"

The group exchanged curious glances and they all shook their heads in disagreement.

"Noah, no one can hear them. That's why they went in the room."

"I can hear them, though! I can!"

He took my free hand and gently lowered it onto the mattress. "Noah, you're hallucinating. You're stressed, you're tired, it's gonna trigger them."

I scrambled onto my knees and dragged the handcuffs up and down the pole in agitation. "No, I'm not! I know they're talking about me, I know it!"

He kept his manner relaxed as he ushered me to lay back down again. "I know what they're talking about, Noah. They're going over your MRI results. They're not allowed to do it in the open in case someone outside of our little group here finds out. It's to keep your privacy."

"W-Well, y-yeah. That's what they w-were saying!"

"Okay." He gave a gesture to the other doctor. "Can you still hear them now?"

My eyes fluttered as I tried my best to listen, but there was a continuous growing of noise coming from the outer corridors. It sent my body into a shudder, and I scratched violently at my neck and temples.

"It's too loud." I shuddered again and the insides of my ears began whistling. I crawled to the man for help, and he cradled my head to protect me from the overwhelming surroundings.

"Alright, okay." He muttered to his co-workers.

They rustled about, metal clanging against each other as they sorted through different items.

I retracted from the man's embrace and gently tugged at the handcuffs. "Can you take this off?"

"Noah, you know that we can't do that."

"Please. I won't go anywhere! You can stay with me."

He glared at me. "Noah. No."

His sternness frightened me, shying me further away from him and laying down on my side, curling into a ball and closing my eyes.

Later, Olsen and the woman returned. I leant forwards as the man approached them and began whispering to Dr Olsen. He was told my actions and I watched as his expression fell further into disappointment. I turned away in shame as he joined me. He scratched my cheek.

"Hey," he said softly. "How you feeling?"

I shrugged.

"Are you still hungry?"

"A little, yeah."

He smiled. "Alright." He called to the nurse who was stood anxiously by the far wall. "He can have that tray now."

She quickly shuffled over with the covered tray in her hands and the doctor took it from her. He swung a small table across from the side and placed the tray down. I pulled myself up and inspected the different foods as Olsen lifted the cover. I don't know what I was expecting, it was food. I picked up the plastic fork and poked at the different pieces. With nothing else to do, I ate what I was given.

Olsen returned to his original seat and the rest of the group dispersed. The guard stepped outside, and I watched through the half-covered glass as he positioned himself beside the door. The nurse followed him out, but didn't return, whilst Toby and Paige simply paced around the space.

A little bit later, Toby approached the window that overlooked the car park and groaned.

"How the hell did they find out we were here?"

"Who?" Olsen questioned.

"The protestors." He began pacing again as Paige checked outside.

"I swear, one comes along and then you see ten more a second later," she said.

I turned to Olsen. "What's a protestor?"

He dragged his chair closer. "Well, usually, it's a group of people who share the same opinion and want to make a change to something."

"What are they protesting?"

He glanced over at his colleagues quickly. "It could be anything. Everyone has the right to free speech. Even you." He flashed a hesitant grin.

I nodded then turned back to my tray. I stared at it then lowered my fork in disgust.

"You don't want any more?" the doctor asked.

I shook my head.

"I thought you were hungry?"

"I was..." I said meekly. "But not anymore."

"You barely ate any of it," he replied as he poked the remaining food with my cutlery.

"Sorry..."

He sighed and sat back, taking the tray away. "It's alright." He placed it down on a table beside him.

"I'm tired..."

He nodded. "Me too, mate."

"When do we go back?"

"Soon. Very soon. We've just got to wait for some people to come help us move you. And the good news for you is that they lost the straitjacket, so it's just handcuffs on the ride back."

"I don't like the handcuffs, though."

He gently rubbed the marks around his wrist. "Yeah, neither do I, but this hospital doesn't have straitjackets 'cause they're not trapped in the middle ages like us." He chuckled.

I nodded, not quite understanding his joke.

"You're doing well today." He rose and checked over by the window.

I watched through the gap in the side curtain as he left.

He whispered. "How long's it gonna take the driver to get through that, d'you think?"

"He should get to the area pretty easily," Toby replied. "It's us that I'm worried about. You know they're gonna swarm us. There's no other way to get him to the van with a safe perimeter. It's not so safe anymore, mind you."

Dr Olsen sighed. "I'm all for justice and everything, but I don't think any of them understand the other side of the situation."

"Neither do I."

"Mm." The doctor stepped back around the curtain and joined my side again.

I swallowed anxiously and picked at my nails. "Doctor?"

"Yeah?"

"Do you know why I hurt Dr Wilks?" I asked sheepishly.

His expression drained and he sat down. "Do you?"

I shook my head. "No."

"Well, then. Neither do we. You know we can only theorise about what goes on in your head. We don't know what goes on in there." He smiled.

"But you still know what I did – everyone does – so why are you being so nice to me?"

He leant back. "Because you're still you. No, we don't like what you did, and we *especially* don't like that people were hurt because of it, but it's a part of our jobs. We get told it's dangerous, we get told it can be scarring, but if it weren't for us then you'd be out lost in the world, so I think it's worth it if it means I can protect and help people. It's our jobs to find out what's wrong with you."

I nodded. Wrong, wrong, wrong. Everything's wrong with me. There's never been a right. Not once. All I am is broken. I don't even know what I am. I'm a patient, I'm a suspect, I'm a disappointment. People have lots of reasons to hurt someone – I had none. I just did it. No recollection of it, but I did it. And those protestors? They all thought I was just another deranged maniac who kills to pleasure his deep desires, and who most definitely deserved worse than what he was getting, but as I was escorted past them, their shouts faded.

I was chained up tightly to a wheelchair with the streams of guilt running down my cheeks. I was trying desperately to shield from the hoard of justice seekers, but they were everywhere I turned. Each of them stood in an awed silence. I cowered underneath the small blanket I had been given and trembled, Dr Olsen keeping his hand beside me for me to hold it close and pray the glares away. I deserved them, each and every one of those hateful, burning eyes that seared into me. They murmured, they whispered, all words they didn't think they'd end up saying.

"He's not what I expected."

"He's not as threatening as I thought he would be."

"He's probably got another side to him."

"I bet that other boy's lucky he got out alive when he did."

106

"If he was in a proper prison, he wouldn't have been able to get to anyone."

Then as we grew inches from the van, a woman leapt the barricade with a large sign gripped in her hands. She thundered her way through to me and began slamming the sign against my head. The cardboard had little effect on me, but the wooden beam certainly did. She got in several blows before she was ripped back by the police screaming as the crowd cheered for her.

"YOU DESERVE EVERY BIT OF HELL THAT'S WAITING FOR YOU! I MEAN IT! I HOPE YOU GET YOUR NECK SLICED OPEN, JUST LIKE YOU DID TO MY MUM, YOU FUCKING FAGGOT!"

The doctors quickly whisked me to the safety of the van and sealed the doors tightly as I panted in and out frantically, clawing at my chest as my head pain crushed against my skull. I wasn't even out of the wheelchair yet and the van was already moving. I guess they wanted to escape the fiasco as quick as they could to retreat to a calmer area to fix me up.

I was left in the corner sobbing and clutching at my right eye. Dr Olsen, Paige and the guard all uncuffed me and inspected my injuries. Olsen carefully lifted my hand away and revealed the battered and already swollen area beneath my eyelid. He gently tried to feel the burning patch, but I pushed his arm back each time to stop the pain from furthering.

"D'you think we should go back in there?" Paige asked.

"No, no. It's not worth all the hassle, he'll only get beat again. We can fix him up on the way back." He began wiping the small drops of blood with a cloth. "Shh, Noah, it's okay."

I shook my head, still sobbing. "No, it's not. It's not!"

"Come on," he said. "Let's lay you down."

The group stepped me towards the bed then, together, hoisted me onto it. I flopped onto my back and was strapped in. They didn't even bother with the extra restraints this time. They just slung the chains to the side and were done with it. I guess they thought there was a more serious issue at hand. Dr Olsen rifled through one of the first aid kits and pulled out a small plastic pouch. He squeezed it then placed it in my hand. It was slowly falling to freezing.

"Hold that on your eye, mate."

I nodded and rested it in position as they finally got a chance to relax, and the van was able to set course for home – the sirens of the police cars echoing around us.

"They were protesting against me then…" I muttered.

"Yeah," Olsen replied sorrowfully. "We didn't think they'd manage to get to you, though. And what that woman said *definitely* isn't true. It wasn't your fault, Noah. You're sick."

"Doctor?" I began quietly.

"Yeah?"

I glanced over at him. "What did she mean when she called me that word?"

His cheeks drained of colour, and he forced himself to turn his head away from me. "It's… It's not a nice word, Noah. It's used against gay people. People like you."

I retreated inside myself, my head lowering further into the pillow and shrouded myself beneath the blanket. "Oh… Why?"

"Don't worry about it, mate. There's no need to learn why. Just know that there's nothing wrong with you and Aaron, okay?"

"No. Why does me being gay have anything to do with it?"

He shook his head. "It doesn't… Some people they… they think it's the reason why you're the way you are, when really, they'll make any connection they can to try and prove you shouldn't be cared for."

I nodded shyly. "Okay…" I gazed out of the small side window as we shot past a stream of fences before I turned back to the others. "How did she know then? That I was gay?"

He bit his lip and shrugged. "I couldn't tell you, mate. Dr Wilks probably knew from your files and told her daughter about you."

I gritted my teeth and tossed over. "I knew she bloody would."

He was taken aback. "It's not like you to talk like that, Noah."

I tossed back and aggressively gestured the ice pack around. "Well, I— I'm just—I knew she would! I knew she'd go home and tell the world about me. I'm just a story. A whole crazy story that no sane person could ever experience, so they take my life and make it a fantasy. Until that fantasy became reality. That's why I'm the villain. I'm not worth anything. I'm not even worth this stupid thing." I chucked the ice pack to the floor and faced the window again. I shuddered and gripped at my blanket, pulling it over myself and hiding from the group.

The rest of the journey was silent. All the way through 'til processing. They inspected my battered eye – assuring that I wasn't blinded – then returned me to Riptide. They locked me back up in isolation for another

108

week with nothing but questions being thrown my way. The MRI results were finally collected together, and the doctors did what they could to make me understand. I couldn't. Not really, anyway. The different images just looked like a blurred mess.

I was told what I overheard. That when I became overstimulated I broke the machine. That's why some images were worse off than others. Nobody was able to comprehend how that happened, so at least I wasn't alone in my confusion that time. But from everything else, I gathered what I could. My brain injury caused my amnesia, as well as possibly my other problems, and my fugues were the result of stress. It seems rather simple when you just see it like that, but it's really not.

The detectives returned after, but they didn't speak to me. They watched me through a camera and talked to the doctors, but then they left again. I couldn't tell you another thing. Nobody told me a word.

After my final day of punishment, and the case wrapped to a close, I was released back to my room with the news that I'd not to go anywhere outside my room without an escort. I stepped in with the doctors to see the room stripped bare. All of my belongings were crammed inside cardboard boxes that were waiting for me on my desk. I rummaged through one and pulled out Aaron's knitted blanket. I brought it close to me and snuggled against it as a doctor stepped over.

"We had to search through all your things after your isolation. We didn't take much, just a few contraband items like your sharpener and razor. We left all of your art and your gifts."

"How am I meant to sharpen my pencils or shave?"

"You ask," she replied bluntly. "You're not even meant to have them in your room, you know that. You need permission from someone, and they have to watch you do it. It's not like you need the razor anyway, baby face."

They approached the airlock.

"Free time's coming up. You're to wait in here until your counsellor arrives to escort you."

The door lifted.

"Jaiden?" I questioned.

"No," the woman replied. "Dr Hudson."

"Right…" I cradled the blanket as the duo left.

I turned back to my stuff and rummaged inside. I found my bathroom items and brought them through. I returned them to where they once stood then glanced up at my reflection, seeing the large bruise surrounding my right eye. I lightly tapped it and winced as an aching pain shot through me. I exhaled slowly before continuing to organise my toiletries. There wasn't much there, only towels, my toothbrush, toothpaste, soap, and my two-in-one shampoo. I mean, what else goes in a bathroom, really?

After sorting out another box, the alarm sounded for free period. I did as I was told and waited for Caleb to arrive. I missed out on ten minutes of freedom, but he came eventually, along with a guard. They walked me outside and towards the common room. I didn't want to go, but I hadn't anything to do. It wasn't fun, though. With each person we passed, a judgemental, steely glare was shot my way, especially upon entering the social area. I stepped in the door and froze, my attention only drawn to the disgust in the air. I was only broken free by Caleb pushing me forwards.

I quickly shuffled away from him and settled by the window. I stared across the car park at the outer wall, noticing a feint orange creature fluttering over the razor wire, shining brightly against the bleak weather. It bounced back and forth until it met with a large bird. The bird pecked at it with its beak until the orange creature sent it off with its sudden, rapid movements. The creature then rested on the tip of the next fence. I turned away, deciding to inspect the room I hadn't seen in weeks. It was exactly the same. All that was new was the fact I was being watched intently from the other side. Caleb and the guard were stood together with their eyes fixed on me.

I turned back and faced the TV, distraught over what was playing on the screen. It was the news. They were showing what seemed to be an arial shot of a large crowd. They were yelling loudly, and as the reporter explained, my past self-appeared. The scene flashed back in my mind and the echo of the daughter's words unpicked the stitches of my emotionless front. I yanked my sleeves down nervously and threw my hood over my head as I stared at the screen.

"We received more on the Ocean Cliff murder last night after authorities confirmed the closure of the case. The patient responsible for the crime was originally kept from the public due to confidentiality, but after the victim's family was told of the murder, the patient's identity was revealed as Noah Coleman – a twenty-four year old man who is incarcerated at the hospital where Dr Yvonne Wilks worked."

The screen quickly cut between two images. The first was of the doctor.

She was joyful and surrounded by similar bright-faced figures, each of them showing love to one another. Then the second was of me. It was my intake photo – the only photo the hospital had of me, and the only photo the public would ever see. My eyes were grey and puffy, one eyelid droopier than the other, with my hair greasy and casting out at multiple angles, and the final touch being my broken, chapped lips. It was obvious who was meant to be the villain in this situation.

"The footage caught from a police helicopter shows Coleman being discharged from a public hospital and being beaten by the justice-seeking protestors. These protestors included the friends and family of the victim who were desperate to see a more fitting punishment than the one they heard.

Coleman was not taken to court and did not give a plea. This was due to the fact that he was not in the right frame of mind. Doctors and authorities both concluded that Coleman was guilty through reasons of insanity, stating that the patient did not consciously do the act.

This was not taken well with the family of Dr Wilks, as Coleman's sentence was not altered as he was already being institutionalised indefinitely. Since this was revealed, protests have been occurring at both the courthouse and the Ocean Cliff Psychiatric Hospital for Coleman to receive further punishment."

I shuddered, my skin and eyes burning as patients turned over the back of the sofa to face me. I whimpered and bolted from the room, slamming the heavy door into the cushioned wall-pad as Caleb's voice called desperately after me.

"Noah! Noah, come back, please!"

I glanced over my shoulder and saw him rushing for me, radio in hand and his keys swinging from his belt. I turned back and sprinted faster, panting with sharp breaths as I fought not to cry out. I passed Jaiden's office and she caught sight of me as I tripped and skidded across the tiles.

"Noah!" she jumped out of her door towards me. "Noah, are you—"

I scrambled up and backed away with my arms out frontwards, shaking my head. "NO! LEAVE ME ALONE!" I headed for the rooms, hearing her voice as she questioned Caleb.

"Caleb, what's going on?"

He sighed. "God, I don't know. His case was on the news."

"What? His first case?"

"No, no, the Dr Wilks case. They didn't mention anything about Ryan, thankfully."

Their voices faded as I skidded around the corner, slamming against my door upon reaching it. I rattled the handle and tugged violently for the airlock to release, but it didn't budge. I kicked at the metal and threw my body against it, sliding down to my knees and sobbing as the staff gathered around me. Caleb crouched beside me and held my arm.

"Noah, Noah, calm down, deep breaths, okay?"

I clawed at his shirt, causing him to flinch. I noticed his pain and quickly shot back. "No, no! I can't stop it! I CAN'T... STOP! PLEASE!" I buried my head in my knees. "I don't want to be like this anymore..."

Caleb patted my shoulder. "It's okay, it's okay. We'll figure it out."

I peered over my knees at the doctors looming above me, instinctively rolling onto my front as I saw the needle in a man's hand. "Just get it over with..."

As I nuzzled against my forearms, the staff knelt down and shimmied my layers up to my shoulders. They pinched my lower back, and the sedation sensation began. Before I was completely out, they unlocked the door to my room and dragged me towards my bed, slumping me onto the mattress and waiting. Through my drooped eyelids, I saw Jaiden. She gently removed my shoes then tucked my blanket around me. With what energy I had left, I lightly placed my hand above hers. She sighed and stroked her thumb across my skin.

"It's gonna get better," she whispered. "Trust me."

I gave a sluggish nod, and she rested my hand atop my pillow. "I'm... sorry..." I murmured.

She sighed. "I know you are."

I wasn't out for too long but fell asleep for good at around eight. But even then I couldn't escape the day. Through 'til midnight, I was taunted by it. By all of it. Ryan, Wilks, each memory playing with me, contorting my dreams into a corrupted nightmare. I'd wake up shrieking with tears soaking the sheets, only to be pinned down with guilt. I ripped my sheet from my bed in agitation, hurling it to the carpet, and curling up as I gripped desperately at my pillow, begging for everything to stop. But it didn't. Not on its own. The only way I could bring it to an end was to get the pain I deserved.

There was no watch on me at night – aside from the bed check guard that came an hour or so after lights out – plus, the camera can't pick up every angle of my room, so this gave me ample time to do it. There wasn't much I could use, in fact, there wasn't anything, except for the one part of me they couldn't confiscate.

I sat up, brought my nail to my forearm, and sliced it down my skin. It stung, and once the deed was done, I cradled the injury against my chest. It was quick, but the pain lingered. So did the guilt, but at least the public got what they wanted. People pray to see punishment but scream when they see the suffering. So why should I give them that pleasure? One person suffering is enough, so give it to the guy who deserves it, and no one else needs to know it.

After a minute of clutching my arm, I tore it away to inspect the damage I caused, only to break into a further spurt of tears when there was nothing there but a few flakes of broken skin. So I tried again. Then again, and again, and again, until my arm was burning and swamped with light red scratches. Not one cut deep enough to do the damage that was needed, so I slumped back and stared at the ceiling in defeat. If I can't even be here to suffer then I shouldn't be here at all. What's the point in wasting time on me when the doctors could be caring for somebody who needs it. It's not like they ever wanted me here in the first place.

When the sun rose and casted its stunning amber glow through my window, I took in a breath, holding it for as long as I could until I exhaled in acceptance of what I planned to do. When the time came for my medication, Dr Phillipson stepped in with her same bright smile.

"Good morning, Noah. You doing okay?"

I smiled. "Yeah."

"Good. Let's get you to your meds then, shall we?"

"M-hm."

I followed her out of the room and waited alone in the airlock as the slot in the second door slid across. I rested my wrists on the plate and held my sleeves down as the handcuffs were locked onto me. I took my arms back and met with the staff in the corridor. Together, we headed for medical. I kept my eyes fixed ahead as we passed each inch of the hospital until we reached the door. Phillipson unlocked it, edging me inside as it swung inwards. I scanned the room, searching for what I needed, when the man across the countertop passed the two cups across. My restraints were removed shortly, and I took the one chance I had. I reached for the pill cup and knocked it to the ground.

I jumped in my falsified panic and scrambled to pick up the scattered pills. "Oh, gosh. I'm sorry. I didn't mean to—"

"That's quite alright, Noah," Phillipson replied as she took my arm and moved me away. "We all get a bit clumsy sometimes." She positioned me in the corner of the room by the half-opened cabinet of medicine. "You just stand there a second whilst we get you a new pot, alright?"

I smiled. "Yeah, yeah. Sorry."

"It's okay."

As hers and the man's backs were turned, I gently slipped my hand inside the glass case. The hinges squeaked and I pulled my hand back on instinct, hoping no one heard before I tried again. Through the corner of my eye, I read a packet label.

Penicillin.

I fumbled with the boxes before I had a grip on one then swiftly slipped the packet into my waistband, just as Phillipson turned around. I swayed anxiously back and forth to cover my movements as she caught sight of me.

"It's alright," she said. "We've added a pain killer to the usual lot for your eye, so don't worry."

I slowly stepped back to the counter, staring down at the paper cup. I tipped them into my palm, and one-by-one I swallowed them. They shone their light into my mouth, and I was given the all clear, which meant I was to be sent on my way back to my room. To be alone.

Once the door was sealed, I glanced over my shoulder at the camera. It was green. That meant they'd see me, and I'm not allowed in the bathroom without permission until an hour after meds, so that ruled that out. Instead, I hid in the blind spot. They didn't know it was there when the cameras were installed, and they haven't the time to move each one to the other side of the room, so I clambered onto the left side of my desk and shuffled close to the corner. My legs were still on show, but that didn't matter.

I turned my face to the wall, pulling the packet out from my trousers and staring down at it. I ripped the box and slipped the two film packets out. I ran my thumb across each pill, thoughts counteracting each other in my head. I inhaled deeply then pushed each one out to my left. They rattled as I dropped them on the surface before I scooped each of them into my hand. I pulled my journal over to cover my actions then slowly, one-by-one,

I swallowed them.

I don't care what it does to me. However it happens, it doesn't matter. I don't deserve to go out easy. This was the worst way I could think of to punish myself, and I deserve it. I pulled a pencil out from the pot and hesitated over my book. I guess what I'm writing will be the last thing I'll do…

…but there's nothing to say.

Chapter 5

Straying from the Path

I thought I was dead. I felt like I was dead. I mean, I've never been dead before so how could I know? Every molecule of my body felt lifeless, so that concluded in my mind that I was too. But then I managed to move my arm and I caught myself breathing. My eyes flickered open, and I lopped my head side to side.

I wasn't dead. I was in a medical room. Not just any medical room either, I was in the emergency one. I'd say how I felt, but I didn't really know. I still don't. I wanted to be dead. I wanted to go. I didn't want to be here any longer, but now it looks like I'm gonna be. I wasn't sure if I was angry, or sad, or maybe even slightly relieved. I didn't want to die, but I didn't want to live either. My head was so fuzzy that I could hardly feel alive enough to have any emotions.

The doctors spotted my opening eyes from behind the counter and quickly gathered together what seemed like paperwork and supplies. I really couldn't tell, all I could hear was rustling.

Then a voice came from beside me. "Noah?"

I rolled my head back across the pillow and tried to make out who it was that spoke.

She stroked my forehead and rubbed my left arm softly. "It's okay. You're okay."

My vision started to clear, and I managed to see the figure. "J… Jaiden?" I said breathlessly.

"Shh," she replied still stroking my head. "Don't say anything." She glanced at the doctors who were stepping forwards with their equipment.

"Wh… wh…" I tried to speak, even my voice had given up. There was nothing I could do.

"Shh, Noah," she continued in her soothing tone.

I sluggishly gazed down at myself, noticing a bandage around my left arm and both my hands covered with flat gloves. I brought them closer into view and tried to clench through the fabric to take them off, but they were strapped onto me tightly.

Jaiden separated my arms. "Stop, Noah. Don't move them. You've got to keep them on."

"What… What… are… they?"

"They're to stop you from using your hands. We found the scratches on your arm, Noah. It was red and the skin was peeling."

I rested my covered hand atop the injury, shying away.

She was stern. "Did you do it to yourself?"

I couldn't look at her. "No…"

She sighed as other doctors surrounded me. "There's no point in lying, Noah. We already know. We checked the recording of your room, we saw you do it."

The doctors adjusted my position, bringing me more upright. They propped my back with lines of puffed pillows then started to rush back and forth around the ward. I let my eyes drift almost to a close.

"You could have said something, Noah. We would have helped you if we knew what you were feeling."

"I didn't want your help…"

"Noah—"

"Why couldn't you have just left me there?" I interrupted.

Jaiden held my gloved fingertips in her hand. "Because we care about you, and we didn't want to lose you."

I took my hand away as the doctors returned, strapping me up with all kinds of devices and tubes. I didn't even realise before that I was already covered with some, but now that they were changing them I felt strange.

"Noah, because of your suicide attempt, we are going to have to keep you on a constant one-on-one watch," Jaiden explained. "Unlike before, a staff member will be with you at all times."

I exhaled deeply in annoyance. "Why?"

Her expression was sorrowful. "Noah, it's to keep you safe."

I went quiet and drew my attention to the other doctors, who were beginning their line of questions.

Jaiden rose from her chair. "Dr Lloyd should be with you soon." She patted my hand then stepped out of sight, the right side of the room being blocked by a blue curtain.

I let my head sink into the pillows as I was examined. They didn't ask me too many questions for once. They just explained what they did. They saved me. They removed the pills from my system, saved me from anaphylaxis, and left me here to wake up. They were surprised I wasn't asleep for very long – apparently it was only three hours – but they were thankful I was awake. They told me I was likely to feel nauseous, which wasn't new to me, then Dr Lloyd arrived. I didn't recognise him from the MRI trip, but I did now. It was Toby. He took Jaiden's seat, and the watch began.

I was stuck in the hospital wing for a week. I wasn't allowed to leave the room, except to go to the bathroom, and even then I had to have someone watch me. It wasn't exactly good for dignity. I had never been so bored at the hospital. We did have the radio, but because of the growing storm it was mostly static that came through.

I don't know much of what happened after I wrote in here. As I scribbled each word down, I grew gradually more drowsy. The tips of my fingers faded blue, and my hands started to tingle. I struggled to keep a grip on my pencil as my senses snapped. My chest tightened, my breathing slowed, and I felt myself dissociate. I felt my mind retreat within itself then several minutes later I blacked out. I couldn't see a thing, but I could still hear. There were a rush of footsteps and the clamber of equipment with voices ordering to each other across the room. One voice stayed close to me, and I felt their hand touch my cheek.

"Noah? Noah? Come on, buddy. Stay with us." It sounded like Caleb. "Stay with us, Noah. Stay with us."

He kept repeating those words to me, but it was too late. I'd given up. I was ready to go, but here I am, I live to write another day. On my last day in the emergency wing, I was given my new regime – only a temporary one. It was almost exactly the same as my old one except it had a new line between two others:

Group Therapy: 1PM – 2PM

Group therapy has been here since the beginning, I've just never gone to one, which is why I didn't mention it in here before. From what I've heard, the patients involved in it are always having fun, so are the doctors. I never wanted to sign up to a group because I didn't want to disrupt anything within it. Everyone in there seemed like they had deep connections with each other and if I went I'd ruin the flow.

I questioned Jaiden as to why I was being placed in the program. At first, she seemed hesitant to give me an answer, but after her stutters she replied telling me it was to help share how I was feeling with people who felt the same. I begged her to remove me from it, but she refused.

When the time came, Jaiden took me on a slow and hesitant walk towards the common room. I kept my hands firmly in the pockets of my hoodie after being told I was to wear a pair of black gloves. It was to stop me from using my nails. So that added more to the strange looks I was getting. As she opened the door, I was brought over to another woman. She seemed familiar, the way she spoke and the way she looked, but my brain was frazzled.

"Hello, Noah. It's nice to see you again," she said, seeming to try her best to be polite towards me.

I glanced back and forth between her and Jaiden, filling with shame that I couldn't recall who she was.

I saw as her smile faded away in a slight confusion then turned to Jaiden who was whispering to her beside me. I tried not to listen so instead scanned around the room, watching the other patients laugh with each other and move about. Across from the television area was a large open space where the craft table usually stood. Instead three patients were stood in a line with a man in a tracksuit beside them. A black-haired patient slid over to a small speaker and pressed a button. He slid back into the line as an upbeat song played and the three of them broke into dance whilst trying to teach the man the moves.

I'd never seen anyone in Riptide be so active. Everyone was actually having fun. Maybe this was where all of the saner people hang out (since sane people are apparently meant to be upbeat and social). Aside from the dancers, there were two patients who were playing snap on the floor whilst another was reading. I didn't recognise any of them, maybe they hide away when us lot emerge from the depths.

Jaiden brought my attention back to her and the doctor. "Okay, Noah. This is Dr Phillipson. She's the one who does your medication, do you remember?"

I tilted my head as I tried to recognise her, but nothing came up. I was so withdrawn from reality that my memory had reset with it. I turned around, trying to avoid the conversation, but Jaiden pulled me back.

"Come on, Noah," she whispered. "Please, give it a go."

119

I looked down at my shoes.

"Noah? Please?"

I shifted my gaze back up and nodded before drifting it back down again.

She sighed. "Thank you, Noah."

I was then passed over to the hands of Dr Phillipson and the group gathered around, each patient grabbing a plastic chair from the corner and placing them in a circle. I was instructed to do the same and I followed the movements of the other patients. I had no idea on what to do or how to act, so I gathered that mimicking them was the best way to blend in. I positioned my small, plastic chair beside a rather fidgety patient who was somehow half the size of me. I kept my hood up as the group began and kept note of how everyone was acting.

I glanced at the man in the tracksuit, and he looked rather similar to Dr Phillipson, and about the same age. I later went on to learn that they were actually twins and they both got a job here together. The man introduced himself to me as Jacob and asked for me to share my name with the others. I was hesitant to begin with. I didn't want them to connect the dots about who I was, so I shrugged and the patient next to me questioned such an action.

"You don't know who you are?"

"Go easy on him, Carson. He's new to this," Dr Phillipson replied almost warily, of course knowing more than the patients did.

Carson shot his head to look at the floor. "I'm sorry, I'm sorry."

Another patient poked fun at him and Carson returned the favour by flicking the patient's upturned collar.

"It's alright, Noah," Phillipson said softly.

I pulled at my sleeves, trying to cover myself up as much as I could as if moving my clothes over my skin would stop them from seeing me. "Um… My name's Noah… She said it for me really."

There were a few scattered laughs, and a small smile broke through my sheltered exterior as my humour made its way to the others.

"Do you have an ark?" one of the men asked.

My eyes jumped from one person to the other as they all laughed more. "Um… I don't… I don't know what that means."

"Do you know anything?" Carson questioned.

"No, never met them," I replied bluntly.

120

The patients continued to laugh at my bland attempts at jokes and Carson sat back in his chair in confusion as he tried to work it out.

"Okay, guys. Now, the reason we're here today is to what?"

"Bully Carson," a man replied.

"Hey!"

"No, not to bully Carson. That's on Wednesday's."

More laughter occurred, even from Carson, although his was more sarcastic. I didn't actually catch what we were there for, I got caught out by the sight of Caleb and Jaiden talking on the other side of the door. They kept looking through the pane in the door at me, and it was really sparking my anxiety. I hadn't realised how long I was watching them for until the doctor called my name.

"What?" I said as I swung back around to face the group.

"It's your turn."

"Oh, um…" I gave a short mumble into my hoodie, definitely not loud enough for anyone to hear, then glanced around the room.

"What was that, Noah?"

Use your defects to save you.

"I, um… forgot what we were talking about."

"That's okay. I think you have a valid reason to be excused from that. We were talking about different pets we had as kids."

I stuttered and picked at my nails as he spoke.

"I know your circumstances, so you can just say what pet you imagine you had."

Before I could answer, Carson raised his hand. "Can I ask a question?"

"Apparently so," another patient muttered.

"Sure, Carson," the doctor said as he let out a breath.

"Why does Noah get special questions?"

He stuttered. "Noah, are you okay with me telling them? That's why we're all here, to talk about our experiences."

I nodded and hid my chin in the bottom of my hood.

"Noah has amnesia," he said. "He doesn't remember things quite as well as we all do."

That was then followed by a rather long discussion about the subject, the different patients throwing theories in the air that I couldn't be bothered to debunk. I wish I was allowed to leave. I hated every second that I was in there. Everyone else seemed pretty happy to bounce remarks off of each other, but I wasn't into it. I admit that some comments were pretty funny and did make me smile, and at one point they all joined together to sing a song about life going on. This chaos was sparked by someone suggesting that I should have a whale as a pet.

I think at this point I was actually losing it and was so relieved once it was over. Each day I had to go back and relive the experience only with a different ending. I did learn a bit about everyone each time though. Carson and Mike had ADHD, but they were both polar opposites of each other. Carson needed to speak each time he had the urge to and if someone said something that would remind him of an incident, he would go on about it until the end.

Meanwhile, Mike barely says anything. He's as quiet as me. He just sits chewing on a piece of rubber around his neck whilst staring into space and keeping the hundreds of scars on his arms hidden from the others. Randy – the one who asked about the ark – is pretty slow in catching up to what's going on, but he's actually the smartest out of all the patients, he just needs to take his time. Then there was Arty and Mason – the two who were playing snap. They both have anxiety with Arty having PTSD. Then the final guy was Levi. All I know about him is that he has a stutter. Literally, that's it. They're all nice enough, but they're just a bit too much for me, and they really make me question whether Riptide is all that calm after all.

All I did for the week was go to the group just to come back and lie in bed. I told Caleb and Jaiden about it in my meeting. Caleb was fine with me dropping out of it, but Jaiden wanted me to keep going with it just for another few days. I did, but all it did was make me share less. This was becoming increasingly noticeable to those monitoring me, Toby was the main person, especially when they came to actually trying to talk to me.

We were in the canteen, sat beside each other at a far table away from the other patients. I rested my head in my arms and pushed my tray away.

Toby sighed. "Come on, Noah. You can eat a bit more than that."

I kept my head on the table, picking at my gloves.

He pulled my tray back. "Come on."

"I'm full," I muttered.

"You only had a few bites."

I sighed and closed my eyes.

He sighed. "If you have the rest of the bread, we can go. How 'bout that?"

I scowled at him then sat up, dragging the tray across the surface and nibbling at the slice of bread.

He rubbed my back. "Good boy."

I slowly ripped the bread apart, flakes falling off and covering half the space in front of me until I looked to Toby and the two of us stood up.

"Alright," he said in defeat. "Well done. Let's go." He took my tray and placed it with the others, and together, we left.

I ambled down the corridor beside him, approaching the wall pad and picking at the stitching. Toby quickly pulled me away and adjusted my gloves.

"Come on, Coleman."

We returned to my room and stepped over to my desk. I searched through one of my boxes and found part of a pencil lead inside. I picked it up and tapped the pointed end against my fingertip, only for Toby to swiftly snatch it out of my hand.

"Ah, ah, no. You can't have anything like this, alright?"

"Well, there's not much I could've done with half an inch of pencil..." I said under my breath as I slumped myself on the floor.

The doctors obviously noticed my downward spiral, and so pulled me out of group therapy to talk. I was taken into an office and sat with about four doctors as they tried to work out what was best for me. They bounced suggestions at me, but each time I'd shake my head and deny them. Because I was one of the highest risk patients at the time, they were all desperate to distract me from both what I'd done and how I was feeling. If I'm distracted then I won't cause trouble. All I could do in response to this was to break down crying.

"I don't want to hurt anyone!" I sobbed. "I just want everything to go back to how it was!"

Jaiden went to comfort me but was kept back by another doctor to protect her.

"No," the doctor whispered. "You're not getting in his line of fire."

"He's crying," she replied sternly. "He needs to be comforted not contained like some rabid animal."

"He killed a doctor with a piece of wire. Think what he could do to your baby."

As the two argued, Caleb jumped forwards and concealed me in his arms, rocking me back and forth as I gripped at his jumper. "Hey, hey, calm down. It's alright."

He stroked across my arm as I choked on my own tears. He gave me a few pats as I sniffed and coughed until the mess became slowing breaths.

"That's it," he continued. "Calm down."

I nuzzled my head against him and closed my eyes, speaking softly. "I... just... want... everything to... go back... to normal."

"We want that too, Noah. We really do. We just need to find a way to get things to how they used to be."

Jaiden approached, crouching to my level as she reached out for me. "Noah? Hey."

I recoiled from her touch, edging closer to Caleb. He held me close and shook his head as Jaiden took her hand away.

"Come on, Noah," she said in concern. "It's only me, I'm not gonna punish you or anything like that."

I glanced back and forth at her in panic before Caleb gently pushed my head away and rested it against his shoulder.

"Noah?"

When I didn't reply, Jaiden rose and stepped away.

"Well?" one doctor said.

She sighed and whispered back. "I don't know. He's never acted this way to me before."

I covered my ears from the conversation. I didn't want to hear what they had to say about me, I already knew that from the way they treated me, but one person I couldn't block out was Caleb. I was clinging to him for dear life, it would have been pretty hard to ignore his voice.

"His system's very broken," he began. "If we want him back to normal then we make it that way."

"That's impossible," another replied. "We've got too many changes that need to happen."

"Exactly." Caleb stroked my hair out of my face then took my hand as I reached for his. "You've battered him into the state he's in now. You took his job, you punished him for having an allergic reaction, treated him like a dog with mange when he had a psychotic break, then somehow managed to miss the fact he stole a pack of Penicillin and practically died."

His tone was rather getting to me. It made me whimper and shudder as my actions were listed. He obviously noticed and muttered an apology back at me before he continued.

"What I'm trying to say is… his system was so damaged that he had no choice but to deteriorate. He needs to get that system back."

"How?" a woman questioned. "Wipe his memory?"

I tensed up and clawed at Caleb's back, my nails being blocked from hurting his skin by my gloves.

"No," he returned. "We just put what we can back in place."

That conversation is how I got reinstated as the unofficial tidier of Riptide, except only for three people and I'm not allowed near the cabinets ever again. Not without someone's eyes fixed on me. I could tell that even after Sector 3 started to cool down after the whole incident, the staff still didn't like me, but I kind of started to get used to it, it was becoming the new norm for my system. Riptide's waters have been rougher than they've ever been at the start of this year.

Speaking of years, I passed my one-year anniversary. I hadn't even realised – my calendar was still in December, and it was almost through February now. I was pretty content until I realised that Jaiden was leaving today. I wasn't as broken up as I thought I was gonna be since me and Caleb had actually sparked a pretty good balance between us.

When the day came, I saw several of the patients give her gifts as a goodbye and all of them had come to terms with her future absence, but I couldn't bring the courage to give her what I made her, so I sat with it at the craft table just staring at it until I was ready, the eyes of my observer blaring from the corner – they'd lightened up slightly due to the lack of staff around.

Then the universe must have been trying to speed things up a little since Jaiden had actually come to find me. I caught eyes with her, and she smiled as she approached me. I lifted my head from the table as she stopped at my side.

"Hello, Noah," she said happily.

"Hi," I replied, hiding the card underneath the desk.

"How are you doing?"

"Okay, I guess." I cleared my throat and shakily pulled the yellow card out again. "I made you this."

She took it and with a thankful grin she opened it, reading through the short message. "I love it, Noah. Thank you."

"That's good," I said with embarrassment. "I was worried in case you were sick of getting things."

"Not at all, Noah. I'm happy that you took your time to make it."

I chuckled. "I haven't much else to do."

She smiled back. "There's someone here to see you."

I perked up. "Who?"

"Head to visitation."

I scrambled from the table and pleaded to my guide. They glanced at Jaiden and escorted me to the visitor area.

I've been in Riptide's visitation several times. It's a room with a single wooden table, a couple of cushioned chairs, a sofa, a games box and steel-bolt doors on either side. I shouldn't think it makes visitors feel better about seeing their loved ones whilst being locked in a metal box. One thing I could never understand was that if the doctors worry we'll hurt our visitors then why lock us in a room with them? I mean, there are guards in there and the occasional doctor, so I guess it's safe. They can just pounce on us if we get hostile.

Visitation is also the furthest place from the rooms. The whole hospital was built in strategic ways to restrict any chance of the patients escaping or getting lost, that's why when one of the few ways to get to the outside was built, it was constructed highly secure and far away. Of course, I could have made up the reasoning, but it took us a fair bit of time to reach the door to visitation, so the theory matched up.

They pushed me into an airlock and fixed the handcuffs to me. I took in a breath, holding it as the door revealed the room. Waiting anxiously on one of the sofas was Aaron. We locked eyes and he jumped up, the both of us running to an embrace. He wrapped his arms around me, and I nuzzled against his chest. Together, we cried.

Aaron's speech was broken as he spoke. "I—thought—I—lost—you."

I shook my head rested my weight on him. "I'm so sorry, Aaron," I sobbed. "I'm so, so sorry."

"They told me everything that happened. Start to end. I couldn't bear it! I asked day after day to come see you, but they wouldn't let me."

"Aaron, I'm s-so sorry."

He rocked me back and forth. "Shh, it's alright. I'm sorry too."

"For what?" I questioned, sniffling and wiping my nose.

"I should have come seen you more," he replied whilst gasping for air through his tears. "I should have asked to call you, but I didn't! I left you alone."

I nuzzled closer against him, gripping the best I could at his shirt to

126

keep him as close as I could. "It's not your fault, it's mine! I—should—have—never—worked—at that—stupid—bloody—school!"

He sighed and held me tighter. "I know," he said, his voice low. "But there's nothing we can do about it. Something like this would have always happened, whether you took that job or not, one of us would've still fallen into something like this."

Finally, we separated, keeping our eyes fixed on each other for moments after, Aaron holding my hands in his.

"It probably still would've been me."

He chuckled softly. "I dunno, I mean, I nearly got dragged into quite a few scraps after Wyegate, but I s'pose you don't remember, huh?"

"No," I said sheepishly. "What happened?"

He shrugged and glanced at the guard in the corner. "Eh, I think it's best left for another day."

I grinned, but the smile slowly faded as I saw the glum look across Aaron's face, his eyebrows arched down, and his lip bitten to keep from breaking down further – a trick he taught himself in Wyegate to keep himself suppressed. It's why his lips aren't exactly perfect. Biting your skin for so many years really leaves a mark.

"Are you okay?"

He adjusted his demeanour and straightened his arched body out. "Yeah. Yeah. I'm fine. It's just, I'd kinda take a scrap with the guys if it meant I could talk to one of them."

"What d'you mean?"

"Well, you know I said that my mates were kinda ignoring me, and that there was probably something going on?"

"Yeah."

"Well, there's nothing going on, but nobody's said a word to me. I've tried over and over to talk to them, but nobody ever answers – they don't even read my messages. And they're not back in Wyegate, they're not even in *any* prison, they're just... gone."

I shuffled back in confusion, fidgeting with my handcuffs as I processed possible reasons. "Are, are you sure? Like, are you sure they're not just hiding out somewhere?"

He shook his head. "I don't know, Noah. But with all of this going on, and nearly losing you, I—I'm just so messed up."

I jumped back into his embrace, clamping tight to him and lightly kissing his neck. "I'm sorry, Aaron. I'm so sorry."

He sighed and ran his fingers through my hair, stroking the top of my skull. "I love you." His voice was a sincere whisper.

I inhaled shakily. "I love you too."

Then a new voice broke the atmosphere. "Coleman, it's time to wrap it up."

We both turned to the guard before separating and sniffling together. Aaron reached into his jumper pocket.

"I've got you something," he said quietly as he pulled out a stack of paper. "The staff say you can finally receive letters now. Every one that was sent got returned to our house so there's quite the collection. They've already read through them all so anything dodgy's gone."

"Right." I took the stack from him, staring down at each ripped envelope.

"They're from your family."

My head shot up at him in shock. "What?"

"Yeah. Your parents sent loads of letters when you got taken away until they gave up after realising not one made it to you."

"Then why can I have them now?"

He shrugged. "I don't know. Your counsellor signed off on your good behaviour and thought you deserved it."

"Jaiden…" I muttered.

"I don't know, but they said you deserved to know."

I stuttered before giving him one final hug. We swayed back and forth before the guard separated us and edged me towards the airlock.

"I love you," I called to Aaron.

"I love you," he called back before his face was covered by the metal door.

I sighed and turned to leave, the guard unlocking the handcuffs and glancing at the letter sceptically.

"What?" I said carelessly.

He shrugged me off. "I've received word that you need to swing by Dr Olsen's office."

"What? Now?"

"Yes, now."

He marched me back down the halls, twisting and turning me as we passed other patients until we reached the door to Olsen's office. I was sat on the bench firmly and the guard knocked against the wood. He peered through the opened crack, muttering to the people inside, before ducking back out again. He lightly closed the door and sat to my right.

"He's just talking with someone. He'll be out in a minute."

I nodded and leant against the wall cushion, flashing back to the scenes of the MRI visit. I could hear them talking. I swear I could. All that's between me and this conversation was concrete wall. Nothing else. I held in a deep breath and listened.

"Toby, this is serious," Olsen began. "He's out there now, waiting for us to talk to him about it."

Toby gave an annoyed groan. "I know, but he won't even know what it means! He doesn't remember these types of things. I bet he won't even know what it means to be prejudice!"

"That doesn't mean it's right!"

"I know that. It's disgusting what people to do, but I'm just saying that it might be for the better if he doesn't understand. You can't take offence to something you didn't know was meant to be rude."

"Toby might be right, Joel," added Jaiden. "He didn't even understand the word her daughter used against him, how could he even grasp homophobia?"

Dr Olsen let out an exasperated sigh. "I don't know. I don't *want* him to know, but it feels wrong that the world knows what's happened and he doesn't – and he's one of the main victims."

"Joel, listen," said Jaiden calmly. "We've got quite the number of... I don't really know if I'm allowed to say queer, but there's a number of patients here who are indeed not straight and not cisgender, and I dread to think how many of them fell behind in their care because of her. Explaining to Noah what's been found out may ease his guilt."

"This is why I suggested removing the information from their files," Toby exclaimed. "I don't know why it was necessary to have their sexualities stated. It can sway people's views and patient care."

"I wish I could agree," Jaiden replied. "But the reason it's stated there is because this is an all-male facility." Her tone became slightly awkward. "We need to be aware of which patients are... more likely... to... engage with each other. We've had incidents before. Of course, we know Noah is likely to never be involved in something like this."

I gave a stiff chuckle, biting the inside of my cheeks to prevent an outburst of seemingly unprovoked laughter. I glanced at the guard. He did indeed spot me jolt forwards as an amusing memory came to mind. Yeah, sure, I wouldn't get up to much of *that* kind of thing here, but if only Jaiden knew the adventures of Wyegate. Okay, there were only two adventures... and I hated both of them. Me no top, please and thank you.

I covered my awkward memories and returned to their debate.

"Does his family know?"

"I met with his partner, Aaron," Jaiden replied. "He was just with Noah, but I guess free period is getting near its end, so he got let out early. I had a chat with his parents, too – his brother didn't show. His parents weren't surprised by that, though. Either way, they were worried for him. They asked if Dr Wilks had ever been physically aggressive to him, which I told them 'no', but obviously, we don't know now if that's true."

"Which is why I want to tell him," said Olsen.

They fell into a thoughtful silence until Toby broke through with his query.

"So we tell him?"

Jaiden sighed. "Joel?"

"Mm?"

"It's your decision."

"I think we should. It's only right."

There was slow movement towards the door, and I watched as the handle sloped down. Olsen revealed his face to me, showing a smile.

"Hey, Noah. How are you?"

I nodded, tucking the letters into my waistband. "I'm good."

"Good." He stepped to the side. "You can come in now."

I glanced back at the guard before hesitantly entering the office. Olsen was close behind me as he closed the door. The others gave me a smile too, Jaiden presenting an armchair to me. I perched on the edge, staring up at the trio in confusion.

"What's going on?" I asked.

Dr Olsen led the questioning. "Noah, I don't like to open old wounds or anything like that, but there's been new evidence about the Dr Wilks case."

I slipped my hands under my thighs, rocking back and forth gently. "Oh, yeah?"

"Yeah." His voice was gentle and considerate. "It's been on the news, but I don't know if you've seen it."

"No, I haven't really been watching much TV."

"I didn't think you had." He crouched in front of me. "But because of what's happened, we need to ask you some questions, okay?"

"Okay."

"Good. Okay." He seemed wary. "Did Dr Wilks ever show any sort of... displeasure towards you?"

I glanced over at Jaiden. "Um... I..."

"It's okay, Noah," she said. "You're not in trouble."

I turned back to Olsen and gave a timid nod.

He sighed. "Right. Did she ever hurt you in any way? Physically or emotionally?"

I shrugged. "She gave me Penicillin... and... generally didn't like me."

"The Penicillin. The first time we assumed to was an accident, yes? Noah, honestly, do you think she did it on purpose?"

I took my hands out from under my legs and picked at the pillow beside me, merely giving the doctor a shrug.

He returned to standing, lightly patting my shoulder before he turned away. "It's alright, mate." He gestured to Jaiden.

She then took his place, reaching for my hand. "Noah?"

I recoiled from her, the thought of her lie still clinging to me.

She seemed to understand. "Noah, we need you to help us. We've spoken to other patients like you about Dr Wilks and they have all had similar responses towards her. We're trying to figure out if her aggression towards you was the trigger of your fugue."

I shuffled and swallowed, my mouth falling dry.

"Noah. Was Dr Wilks ever homophobic towards you?"

I glanced in confusion to each doctor. "What?"

"I told yah he wouldn't know," mumbled Toby.

"Stop," Olsen ordered back in a whisper.

Jaiden adjusted her jumper. "Do you know, Noah?"

My gaze sank to the carpet. "Yeah..."

"Don't lie, Noah," said Toby sternly.

I rubbed the tops of my arms and shivered, my legs ever-so-slightly twitching. "I, um..."

"It's okay, mate. You shouldn't have to know." Olsen flashed a reassuring smile. "But it's the reason Wilks never liked you. It's why she didn't like a lot of patients. It's also why the protests have eased off. There's still some, obviously, but they're not going for you anymore. It's about all the patients who were ever a victim because of her."

"But I'm not the victim," I said. "She was. I killed her."

"Yes, well, it seems you're both victims *and* perpetrators."

"That doesn't make me feel any better," I mumbled.

"I know, mate, but we have to ask. It's either us or the desperate reporters that flood the front gates every day. This is a big thing, Noah. Your whole case is."

I bowed my head.

Jaiden sighed. "Noah, sweetie, you can talk to us. We won't shout at you, we want to help."

I scratched at my forearm harshly before sitting on my hands again as the doctors spotted what I was doing. "Sorry..." They all remained silent. "Please... I just want to go back to my room."

They glanced to one another before Olsen nodded and stepped over. "Alright, mate. Let's go."

He took me by the arm, and we left together. Along with the guard, we headed down the corridor towards my room. The doctor scanned his card, and I entered the airlock.

Before it closed, Olsen spoke. "I'm sorry about what happened to you, mate. Even if you don't understand it..."

Without my chance to reply, I was sealed inside. I slowly ambled across the carpet before I took the stack of letters out from under my top. I stared down at them. I didn't know what to feel. I wanted to know more than ever who was a part of my life, but it's been so long since I haven't known that I almost didn't want to. What good would it do anyway? I can't go see them. I can't go talk to them. How is it going to help?

I friskily marched over to the right-hand wall, hiding behind the mountains of destroyed cardboard boxes that were left over from my searched items.

A guard then startled me as he spoke through the speaker. "We're still watching you, remember that."

I nodded and dropped to the floor staring at the first piece of paper. It had my name scrawled across the middle in scruffy handwriting. I crumpled it up and threw it across the room then glanced down at the pile. The first out of the stack was a torn open envelope. The address had been scribbled out with thick black ink, as were most of the lines on the letter itself. I couldn't read a word of it, even the lines that weren't covered up. It seemed to have been written in anger as the whole page was crumpled and smudged. I let the paper drift out of my hand and land on a stray box.

I gazed down at the next item in the pile. It was a postcard of a tent and a lake. I turned it over and read across it. Although having very few printed space, the writing was squeezed tightly inside the box.

'Hey, Noah. We are all on our usual trip in the Lake District. It's not the same without you here, you always gave the boring parts your own spark. I suppose you don't remember it, but this picture was always your favourite and I know how you liked postcards. I don't know if you still do. I hope that whatever is going on with you gets better soon. – Dad'

I turned the card back over and gazed at the image. It was bright with colour, the sunset shimmering in the reflection on the water. It was a nice photo. It made me smile.

I lowered it carefully and moved to the letter underneath. It folded out from the small square to a larger A4 piece. It was much better preserved than the last and the writing was actually understandable. Clipped to the bottom was a photo. I was in it but seemed much younger – probably late teens. I was in the centre of a gathering. An older, lean man with ash hair was stood behind me with his arm around my shoulder, his shirt buttons slightly undone. To my right was a woman with slightly darker hair and wrinkles around her blue eyes. She was plump, but proudly wore her striking skin-fit dress. To my left was another man, seeming a bit older than me, but looking oddly similar. We had the same nose, the same chin, the same eyes, even the same dimple when we smiled. I noticed he had a silver ring on his finger, and I matched it with the woman beside him. In her arms was a small boy, who was reaching over to the man. There were many people in the background and around us, but the rest was too blurred for me to make out. I pulled the photo off of the letter and began to read.

'Dear Noah,

I have never been quite as scared for you as I am now. That final day in the courtroom was terrifying, I wanted more than anything to just rip past the officers and hold you in my arms, but we were all dragged back out to the hallway and forced to wait without being told a word about what had happened. The guard's refused to let me see you, they said you were too big of a threat to be contacted. I received a similar response from the hospital.

The doctors say you are too unstable for me to visit and don't want me to disrupt any progress in your rehabilitation, so I just wrote this letter instead. They described your coping mechanism to me as falling back to the ways of a child. If you're anything like you were as a kid then I feel for the doctors who look after you.

Seeing you in so much pain broke my heart, and I can only wish that you are on the right track for getting better. Aaron told me about your amnesia and said you might not ever remember me, your father, Jac, Jessie or Asher, so I dug out this old photo of us all together. It was the last time I've ever seen us smile together, and I'm scared we won't get a moment like this again since that night you disappeared. Do you remember this night? It was New Year's Day in 2015. You and Jac were setting off the fireworks with dad in the garden for Asher. It was so cold, I remember you almost turning blue.'

Several lines after were blacked out. I scrambled underneath the light to try and see them through the page, but it was useless. I sighed and fell back on my knees as I finished.

'... and I may not ever get to see you again. Nevertheless, your actions don't define who you are to me. You clearly needed help from the start, and I refused to give it to you. Now we both have to pay the price for it. I pray every night for you to get better, so that you can come home, and I can hug you one more time.

I love you more than you know. – Mum'

I took in a deep breath then fell onto my back, holding the letter close to my chest as I burst out crying. I rolled onto my side and curled my legs towards me, forming myself into a ball. She seemed like a good person. No. She was better than that. She was my mother, and I let myself forget her. Anything she had done for me, anytime she had been there for me, I couldn't recollect. The only part of her that I could recall was the day I hurt her, but even then, she is just a blurred vision of something I wasn't even convinced was real. And what's worse is she knows what I did to her more than I do. She has to live with knowing all of the devilish things I've done in my life, whereas I only have shards. Shards that rarely fit together. Shards that might slice through me if I get too close.

This was only the third letter, and I was already in a state. The stack had so many more to go, but I wasn't ready to read them, so I opened my hide-away slot and hid the rest behind the opened panel. I took in a deep breath as I gently closed it then wiped my eyes.

I had a whir in my head. I guess my guilt was somewhat relieved from the reminder to myself of who I was. I know what I did was wrong, and the reason I'm here is to work out what causes me to do it. I keep trying to tell myself that. Although, the guilt wasn't really helped when I returned to the common room the next day to see about ten patients all huddled around the sofa watching the news. Before joining the group, I grabbed a cup of water from the machine then leant over the back of the sofa to watch the screen.

Kyle looked up at me, tapping my hand to get my attention. "Hey."

"Hey," I replied, almost in shock. I wasn't expecting the attention, I didn't think any patient would dare to go near me, let alone talk to me. I cleared my throat and gripped at the cup. "What's going on?"

"They're saying that people all over England are going missing," he said quickly.

"What?"

"It's not just random people," Justin called from the sofa arm. "Everyone that's been taken have criminal records."

I took a sip from my water and stared at the reporter on the screen.

"The disappearances first started to occur from the outskirts of London, including places like Watford, Luton, Harpenden, and Hemel Hempstead. Although originally thought to be an uprising from the unbalance of criminal justice, law officers are now stating that the missing people have had no reason to and do not correlate with the original evidence."

A graph appeared beside the woman, showing the increase in missing people over the past two months. There were two lines – one blue and one red. The blue line was at a steady decline from the teens, but the red one kept increasing, reaching up into the fifties. Across the bottom each were labelled, the red being those with a criminal past and the blue being the rest.

I bit into the polystyrene cup, trying to keep my composure.

"The first to be reported missing was a young boy in his teens who was called for a court hearing on the twelfth but was then recorded as missing the next day by his parents. His last sighting was by the steps of his home where he seemed to be in some distress with pain in his neck before returning the way he came."

I ran my hand across my scar, my heart rate beginning to raise.

"Since that day, the numbers only rose and other areas started to fall

victim to it. There have been very few witnesses at this time due to the disappearances occurring mostly within the walls of police stations, prisons and mental hospitals."

The patients murmured frantically between themselves, half becoming overwhelmed with nerves. I stood up straight, clenching my now empty cup as one of the security guards marched over and switched the TV off. Everyone groaned, all giving reasons for him to leave it on.

"No. There's been enough of that today. All of you scatter!" he ordered.

Most kept pushing for him to let them watch more, but he spat threats at them and forced them to move. We all dispersed, heading to different corners of the common room. I pushed off the back of the sofa and approached the bin by the stairwell door. I discarded my cup then turned to see Kyle and Shawn behind me.

"Can you believe that?" Kyle began. "What if they come here?"

"I don't think they will," Shawn replied calmly. "None of us are very useful."

"But what if they do? "

"They won't."

"How do you know that?"

Shawn continued to try and calm his friend's growing erratic actions, occasionally stepping in circles as he tried his hardest to speak. As the two of them debated their points, I shuffled over to the window. I glanced down at the windowsill and noticed a large orange butterfly perched on the ivy that was growing around the bars. It fluttered its wings and started to lift off only to end up on a different vine. I reached my hand out and gently tapped the glass. I expected it to fly away, but it didn't. It just sat slowly flapping its wings up and down.

I guess I was looking for a distraction. I was trying to hide it from the other patients, but the news report kind of rattled me. It rattled most of them too, but I didn't want to add to the hysteria. They were only just accepting me back into the norm. They knew what I did to myself and I'm guessing they knew the feeling I was in. The whole reason we're all here is because we broke the law, some more seriously than others, and if it weren't for our busted-up brains we'd be in prison. Again in some cases.

I was an inmate once. It's a secret I don't like to share, even if it is in this thing. I was only eighteen when I was arrested, and it was barely past my birthday. I was sentenced to four years at HMP Wyegate, and it was only that because I was so young. I was terrified. I think. I don't really know. I'm not even sure if this story is real or not, but it feels it, so I believe it.

After I turned eighteen, everything in my life was pressured onto me more than I could handle. I was already struggling with myself. Struggles that I couldn't tell anyone. If I did, who knows if anyone would have cared about me anyway? They'd probably have told me to 'stop worrying' or 'everyone's in the same boat', which is a phrase I can't bear to hear. Why? Because nobody is the same. Each and every person on Earth has a different brain, meaning no person will have the same thoughts, reactions, or feelings towards something. We're not in the same boat, we're just on the same river. Some people can stand rapids, some people can't, and nobody cares about the people who can't.

I was the one that couldn't. I came home and was teetering on the edge of self-destruction. My parents tried their best to help me, but I didn't listen. I just argued with them, shouting at them so much that they couldn't get a word in. Then when my mother tried to comfort me, I hit her. Right across her face. The face that I will never be able to recognise. Her scream of pain seared into me, it's a sound that won't ever leave me, even from in here. Like I've said before, guilt is a painful thing. You don't need to know the full story to feel it.

After that, I hid away in my room, refusing to show myself to anyone in my house. I never apologized to my mum for what I did to her. Instead, I picked up a call from my friends as the time drew near 11:00PM. I didn't want to. I wanted to keep crying to myself under my bed. I wanted to be alone, but curiosity overruled the rest of my emotions.

"Hello?" I said with a broken voice.

"Noah, mate. You gotta get down to The Lion! We're having the best time!" my friend bellowed. From the way he was speaking it sounded like he'd had plenty to drink already.

"I dunno, man…" I replied.

"Come on, mate! One night! Just one! You never go out anywhere!"

I stared at my blanket in deep thought. Honestly, I didn't like any of the people who I was friends with. I only joined them because I was fed up with being alone every day. They never really treated me the same as the rest of the group, I was always the outcast. They teased and laughed at my misfortunes, never once stopping to ask if I was actually okay. What's worse is they were all forcing me to do things I didn't want to do. Of course, they all assumed I was straight, so they thought I'd have just the same feelings as them when it came to cat-calling the very few lesbians who were out in my class. They even taunted the ones that weren't out. I never joined in with them then. I shied away, knowing how much their views would sway if they found out about me. Looking back now, I regret so many of my actions that were due to them forcing my hand.

I agreed to go. I slung my hoodie over my pyjama top and slipped on a pair of skinny jeans that were crumpled in the corner of my floor. I pulled my beanie onto my head then headed into the bathroom as I flicked the lights out in my bedroom. By now, everyone in my house was asleep and I knew that going out the front door would disturb the crisp silence throughout the house, so I locked the door to the bathroom, jumped out onto the outhouse and ran down the street.

By the time I'd reached the club it was already twenty-to-twelve, and my body was covered in goosebumps from the nippy March night. I pulled open the busted door and was immediately swamped by the thundering of dance music. I stepped in and scanned the main area, spotting my friends in the corner who were sat laughing and swaying in their seats. As I saw them drunkenly try to sing along to the unintelligible songs, I forced a smile across my face. I stepped over to them and they all shouted as they spotted me. I took a seat beside a friend's girlfriend, and they slid me over a drink. It seemed like a coke at first glance with a lemon and a straw, but after a sip I winced as the bitter taste touched my tongue. I didn't want to keep drinking it, but they all insisted, each of them with a cunning smirk. So, I did.

All seemed okay to begin with. We chatted, we danced, we sang. But as the night progressed, I started feeling strange. Lightheaded and shaky. I called a break from dancing and sat back down at the table. I checked the time on my phone to see that it was barely past midnight. I couldn't understand it, it felt like we'd been there for hours. I looked around the room and held onto the table in fear as I saw the walls fade into the floor, the colours washing down like a waterfall and floating around each person, surrounding their bodies with bright pinks and blues.

I shuddered as they slowly streamed towards me, and I shot up from the table and rushed to the bathroom. I stumbled against the sink and gripped hold of the edges so tightly that some of the porcelain peeled away from the cracks. I panted frantically as I splashed my face with the cold water, the droplets curving down my cheeks and splashing against the drain. I tried to focus on myself in the mirror, but I was scared to death by a black mist that I saw behind me in the reflection. I noticed as it reached its bone claw towards my shoulder, the swarming mist surrounding it acting as it's defending cloak. I freaked out and turned to face it, but it vanished and all that was left was an old man in an overcoat staring at me.

"Are you alright, son?" his frail voice asked.

I didn't reply. I just darted back out into the bar, stumbling against the walls and into my friend's arms.

"Wh… What's happening?" I questioned breathlessly.

He chuckled with an overly large smile as he held my arms. "You better take it all in, mate! You're gonna thank me later!" He pounded his hand on my back, making the world around me more and more distorted.

I was frozen for words. I couldn't even manage to let out a breath. Well, I could. But it sure as hell didn't feel like it. It felt like my chest was being tightened by some unknown being in the sky, controlling me with his strings. I didn't feel in control anymore, but as I watched the world pass by me, I started to ease. I hadn't a single dark thought in my head, just emptiness. I was happy. I think. Nothing around me felt real anymore, and as the moon rose higher, so did I.

I checked the time once again and saw that another two hours had passed. I looked up from my phone and realised that I was the only one left, aside from the barman who was likely running a damp cloth across the surface.

I shuffled back against the table in shock and confusion. "Where'd everybody go?" I asked him.

"Wherever they wanted to, I s'pose," he responded.

"Did you see my friends leave?"

"They left about half an hour ago."

I was taken aback. I couldn't understand what had happened. I was with them. I just spoke to them. I glanced back at our empty table then back at the bartender.

"I'm sorry, I… I didn't realise I'd be here so late," I said as I headed towards the door.

He shrugged. "I've had a lot worse. Trust me."

I nodded and trembled as I took to the pavement. By now the air stood still. There was nothing. The outside felt like my insides. Nothing.

139

I made my way down the decrepit alley that brought me to the bar and tried to remember. But I couldn't. There was a flash of bright colours, loud noise and then… nothing.

I kept walking, staring at the cracks in the pavement until I reached an opening and saw the shine of the neon police stripes on a car. I smiled at the two officers as I went to pass them, but they stopped me. This wasn't the first time this had happened though. I admit that I did dress a little sketchy, especially for the late hour it was. They asked me where I'd come from and what I'd been doing. I told them what I knew.

"I was angry, so I took a walk."

"At 02:00AM?" they asked.

"I wasn't keeping track of time." I started shuffling away from them the best I could.

"Where are you off to now then?"

I actually hadn't thought about that. I guessed I was going home, but my feet were leading me in the other direction. "Um, home…"

"You don't sound too certain about that. Are you sure?"

My eyes were now drooping heavily. "Yeah, yeah." I placed my hands in my pockets and felt the blood drain from my face. I fumbled around and ran my fingers across what seemed to be a sheet of paper and a small glass bottle. I stuttered as I then felt a film packet with several pills enclosed inside it. My gaze drifted to the concrete as I tried to stay calm. "I've really got to go. I've gotta, I've gotta go."

I went to turn but caught my foot on the side of a wooden bench and fell against the pavement. My head knocked onto the sharp pebbles, one sticking into my eyebrow and piercing the skin. The officers rushed over to help me up but as they pulled my arm, the items in my pocket spilled onto the ground.

The rest is a bit hazy, but I can only imagine what happened after. Locked in the back seat of the car with my hands tightly cuffed together. Months later I was being marched along a metal grate in Wyegate by a guard towards my cell. I felt the glares of the other inmates through their door windows, each seeming to analyse every move I took. I tried my best to ignore them. At this point, I don't think my anxiety had ever been this high in my life. The only things I knew about prison were from some documentary I watched in school mixed with the stereotypes that people threw around in life.

The two of us came to a stop outside a cell. I watched intently as the officer tapped on the door and signalled to the person inside. I felt my stomach turn as it finally hit me that I wasn't going to be alone for my stay. I don't know why I thought otherwise. The sound of the metal unlatching from itself gave me shivers, I didn't know it then, but I would grow to get used to much worse than that. The woman pulled the door out and nodded her head for me to enter. I inhaled deeply then shuffled in.

The room was smaller than I expected. I knew it was gonna be small, it's prison for God's sake, but for two men to live in that amount of space for years to come was absurd. To the left was an old bunkbed. The bottom had its thin mattress rolled up, revealing the metal slats beneath it, whilst the top was laid out with blankets piled across it.

Across the back wall were two small cabinets, one in each corner. To my right was a half wall, behind that was a toilet and a sink with a very smudged mirror above that. I turned back to the final part of the room. It was a steel desk and stool centred opposite the door underneath a windowsill, fixed between the two cabinets.

That's where I met him.

He was stood leaning against the metal surface with his arms crossed. He was much scruffier than he is now, his hair was greasy and sprung out from all angles, he was also slightly slimmer in his arms and legs. Then as the guard locked us in, the shred of remaining light shimmering across his silver-framed glasses.

There was a lot to say about him. He was a bit of a magpie. He still is. Anything shiny or that gave off a glimmer, that was for Aaron. It's what landed him in Wyegate. All through college he was getting into places he shouldn't be, and robbing people blind of whatever shone his way. The thing was, he stole right in front of them. He'd take something, pretend it was his, drop it in plain sight, then get his victim to give it back to him. Then he'd run back and store it in his den. He never sold one piece. He just stole it to look at it.

Of course, they tracked him down in the end. In the midst of July, Aaron was forced onto a family holiday to Paris. He made it there and back just fine, but in his absence, the police had made the link to him in the investigation. When he got home he didn't even make it through the front door. He was taken by the officers and his collection was either returned or kept in evidence.

Fast forward a year and that's when I joined him.

I wasn't sure about what the atmosphere around us was, but I will say it could have been worse. We stood in silence for quite some time before he broke the ice.

"That's your bed," he said bluntly, waving his hand towards the bottom bunk.

"Okay," I replied, cautiously lowering my bag onto the frame.

"You done this before?" he asked.

I shook my head as I rolled out the mattress. "No."

He nodded then seemed to let out a sigh of relief.

"Have you?"

He unfolded his arms as he turned back to the desk. "First time."

I nodded and pulled out my bed sheet and threw it over the bed pad. For what little material there was, I was surprised at how it managed to overhang so much. I tucked it underneath the best I could then repeated the process with my two blankets. I glanced up at his bed, realising that his blankets were much different to mine and that they weren't even prison issue. They were hand-made from different patches of material and wool. This blanket was more well-travelled than me, and it ended up being the one Aaron gifted me when I was taken to Ocean Cliff.

I sharply turned back as he spoke again.

"What's your name?" he said, flicking through different pieces of paper.

"Noah. Coleman."

He turned around and smiled. "I'm Aaron. Wickers. How long you got... Noah?"

"Four years."

He nodded and looked down. "That's okay. Could be worse." He turned away again and crouched down to open his cabinet.

"What about you?"

He glanced over his shoulder. "Five left."

"Left?"

"Yeah..."

"How... How long have you been here?" I asked sheepishly.

"Ten months."

"Oh."

"How old are you?" he asked as he pulled out an unravelled mess of

142

wool.

"Ei-Eighteen."

He shrugged. "Okay."

"How old are you?"

"Turned nineteen in August."

"Right."

Aaron closed his cupboard and stepped over to the bed. "It's not so bad once you get used to everything." He jumped up and slipped his shoes underneath his mattress – his stashing habits staying with him way past Wyegate. "The best thing to do is stay out of the way and not be a prick." He smiled at me and laid back on his bed, resting his head on his pillow.

I nodded and sat down on my scratchy sheets. I crossed my legs and rifled through my bag and pulled out a picture. Back then I knew who the photo was of, but now I couldn't say I recognised anyone, that part of my memory was still blurred. Of all the things I can remember from my life, it's prison. As if I needed to punish myself further. But to be honest, I had some great times there. Most were only small moments that normally I wouldn't have thought twice over, but with each tiny bit of amusement that came, it made the day better.

I guess I took that lesson with me. I do enjoy the little things. I enjoy anything that's worth the time. Even if that includes watching butterflies sit outside the window.

Chapter 6

There's Reasons You Forget

So the week without Jaiden was pretty peculiar. It was weird not seeing her in the halls and around the hospital, but I did get to see a lot more of the other doctors. Caleb's kind of like Jaiden when I have my meeting only with a tad more professionalism. I think that's just a part of who he is. We joke about it in the meetings, and he manages to distract me from the fact he's trying to pry into my brain. Both Caleb and Olsen let me sit in their offices with them when I ask it, and as long as there's no serious business going down in there, then I'm good to stay.

Earlier on, I was sat swinging my legs back and forth on Dr Olsen's desk, watching him as he carried these cardboard boxes into his room from the corridor. There were so many that they basically towered over him, each stacked on top of one another. He lifted one up, stumbling backwards from the weight.

"What's in there?" I asked.

He grunted as he placed the first one on the ground. "Files, files and more files." He dragged in the next set, this time not risking the heavy carrying.

"Files for what? There can't be that many patients here, can there?"

"I don't think it's all patient files," he said, straining as he pulled in the last three. "They've got all kinds in them. Costs, building repairs, taxes. I imagine it's like a game of *Monopoly*, only with less family destruction." He looked up at me and chuckled.

I smiled back at him, not sure whether I was supposed to laugh or not, as he turned to close the door.

"How're you feeling, anyway? I'm glad to see you getting back to your old self."

I shrugged and my smile faded, my head sinking down. "I-I don't think I am…"

He pulled out a chair and sat down on it backwards, resting his arms on the back as his face turned concerned. "What makes you say that?"

I moved my hands underneath my thighs and swayed my head back and forth. "I don't know... I just... I can't get it out of my mind."

Dr Olsen sighed. "I know it's hard. Something like this can take a toll on everyone, especially you. We both know that what you did wasn't good, and I am in no way trying to say otherwise, but it was a mistake. I know you."

"How? I don't even know myself anymore! If I can't know who I am then how can you?"

He rose from the chair and leant on the desk beside me. "I know that you never meant to hurt Dr Wilks, and I may not have been there when you hurt that kid, but I have a feeling that you didn't want to do that either."

"But what if I did?" I said, tears building up in my eyes. "What if there's this whole other side of me that I lose control of and I'm suddenly some psycho who just tries to kill the first thing I see?"

He placed his arm around my shoulder and hugged me. "Well, if that's the case then I will be there to stop you and bring you back onto the right side. Yeah?"

I smiled at him and nodded. "Yeah."

He smiled back in a comforting manner. "Good. Now, I'm gonna get to the bottom of what's happening to you, as is the rest of us here, that's why we're trying all these different things with you, but I want you to keep your head up as much as you can, alright?"

I nodded again.

"And I want you to know that you don't have to if you're getting close to the edge. It's okay to step back and call for help, even if you don't think there's anyone there to hear you, someone will."

"M-hm." I wiped the tears from my face.

He hugged me tighter then pushed forwards onto his feet. "Now, then. We better get started on these otherwise Dr Hawthorn will be on me like a ton of bricks."

I ruffled my hair and cleared my throat. "What're we doing first?"

He spun around the mountains of cardboard then settled by the largest. "I guess if we get this one out the way then the rest'll be much easier." He gestured at the table by the window. "Grab me that green box by the windowsill, would you?"

I slid off the table and slowly waddled over, anxiously picking at my nails as I did. I carefully dragged the woven box towards me then stared through the glass. I watched as another shimmering orange butterfly swirled around in the wind.

Whilst keeping my eyes on it, I spoke. "Hey, have you seen all the orange butterflies lately? I've seen quite a few over the past few days."

"The what butterflies, Noah?"

"The orange ones. They keep flying around outside."

Dr Olsen stepped over and joined me by the window.

I placed my finger on the glass. "See? They're everywhere. What are they?"

"I think it's called a monarch," he replied.

I slid my finger down. "Oh."

"Don't worry though, I have been seeing them too. I was surprised by them being here in the peak of winter, but the climate is changing so maybe it's affecting them. I dunno though, I watched a nature documentary last night and they were on it. They're a whole lot bigger than they're meant to be." He took the box from my hands. "Now, come on. I'm sure that Mr Monarch doesn't like being watched when he's trying to relax." He shuffled back and took a seat on the sofa, unzipping the top to the green case.

I took one last glimpse at the butterfly then turned back to join him. I settled on the sofa beside him and watched as he tore the tape from the seal. He let it drift to the floor then proceeded to unfold the cardboard.

"Ah." He reached into the box and pulled out a stack of paper and a bag of ink cartridges. "Printer restock." He dropped them back in the box and wiped his hands. "That's good, we just ran out in the staff room." He closed the box again then reached for a marker and the neon sticky notes that were inside the green bag. He passed them to me. "Write on there, 'Printer Paper' so we know what's in each."

I nodded and scribbled on the green paper. I rubbed the sticky part against the cardboard and Dr Olsen kicked it aside.

"One down—"

Before he could finish his sentence, a wild crash sounded next door. We both jumped, but he recovered much faster than I did. I buried my head in my arms as Dr Olsen tried to comfort me.

"Hey, it's alright," he said as he rubbed my back.

I hesitantly lifted my head as the noises continued. Dr Olsen rose from the sofa and approached his shelf. He pulled a blanket out from a box and wrapped it around me.

"Here. Keep this round you and if you get scared you can cover yourself with it. I'm gonna check what's going on, I'll be back in a bit."

I continued nodding as he swung around his doorframe and followed the sound. His door slowly closed, and I gripped tightly at the material of the old blanket. Considering its age, it was still in one piece and was still soft to the touch. As well as this, it was weighted. With the combination of it all, I felt relaxed. I slipped my shoes off and lifted my feet onto the sofa as I swung the cover around me and laid back. I kept my entire body hidden from the world with the only part of me showing being the top half of my head.

I kept my breathing low as I tried to listen to the noises next door. There was a cascade of overlapping voices and the sound of shattering. I turned myself around and rose onto my knees as I pressed my ear against the wall, the blanket falling past my shoulders. I made out Dr Olsen's voice and the movement of what I assumed to be his footsteps approaching the right side. I couldn't make anything out of what he was saying. It was all murmurs and muffled commands until silence fell after more shattering. I shot back underneath the covers and clenched my eyes shut as I awaited Olsen's return, panicking if he was even going to.

After minutes of nothing but me cowering, I heard the door creak. Then footsteps. And finally, the familiar voice returning.

"I'm back again."

I peeped out of the side of the cover and Dr Olsen calmly lifted the rest to reveal my face.

"W-what happened?" I stuttered.

"Another patient broke the window next door. He was sedated and taken back to his room." He sat down beside me.

"Is he okay?"

"I think he will be. He was just having an episode of some kind, he should be back to normal tomorrow."

I retreated back into the blanket. "Okay."

Dr Olsen sighed and uncovered my face again. "Hey, it's alright," he said with a smile. "Everything's back to normal now."

I burrowed out of my cave and let the blanket sprawl out over the sofa as I reached forward and hugged the doctor.

He stroked across my head lightly. "Hey, it's okay. It's okay."

I opened my eyes and saw the flicker of an orange wing circling by the window. I shook my head and buried it again.

"Noah?" Dr Olsen began.

I faced him and picked at my fingers, the sensation of gloveless hands seeming alien to me. "Why is it still there?"

"What?"

"The butterfly." I pointed at it. "It was there."

He approached the window and inspected it. "I couldn't tell you, mate. I'm sure it'll go away. It's just a butterfly, it doesn't do anything to you."

"Are you sure?"

"I'm sure." He sat back down again.

"Okay," I said shakily.

"D'you wanna keep going with this?"

I closed my eyes and trembled, still trying to recover from the fright.

His voice mellowed. "Do you wanna do this another day?"

"M-hm."

"Alright." He stood up and put out his hand. "Come on. Let's get you back to your room."

I grabbed his hand and slipped my shoes back on before we progressed, leaving the blanket on the sofa. We headed slowly back to the rooms, my feet shuffling across the ground as we moved, fearing another scare would come. Dr Olsen kept his hand hovered behind my waist, directing me on where to walk. The halls were mostly empty, the patients all vacant from the area with the only people left being two guards and a doctor. They watched me intently as we passed them.

Eventually, Olsen and I reached my room, and he scanned his key card against the reader, the door sliding upwards.

"Want me to come in with you or are you fine on your own?" he asked.

I stepped into the airlock. "I'll be fine."

"Okay." He pressed the numbers on the keypad and the door slid shut, sealing me inside.

As the next one opened, I stepped through and took a seat on the carpet. I crossed my legs and sat motionless for several minutes. I took in multiple breaths with my eyes clenched shut as I tried to fight the urges that were creeping up on me. I opened my eyes again then sat at my desk, staring out of the window, only to see another butterfly swerve around the corner and smack into the glass. I jumped and crawled onto the surface to get a look at it. It was a pretty hard thud, and as much as I didn't like the bugs, I didn't want it to be hurt. I looked down at it and saw it upside down on the bricks still flapping its wings as it tried to get up. I tapped on the glass and watched as it became manic before it quickly returned to its catatonic position. I quickly pulled a loose piece of paper out from a pile and sketched the creature. I then coloured it, and then I shaded it, all whilst it stayed there. I took the final piece and used the glue dots to stick it to the wall.

It fascinated me. The mystery of such a common animal. It was unknown to the world what they were doing here, or even why they were so different to their ancestors. I backed away from my drawing and slowly clambered onto the surface of my desk, resting the palms of my hands on the thick, frost-coated glass. The monarch was still, its large wings casted outwards and revealing its shimmering colour. The streaks of darkness that flowed between each collection bright scales, along with freckles of pure white throughout its blackened parts.

I turned my head, looking to the clock on the wall. Forty minutes until Free Time. I turned back then slipped my fingertip down the glass. The monarch fluttered. I dragged my hand left, I dragged my hand right. Both ways ignited movements. I sat there, resting on my knees, simply wavering my fingers across the window until the short siren sounded. The unlocking of metal followed, and I gently rolled from my desk, leaping for the door.

I scrambled out into the hall and practically ran to the common room, although the staff swiftly ordered me to slow my pace. I joined the selection of other patients outside the doors as a doctor rummaged their way through as to reach the front.

"Alright, alright," they said, their arms raised with keys dangling from their fingertips. "I'm doing it, I'm doing it." They fumbled with the lock whilst clambering to keep the eager patients back, some even yanking at their jacket. "Come on, guys. Back it up a little, yeah?"

We didn't listen. Instead, we shuffled closer. I'd never actually been to the common room this early before. I've never seen the doors open. I wondered if this was what it was like waiting for a club to open on the outside, but I'm sure that's not as exciting as racing to get the only board of backgammon from the games cupboard.

"There you are, you defiant lot," the doctor announced as they dramatically pulled the doors out.

The men then excitedly rushed in, leaving me and the doctor in the dust. I adjusted myself from the constant nudging and the doctor approached me.

"You alright, Noah? Never seen you here for opening hours."

"Yeah, I know," I replied with a chuckle. "I'm feeling inspired for once. Wanted to get going before it disappears."

"Well, good for you." They smiled and tapped my arm. "Enjoy yourself. I'll be in in a sec. I've just gotta fix these doors in place. We're not allowed them closed anymore."

I swallowed and stepped in. "Right…"

I watched the frantic groups inside. Some were invading the craft station, some were flinging games boxes around, and some were settling together on the sofa. I yanked at my sleeves then headed to the centre, crouching beside the short bookshelves. I scanned over the book list that was fixed to the wood then found a possible success in the A section. I dragged different covers out, inspecting each one before slinging them back in, until I found a rather thick one. It's title read, '*The Animal Kingdom*', so I slumped my back against the shelf and opened to the first page.

It was from 2015, but I guessed it was good enough. I just hoped each one was still around in this day and age. I skipped to the M's and skimmed each section, Manatee, Macaw, Meerkat, until I found the page. Monarch Butterfly. Before I began reading, I swung past the craft table and stole a spare sheet of paper and pencil. I then settled down again and jotted what I saw. There was barely half a page.

'The monarch butterfly is an extraordinary creature, native to North America. Its general habitats are forests or anywhere that milkweed grows. This animal is also known for making ambiguous journeys – sometimes reaching over 2,000 miles, even with its 4 inch wings. The usual trips are made from Canada down to Mexico, but some have even been sighted as far as Europe.

However, despite this incredible dedication, the monarch rarely survives longer than a month and are faced with many threats. Main ones being logging, predators, and harsh weather. These are the main reasons for the declining numbers of the insects.'

I slouched with a sigh and closed the book. I'd heard most of this on the news and radio, so I folded my sheet up and returned the book to its slot, making sure as to keep to its alphabetical order (even though most patients

150

don't care much for that).

I then checked over the book list again, reading over it for a book that maybe focussed on the creatures. I spotted one and slid to the M's, once again flinging books in and out of the shelf on my search for more. Until one book fell from my grasp. It thumped against the gristly carpet and the cover glared up at me.

'MK-Ultra: Reality, Not a Conspiracy'

I lifted it up, glancing around in confusion before re-checking the book listings. It wasn't there. I checked the other books around me, and their names were all on the list. This one wasn't. Of course, this could have just been a printing error, but they've never missed a book from the list. Ever. The staff love to know exactly who's read what.

In intrigue, I investigated. The cover was ripped and the book as a whole was quite short, not many pages at all. Then in the corner I noticed a small graphic. A cluster of monarch butterflies. I quickly fumbled with the pages and read over the introduction, unfolding my notes once more.

'In the 1950s, the CIA conducted an unsuccessful experiment codenamed 'MK-Ultra'. It involved the drugging and torture of many unknowing volunteers and victims. However, the story of MK-Ultra is mostly told through conspiracies and rumours due to the destruction of the official records, the only reason we know of such an experiment is from a few surviving files that were incorrectly labelled.

We know from this that the CIA were trying to master a mind-altering drug, but their motives as to why – aside from the fear of the Cold War – can only be speculated. It could have been to erase memories, sharpen interrogation methods, create a truth serum, or to use people as assassins. It is unclear if we will ever know.

Of course, others would use the drug for different purposes. If it were completed, the world could have been quite different. Would the Cold War have ended faster? Would lives have been saved? Would people feel safer? Or would the world fall under power of an organisation with too much control?'

I lifted my head from the book and checked around me. I didn't understand how a book like this made its way into Riptide, let alone it being so easy access to everyone. I turned back to the page, trying to analyse it. Too many dots were overlapping with me. Drugs, memories, assassinations. What if—No. Don't think that. It couldn't be possible, it was in the 50s. It's

151

2023, for God's sake. It's been seventy years. It's over.

I shut the book abruptly and held it close to my chest. My head was shaking as I closed my eyes, trying to keep myself from spiralling. I spun back to face the shelf and hovered my hand above the empty slot. But I couldn't bring myself to put it in. I gave an exclaim under my breath and rested the book on my lap. I ran my thumb across the title, an overwhelming urge to keep reading filling every inch of my free will.

With a final exhale, I gave into my curiosity and returned to my original position, flicking to the next section.

'The project was alleged to have been established in 1953 after the idea of mind-control techniques were being used by those in China, North Korea and Russia. With the fear it could happen to them, the US took to the CIA to create a project with the same outcome. MK-Ultra. Over the years, they worked towards behaviour modifications and interrogations. They also hoped to achieve a candidate that could be controlled at any point to commit an act they would go on to forget.

How did they do this? The CIA used a range of materials and methods to reach their wanted goals. This included drugging and hypnotising. The drug that the CIA favoured the most was LSD, a hallucinogenic drug that alters a person's reality. Subjects would be unwillingly given the drug and watched through a screen by the doctors. The substance was led to be abandoned, however, as its effects were too great and unpredictable to be able to control one's thoughts. Several projects sparked from the main one, leading to the creation of 'Operation Midnight Climax' and the 'Monarch Project'.'

I gave a silent cry. No. Stop. Just bloody stop reading it. You didn't come to search for this, you just came to learn about that stupid butterfly – have a little fun. Not this. I shakily pushed the cover back down and slung the book carelessly atop the others on the shelf, taking my notes and sitting at the craft table. Keeping my back to the shelf.

I flattened the sheet onto the tabletop then reached for a larger one. There were a few scattered pens around so used them to brighten up the work. I was thoroughly enjoying myself, creating word bubbles and doodles, all in relation to that simple butterfly. But once I'd finished, my attention drew back to the shelf. Back to the battered book that was lying on its side. I pushed back on the chair slightly, turning away from the table. I didn't know what it was, but there was something in me that had a connection to that story. It was like a missing part of me was to be found if I just kept reading.

But before I had a chance, the buzzer sounded for dinner. There was no time to return to my room with my papers, and no time to read that book. One-by-one the staff collected a patient. I darted my eyes as each one was taken then quickly folded my sheets small enough to fit them in my pockets. I chucked the scrap page in the waste basket in the corner, but once again was in awe of the shelf.

I had no idea on what to do. The staff check that book list at the end of every day, making sure that each book is firmly on the shelf, and if that one isn't on the list, it for sure will get taken away. I glanced at the forming line by the door and the remaining few patients getting escorted towards it, so with little thought, I grabbed the book and slipped it into my waistband, covering it with my top layers just as I was collected.

Before exiting, we were each searched, the staff briskly brushing the hands over our clothes. One patient had a sharpener taken, and another lost a piece of string. So when it came to my turn, I certainly held my breath. The guard skimmed his hands across me, stopping as he felt the pouch of items in my hoodie pocket.

"What's in your pocket, Coleman?"

I stuttered and fumbled my hands inside, pulling out the monarch paper I drew and hoping it would be enough for him. "It's just some work I was doing."

He ripped it from my hands and glossed over it, ending with a shrug. "You've been watching the news then?" He passed it back.

I nodded and held the A3 paper in a chaotic relief. "Y-Yes, I have. I thought that maybe I could find out something."

He scoffed. "Good luck with that, but I'm glad you're doing something productive."

I bit my lip and forced a smile as I stepped out to the hallway, following the stream of blue outfits towards the canteen. I folded the page back into a small square and shoved it back in my pocket, gaining enough space from the staffs' field of vision as I trotted along.

Soon after, I slipped away, almost at a run, and headed for the rooms. I couldn't risk anything happening in the midst of dinner that could result in me losing the stolen item. Running around with contraband under your clothes is usually not a good thing to do. I passed several people on my way, all of whom were going against my grain. Most didn't notice me, but the doctors definitely did.

They called out, "Noah! Where are you going?"

"Just to my room!" I called back, rushing off before they could reply.

I weaved in and out of each corridor, losing the tail of the staff so that I could reach my door's hallway. I glanced around the corner and spotted two doctors talking down the corridor that my room was off of.

I shuddered as I felt the scratching of the pages against my skin and took the book from under my shirt. I took a step back with it in my hands and collided with Dr Olsen. I stumbled back and gripped at the book in shame of being caught.

"Noah, you know it's dinner time, right? What are you doing down here?" he questioned.

"Um..." I tried to hide the book behind me, but he had already caught sight of it.

"What's that you've got there?"

With my head hanging, I presented the cover to him.

He read the title and quickly became very tense. "Noah, I need to take that, mate. You're not allowed it." He tried to reach for it, but I backed away.

"I just wanted to read it," I muttered. "It's interesting."

"I'm sure it is, but you can't have that one, mate. I'm sorry. I don't know how you got hold of it, but it definitely isn't meant to be here." He placed his hand on the top of the cover and tried to take it away, but I pulled it back. "Noah." His tone became stern. "Please, mate. I need to take it."

We stared in silence as I dug my nails into the cover, pressing so harshly that permanent dents were formed across it. Olsen kept his grip too. Whatever the reason was, he would have given anything for me not to have even a peek at a single page.

With another shudder, I lifted my grip and allowed him to take the book from me.

"Thank you, Noah." He held it under his arm. "You know that you're not allowed to take books in your room, mate. It doesn't matter what it's about."

"I know..."

He sighed. "Go on. You better get to dinner before all of the good stuff's gone."

I nodded then headed back the way I came. Olsen watched me leave,

154

keeping a tight hold of the book I had now lost.

I met with Shawn and Kyle at our table and sat beside Shawn with my tray. I listened to their conversations as I sat with my hood up, not touching a speck of food.

Shawn nudged me and I turned to face him. "You okay?"

I nodded. "I'm fine."

"Are you sure?"

I turned away again, replying slowly. "Yeah."

Even though we were all friends again, Shawn and Kyle have certainly been treating me different ever since the Wilks incident. Honestly, most patients were overjoyed that she was gone, but didn't like the idea of why she is.

I cleared my throat. "Hey, um... Do you guys know anything about MK-Ultra?"

Kyle shook his head. "It sounds like a spaceship."

"Never heard of it," Shawn added. "What is it?"

I swallowed and rose from the table. "I don't know." I took my untouched tray and placed it with the finished ones then headed back out to the halls.

I had one thing on my mind. Getting that book back. If it wasn't meant to be here to begin with, it's likely he didn't take it back to the common room, and the most logical place I could think to look was his office. Since it was dinner, I knew he wasn't going to have anyone in for a meeting so that's where I started. I don't know why I was so drawn to getting it back, I hate breaking rules, but when something's important to you, nothing else really matters.

I hid behind the different walls to avoid any of the staff seeing me until I saw the door for Olsen's office. He was stood outside it talking to Caleb. Neither of them had the book, so maybe it was already in the room, I just needed a way in. I watched and waited as they both continued their conversations. Dr Olsen had placed his hand on his door handle, ready to enter, but both men were called urgently away by a woman who had emerged from a patient's room. As they rushed to assist her, I skidded over to the office. The door was unlocked, and I gained easy access to the room. I quietly closed the door as I scanned my surroundings.

I checked across his shelves then across the back tables until I found it inside a box with a few other contraband items. Just as I celebrated my find, something caught my eye. The amber cover of my file. Dr Olsen had it lying on his desk with a pen readied next to it. It was there. In plain sight. Ready for anyone to take.

The decision I made took a lot of thought. After everything that happened, we all decided that knowing what I did makes things worse, and that if it stays forgotten then I'll get back to normal much quicker. But I needed to know the truth. I needed to stop the stories whirring in my head. I needed to prove that I was just like any other patient.

No. I can't. I can't know.

I groaned and pushed on the door handle. But I didn't leave. I couldn't.

You're just here for the book. If you hadn't lost it before, you wouldn't have seen the file. The file wouldn't be there.

I hesitantly looked over my shoulder at it before making the decision. I took it. I didn't have time to read it there, so I slipped it inside the MK-Ultra book and stepped back out into the corridor. I heard the clatter from the room the doctors were investigating and gathered the amount of time I had to reach mine. Thanks to dinner, most of the staff were monitoring there since that's where most of the patients were, if not there then they were in their rooms. I made a break down the hall and reached my door.

I skidded against my heels as I tried to pry a gap open but quickly gave up, knowing full-well that doors remain locked for the first fifteen minutes of any food hours. They'll let you out, but they won't let you in. In a panic, I fumbled with the pages of my file and tried cramming them through the handcuff slot. Although, somehow, the clips holding the file together snapped and sent a stream of floating papers in every direction, some on my side of the door, some on the other.

In a panicked rush, I chased the ones on my side down. Some had managed to get doors away. This resulted in me noticing the security camera in the corner that seemed to be focusing on me.

They're watching you.

I stepped back slowly as I was caught, muttering as I made my way back to my room. As I reached my door, I noticed two doctors heading my way and point in my direction. I quickly spun myself around again and calmly returned to the corner with the camera before sprinting out of sight of the staff. I heard them pursue me and allowed my feet to take control of the situation and they led me to a secluded area.

I sat down behind the wall and quickly ripped each page out of the now crumpled book. I found it would be easier for me to hide the pages than it was to simply keep it as one. After I removed each page, I folded them and hid them all over me. As for the cover, I approached one of the bin panels in the wall and dropped it inside. It clanged against the metal as it fell.

All that was left were the few pages I had recovered from my file. I perched on a bench and tried to find the beginning. Most pages were incident reports, so I slung them to the side and cowered at the words on the remaining two. I gently lifted each page as I read across each one, twitching back and forth at each sound that echoed down the halls. There was little time, so I read what I could.

'*REASON FOR ADMISSION:*

Coleman was arrested on 23/01/2022 for the attempted murder of Ryan Axel, 17. The attack was proven to be unplanned, and so fell under the third-degree. Ryan Axel was a Year 12 student at Layset Secondary School where Coleman was employed as the librarian. It was on this date that the patient fell into a fugue state. Whilst in this state, the patient tried to strangle Ryan Axel with a piece of piano wire that he obtained from the music department.

Witnesses described Coleman as seeming lost and that he wandered the grounds of the school in a dissociated manner before returning to himself whilst he was strangling Axel. Coleman was manic and quickly released the student once he realised what it was he was doing. He was restrained shortly after then continued to scream about a teacher by the name of Blake Hayes. The patient believed that his colleague was involved in a mind control project as well as believing that he was being controlled by him. Later, Coleman stated that he found information on a USB, and that the USB had a printed marking on it of three multicoloured ovals.

When he was taken to the police station, he was originally ruled deluded, but was later found sane by the station's psychiatric team with his mania being caused by Lysergic Acid Diethylamide which was found in his system after a drug test.

It was led to believe that the patient's memory loss and psychosis was caused by the heavy use of the drug, along with several others that were found, but his family suggested otherwise. It is unclear what caused the incident to be so sudden as not only were the drugs firmly out of his system by the time his memory relapsed, no known drug has been recorded to cause such a sudden reaction.

As for the teacher the patient accused, he was later cleared of any suspicion due to the patient being under the influence of LSD and his delusions.'

I felt as each cell of my insides shrivelled into dryness. I fell paler than the piercing white tiles that covered the hospital. I had my ribs rattling as my heart skipped into a constant pounding.

This isn't true. It's not true. They knew. The staff knew. Everybody bloody knew. Even Dr Olsen. That's why he took the book. That's why he couldn't bear for me to even touch it. They all knew that if I read one page I'd figure out what really happened. LSD, wiped memories, fugues, murder, mind control. Too many dots connected. Too many.

But before I had a chance to read further, the doctors found me, and I shot up from the bench. I went to run, but I was trapped at either end. I paced back and forth between the two sides as the two groups persisted in their trap. One woman reached her hands out and tried to take the pages from me, but I pulled away from her.

"Coleman. Give me the paper," she said sternly.

I shook my head. "No."

"Coleman." She laid her hand out. "Give me the paper."

I glanced behind me and there were now two security guards readying to pounce after one hint of aggression. I turned back and saw another doctor take the sheets from the bench and pass them to another. I gripped at the sheet and closed my eyes, bracing myself for whatever they were going to do.

"No!" I yelled.

The guards then grabbed me from behind and pulled me down, resulting in me being dragged across the tiles before the scene was interrupted by Caleb. He pushed through the crowd and ordered the guards away. At first they remained, but after a second demand they released me. I curled up in a ball, the paper being protected by my stomach, as Caleb carefully crouched beside me.

"Hey, buddy," he said softly. "You okay?"

I shook my head as I curled up tighter.

"What's the matter?"

"They... they knew," I muttered.

"Knew what, Noah?"

I gestured at the doctors behind him. "They knew what really happened

158

to me. They know why I'm like this and they won't tell me!"

He glanced back. "It's not like that at all, Noah. Yes, we knew of your crime, but we don't know why it happened that way. We don't."

I loosened my position then fumbled with the paper.

"Can I have the file?"

With a final breath, I passed the crumpled sheet to him, and he quickly passed it to the woman.

"There we go. That's all they wanted. Are you gonna come with me to your room now?"

I nodded and Caleb reached his hands underneath my shoulders and hoisted me up off the floor. I stumbled slightly from the bang to the tiles but managed to recover. Caleb kept contact with me as we headed through the group together, hatred-fuelled stares glaring at me.

Before I was locked in my room, I was patted down by the guard, and he found the majority of the papers I had stashed from the torn-up book. They were confiscated, as was the mess of the file that was still trapped in the airlock. Whilst I waited for the system to engage, I heard the staff muttering from the corridor.

"Where did he get it from?"

"This was in Joel's office."

"He must have broken in to steal it."

I only heard what must have been the beginning of a very long line of questions before I was left alone in my room and the door sealed. As the clock turned six, I sat hidden behind the side of my bed, blocking a part of me from the camera in the corner and the mirrored glass.

Thankfully, I was ahead. They hadn't found everything. There were still three or four pages left over that I had stored in my socks. This included the section that deemed most important. *'The Monarch Project'*.

'The Monarch Project was named after the monarch butterfly – a symbol of rebirth and transformation. This was the main goal for MK-Ultra. The creature holds a hardwired behaviour to follow a set migration period that has little to stop them from doing so. This is similar to how the CIA wanted their conditioned subjects to act – without consciously thinking – it becomes an instinct, not an action.

The subject will receive a handler, someone who has full control over the subject's mind, and will have triggers that can ignite the behaviour in a person. Those in the programme have no knowledge of their trigger and may not even realise they are in the project at all, but when a trigger is used, the subject will have no choice but to comply. They will become cold, and unable to form compassion.

This is similar to the quote by the Dalai Lama about the butterfly; 'The butterfly never meets its mother. It must survive independently and remains a stranger to affection. An animal nurtured by mother's milk, however, is dependent on another for its basic survival. A child who grows up in a cold and detached home environment is similar to the butterfly, in that kindness is sparing. Once an adult, it will be very difficult for that person to show compassion'.

This was the goal of the handlers. To programme their compliers to be as void as the butterfly.'

With this, I shot from the floor over to the window to spy for the stalking creature, only to find it exactly where it was the last time. It was still alive. It was still sat on the bricks with its beauty flashing through its wings. I frantically banged on the glass, desperate to scare it off, but it remained. It always remained. I panted harshly as emotions and thoughts raced in harmony.

They want you that way. They want you void. It's why they never tell you anything, it's why they never care. They want you void. They want you compliant.

I continued battering the glass, throwing each page I had scribbled on in its direction, but it merely fluttered. As I tried and failed to rid the monarch, my door re-opened, and Dr Olsen stepped in. He spotted my actions and rushed over to me.

"Hey, hey, mate. Calm down. What's the matter?" He pulled me away from the window.

Knowing that my last piece of evidence was at risk, I tried to deter my reasons for why I was so untamed.

"I, um… I was playing with the butterfly."

He glanced through the glass and saw the monarch. "Hm. It seems to have taken a liking to you." He stepped back. "But I wouldn't aggravate it, mate. It won't make it very happy."

"M-hm," I said as I crumpled the MK-Ultra pages in my fist behind my back, the noise not noticeable to the doctor.

"Noah," he began with a sigh. "I need you to be really honest with me. No lies, okay? Complete honesty."

I nodded, fearfully glancing between him and the mirror.

"Did you break into my office?"

He didn't sound angry, but nonetheless I felt a cascade of guilt fall upon me, making my stomach churn and my skin crawl. It wouldn't even allow me to speak.

"Noah? Yes or no? Did you break into my office?"

With a shred of movement, I nodded my head and drew my eyes away from his.

He sighed deeply. "Did you steal the book I took from you?"

I nodded.

"Did you steal your file from my desk?"

I nodded.

"Okay." He patted my shoulder. "Thanks for telling the truth, mate. Listen. How much of your file did you read?"

I was very hesitant. If I said everything I read, he'd for sure increase watch in me. Keep the camera manned and not let me out of sight. I couldn't tell him. I couldn't comply. "Not much... I read... about... Blake Hayes and... the LSD."

He rubbed his tired eyes. "Right, okay. What do you know about it?"

I shrugged. "That I said something about him to the police, and that I was on drugs..." I looked back up at him. "I only had two pages of it. I don't know what it was I said about him."

He seemed relieved, although that could just as well be the exhaustion. "Alright, Noah. I know the staff got a little bit too harsh on you out there, didn't they?"

I chuckled out of awkwardness then pulled at my sleeves. "They rattled me a bit, yeah."

"Don't worry. I've spoke to them about it. They wanted to apologise for how they treated you."

I swayed my arms back and forth. "Tell them I'm sorry too."

He smiled. "I will, mate. They've had to go on a scavenger hunt for your file now." He laughed shortly. "It's why I came to ask you about it. We couldn't be sure what you'd seen and what you hadn't seen."

I flashed a grin and forced a chuckle. "Yeah, I kinda missed my chances at reading much."

"Maybe that's for the best," he replied. "Now, get some rest. Let's hope tomorrow will be calmer."

I wish that could've been true. But after the doctor left, I couldn't settle on anything other than three things. My file, MK-Ultra, and that butterfly. I had such a mixture of feelings fighting inside me. Some being the voice of reason, whilst another was the voice of delusion. In fact, I couldn't tell you a straight thought. Everything was battling for a place in the spotlight, and as midnight chimed, nothing felt real. Nothing was normal. The only normal thing there is about life is how queer it can be. And I mean that in every sense of the word. I writhed around under my covers, forcing myself over and over to at least try and shut my brain down, but I couldn't. Everything was there. Colours, shapes, voices.

I tossed and turned in my bed for hours until I'd had enough and clambered onto the desk. The butterfly was still there. Still waiting. I analysed its movements, its patterns, each of its different markings until I had an idea spring. I pulled my notepad from the drawer and yanked the pages from earlier out from my hidey hole (the loose panel that surrounded my window).

Every little piece I had – no matter how small – was added to the pile of growing paper on the floor. I wrote about me, about my link to the project, about how it could all be connected. I wrote about Blake Hayes. I had no clue of who he was, but he was a teacher. A teacher at Layset. Layset. I wrote about that too. Every shred of my life that I could recall was scribbled down, and by the time the sun came to rise, I had the whole theory mapped out on my floor. There was even a symbol. It was a symbol I had never seen. Not in this life, anyway. It was three ovals. Each drawing different to another as I racked my brain for a similar image until I found one. Twenty-three symbols later, I found it. Three stretched ovals overlapping. One red. One blue. One grey. I plastered it Then as the buzzer sounded for breakfast, I finished.

I wasn't tired the whole night, and I wasn't tired by the time dawn had well-and-truly passed. I hadn't realised how long I'd spent on it – the floor was covered, not a single bit of carpet was visible, so I began moving it to my wall. But as I crouched for the first piece, I caught sight of a guard staring through the opened slot in my door. I only saw her eyes, but they were deep with concern. She quickly slammed the slot across, and the outer airlock sounded.

I ignored her and rapidly sprung back and forth around my room, the papers swirling from the gusts of my speed. Soon enough, the airlock opened again, this time Olsen and Phillipson stepped through, the guard behind them. Each held startle in their eyes.

Olsen stepped first, brushing a page with his foot. "Noah… when did you do all of this?"

"Last night," I replied bluntly as I jumped between each gap in the papers.

They glanced at each other, and Dr Olsen took another step towards me.

"Um, Noah, how long did you spend on this?"

"I don't know. From one 'til breakfast, I guess." I stuck one of the symbols beside the monarch sketch.

"Did you not sleep at all last night, Noah?"

I shook my head then approached the window. It was still there. It was still watching. I tapped on the glass and the bug flapped its wings. I stepped back then searched around me for a pencil before scribbling another note onto the wall.

"Noah, what… what's going on, mate? All of this, what you've done, it's a bit worrisome."

He gestured at one of the papers next to me and I slammed my hand forcefully on the wall. He couldn't touch it. Nobody could. From shock, he quickly retracted his hand then signalled to the other doctor.

"Noah, we're going to take you to get your meds now, okay? It's that time of the day." he continued, this time with a much more cautious manner.

"No, it's not," I replied sternly.

"It is, Noah."

I aggressively pointed at the clock. "No, it's not. Look!"

They turned to see the time.

"See?" I continued. "8:13. That's an hour until meds."

Olsen turned back. "That's right, mate. But we're just a bit worried that your dose is off ever since giving you those painkillers for your eye. Remember them?"

I felt across the near-faded bruise then turned my backs to them. "I'm not going anywhere."

He chuckled weakly. "Come on, mate. I know that your pills aren't the best thing in the world to take, but they'll stop all this floating around your head and you can relax."

"I can't," I said bluntly. "I can't leave it. They'll take it down once they know I'm not with it. I need to stay, or they'll trigger me."

"Who's going to, Noah?"

"The handler. I don't know who they are. They might not even know that I know yet, but even so, they could take me at any time so I can't leave this."

The two doctors exchanged glances again, this time with much more concern as shown by Phillipson reaching for her radio. She pulled Olsen to the far corner and whispered.

"What do you suppose we do?"

"I don't know. He needs his emergency meds, we can't let him go on like this with his normal dose. His mania will get the best of him."

With a sudden burst of aggression, I launched the pencil in their direction, causing them to flinch and the guard to lunge my way. I ordered her back.

"Stop! Don't touch me!" I turned to the doctors. "I'm not manic! I'll prove it to you! I can live, I can be normal! Or whatever normal is to you! I'll prove to you!" I angrily marched through the waves of paper, pushing past the guard and slamming my hand against the door. "I can prove it! Let me out!"

Olsen and Phillipson rushed for me, pressuring me into the corner.

"Noah, please. Calm down," said Olsen, raising his hands.

"I'm trying to cooperate! You wanted me out, so I'll go out!"

"Alright, we'll take you out," he said calmly, gesturing to the guard waiting behind the glass.

The door then unlocked and the four of us waited inside, each filled with intensely different emotions. As door one slid down, the second opened, leading me to step out in the same agitated manner as I stepped in. Dr Phillipson went to take my arm, but I shoved her away and stormed through the halls.

We arrived at the door to medication and bumped into two other patients who were waiting outside. I groaned and began pacing back and forth between the two walls that lined the corridor. Phillipson politely edged past the other patients and entered the room, the guard then directing them further back. Olsen then slid in front of my stride, trying desperately to calm me.

"Please, mate. It's alright if you're upset, I know this isn't how your schedule usually is, but we don't want you getting worked up about what

164

you found."

"Why? " I cried, slowly stalking towards him. "Why don't you want me to know? Why would it be so bad? "

He began stepping back. "Noah, please—"

"Why did you never tell me what I did? Why didn't you? "

"Noah, stop it now." His tone was becoming demanding.

"No! I won't! Because. I. Am. Done. COMPLYING. TO. YOUR . RULES!"

Without my realising, my hand swiftly lifted, and I struck my palm against the doctor's cheek. He stumbled back from shock, holding the area in pain as Phillipson and the guard witnessed the action.

"NOAH!" Phillipson screeched, sprinting my way with the guard behind.

I trembled, glancing between my hand and the injured Olsen in shame. "No, no, NO!" I turned from them, ripping at my scalp in regret as I was scarred by the doctor's betrayed eyes. Then as I glanced back, the guard tackled me to the floor, bringing my head to the tiles. With the help of the others, she kept me pinned in position long enough for newly joining staff to reveal the skin on my back and drive a needle through it.

They kept on top of me for as long as they could for the drug to take effect, leaving me just enough time to overhear the growing crowd. One gave Olsen an ice pack, which he rested on his red face.

"Thanks," he said.

"It's alright," she replied. "What set him off, anyway?"

He sighed. "I did. I was being too hard on him. He never responds well to stuff like this."

Their voices began fading.

"Are you okay, though?"

He shook his head. "He's never hit me before…"

"Well, if he's done it to you once, you can rest assure he'll do it again."

Olsen took the ice pack away and we caught each other's eyes. His seemed sympathetic, mine were just of burning sorrow. I dug my hand out from the pile and pleaded in silence for him to accept my apology, but he simply walked away.

Later, I awoke. I could barely move and felt stripped of any connection to the world. I sluggishly writhed beneath my layers of blankets, kicking them off the best I could. I brought myself to sit up and rested my head in my knees once I realised I was in my room. I then shot back up again. I was in my room. I stumbled off of the mattress and scrambled towards the bare floor. I spun in frustration as a delirious whir ran in my head.

I stamped my tired legs on the carpet. "No!" I then kicked my chair.

It was then that a voice came through my overhead speaker. *"Noah? Can you hear me?"*

I turned to the mirror as I matched the accent. "Dr Olsen?"

"Yeah, mate. It's me."

I quickly leapt over to the screen, placing my hands on the mirror's plastic. "I'm so sorry, doctor. I didn't mean to—"

"It's okay, Noah. I know you didn't mean to hurt me."

I gave a sigh of relief.

"I get that you're probably upset over us taking your work, right?"

I scratched at the plastic. "Why do you care?"

"Because I didn't want to have to. I don't like taking your things, Noah, but sometimes it's necessary."

I returned to the empty space.

"Noah, do you want to know why I wasn't allowed to give you that book?"

I swung back around.

"First off, it wasn't a book that was registered, so no matter what it was about, you couldn't have had it. Just in case. Second, MK-Ultra is a forbidden topic at the hospital. It falls under a conspiracy. We don't allow conspiracies because they provoke delusions. Especially if it's caused one in the past."

I grunted and paced from end to end of my room.

"Noah, what's going on is made up in your head. You're safe. MK-Ultra doesn't exist anymore. There's no handlers, there's no drug, and there's no mind control. And if there was, I'd protect you from it. I won't let anyone hurt you, Noah. Okay?"

I ignored his query then glanced up at the clock. 12:32. I brought my pace to the door and shook the metal. It gave a rattle and so mashed at the call button beside it. It didn't budge.

"Noah, the door won't open."

"What? Why not?"

"The staff have put you on a 48 hour lockdown."

I gave a louder groan and kicked the broken wheel of my bed. "Gah! What for? "

"For attacking a staff member, and unruly behaviour, mate. 24 hours for each."

"I didn't mean to hurt anyone!"

"I know, mate, but even so, you broke the rules. Luckily, I talked them out of putting you in iso."

I slumped myself on the floor and rested against the wall. "I bet they *loved* that…" I muttered.

He brushed off my remark. *"You'll get your meds and food brought to you, but you won't get any tests and your privileges have been revoked. That means no visits or phone calls, Noah."*

"No different, then…"

He gave a sigh. *"Goodbye, Noah."*

The speaker crackled and I was left with the silent room. I groaned and aggressively ran my fingers through my hair before staring up at the window. I pushed myself up and crawled onto the desk, leaning against the glass. I grinded my teeth as I saw the butterfly perching on the bar once more. I scraped my fingers downward then struck the side of my fist at the plastic surrounding, causing a slight rattle which led me back to the hidey hole.

I hooked my nails into the plastic and pushed the top layer forwards, revealing the opening. I reached inside and dug around, pulling out the stack of letters I had forgotten were in there. I rifled through them, scanning the handwriting on each one, until I stopped at one that was quite the bit crisper than the others. It hadn't been opened prior; the seal wasn't ripped. And somehow I missed a crucial part. There was no address. Not to me, or to the return. It was just my name.

I slid underneath my desk and wrapped myself up in my blanket that was hanging off of the chair. I carefully unpicked the envelope, fearing that I'd ruin the contained letter if I continued in anger. A minute later, a small letter slipped out. It wafted onto my lap, and I folded it out.

'Hey, Noah.

You're probably wondering how I got this letter here, huh? Well, I've still got plenty of slight-of-hand tricks up my sleeve. I was worried you'd never get to read this one, thinking the staff would take it away for scanning, but if it got to you in one piece then I'm glad. I read over your other letters, and they blacked out any relation to Wyegate or Layset, I guess they still don't want you knowing, and I want you to get better and everything, but I couldn't not tell you this.

Whatever you found out at that school was real. I couldn't tell you what part; I don't know anything about it, but it's connected to Wyegate. I've been going over everything in my mind ever since the day you were taken to Ocean Cliff. You're the only one I have left and I'm sure that whatever happened with Wilks and Ryan was not because of you. Remember that. It's not your fault, it's the ACC's. – Aaron'

I crumpled the paper against my chest as it fluttered, wishing that the paper was really him. I cuddled against the blanket, thinking that if I brought it close enough then Aaron might get the message.

I'm gonna find out what happened, Aaron. I will. I won't let them take you.

I gazed over the scribbled last line. The ACC. I knew that name. I bloody knew it. I'd seen it. I'd seen it with *that* symbol. But what the hell did it mean? I don't think I ever knew. But they did something. Even Aaron knows they did something. I'm not letting them get to him. To either of us.

Chapter 7

We've Been Here Before

So many days passed, I couldn't tell you how many. The calendar's been abandoned. It's covered by the slate of other paper. Of information. They soon became repeats of themselves. Ten pages all the same, each line connected to another across the room. The centre to it all, that symbol. The ovals and the ACC. They were the root to all of this. They had to be. They were the ones in control.

I tried to keep this hidden, but there was no chance of it. There was too much to unfold. Too many connections. I refused to leave that room. I refused everything. Trust me, I wanted nothing more than to leave that pit, but I was dragged back. Dragged back by my own tormented brain. Over and over again. It was obvious that I was becoming erratic. Not sleeping, barely eating, leaving my life in the hands of this project.

The doctors had no choice but to bring what I needed to me. My food, my meds, even my meetings. They dare not stay long though. Any time they'd come towards me, I'd freak out. Then, in turn, they'd freak out. Although, they were better at hiding it than me. Every day it's 'Noah, please, talk to me,' or 'Noah, stop. We can help you.' But each time I heard them, it only drove my desire to defy them.

Even the news was on my side. Before this all got too deep, I was forced from my room (if only for a short while). So I hid away in the corners of the common room watching TV. They kept on about the increased amount of the butterflies around the country. They'd taken one in for examination and found that the reason they seemed so impossible is because they were. They weren't formed from a caterpillar, they were made. Mutated from the genes of a single monarch. The reason they're big, the reason they survive, is because of what it's made of. Metal. Metal, monarch, chemicals and blood.

That last part was the most shocking for some reason. When it was analysed, it was proven it was not blood of a butterfly, but blood of a human. Human blood mixed with an unknown substance. Before they tested more, the creature escaped. It was fast. It didn't stick around. That drove me back to the wall. To add to it. The staff grew ever more worried about me, almost fearful – if they weren't already. They daren't touch what I'd made. I was like this every day. For weeks. Or days? See? Time was useless now. Everything was. Until the staff finally had enough.

I was scampering back and forth across the room, dragging paper from different corners and scribbling information over the old notes before I froze in place as the door buzzed. I remained crouched on the carpet with a sheet clutched to my chest as the footsteps entered. I twitched about slightly as I glanced over my shoulder at the three figures in white before I broke free of my stillness and slumped to my knees.

"Hey, Noah," Dr Olsen began. "You alright?"

I ignored his query and yanked the work that was floating around their ankles away from them.

"Noah?" he repeated.

I straightened out and stumbled loosely as my energy levels brought me to my knees again.

"Noah. Look at me."

I crunched a page in my hands as I reluctantly peered over my shoulder.

He crouched beside me and spoke softly. "You didn't eat breakfast."

"I'm not hungry," I replied sharply as I returned to the image of the harshly drawn ovals.

"Noah, you need to have meals. You need to eat, or you'll get ill."

I continued in my stern tone. "I don't want to eat."

"Why not?" he questioned.

"I just don't want to." I crawled away from him and curled up in the corner by my desk.

He followed my trail. "Noah, you can't not eat. It's dangerous. You need to eat otherwise your body will run out of energy."

I gripped at the edge of the surface as I rose to my feet, swaying back and forth. "I'm fine!" I shouted as I rested my head against the wall and my breathing staggered.

Olsen approached and gently touched my back. "Noah, please, mate—"

I quickly shook back and forth as he formed a grip around my arm. "Let go of me."

170

He spoke with sorrow. "I can't, mate. Not if you're not gonna eat anything."

Although drowsy, I jerked about, flailing my free arm in his direction. "Stop. Get off!"

"Noah, listen to me—" He reached his hand towards me.

I smacked it back on instinct and shouted more. "NO! STOP!"

The other doctors finally jumped forward and tried to pin me back.

I stumbled from their grasps. "DON'T TOUCH ME!"

"Noah, stop. Calm down," Olsen said calmly as I paced away from them.

"NO!" I dodged one of their attempts to grab me, but as a result, slipped on the loose pages and collapsed against the metal end of my bed.

The staff then took their chance. They grabbed my collar and yanked me into the open space (if you could call it that). I jolted all around as they pressed their weights on my side and as Olsen removed the handcuffs from his hidden belt.

Stepping over, he spoke. "Lay him on his front. We need to get him to the emergency wing."

"NO! I'M NOT GOING ANYWHERE!"

As I cried, the doctors rolled me to my front and pinned my wrists to my back. I writhed about violently as Olsen knelt beside me, cuffing my hands in place.

"Stay, calm, Noah," he said. "Stay calm."

I kicked my legs out. "NO!"

"Radio the wing," the doctor ordered. "Tell them to keep on with the preparations."

One doctor hesitantly lifted their grip. "Alright. You got him?"

"Yeah, yeah. We've got him."

The woman then stepped away and spoke into the radio as the two remaining staff kept up their fight with me.

"I didn't want to have to do this to you, mate," Olsen said as I kicked him back and forth. "But it's for your own good. You need to eat."

"I CAN'T LEAVE! GET OFF ME!"

He sighed and glanced up at the radio doctor.

"They're nearly done," she told him.

"Alright, let's get him there."

The second woman brushed against my lower back. "Should we sedate him?"

"NO!" I screamed. "I DON'T WANNA!"

Olsen gently rubbed me and lowered my top. "We won't get it prepared safely in time. Plus, I don't wanna risk him not waking back up again. Not until we get him somewhere under control."

"NO! I DON'T NEED CONTROL! I'M FINE!"

The first woman returned. "They've readied the wing."

"Alright," Dr Olsen replied. "Let's go."

Together, the trio wrapped their arms around me and hoisted me to my feet. Refusing, I let my knees buckle. "NO!"

"Come on, Noah," said a strained Olsen. "Stand up."

I began sobbing, tears getting absorbed into the paper by my feet. "NO!"

He sighed. "Lift him up."

The doctors dragged me towards the door, twisting me into position, and lifting me from the ground. I felt my centre of gravity slide from one end to the next as I was carried through the airlock.

"PUT ME DOWN! STOP IT!"

Once the door rose, we were met with a number of other staff. The doctors gently lowered me for a second, only for a group of guards to yank me down the hall. The doctors hurried behind.

I kicked my legs in a panic as I grew further from the floor. "LET GO OF ME! GET AWAY!"

"Noah, Noah, stop," Olsen pleaded.

My energy was plummeting, I had no power against any of them. Even a kick at all my force was nothing but a tap. I panted in and out, and as we approached the emergency wing, I was forced to witness a dark mist creep from the outskirts of my vision until it cloaked my sight. I gave another deafening cry and slipped from the arms of my captors.

"I can't see… I CAN'T SEE ANYTHING! I CAN'T, I CAN'T—" My pants become wheezes of desperation, worsening as I was grabbed at different angles by unknown hands.

Olsen's voice was by my side as I was rushed closer and closer to what I assume was the allocated room. "He's gonna pass out. He needs food."

I drooped my head against somebody's shoulder and felt as my limp legs were drifted across the floor. It wasn't until I heard metal clanging and machines beeping that my vision returned. I refused to go unconscious. I was not giving them a chance to control me.

I dug my heels at the tiles as I reached the edge of the large bed, staff and curtains blocking the view to everything but the scene I was about to experience. There were voices calling from every direction, all orders, each one being followed. It was then that the clamps around my wrists were removed, and I was lowered onto my back on the raised mattress. I jolted at each noise and gesture, flailing to escape what I knew was to happen.

They strapped my limbs down, keeping them spread to the rails, giving me no leeway to fight further. I was sat up far enough for me to see straight ahead at the closing curtain. There were trapes of wires in the surroundings, one man unravelled a small one with a clip at the end, which he attached to my index finger. He tapped across a device and a pulse appeared just out of my sight.

He called to Olsen. "He's at 62 BPM, and it's likely that it would be lower if he wasn't panicking."

"What's his blood pressure?"

Another doctor came close, leaning over the frame to reach my jolting arm.

"GAH! Stop!" I still couldn't move.

The cuff was fixed and began to tighten.

The doctor shook their head after staring at the reader, the stethoscope swaying from side to side as they did. "It's hard to tell. It's jumping from 80/50 to 90/70."

Olsen sighed. "Are the tubes ready?"

"Yes," they replied morosely.

I rested my head back and let out a stifled whimper.

Olsen bit his lip and inhaled deeply. "Let's do it. Come on."

I shook my head, staring defeatedly at him with tearful pleas. "No..." I said shakily. "Please, no!"

The equipment prowled closer, the metal scraping against itself and the rubber attachments flailing from one nurse to the next. One man dragged the main tube out, his latex gloves squeaking against the material. He gazed up silently for Dr Olsen to give the word.

"The quicker we do it, the quicker it'll be over," he said in the same sad tone as the others.

I swung to face the man. "NO! PLEASE, I'M SORRY! I'M SORRY!"

He squinted his eyes, gaining second-hand pain of what he was to bring to me. He turned to his colleague. "Have you got the painkillers?"

She presented another tube from my right, and with the help of Olsen, speared it through the skin of my hand. I screamed and shot forwards, the sharpness crawling up my arm before I was rested back again. The nurse fiddled with her tubes for what seemed like hours, the constant, whining beeps droning into my skull.

Once the painkillers were in for certain, the other staff leaned close. They brought their long, thin stretch of wire towards my throat, a light shining from the side of it.

I tossed my head about, straining to avoid it. "No… please!"

Olsen gently held my hand. "It's gonna be okay, mate. Don't speak."

I faced him, eyes puffy and skin pale. "Please… I don't want… I'm sorry."

I saw as water built up in his eyes. He nodded. "It's okay. It's gonna be okay."

The nurse turned my head back, holding it still as the camera entered my mouth. As it backed into my throat, the thought of what it could do causing me to gag. Olsen continued to stroke my hand as tears rolled down my cheeks and landed in my mouth, the salty taste making my throat clench. The staff gave remarks to each other, none of which I understood, and once they confirmed the placement of the wire, they forced the main tube up my nose. I wacked my hands at the bedding as the sensation of the silicone joined with the other devices.

They kept forcing the tubes down me anyway, the constant gagging causing my chest to jerk forwards which, in turn, led to the devices having to be readjusted and shoved down more, all whilst the rest of me was being pinned in position by the remaining staff. I couldn't move, I couldn't speak, I couldn't even have a say over my own well-being. If they're all so worried about us over-reacting about food then my suggestion would be to not scrape our throats out with cameras and plastic. That probably wasn't what was actually happening, but I'm the one who felt it, okay? I was the one cuffed to a frame six-ways-to-Sunday having his insides flooded with whatever mutated chunks that managed to slide through the silicone.

Then, as the camera was dragged back up me, the ceiling above seemingly shattered. It crashed and the shards cascaded down. I shrieked and slammed my head against the side bar to avoid it, only to be twisted back to see the normal tiles.

I trembled. "Oh, God..."

I glanced over at the doorway to watch as the bricks above melted over the frame and consumed the door, sealing the exit as it hardened. I took in rapid sharp breaths as voices echoed each action I took.

Tapping your fingers. Twitching your leg. Flailing your body.

I shuddered as the staff fixed the tube in place, the tape yanking tightly at my already cracking skin. I let out a whimper as I tried to explain what my brain was doing to myself, but nobody was there to listen. Sure, they were in the room, but their minds were all too busy elsewhere to understand what my new pleas were about. All the pain, it grew. It grew to burning, piercing, singeing. Until, for some reason, it all submerged. The tension in my muscles released and my vision clouded over as silence fell.

It was sometime later before I became conscious. The pain remained, but it wasn't nearly as bad as what it was. I sluggishly tossed my head back and forth across the pillow as I inspected my surroundings. I lifted my hand to my face, the weight of it heavy as I ran my fingers over my covered nose. I then noticed that my hand also had that same tube attached to it. I rested it back down and followed the trail to a large stand beside me. It was connected to a clear bag that held a large amount of liquid. I went to pick at the bandage holding the tube in place when Olsen's voice came from just behind a curtain.

"Noah, mate, don't touch that."

I quickly lowered both arms. "S-Sorry, doctor..."

"It's okay." He sat in a chair to my left.

"Y-You al-ways seem to know when I'm..." I inhaled shakily. "... doing something... huh?"

He smiled gently at me. "It does seem that way, don't it?"

I lowered my head and breathed jaggedly as I continued to fiddle around my nose. "W-What... happened... to me?"

He reached for the clipboard hanging from the wall ridge. "Well, a lot." He flipped through the pages, quickly scanning over them as he spoke to me. "Do you remember anything from yesterday, Noah?"

I shook my head. "Not... really."

"Alright, that's okay." He scribbled across the notes. "Well, yesterday and the day before you were refusing to eat, and from the looks of you it's likely you've skipped more than just those. Do you remember anything about that?"

175

I stuttered and slid down the pillow slightly. "I, um… y-yeah."

His interest sharpened. "Do you know how long you've been skipping meals for?"

I glanced back and forth at him shamefully. "A w-week…"

He exhaled and added to the notes, his tone seeming disappointed. "Okay."

I cupped my hands together and stared at the sheets.

"Well," he continued sorrowfully. "Because you were refusing to eat, we had no other choice but to force-feed you. That's what that tube is for. Without anything your body would have shut down. It nearly did."

I nodded sheepishly.

"Whilst we were attaching the equipment to you, you were violent, and we had to strap you down – another thing I didn't want to have to do. Then because of how stressed you became, you had a panic attack and passed out. The panic attack probably made the ordeal at lot more painful than it already was. We tried to wake you up, but each time you opened your eyes, you'd have another attack, and the process would repeat.

In the end, we finished up as quick as we could and let you wake up naturally. You kept drifting in and out for a while until now. This is the first time you've been able to put two words together, which is good."

I brought my gaze to the ceiling in a dazed state then glanced in the direction of the door, only for it to be blocked by the turquoise curtain that surrounded my station. Olsen followed my eyeline before turning back to me as I spoke.

"W… What… about… the door?" I questioned breathlessly.

"What do you mean, mate?" he said with his considerate tone.

I pointed to my right, limply. "It… was… it melted."

The doctor stood up and stepped towards the curtain. He reached his hand underneath it. "No," he began as he lifted the material. "It's still there. See?"

I peered out and felt embarrassment consume me as I spotted the door exactly where it was meant to be. "Oh…" I closed my eyes and turned away. "So the ceiling didn't shatter either?"

Dr Olsen slid the curtain back then returned to my side. "No, Noah. It hasn't moved an inch."

I buried my face in my hands and sobbed. "Oh, God!" I let out several stifled breaths as I accepted the delusion and Olsen wrapped his arm around me.

"Hey, hey. It's alright," he replied softly. "Shh, it's alright."

I shook my head. "It wasn't real. It wasn't real."

He gently ran his fingers through my hair as I laid my weight against him. "I know, mate. It's scary."

I sniffled, only partly before wincing at the moving tube inside of me, then sat back to an upright position.

Olsen picked up the clipboard once more and rested his hand atop the paper. "Just for the notes, mate, I need to know what you hallucinated. Is that okay?"

"M-hm. It was... um... the... ceiling. It... shattered and... fell on me. Then the door, like... melted away."

He nodded up and down as he jotted the information on the page before he placed it to the side. "Okay. Good boy. I'm glad you told me that. We already put you on your emergency meds in that IV, so you shouldn't get any hallucinations for a while, especially if you stay relaxed, then it won't trigger anything, alright?"

"M-hm." I glanced up at the drip then let my body fall limp and slide back down the bed. I rested my head down and stared at Olsen. "I'm really tired..."

"That's not too surprising," he replied. "The sedative in your meds is probably effecting you more than usual due to how little energy you had in the first place."

I drowsily looked at the machine connected to the end of the feeding tube. "When do you... feed me?"

"Are you hungry?" he asked as he rose from the chair.

I shrugged. "I don't know... I can't... tell."

He bit his lip and nodded. "That's okay." He checked his watch. "Lunch is in an hour, so we'll come back then, alright?"

I leant forwards in concern, gripping at my sheets. "W-Where are you going?"

He lifted the left side of the curtain. "I need to inform the other staff that you're awake. Don't worry, you're not alone. If you need someone you can either shout really loud or press the help button on the panel to your left."

I glanced to my side and lightly scratched the emergency panel with my nail before turning back to Olsen. "What... am I meant to do here?"

177

"Just rest, mate." He checked behind the curtain quickly. "Lay back and relax." He then swung away, the blue sheet curling back to position as he left.

I sighed and slid down my bed until my head was buried in the soft layers of pillows. I gave a deep sigh and returned to inspecting my small, enclosed pod. My sides and front areas were blocked by the curtains with behind just being the same wall that lined the rest of the hospital. Inside my little space were the few machines that tracked how alive I was, as well as the table and chair that Dr Olsen was sat by. There really wasn't much else. Anything that wasn't necessary wasn't there. Not even entertainment.

Well, I say that. I could still hear things. Paper doesn't block out much noise. There were definitely other doctors in the distance and there was definitely another patient in the vicinity – I just couldn't tell where. His voice was familiar, except it sounded a little drowsy – if not, a lot drowsy. I wasn't sure if he was talking to someone or just himself, but either way, he sounded delirious.

"Really, there should be a word that's the same in every language that means 'what language do you speak?' I think it would help out a lot of people."

Nobody replied.

"Do you not think so?"

"It's a very smart idea, Kyle," another voice returned. "But I don't think many people would take you up on it. People don't really like changes."

Kyle. It was Kyle. I hadn't seen him for weeks. I hate to say it, but I forgot about him. I forgot about Shawn. I couldn't remember when we last talked.

I cleared my throat and called for his name. "Kyle?"

No response.

I inhaled and tried again. "Kyle?"

"Hello?" he called back in confusion.

"It's… It's Noah."

"Noah? " he yelled back. "What the hell, mate? I ain't seen you for ages!"

"S-Sorry," I stuttered. "I've just… had a lot… g-going on."

"It's alright. Me too."

"Why are you here?" I questioned, trying to steer away from the topic.

"Eh, you know me, heh. Seeing things wrong. I, uh… I tried to jump

178

down a flight of stairs."

"What happened?"

"I sprained both my ankles. Lucky it was just that, really. It's alright, though!" I heard him tap against something metallic. "I got the good stuff, so I, uh… can't feel a thing."

I gave a weak chuckle. I missed him. I don't know how, it's not like he went anywhere. He just made me feel a bit more normal when he spoke. And that's nothing against him. I'm not saying he's the weird one or anything. He makes us both feel normal. And that's good enough for me.

"So?" he continued.

"What?" I replied in confusion.

"Why are you here?"

I pulled my blanket further up my body and held it close as I rolled to my side. "Forgot to eat…"

"Yeah…" His tone dropped. "I haven't been seeing you around a lot."

"Yeah, I, uh… haven't been doing so well." I laughed through my strain. "I can't even feed myself these days."

Kyle cleared his throat and spoke softly. "Yeah, well… I'm gonna do what I do best and… go to sleep." I heard the bed rattle as he turned over. "Don't blame yourself. We're here 'cause we're sick. We're allowed to mess up."

"Right…" I rolled onto my back and stared lifelessly at the ceiling – each tile in perfect position.

It was quite a while before a doctor returned to me. Of course, I couldn't be sure on timings. The emergency meds really messed with my senses and distanced me from the world. It was kind of like watching a movie. A really, *really* boring movie. I've met a number of people here who know that exact feeling. In fact, it was more rare if this phenomenon didn't happen.

As lunch arrived, so did the staff. They adjusted my position, bringing me upright, then propped my head in position with the many pillows I had stuffed behind me. One nurse tapped at the main machine and adjusted what I assumed was my food, but Olsen quickly diverted my attention away.

"Hey," he began. "How're you feeling?"

"A little better," I replied.

"Have you had any hallucinations? Delusions? Things like that?"

I shook my head.

179

"Okay, that's good. Do you still know why you're here?"

I nodded. "Y-Yeah."

"Alright. Good," he said with a smile, but I kept noticing him glance away and towards the machine, which definitely made me feel a little uneasy.

"How long am I staying here for?" I asked.

Dr Olsen sighed. "We're not too sure, mate, but no more than a month."

"A month? " I replied in shock.

"It may not be that long, Noah. We just want to make sure that your body is functioning the way it should be and that you're well enough to make the decision to eat on your own."

I jerked forwards, the tubes connected to me tugging briefly. "I can eat. I *will* eat! It was just this once! I can do it on my own-"

"And I want to believe that," he interrupted. "But I've dealt with patients like this over and over, Noah, and they all said the same thing. It's my job to make sure you're safe. If you've developed an eating disorder and I just ignore that then that's not keeping you safe, is it?"

"I don't have an eating disorder..." I mumbled as I lowered my head.

He sighed. "I'm starting to think you do, mate."

"I'm fine..."

"Noah, we've all been keeping track of your eating habits, we know you don't eat properly. We never had the resources to intervene before, but now it's too far for you to go on without help."

I gritted my teeth. "I'm. Fine."

Olsen shook his head and adjusted the notes in his hands. "Noah, have you ever heard of ARFID?"

I rested my head back, exhaling deeply. "No..."

"Well, it stands for Avoidant Restrictive Food Intake Disorder. Your symptoms match to it more than any other eating disorder, but we can't diagnose you yet."

"Why not?" I said sleepily.

"Because it can take weeks to find a correct diagnosis, even months. You know how long it was to find your schizoaffective disorder. That took us half a year. Even your amnesia took time."

I turned to the nurse, watching as she readied my food in a syringe. "What's that?"

She gave me a smile. "Nothing exciting. Just fruit and milk, really. Just think of it as a smoothie."

"Okay…"

Olsen drove my attention away again. "Noah, we're gonna keep you on the feeding tube for a week, okay? Then we'll reassess whether you can come off it after."

"A week?"

"Yeah, mate. It's just to monitor you. You might get to come off it afterwards, but if you still haven't improved then we'll have to keep you here."

I gave another nod, closing my eyes and straining as I felt clenching in my stomach. I fell forwards and scratched at the back of my neck.

Dr Olsen edged me back. "Sit up, mate. Sit up."

I glanced at the nurse through squinted eyes, watching as she reached the end of the syringe.

She gave another smile. "Almost done."

I scowled at her. I didn't mean to, but haven't your stomach filled by some random stranger is not a nice sensation. Olsen held me up to stop the tube from bouncing around too much as the 'smoothie' slid down it. This was followed by water. The nurse injected the full needle of it through the tube – the excess food being swamped up with it. All I can say is, I'm glad I couldn't taste it.

A few days passed and I was allowed to move around a bit more freely. I wasn't allowed to leave the wing, but the staff let me roam the room I was in. I did have to drag my IV and other tubes around which wasn't very fun, I kept getting twisted up in them all. Oh, and word of the wise – don't stand on the frame. I had to learn that the hard way after I snapped the wheel off and went flying through some guy's curtain. The nurses weren't happy. Neither was he.

When I wasn't accidently harassing people, I'd sit at the tables they had dotted in the centre of the wing. There wasn't much to do then either, except maybe read the etchings that were carved into the wood from past patients. A day or two after I was given the green light to walk around, so was Kyle. Well, not so much walk around as wheel around. With two sprained ankles, he wasn't gonna get very far on foot, so the staff stuck him in a wheelchair. It was quite entertaining watching him try to work it out, but he caught on quite quickly. He wheeled over to join me with his food tray balancing on his lap.

"Hey, how's life?" he said, bumping his knees against the tabletop.

I glanced at him and shrugged. "I don't even know…"

He nodded and lowered his voice. "Look, I… I never knew whether to ask you about this or not but…"

His hesitation made me tense.

"… I overheard the whole thing the other day when they brought you in – it was pretty hard not to."

I felt across the tape on my nose. "Oh…"

"You were really out of it, huh?"

I looked to the floor. "Yeah."

"Don't worry," he said with a smile. "Us psychotics have our moments, don't we?" He leant close and whispered. "Wanna hear a story?"

I looked up and shrugged again. "Sure…"

He placed his tray on the table. "So you know how I like sprained my ankles, right? Well, the story started with me near the common room. You know the stairs down to the outside bit? Yeah, those.

Anyway, the episode started when some *genius* decided to order the staff into a game of blackjack, so there was nobody watching the rest of us. So when I trundled up with my head in the clouds, I fell into wonderland. The room shrank, people had their own weird-as-heck languages, so I decided the best way to escape was to leap from the top of the stairs to the bottom. Of course, to me those stairs were inches down, when really they were an entire flight."

We both chuckled, Kyle more than me.

"See? No need to feel embarrassed. I know how it feels when you're in that state. I was always embarrassed, especially after my time in Freefall. They made me feel like a right looney, saying there's nothing wrong with me. Worst time of my life. Worse than Riptide."

"Really?" I questioned, a pinch of energy surfacing.

"Yeah," he replied. "They wake you up at four, take your vitals, then don't see you again for another few hours. They don't care about you up there unless you say you're suicidal. I wish I did, maybe I wouldn't have gone and hurt anyone."

That was when a voice called from my cubicle. "Coleman!" I glanced over my shoulder and saw Caleb stood beside the curtains with a clipboard in his hand. "It's lunch, buddy."

I rose from the chair, speaking drowsily to Kyle. "See yah…"

182

He watched me leave. "Bye." I traipsed across the wing, dragging the rickety IV behind me until I met with Caleb.

He smiled gently then pushed the curtain back. "It'll go quick, I promise."

As he hid us behind the blue sheets, I shuffled for the bed. I let the IV drift from my hand into position then clambered onto the mattress. Caleb quickly adjusted me, making me as comfortable as I could be, then sat in the chair.

"The nurses are just getting it ready," he said.

I nodded and pulled my blankets closer. We remained silent for a few moments.

"Um… Caleb?"

He turned to me with another reassuring expression. "Yeah?"

"Do you believe in the project?" I asked sheepishly.

He shuffled in his seat. "Which project?"

I cupped my hands together and buried them beneath the sheets. "MK-Ultra? Do you believe it's real?"

His shoulders relaxed and he sat back. "Well, it was something that happened, so I believe *that*."

"Do you believe it's back, though?"

He sighed. "MK-Ultra? No. But if there was a project like it, I think the safest thing to do is to avoid it."

"What do you mean?"

"What I mean is, if you investigate into something and shout it to others, you'll probably be more of a target. People will know you know. But if you ignore it, you'll be safer because then the group in charge won't have a reason to come for you. Think of those movies you've seen in the common room. Granted, you didn't see the end of one after the crayon incident, but still. The people in those movies were put in danger for knowing things they shouldn't. If there is a project out there, you'll be safer to act like you never knew about it."

"So you think there *is* a project?" I blurted out.

"Noah—" He scratched his neck, revealing a small chain that was once covered by his collar. I became distracted by it.

"What's that?" I asked, pointing towards it.

Caleb felt across the metal before pulling the full necklace out into view. Swinging on the end was a pristine golden ring. He held it in his

183

hands. "This?"

"Yeah."

He smiled blissfully as he stared at it, running his thumb gently over the diamonds that wrapped around the centre. "Well, quite a few years ago, my wife and son passed away."

I lowered my head. "Oh… I'm sorry."

He shook his head. "It's okay. It's not your fault."

"Do you miss them?"

"Yeah. But that's why I had this ring made. When they were cremated, I had a part of them made into this ring so that whenever I *do* miss them, I know that they're near."

"How old was your son?"

"Two."

I swallowed and turned away.

"It's alright," he continued. "It took me time, but I came to accept it."

As he tucked the necklace back underneath his collar, the nurse arrived. She gave the two of us a smile as she brought in the needle.

I turned back to Caleb. "So… about the project," I muttered quietly.

"Yeah?"

"I should just ignore it, and I'll be safe?"

He shrugged. "It's your choice, but it'll be safer for everyone if you do."

I sat back in the bed as the nurse gently pulled the feeding tube towards her.

Weeks passed in there, and Caleb's words played over in my head. I was given test after test, until they deemed me capable of surviving without the assistance of their equipment. They sat me down and removed the tube from both my hand and nose, both stung, and I got to eat my first proper meal again. I never thought I'd be so happy to eat the food here. It didn't make me feel any better though. With how many meds and food that were being pumped into me, let's just say my body wasn't happy with it, but it wasn't long until my weight fell back to its usual spot.

Once tests were over, Dr Olsen joined me in escorting me back to my room (as well as some other staff). I followed the yellow lines home, keeping my eyes and feet on them until we made it to my door. It scraped up and I ambled into my once again bare room. I slowly ran my hand across the wall, feeling the remnants of the glue dots and torn corners of missing pages. I peeled one off and fiddled with it as Olsen spoke.

"Noah, if you need to talk to anyone, just press the call button, okay?"

I let the paper corner drift to the floor. "Am I allowed to use the phone?"

"I'm afraid you've still got a few more days until you get your privileges back, mate."

I nodded and wrapped myself up in Aaron's blanket, approaching my bed drowsily.

Olsen sighed and followed me. "Noah, you've been in bed for over two weeks, I didn't think you'd want to go back to one."

I shrugged and slipped my shoes off then burrowed beneath the sheets, half of my body hanging limply over the edge.

The doctor perched by my feet. "Noah? Are you okay?"

I exhaled into my pillow. "M-hm."

He pressed on. "Noah."

I peered over the blanket at him.

"You know I'm here to talk, right? You can say anything you want to me."

I nestled back into my surrounding sheets. "Don't got nothing to say."

He chuckled slightly. "You're starting to sound like Kyle."

I smiled weakly. "People already think we're the same person." My expression dropped and I quickly sat up. "They think we're the same person."

Olsen shuffled back from my sudden movements. "Yes, some of the staff do, but they're getting better."

I stumbled to the floor beside my bed and rushed to the door, my blankets tripping me up and intertwining with each other. I fell shortly to the carpet, Olsen chasing after me in concern.

"They think we're the same person!"

The doctor carefully lifted me up. "Hey, mate. It's alright. Calm down. Who are you talking about?"

I battered my fingers against the call button, the lights on the door flashing as I waited for the door to open. "I've gotta tell him! They're gonna take him!"

Dr Olsen directed me back, cancelling the door call, and swinging me to face him. "Hey, look at me. Deep breath. Now, tell me. Who's gonna take

Kyle?"

I gripped at his sleeves. "The people! The ACC!"

"Who are the ACC?"

I stuttered, staring at him as my eyes watered, my grip loosening. The words ran in my head again. I inhaled shakily. "If I ignore it... we'll be safe."

Olsen gently ran his thumb over the plaster on my hand (the remains of the IV). "What are you ignoring, Noah?"

"If I ignore the project... we'll all be safe. If I ignore it, the butterflies will go away, the handler won't choose me, and everyone will be safe... because I... am... ignoring it." I sighed and fell into his embrace.

He stroked my back, rocking me side to side. "That's right, mate. That's right..."

I sniffled.

"Did you learn this in the emergency ward?"

"Um... C-Caleb—Dr Hudson, he helped me. He said that it didn't matter whether a project existed or not, if I don't know anything then I will be safe from them."

"I see," he replied, a sense of intrigue in his tone. We separated. "I'll have to have a chat with him about it. If he's found you a coping mechanism then that means he's doing well with you. You're making progress again." He scratched my chin, making me smile. "I'll have to go catch him now." He stepped to the door. "I'll see you after dinner, okay?"

"Okay," I said just before he disappeared.

I then hesitantly gazed over my shoulder at the window, the glass reflecting the sunlight from the wire in the distance. I stepped over carefully then leant on my desk to spy for the monarch. It was still there. I shuddered and closed my eyes, edging away with my hands raised.

"If I ignore it, I'll be safe. If I ignore it... I'll... be... safe."

I returned to my bed, crawling onto it and cocooning myself in the blankets to hide from the fierce cold air that hung throughout the hospital. It was colder than it was in Winter, it's edging on Spring now. I get told over and over that it warms up after January, but that was a blatant lie. Honestly, I'm not usually thrown off but low temperatures, but today was strangely brisk. It was later revealed that the boiler in our sector had packed up, so we can't even have warm water to make up for it.

When dinner came, all us patients were huddling against each other,

186

desperate to hold onto the remaining warmth. The food was the saving grace, though. I'd never seen anyone in Riptide so eager to eat blended chicken. I settled down at a table with two other patients. They were sat shoulder to shoulder as they shakily lifted their spoons. I reached for my slice of bread and began ripping the crust away.

I looked over at the doors, spotting as Dr Olsen entered with a few patients trailing behind him, all shivering as they blurted words at him. He passed them over to another doctor then scanned the canteen. He caught eyes with me and approached with a smile. His skin was pale and drained of colour, and despite his extra layers, he was still covered with goosebumps.

He sat opposite me. "Alright, Noah?"

"M-hm… Are you?"

"Yeah, yeah. It's a bit chaotic in the offices lately. I don't wanna bore you with admin stuff, but I can't find anyone to fix the heating – I still haven't found anyone to fix that bloody door to the transfer wing."

I gave a short smile. "They won't want to be coming now with all the news, huh? They're probably scared they'll get stabbed." I nibbled at the bread.

"Don't think that, mate."

I shrugged. "It's true, though. No one wants to come to a place packed with mentally ill convicts."

He smirked. "Although I'm not a fan of your comments, I am glad that you're perking up a bit."

I dipped the bread in the bowl of chicken, swirling it around the edges. "I guess so…" I scanned around the hall. "Do you know where Shawn is?"

"Shawn?" he said with surprise. "He's, uh… he's gone, Noah."

My heart sank. "What?"

"Yeah. He got released."

"When?"

"About a week ago. He made a good recovery, his crime didn't require him to do any time in a prison, and he got to go home."

I lowered my head, tears welling up in my eyes. "No one told me he was going…"

Dr Olsen sighed. "I know, mate. It's sort of bittersweet when people go. I know you two were good friends. But look on the bright side, he's okay. He's living a new life."

187

I felt a quivering up and down my throat. "He's gone…"

Olsen stepped around the table and sat beside me. "Come here, mate." He wrapped his arm around me, and I huddled against him. "I'm sorry, Noah."

At this point I wasn't sure if I was gripping to him out of comfort or for sheer warmth. Either way, I didn't hug him too long – the other staff in the corner were already giving looks of concern. I sat back quickly and returned to picking at my food.

Dr Olsen rose from the circular seat and gave a smile as he pointed to my tray. "Well done."

I nodded and gave a shaky smile back just before he got taken away by the frozen sea of patients. They all murmured out their words, the doctors seeming pristine compared to that sedated lot. They were all piling up on one another until the canteen was shot with a silence after a force slammed against the large side windows. Every head turned. Not just one or two. All of them. No matter how drained and shrivelled our bodies were, we all had to see.

"What was that?" said a man, the sound of a voice seeming unbearable in this echoing chamber.

A select number of patients rushed to my right of the room, jumping the barricade to the queue, and crowding around the glass. The staff followed them, trying their best to urge the men back to their seats.

I noticed as the doctor I only knew as Paige called to the group. "Boys! Get back from the window!" She ducked beneath the barricade as they refused. "Guys, come on—" She was then caught in their awe.

"It's… It's a butterfly," said a young sounding patient.

I jolted up. Olsen flicked his head my way. I clawed at the table, glaring over at the glass, only to see the thunderous clouds in the distance. I swiftly swiped my unused knife from the table and sped for the creature.

"NOAH!" Dr Olsen yelled, his footsteps instantly bolting for me.

The patients all scattered to the perimeter, not one risking getting near mine. I hurtled over the barrier and skidded against the plastic wooden floor as the monarch stood still. I immediately jabbed the pathetic knife at the glass, carving slices into it.

Dr Olsen was quick to hook his arms beneath mine and yank me back. "Noah, Noah. Stop. Calm down." He gripped his hand over mine as we slowly slid to the floor. "Remember what Dr Hudson told you?"

I panted harshly. "Ignore it."

"That's right. Ignore it." My grip loosened and he slipped the weapon from my fingers. "Ignore it."

I glanced over at the other patients. At their faces. There was a mixture of fear, entertainment and sympathy. No matter how they felt, I was nothing but embarrassed. I stumbled to my feet and adjusted my clothes, then with a final look at the crowd, I scampered off. The doctors called after me and I broke into a run. I had no destination, I just let my legs take me. We weaved in and out, the feeling as though I had been magnetised to the floor lines. The staff kept chasing. With each corner came a new confused pursuer and a constant glance behind from me.

Dr Olsen was shouting, waving his arms frantically as he skidded to a stop. "Noah! Noah, STOP! WATCH OU—"

I wasn't sure what hit me first. The door or the noise. The metal clanged abruptly as my skull had my momentum crashed against it. My legs buckled soon after and I sprawled across the tiles as the pain wrapped inside itself. Two figures crouched beside me. Their identities remained a mystery; they were only blurs in my eyes, as was the corridor.

I gave a rapid twitch, the metal around me creaking. My eyes shot open to be met with the sight of an upper bunk. I scrambled to a seated position and panted viciously as I backed to the corner of my very small bed. I ran my hands against the bitter bricks, darting my head to different parts of my equally murky cell, gasping for whatever air I had.

"You alright under there?" came Aaron's voice from above.

I nodded even though he couldn't see me. "Y-Yeah, yeah. I'm fine." I gripped at my tracksuit, almost searching for something to prove I was real. To prove where I really was.

"You sure?"

"W-What?" I said, still panting.

He swung his legs over the side and crept to the floor. He took his glasses from the desk then settled at the end of my bed. "What's wrong?"

"I, um…" I sighed and looked up at him. "It's stupid really but… I'm scared to go home. The last time I was there I…" I shook my head and turned away.

Aaron shuffled closer and placed his arm around my shoulder. "You'll be alright. Your parents are gonna be thrilled to see yah. You're gonna get to do everything you've wanted to. Well… maybe not everything – but you get the point."

"What about you?"

"Eh, I'll be fine. Not too long to go anyway. You better come see me at the gate, though!"

I chuckled. "I'll try. I dunno if I'll be let out of sight of my family now."

"Bring 'em along."

I shook my head. "You know I couldn't do that. They don't know I'm gay. According to them I'm as straight as…" My mind fell blank.

"See? You're so gay you can't even think of something without a bend."

I gave him a light shove and he laughed shortly before covering his mouth, hearing the sound of movement from outside the cell. I shooshed him whilst laughing stiffly myself. When the footsteps seemed to slow past our door, I quickly laid back as Aaron jumped up and over to the sink. I covered myself with my blanket as I watched him pretend to dry his hands on the hanging towel. The guard peered through the door window and stared at Aaron.

He gave a wave. "Evening."

The guard glanced at me then rolled her eyes. She then continued her patrol.

Aaron slyly stepped back over to me, and I sat up. "Won't have to do that anymore, either," he whispered.

"Honestly, that's my way of getting a high. That little adrenaline rush."

"I dunno. I think that time we did acid with McIntyre and Prince was pretty entertaining."

"Oh, God." I leant my head back against the wall in embarrassment.

"Remember that?" Aaron began to mimic my past behaviour. "You running around going 'Look out! I'm gonna get eaten by a custard cream!'" He continued to giggle to himself.

"Yeah, yeah, alright."

He rested his back against the bricks, and we sat shoulder to shoulder. "I am gonna miss you."

I leant my head against him. "I'm gonna miss you. I didn't think they'd let me out *this* early."

"Well, you're a good boy, aren't you, Noah?"

I lightly swatted his leg. "Twat."

190

He chuckled and kissed across my neck. "I love you!"

"Mm." I twiddled with his fingers. "I guess you're alright."

He shot back up with an exaggerated gasp. "I have *never* been so offended in my life."

We both giggled, rocking back and forth until we laid side by side. It was cramped. I was left teetering over the edge of the bunk as Aaron was left with bricks scraping against his back. I groaned and shuffled back and forth.

"This bed isn't really built for two."

"Course it is. That's why it's a bunk bed," he replied, removing his glasses and hooking them to the above frame.

I chuckled as he wrapped that same arm over me and cuddled against my back. He nuzzled against me, his body warming me from the cold night. I took in a shallow breath before releasing it and cupping his hand tight to my chest. I could tell he was slowly drifting off from the world as he fell limper.

"Aaron?" I said.

"M-hm?" he murmured back.

"You'll get out of here, right?"

"Yeah."

It was almost like I didn't sleep at all. It was just a close of my eyes, and when I opened them again, the sun was filling the cell with its warm amber glow. I nestled out from Aaron's limp embrace and swung my legs over the edge of the bed. I stretched out my shoulders and twisted my neck as the usual thoughts of the morning gradually built up.

I glanced back at Aaron, smiling at his adorable curled up position. I wasn't sure whether to wake him, doors will open within the hour. It was a part of our protection pact we made. Fall asleep in the other's bunk and wake them before doors unlocked. Obviously, the other inmates knew about us, but not all of them – not all of the guards either. Why risk spreading more rumours about us just for a lie in?

I reached my hand towards him and scratched the tip of his nose. He wriggled about, swatting his hand loosely at what he thought was there before he finally opened his eyes. He sat up, vision most likely blurred, then unhooked his glasses from the metal above. He slung them on then smiled at me.

"Morning," he said in a croaky voice.

"Morning," I replied.

"Today's the day."

It was. I wasn't sure what to feel. Happy? Sick? Tearful? God, if I'd have known what the future brought, I would have incited a riot just to stick around. But, of course, no one was to know what happened once I stepped out of that gate, running into the arms of my family and leaving the rest of it behind.

Bright light. All around. The straining of a fluorescent light bulb was the cause of it. I pushed myself upwards, my arms shaking below the elbows as they took the throbbing pain from my head. I groaned loudly, clasping at my forehead as ringing shattered my eardrums. I patted across the sheets around me, the material registering with me as my bed. I peered through the slits in my eyelids and ran my fingers lightly across my body, feeling my pyjamas and wristband – understanding that what I saw was that of a memory.

I sighed and checked the clock. 07:47AM. I checked my surroundings then dragged my journal from the counter beside me. I skimmed to the next clear page, jotting down until now. I couldn't be sure what happened to me. I… I can't remember. I guess I sacrificed a current memory for one of the past. A good memory. A memory I wish I could go back to. It's rare I find myself with such a feeling, usually I just torment myself.

I edged off the bed, my body telling me not to as I pushed onto my feet. I groaned as I stumbled against my bathroom wall, gripping at the plaster as I fumbled my feet around. I slowly dropped to my knees and crawled across the carpet towards my desk. I used the wood to clamber back up and broke the seal to my window frame. I reached in and pulled out the torn apart letters, forcing the plastic casing back down as I slid to the floor. My head fell against the drawers as I pathetically yanked out another letter. Then another. And another. I analysed each one, whittling through both paper and time – not realising that the call to breakfast had sounded.

I trailed through the loose paper, falling to the door with the remaining unopened letters in my hand. I buzzed the door and swayed on the black line as I waited for it to open. It took longer than I expected but was soon released into the hall of mindless patients, each one trudging towards the canteen. I turned right to join them before meeting with Dr Olsen and Caleb.

"Sorry, sorry…" I muttered, not realising who they were at a first glance.

Dr Olsen grabbed my arms and tilted my head to face him. "Whoa, whoa, Noah. What are you doing up, mate? We told you to stay in bed."

I rubbed my eye and wobbled on the spot. "What?"

Caleb grabbed me from behind before I fell over. "Hey, bud. It's alright, I got yah."

I readjusted my stance and held onto the counsellor's sleeve. "Thanks…" I turned back to Olsen. "I'm goin' breakfast…" I took another few steps forward.

He blocked me, placing his hand on my chest. "Noah, we told you this. You don't need to get up. We were gonna come to you."

"No, you didn't."

Their faces were concerned.

"Yeah, we did, mate. Last night, remember?"

I shook my head. "No."

He glanced back at Caleb who whispered, "That's not good."

"No," Olsen replied, taking my sleeve and noticing the letters in my hand. "What've you got them for, mate?"

"I wanna see my parents," I blurted out. "I wanna see 'em."

He gave a worried chuckle. "Noah, your parents aren't here."

"I know that," I returned in annoyance. "But I should be able to see them. Shouldn't I? They'll wanna see me?"

Caleb came into view. "Noah, we can't just magically bring a visitor here – especially one that hasn't visited before."

"You let Aaron visit."

"We let Aaron visit because you remember him."

"I remember my parents!"

"You do? " They both questioned in a panic.

"Well… no."

They both sighed. Olsen put his arm around me. "Noah, I know you're probably a bit confused right now – you took quite the blow to your head."

I stepped away. "But I remembered… a part of them. They were there when I got out of prison. I… saw them."

The doctor took the letters from me. "Noah, I think we should have a chat in my office."

I sat on the edge of the fuzzy sofa, kicking my legs back and forth as I watched Dr Olsen pace around reading over my letters. Once he finished, he placed them down on his desk and sat opposite me with a sigh.

"What are we gonna do with you, ay?"

I shrugged.

"Well, the fact that you don't remember last night at all after your injury is quite concerning."

"What happened?"

"You were running, and someone opened a door in front of you and knocked you out. We took you to the emergency wing to check you over and you woke up fairly quickly. You were quite dissociated, but you were able to respond well enough."

"Doctor, I... I remembered my family. I want to see them. I want them to know I'm okay."

"I can understand that, I'm sure they want to see you too, but the thing is, Noah..." He shook his head. "We don't want your family getting their hopes up. Your parents have basically lost a son, mate. If they started to believe that there's a chance at getting you back then—"

"Is it so wrong for them to believe that?" I interrupted. "Is it wrong for them to want to see their son?"

"Of course not."

"Then why can't I see them?"

He sat there, gazing over me, conflicting thoughts reflecting in his beaming blue eyes.

"So?" I said, teetering on the edge of the sofa cushion.

He exhaled and forced his head away. "Fine."

A grin surfaced on my face, and I gave an excited giggle.

"I'm not promising anything, I've really got to test that you're okay after yesterday, but if everything goes well, then yes, we can bring them here."

I leapt from the sofa and swung my arms around him. "Thank you!"

He flinched at first but soon hugged me back. "God... You are a sappy thing, aren't you?"

I chuckled and stepped back. "Sorry."

"It's alright." He stood up and patted my arm. "Sometimes I think the world would be better if people got excited over little things."

"I'd have thought this was quite a big thing."

"I suppose you're right." He grinned with me. "Now, before we get ahead of ourselves, I'm gonna take you to have another physical. Just in case."

"What about breakfast?"

He chuckled. "*After* breakfast."

So *after* breakfast, Dr Olsen brought me down the halls to Dr Jones. He set me down on the bed and checked over me. He ran the drum of his stethoscope up and down my skin, wrapped my arm up in the blood pressure cuff, then shone a light into my eyes.

"He seems normal," Jones began. "He's a bit sensitive to light, but that's a regular for him."

"Any thoughts on the delayed memory loss?" Olsen asked.

He shrugged. "Couldn't be sure. It's likely that he didn't process anything when he was dissociated and only really came out of it once he woke up this morning. Since he's aware now, I doubt the Anterograde is here to stay."

He gave a sigh. "Well, that's a relief."

"Yes, it is. His reflexes are quite good too."

He tapped my knee quickly with a hammer and my leg kicked forwards. "Hey!"

We laughed together and the two doctors helped me off of the bed.

"You're gonna be alright, Coleman."

I stumbled against Olsen. "Great. See yah." I headed for the door only for the doctor to pull me back.

"Not so fast, mister." Olsen gripped to the end of my sleeve. "You've got pills to take. I'm not having you run off and miss a dose."

I grumbled. "I wasn't gonna go anywhere!"

"Just as well." He turned to Jones. "I'll see you later to talk." He led me through the door.

"See you then," Jones called as I bounced down the corridor.

Olsen jogged after me as I skipped across the yellow lines. "Hey, mate. Slow down. You're meant to be taking it easy."

"Don't wanna miss the pills, right?" I replied, spinning around and walking backwards.

"Hey, watch it." He pointed for the bench coming up on my right.

I spun back with a stumble.

"Noah?"

"Yeah?" I said happily.

"What *do* you remember from yesterday? Any of it."

My pace slowed as I fell into thought. "Not a lot." I chuckled. "I remember how much that door hurt, but not a lot else."

"What about before then?"

I shook my head. "No."

He exhaled, the air around him so cold that you could almost see his breath turn to ice. "Well, you didn't miss a lot," he finally said with a smile. "Come on. We've got a lot of things to get you to."

The next few days carried out as normal. Me and Kyle managed to spend time together quite a bit and the staff seemed quite happy about that. I was able to beat him in a game of Snakes and Ladders. I guess I'm quite good at dice.

I applied for some new art supplies too. The staff were hesitant to agree but quickly scraped a few bits together to give to me. I spent most of the following day scribbling chalk across a blank page, hoping that it would come to look like something, until I distracted myself as I somehow flung the rubber from my hands and watched it land just under my bed.

"Whoops."

I lowered the chalk and crouched against the carpet, scanning for the small cube and tapping my sock-covered feet up and down. I reached my hand under the bed and grabbed it.

"Aha!"

But as I pulled it out, I spotted something. It was almost impossible to see but its bleak colouring floated across the dark floor. I strained as I dug my arm under further, the tips of my fingernails scratching the end until I was able to yank it out.

It was a page. It was small and crumbled. The edges ripped apart with the words barely perceivable in the state it was in. I stood up and paced around as I folded out the crimped centre. Then before I got a chance to read it, the door buzzed.

I froze in position and stared over at the door. I watched anxiously as it opened. It was Dr Olsen. A stream of relief flushing over me as he entered alone.

"Hey, Noah," he began.

I sighed. "Hey."

"How are you doing?"

"I'm okay."

"Good." He smiled. "I think you'll be pleased to know that there's some people here to see you."

"Really?? " I gave a short gallop forwards, letting the page slip from my fingers and drift to the floor.

"Yeah." He gestured for the door. "I take it you're coming?"

I nodded, bounding in his direction.

"Where's your shoes?" he asked before letting me leave.

I glanced around then waddled over to my desk and pulled them out from underneath. I slipped them onto my feet and approached the floor line.

"Okay," Dr Olsen said with a smile as he entered the airlock.

The door slid shut and the series of metal sounds and mechanisms followed before I was allowed to enter the airlock myself. As I expected the exit ritual to be over, the slot in the door slid across. I heard a stern woman's voice speak to me through the gap.

"Place your hands in the opening."

"Um…" I shook my head back and forth, even though the only people who could see me were the ones manning the camera.

"Noah?" I heard Dr Olsen call. "I'm sorry, but it's for the safety of your visitors and for you."

I let out a whimper, not realising that the doctors could hear it too. My mood was drastically falling.

"It's okay," he continued.

With extreme hesitation, I placed my hands through the gap. I felt the grind of steel click into place against my skin and I pulled my hands back out to see the thick handcuffs that had now been forced upon me. Then finally, the door slid up, revealing my frightened face.

I shook my head, backing into the doctor. "I-I don't think I can do this. I've changed my mind."

Dr Olsen gently touched my shoulder and edged me out to the corridor, joining with the other escorts. "Don't be scared, Noah. Everything's going to be just fine."

At the slowest rate I could go, we headed on down to visitation. I thought I'd be overjoyed, but the realisation of what I was suddenly hit me.

"Okay," Dr Olsen began as we reached the door. "If you need to leave at any point, tell me. Anything you need you can tell me. I'll be in there with you the entire time, okay?"

I nodded and in return he flashed me a smile.

"Who's in there?" I asked, anxiously pulling at the handcuffs.

He took in a breath and looked away. He had an atmosphere around him that I couldn't make out, he seemed concerned and spoke hesitantly. "The people you wanted to see."

The door unlocked and I stepped back as I flinched. The woman beside me held a tightened grip on my arm.

"Noah, it's okay." Dr Olsen rested his hand on my shoulder and gently rubbed my back as we stepped into another airlock, this one much larger.

My body grew tense and my skin tingled, all the aspects of my anxiety merging into one big mess that held me in place outside the visitation room.

I turned to Dr Olsen with tears in my eyes. "I can't..." I said breathlessly. "I can't do this. I was wrong, I'm not ready to see them. This isn't Wyegate. It's not the same! Prison and hospital are not the same—"

He reached for my hands. "Noah, listen. Give it a try. We can go in and come right back out if that's what you want. We did this because you asked, and I think you're strong enough to do it. Then after, you can go back to your room. Are you with me?"

My body shuddered as I moved my head up and down.

He smiled. "Good boy. You'll be great."

He let go of my hand as the door in front of me slid across. It revealed the same industrial room with the same furniture, upon which were two of the people from my memory. As I became visible, the woman stood up. Her breathing was similar to mine. We were both in distress. She approached me, her hands reaching out towards me before she retracted them from shock. I stared at her, my feet frozen to the floor as she continued to step forwards.

"Noah?" Her voice was calm.

"Hello," I replied quietly.

She stopped in front of me and chuckled in disbelief. "You look so different. You look so much more..." She trailed off.

I had a lump growing in my throat as she lifted her hand.

"Am I allowed to touch you?"

I glanced behind at Dr Olsen to ask the same question. I didn't say a word, but I hoped that he understood my look.

He smiled. "If you're okay with it, Noah."

I turned back and gave a quick nod.

The woman let out a stifled breath as she reached her hand out and rested it on my cheek. I closed my eyes and nuzzled against her palm.

"I'm so sorry," I trembled, tears seeping down to the floor. "I don't remember you."

She inhaled sharply. "I know you don't, honey. It's okay. I'll love you either way, you know that right?"

I jumped back as I caught a glimpse of the man rising from the sofa, making the woman flinch and retract her hand.

Dr Olsen shuffled forwards in caution. "It's okay, Noah. Remember what I said."

I faced him.

"If you need to leave, you can."

"No. I'm okay." I turned back as the man stopped beside the woman. "Hi."

"Hi, Noah. How… How are you feeling?"

"I, um… I'm good." I wiped my eyes then fiddled with the bar that was connecting the two cuffs.

The woman cleared her throat and called to the doctors. "Does he need to have those on?"

"I'm afraid so," Dr Olsen replied. "It's either those or a straitjacket."

She shuddered and I looked back up at her. She smiled through her pain and took my hands in hers.

"I miss you. Every day." She glanced back at the man. "We all do."

I remained silent. My eyes drifted down to my hands again and swayed them from side to side as I held her fingers. I didn't have a clue on what to say, but I knew this, I wasn't scared anymore. I was continuing to sway the woman's hands when I let out a smile of glee. I even chuckled. I looked back up at the two of them and smiled more. They smiled back. We didn't say a word, we just stared at each other in hope and excitement. That was until my face turned to despair and I looked away in shame.

"I… I'm sorry."

"What about, honey?"

"I'm getting your hopes up, aren't I? That I'll remember you?"

She sighed. "Would it be wrong for us to give up on that?"

I quickly looked up at her then shrugged. "That might be a better idea. I don't think I'm coming home…"

"Why not?"

"Because I'm… I don't really think you ought to know who I am."

She lifted my chin. "I know exactly who you are. You're Noah. You'll always be Noah. Our little Noah... who might be a bit littler now." She laughed nervously.

I laughed back, settling the tension between us. "We could... always... start again?"

"Again from where?"

"Um... what's your name?"

She grinned and flicked her hair behind her ear. "Maria."

I looked up at the man. "And yours?"

He spoke softly. "Richard."

I nodded. "Okay." I backed away, letting Maria's fingers slip from mine. I turned and approached Dr Olsen.

"You alright, mate?" he asked.

I smiled and grabbed the edge of his sleeve, bringing him over to the others. We stopped and I let him free. "This is Dr Olsen. He looks after me."

They exchanged looks of appreciation, Maria and Richard both understanding the tension that Dr Olsen held.

"Hello," he said with a raise of his hand.

I grinned happily before darting across the room towards the games box. "We should play something together. There's not much of a selection, but we can find a way to make them fun!" I pulled one of the boxes out from the stack and turned to face them again. "Snakes and Ladders? It's the only one I know how to play."

They all remained still with a sense of intrigue on their faces that was only noticeable through the looks in their eyes.

I lowered the box. "No?"

Dr Olsen smiled. "We can play whatever you want, Noah."

I dashed over to the table and dropped the box onto it. I lifted the lid and awkwardly dumped the items across the surface.

I glanced over my shoulder. "Are you playing?"

The group approached and sat down. Dr Olsen took his seat beside me, briefly placing his hand on my back as he gave me a short hug. I watched happily as we each took our coloured pieces and offered Maria the die. She cautiously took it from my hand and shook it in hers. She released it and the cube rattled across the tabletop, she then moved her piece accordingly, before passing the die to Richard.

He took his turn, and I attempted an applaud as he received a six. It then reached my turn, and I threw the die to my left, in the direction of Dr Olsen. It skimmed off of the table and landed on the floor. We both chuckled as he bent over to reach it.

"Sorry."

"That's okay," he replied. "You got a five."

We continued happily, playing the game over several times. I won twice, but I think somehow they were all purposely letting me win – I don't even know how you can manage that when playing a dice game. Or – like I said – I'm just amazing with dice. After a while, we decided on trying something new. So, I rose from my seat and shuffled over to the games box again. Whilst I rifled through the broken pieces, I heard the group mutter quietly to each other, but I wasn't paying attention to what they were saying.

Instead, something caught my eye. It perched on the old bars. It made my blood run cold and my hands fall so clammy that the game slipped from my fingers back into the box. I jerked forwards, gripping my nails on the windowsill. I shook my head back and forth as I became transfixed on the insect that rested on the metal.

"Noah?" I heard Dr Olsen call. "You alright, mate?"

I didn't respond. I just stared.

Then from behind, I heard footsteps. They were approaching very carefully. "Noah?" came a female doctor's voice.

My throat turned dry as I rapidly pounded on the glass for the butterfly to leave, yelling loudly and shocking the group in the room. "Go away!"

Dr Olsen shot towards me and placed his hands on my arm. "Hey, hey. Noah, calm down, calm down."

I continued hitting the glass, but the monarch remained. "Go away!"

He pulled me back. "What is it, Noah? What's the matter?"

"Wherever I look, they're there. They won't leave me alone! How the hell—HOW THE HELL DID I FORGET? I'm telling you, they're watching me! I swear!"

He glanced outside at the butterfly then directed me away from the window, my body becoming overwhelmed with adrenaline and causing me to bounce from side to side.

"Okay, okay." He retained my attention to him by holding the back of my neck. "I'm gonna take you back to your room, alright? You're gonna fall into an attack."

I shook my head violently. "No! I'm fine, I just… I'm fine, please, I wanna stay longer!"

He sighed. "I can't, Noah. I don't want you working yourself up."

I pulled away from him, but he kept a grip on my handcuffs. "I'm fine. Let me go!"

Maria began to approach us, tears of panic in her eyes. "What's wrong with him?"

"Nothing!" I shouted as the other doctor grabbed my arms and dragged me back.

"Stay there," Dr Olsen ordered, and Maria froze. "We need to take him back, he's becoming deluded."

"Deluded? What—What's making him deluded?" Her voice became panicked.

"I'm fine! I wanna stay!" I pleaded as I was forced back to the airlock.

"He's formed a new trigger – when he sees butterflies – it's too much to explain now. We thought it was over, he had an accident about a week ago – damaged more of his memory – we've tried our best to keep him away from anything that could remind him, but obviously we can't control everything."

"WHAT? YOU'VE BEEN—" The other doctor cut me off.

Olsen gave a strained groan. "God, I shouldn't have said that." He gestured to the doctor holding me and switched places with her. "I'll take him. You radio ahead and escort them out."

She nodded and moved Maria back towards the table. "Come on, Mrs Coleman. You need to leave."

"No, wait! Can't we say goodbye?"

"I'm sorry, you can't."

Dr Olsen edged me into the airlock, the door sealing us from the room. The chaos that ensued was silenced and I burst into tears once I realised I wasn't going to the other side for a long time. I nuzzled into Dr Olsen's shoulder and sobbed as he led me back to my room.

He lightly stroked my head as we walked, speaking softly. "It's okay, mate. It's alright."

We shuffled at a very slow pace back to my room and were joined halfway by several other doctors, including Caleb. He was a lot calmer than the others that arrived and actually told them to be less strict with me. When we reached my airlock, the other doctors dispersed and the only two that remained were Caleb and Dr Olsen, one on either side of me. They removed my handcuffs once the door sealed and brought me over to my bed. We sat together on the end as I continued to cry and pull at Dr Olsen's coat.

"Why won't they leave me alone? "

They both gave their best attempts to comfort me, but neither of them gave a solid reply. My delirium was taking over my body and I felt a schizoaffective attack coming over me. The room began to glow with mixes of colours and the narratives in my head started to form, the voices telling me every move I made.

You're crying.

You're holding his coat.

You're kicking your legs a lot.

You're hugging him.

I was hugging him. Not Dr Olsen, but Caleb. I had switched sides. My head was buried against him as he embraced me. He rubbed my back as I squeezed him tighter.

"Noah?" Dr Olsen said calmly.

I sat up and faced him, his face a bit of a blur from the combination of tears and colours.

"I'm really sorry. I didn't mean for you to get like this. We thought you were out of this."

I jumped up, beginning to shout at him. "No! You lied to me! Why didn't you tell me? " My breathing staggered and I scanned around me, catching the sights of the colours.

"Alright," he replied softly. "Did you take your medication today?"

"Yes, they watched me do it!"

Caleb cautiously stepped closer. "Noah, do you remember what I told you?"

"What?" I said, wiping my eyes.

"Ignore it."

I glared at him and slid down the wall in a huff. "That won't do anything. They're still gonna find me! The whole of bloody Britain knows I'm in here! There's no point in ignoring it! The people in those prisons don't even know what's going on, and they're still being taken! They took Aaron's best friends! They took *my* friends. They'll take us either way."

"How do you know that Aaron's friends are missing?" Caleb asked.

I shrugged and picked at the plastic underneath my chair. "He told me. I trust him. He has no reason to lie to me. And that book…" I swung back

203

to them. "MK-Ultra isn't a conspiracy. It was real and it's gonna happen again! Everything in that book is set to happen again!"

Caleb stepped over and crouched beside me. My head fell onto his shoulder, and he rubbed his hand up and down my arm to comfort me. I gripped at his jacket as I heard Dr Olsen rise from my bed.

"Noah?"

I tried to look over at him but all I could see were the streams of colours merging into each other, so I nestled my head back into Caleb's shoulder.

"I think we need to have a chat about all of this that's gone on."

I nodded, desperate for any kind of help.

"We'll wait until the attack's over. We'll wait with you, even if it takes the rest of the day. Won't we, doctor?"

"Of course," Caleb said softly. "The day's free. I'll stay with you, buddy." He gently jogged his shoulder to direct his speech towards me.

I kept my eyes clenched shut until the episode was over. I had one doctor either side of me as we waited. It was a painful wait, and it was draining. When the ordeal was over, I sent the doctors away. They weren't too eager to leave me.

"Noah," Olsen began as the two stopped by the door. "I'll have a chat later, yeah?"

I nodded, staring blankly ahead as my future flashed its possible outcomes.

"Right." The door slid up. "We'll leave you be for a bit."

They both stepped out. I gave a groan and scratched at my skin, sinking my teeth into my lips. I then brought my hands to the carpet, eyes straight ahead, and noticing the page from earlier. It had gusted to the rim of the bathroom door. I shyly snuck over to it, refusing to move without my feet being firmly on the ground with each new step. I quickly snatched it, uncrumpled the final corner, then turned it over. The final page to the story. The one page I wish I didn't find.

'The Death of Dr Olson.'

I screamed loudly and darted for the airlock, kicking and clattering the metal for it to open.

"OPEN THE DOOR! OPEN THE DOOR!" I panted in a frenzy between yells.

The chaotic pleas garnered a collection of worries as shown by the group of staff waiting outside. I clenched the page in my fist and shoved my way through them to the centre off the hall.

"Coleman!" one doctor called. "What's wrong?"

I darted my head from one end to the other until I saw the man stood with a circle of patients. I sprinted his way, the rubber on my shoes sending screeches as I ran. The gathering heard my thunderous wails and, in confusion, froze in place.

Dr Olsen spotted me. "Noah, what—"

I waded through the patients to reach him. "NO!" I gripped at his coat and yanked him back against the wall. "NOBODY TOUCH HIM!" The men scattered, leaving us and the staff that took their places. "STAY AWAY FROM HIM!"

Caleb skidded to the front. "Noah, Noah, what's going on? Stay calm, talk to us."

"I can't tell you! If I tell you then they'll know I know!" A guard strengthened his stance, and I wrapped my arms around the doctor. "I'M NOT LETTING THEM KILL HIM!"

Olsen squirmed in my grasp, his body stooped low as to match my height. "Noah..." he said raptly. "Mate, what's the matter?"

"They're gonna kill you. They're gonna kill you! It says so on the page!" I snarled at the doctors. "Don't touch him!"

"What page, mate?"

I glanced down at him with teary eyes, whimpering as I presented the screwed up paper. "It was in the book. Everything else is true, so why wouldn't this be?"

He scanned over the words then managed to slip it into his pocket. "Noah, if you let me go, we can sit together in my office, okay? No one else. They won't get to us in there."

I tightened my grip at his coat.

"Noah." He was pleading through his tone.

With guilt and devastation, I released the man. He stumbled to the side but quickly came back to me, halting the guards from touching me.

"I'm sorry..." I sniffled. "I can't protect you from them." I cried into his chest.

He held me close. "It's okay, mate. It's okay. You tried..."

Together, we shuffled down to his office – I couldn't bear to let him go. He sat me opposite his desk, and I rocked back and forth with my hands buried below my thighs. Dr Olsen searched for my file after locking his door.

"See? We're safe in here. No one will be able to get me."

I wiped my nose on my sleeve and nodded.

He tapped against his filing cabinet as he spoke. "Okay, Noah, would you say you believe everything that this book has told you?"

I shrugged.

"You don't know?"

"I do. I just... I can't..."

He gently waved his hand. "Don't worry. It's alright." He continued searching. "I read that page, Noah. You don't have to worry about me."

"I don't?"

"No." He lifted my new yellow file out – the old one too battered to hold the pieces in. He stepped over and sat behind his desk. "Do you know how to spell my name?"

"J-O-E-L."

He chuckled. "No, no, my *last* name."

"Oh... O-L-S-E-N."

"That's right. And how would you spell the other doctor's name?"

I swallowed. "O-L-S... O-N."

"Yeah." He showed me the page. "See? It's spelt different. I'm Ol*sen* not Ol*son*. They are said the same though, I'll give you that. I'm not a part of a mind control scheme, and I will say that I'm flattered you came to protect me."

I gave an embarrassed smile.

"Really, I am, and I can understand your worry. A lot of people believe that if you forget the past, you're doomed to repeat it. So..." he readied his pen. "I think we need to talk about everything else now. What d'you say?"

I shrugged. "I dunno... I, um..." I trailed off.

"Noah?"

I kept quiet.

He lowered my file and rolled around his desk on his chair to sit beside me. I chuckled as he crashed into the side of the wood.

"I'm glad I amuse you," he said with a smile. "What's the main thing on your mind?"

I shook my head shamefully. "I'm crazy..."

"Hey," he rubbed my shoulder. "You know we don't say that around here. You are not crazy, Noah."

206

I looked up at him. "But I am! I'm obsessing over something that I don't even know was true! I'm convincing myself about all of the craziness going on around me – I'm not saying the people are crazy – I'm crazy! I can't talk to Aaron, I can't talk to my mother, I don't trust anyone around here enough to talk to them, and I barely manage to talk to you! I attacked a kid, I could've killed him, I killed a doctor, who knows what I could have done to Olivia! I am not a good person!" I sobbed onto his shoulder, and he cradled my head against him.

"Shh, shh, it's okay."

I whimpered as I spoke. "It's not. It's not."

He rocked me back and forth. "It is. You're not crazy, Noah. You're not crazy."

I continued sobbing.

"Noah... When we collected your file, we realised that you read about Blake Hayes. Do you know much about him?"

I sat up and wiped my nose. "Yeah. He was a teacher at my old work."

"And you said some things about him."

"Yeah..."

"Okay," he said cautiously. "I noticed that you put some things on your wall about him."

I nodded in embarrassment.

"Do you remember anything about what you said to him?"

I shrugged. "No."

"Do you remember what he looked like?"

"Tallish? He had, like, stubble. He had... silver hair..." My gaze drifted down as I started to recall the figure.

"It sounds like you're describing Dr Hudson."

I nodded slowly. "Yeah..."

"I know you have a good relationship with Dr Hudson. Don't you?"

I stuttered. My head felt in a rush, I felt myself retreat into my memory as Blake's image came more into view.

"Noah?"

"He..." I felt across my scar.

Suddenly – I don't know what caused it – but everything that was wiped from my past started to resurface. It was too much. Half my life was coming back to me. Everything I had done, everything that had happened to me, all of it. Including Blake. He was a lot like Caleb. His hair, his figure, his eyes, his voice, they all matched. My body obviously realised before I did. It began to tremble. My pulse skipping into a race, my skin draining from colour as I became cold.

It was him. He wasn't just like him, he *was* him.

I froze in place as the scenes played from start to finish in my mind within the second.

It started at work. I was in the library sat behind my desk, watching through boredom as different students rushed past me, muttering and whispering to their friends about different websites they'd found online. They thought they were being sneaky and getting away with it because I didn't react, but the truth was, I couldn't be bothered. I saw no reason to yell at a kid just because they'd found a video about their favourite actor instead of looking up what the quadratic method was.

Soon, the bell rang – not that the bell plays much of a role at school anymore – and I had to urge the kids who weren't working outside to allow the ones who were a chance to do it in peace. There were a few complaints as I forced them to leave, all of them giving me some pretty ridiculous excuses as to why they wanted to stay. I closed the door and wandered back over to my desk, passing the very few remaining students who were rapidly typing their last minute assignments so they could get to lunch.

I went to sit down, but I caught sight of a piece of paper that was jammed halfway under the staff door. I ambled over to it and picked it up, reading across it to find a name or any connection to who it belonged to, but then I looked over the top of the page and spotted a USB stick hidden underneath a computer cupboard. I crouched down and reached for it, pulling it out and resting on my knees. It had three overlapping ovals printed on it – one blue, one red, one grey. I rose to my feet again then looked around to see if the owner was near, but the area was empty. I read over the page again for a clue – it was only a paragraph – but I started getting an uneasy feeling from what was printed on it.

'... *with this information on the subject, he should respond accordingly. MK-Ultra was a risky project to begin with, as is this one. It is unclear at this time whether he will survive the Other Side, but it is a risk we are all willing to take. Subject D did survive his dose, which gives indication that the new formula is not life threatening at this stage. It is speculated that the dose readied for Subject E will provoke a mind-altering ability. Whether the*

208

subject will be brought in in time is unknown, but a system will be put in place.'

I pulled my phone from my jacket pocket and snapped a picture of the page. I glanced at the USB then hurried over to my computer to check its contents. I guess I was always a bit of the paranoid type. I plugged it into the monitor then waited for the reading. The name came up with 'ASHTON'.

Ashton was a teacher, and I saw him earlier. Whether the sheet belonged to him was up to speculation, but after I opened the device, it made my mind race. It had folders upon folders all revolving around one topic. The O.S. Project. I scanned over a few files. With each read I became more disturbed. It spoke about MK-Ultra, and handlers, and compliers, each as a subheading with sentences below describing its meaning. They were the only three I could read. Someone somewhere was going to bring MK-Ultra back through the use of compliers and their handlers.

Before I could read further, the man I knew then as Blake entered the library from the far door. He waved to the remaining students who were finally leaving for their lunch break. He held the door open as they passed him, and I quickly exited the document as he approached my desk.

"Hey, Phoenix," he said as he came to a stop. That was my fake name. Phoenix Close; twenty-five.

I looked up at him, still in a bit of a whir from the reading. "Hey, Blake. How... How are you doing?"

"I was about to ask you the same thing. You're looking a bit flustered."

"Um..." I handed him the page. "I found this on the floor. I read it to see if I could figure out who it was from, but I think what was on it concerned me a little."

Blake read over the information and nodded in agreement. "I'd say the same."

"That it concerns you too?"

"No. That it would concern you."

I chuckled in confusion. "What?"

He kept his eyes on the paper. "You're too curious for your own good, Phoenix."

He glanced behind me, and I turned to see what he was looking at only to be met with a figure who forced a cloth over my mouth. They pinched my nose shut and I shook violently back and forth as I tried to shake them off, but they'd doused the cloth in some kind of chemical and I faded in and out of consciousness. My grip loosened from the figure's hand, and I passed out.

Moments later I was met with darkness, that's all – matched with a constant high-pitched ringing deep in my ears. I couldn't move. Wherever I was, I was restrained. Every limb was strapped back tightly. My fingertips twitched. Followed by my fingers. Then followed by my hand, until I gained the strength to lift my eyelids.

The room was thin but extended quite a way. Pristine pearl counters lined the left and right walls, each one fixed onto the grey concrete by silver hooks. They were topped with small metallic machines, with more silver objects hanging from the walls. I couldn't make out what they were, they were too far for me to see. I heard the clanging of metal behind me and tensed my head from the sharp volume. I glared out the side of my eyes, my head hanging down loosely, and watched as a figure in a flowing white coat passed me. They stopped opposite me and crouched down to my eye level. His silver hair pulled back tightly to reveal the growing grin across his face.

"Morning, Phoenix." He showed me the page of my old prison file. "Or should I say Noah?"

"Please…" I said breathlessly. "I wasn't gonna hurt anyone… I… I was desperate. I needed a job. Faking my identity was all I had left."

"I see." He gestured to his surroundings. "Welcome to The ACC." He took the file back and flicked through it. "I gotta say, I preferred your alias. 'Phoenix Close'. You sounded a lot more mysterious and interesting than 'Noah Coleman'. I guess we figured out that mystery, ay?"

My whole body was drained, I could barely bring myself to lift my head. "I'm sorry… Please. I'm sorry."

He sat down on a wooden chair and read through each page of the file. "Noah James Coleman. Convicted 2017 for possession of LSD and intoxication. Birthday: 19/11/1999." He glanced up at me. "I thought you looked a bit young." He returned to the file. "Sentence: 4 years. Released early were we?"

My throat became dryer as he found out more of the truth. "Yes," I said croakily.

"How long were you there for?"

"Three and a half years…"

"Three and a half." He nodded, not at all showing sympathy towards me. "And your partner, Aaron, when did he get out?"

My heart skipped and I pulled myself up to look at him. "A few months after, but... How did you know Aaron was there with me?"

He smirked and placed the file on the table behind him then rose from his seat. "There's quite a lot that I know about you, Noah. I've known about you since the minute you stepped foot out of Wyegate."

I obviously had quite the panicked look on my face as my energy started building back up, Blake becoming ever more malicious towards me.

He stepped over to the left counter and fiddled with different pieces of equipment. "I was told about each rejection you received from workplaces, I was told about each probationary hearing you had, I was told about how you acted alone and how you acted amongst others. I will say, I don't blame the stores for rejecting you, why would they want someone with your background working for them. You hit your mum the night you were arrested, didn't you?"

"I was angry," I said sharply. "I lost control of myself, okay? I'd never want to hurt anyone, especially her."

"You lost control?" He glanced over his shoulder.

His glare burned through me, igniting fear and anxiety. "I don't know, I just did it. I don't know why."

"So, you're saying that you didn't feel in control of your actions?"

"Yes."

"I've heard a lot of people say that, not one of them wanting to accept the fact that they had caused harm to another person. None of them really know what it's like to not feel in control because none of them can follow the rules."

Another figure emerged from the shadowy corner and passed Blake a crimson vial. She circled around the centre table, her long blonde hair swaying around her as she walked. I kept my eyes on her slim form as she stopped beside me. I turned back to Blake as he dropped the vial into a black dart gun, the metallic material matching the machines. He pulled different latches back on it then placed a paper thin, two-inch needle into the end.

"Do you know what someone is called when they *do* follow the rules?" He fixed eyes with mine. "Compliant." He stepped back over to me. "It shouldn't be that hard to be compliant, should it? You get told an order and you follow it, why do people find it so difficult?"

Another figure appeared on my left, this time a man. Tan skin and short, spiked hair. Upon closer inspection, it turned out to be Ashton. This was followed by more clanging of metal. I started to grow frantic, my heart rate rising, my adrenaline pumping, but I still couldn't move. My hands, legs, feet, arms, waist and chest were all held back tightly with leather straps.

Blake presented the gun to me, showing off the smooth liquid that was curling over itself in the vial that was lodged inside it. "You see this?" He tapped the glass. "Strong stuff this is. Makes you lose your mind. Almost literally. It's called Otherdoxersiderin. The Other Side for short. Now…" He rose from his seat again. "I rarely lie." He leant close to my face. "I'm not like the others like you who plead innocence for things I know I've done wrong." He passed the dart gun to the woman. "I will confess when I know the truth, so I'll tell you this now." He stamped on a switch on the floor and several spotlights around me flashed violently. "You're in for a wild ride."

Before I had any time to process what he said, there was a shimmering noise – the vial propelling into the gun. It followed with an agonising pain that pierced into the right side of my neck. I let out a shriek as the woman forced the needle deep into my skin. She pulled the trigger on the dart gun, and I felt a gush of freezing liquid shoot into my veins. It shot down my side in an instant, the pain so great that it brought tears to my eyes. I couldn't even contemplate what was happening to me, it was a pain I had never experienced before. It just kept getting worse.

By the time the woman pulled the needle out again – ripping my skin with it – the drug had already invaded my entire right side, now wrapping around to meet on the left. My muscles trembled and twitched as my nerves fought against each other. I yanked at the restraints, but whatever I tried, I wasn't strong enough to fight for power over the war inside me. I clenched my eyes tightly to block out the burning coloured lights.

"Keep your eyes open, Noah," Blake called from the darkness.

I shook my head rapidly, forcing myself to ignore him.

"Open your eyes, Noah!"

I fought against the order as best I could, but it was in vain, my eyelids lifted and kept sight on the raging bulb in front of me. It flashed and flashed and flashed and flashed, each time forcing its way past my skull and building up my already high adrenaline. It went on for so long. My body started to loosen, and I became lost in a scarlet fog. My head swayed from side to side as I kept my sight on the almost forgotten light. All I wanted was to rip out of the chair and fight, but I couldn't move. Well, I could. But my movements weren't of my command. My body was no longer controlled by my own accords. They were controlled by his.

Blake's voice echoed in my mind. He was the only sound I could hear clearly, everything else became void. As did my vision. The room faded away into colours and blurs, colours that were never there before. The dull grey room had now become flushed with spirals of neon pinks and oranges, splashing in the air against the pastel-like green. Just like the hallucinations I get today.

"Say your full name," he ordered.

I spoke drowsily. "Noah James Coleman."

"Where were you incarcerated?"

I hesitated. "HMP Wyegate."

"Hmm." There was the faint echo of footsteps followed by a scratching. "What are your thoughts on your situation?"

I paused. "Too vivid to say."

He chuckled. "I see."

The lights shut off and my senses flooded back, overwhelming me from the sudden switch of emptiness to the instant free will. Blake was stood alone and watched as I was swung back on my chair into a laying position. I was blinded by another light hanging above me and faced with the other two figures who were glaring down with it.

I felt two metal plates get pushed onto each side of my temples and was suddenly jolted with thousands of volts within less than a second. I cried loudly as they repeated the process over and over. My body began to tremble again as the final movement of the drug fought its way to the inside of my brain. My face was covered in tears as the two pushed on with their experiment.

Through it all, I had a constant clicking in my right ear, each click bringing disorientation to me. It was followed with the repetition of a phrase.

'Monarchs fly in the rain.'

With each shock that penetrated my skull I became less and less frantic, the light above me seeming to slow in its flashing. Another shock persisted and my thoughts began to fade. I tried to grasp onto anything that came to mind, but as another shock came, it shattered any hint of an idea. It was then that I realised, I had stopped shouting. My face had lost emotion. In fact, I had lost emotion. I couldn't feel anything, even with the shocks, I gave no reaction. The plates were removed from the sides of my head and was left lying still. I felt the straps around me drop and swing to the floor.

Blake stepped beside me. "Say your full name."

Nothing.

"How are you feeling?"

Nothing.

Blake smirked. "Where were you incarcerated?"

Answer. ANSWER! For goodness sakes, Noah, BLOODY ANSWER!

"Sit up."

As if led by strings, the phantom sensation began to drag my shoulders forwards, slumping me into an upright position, the buzz of the drug casting a sharpness through my senses.

Blake smiled. He lifted my head by the chin and directed me to face him. "Stand up."

I slipped down to the floor, feet symmetrical and hands floating behind my back, holding one in the other as I turned to face him, the grin on his face overcome with pride.

"It works." He laughed loudly. "IT WORKS!"

That was the last thing I heard in that room. What was after that? Red. The world was red. That's the only thing I could see, and my hearing was at a similar level. I'd never felt so awake yet so asleep at the same time. Not one part of my body was with me – it was just a distanced version of myself being dragged through the air.

I had no clue for how long I was in such a state, but suddenly, my vision cleared. The red fog retreating to my peripheral. My eyes batted violently, and my head twitched. Slowly, I felt my senses return – as did my emotions. I became nauseous as I felt my heart beat against my chest until I realised where I was. I was back at school, standing in the canteen, flocks of staff and anxious students staring at me from a fair distance. I swallowed as my nerves returned to my hands and the feeling of wire came with it. A long metal streak was wrapped tightly between my two hands with a weight pushing against it. I glanced to my left. My lip quivered as I found Ryan pinned to me. I then realised that I was the one pinning him. I had the wire tight to his throat, ever-so-slightly digging into him.

I trembled. "Oh, my God…"

I took my hands away in an instant, and he fell to the floor panting and coughing. He scrambled away from me, a woman and his friends reaching for him and embracing him tightly, blood trickling across the floor as he ran.

"Oh, my God." I was so shaken that I couldn't bear to explain myself. I let the wire loose and it curled to the floor.

Before I knew it, four of the teachers tackled me to my front and pinned me in place, gripping at my hair and clothes as they positioned my body.

"I swear, I didn't know what I was doing! I swear! I don't even know how I got here! Please!"

I caught eyes with Blake. He was standing just to the side of Ryan as he was escorted carefully out. He kept his gaze firmly on me as the staff tried to herd the rest of the students away from the scene.

"Blake..." I muttered. "Blake! I know what you did to me!" I screamed, my voice tearing from desperation. "YOU'RE THE REASON I DID IT!"

He shuffled back, acting shocked and fearful when inside I knew that this was what he wanted. Another few teachers joined him and whispered in his ear, glancing at me as they spoke. Blake shook his head and from what I could make out replied with:

"I don't know what he's saying. I have no idea. We need to get him help."

I tried to push myself out of the weight on top of me as I continued my accusations. "Don't lie! I know you wanted this! This is your plan, isn't it? Make me look insane? All so you can work out why your drug here didn't stay? I know it! There's a reason MK-Ultra didn't work in the first place because you used innocent people to experiment on!"

By now I was struggling to breathe and was panting heavily before giving up and accepting the loss. I let out a tearful cry then rested my head to the wooden floor in defeat, my body falling limp as I heard sirens approach from outside. After that, I was taken away. Processed, charged, tested, then questioned.

I was brought into an interrogation room and had my hands cuffed tightly to the desk. They had me wait in there for about ten minutes before a woman showed up with a stack of paperwork, a fact I know because all I had with me in the room was a clock, a table and two chairs – that and the rather large mirror that was fixed on the wall to my right. The woman sat down and began her spiel. Whatever she said was obviously not important to me even then since I blurred over the beginning of the session in my brain.

"Listen, alright?" I began, moving my hands about as I explained. "I wasn't in control. I have no idea what happened between the lab and when I had my hands on that kid. I would never hurt Ryan, nor any of his friends. Please. I know what I saw. I know what I've experienced. Blake knocked me out and I woke up restrained in a chair. He shot me in the neck, and I blacked out only to wake up strangling that poor boy!"

The detective sighed. "Mr Coleman, you were given a drug test, correct?"

"Yeah?" I replied.

"Well, there was no evidence to suggest of this drug in your system, but we did find traces of LSD, and from your record here, it says you were previously incarcerated for having that substance in your possession – and it also says you have a history of taking it in prison."

"No, no, no! I haven't touched a drug since getting out of Wyegate! I swear to you. I know what I saw." I yanked at my handcuffs and winced as they caught against my skin. "I had the evidence. I had the sheet of paper – I took a picture on my phone."

"Mr Coleman, your phone has already been scanned and all that was recovered from it were blurry pictures of the school."

I looked up at her in confusion. "What?"

She laid the images out in front of me from what seemed to be from the school CCTV, and it was true. They showed me wandering aimlessly across the school fields snapping pictures of no significance.

"The students also corroborated that they saw you wandering around taking them before you tried to murder Ryan Axel."

I shook my head, refusing to believe her words. "No, no, no. That… didn't… happen."

"I'm afraid it did."

I sat quietly for a few seconds before replying, my tone becoming less and less confident with my story. "What about the actual paper? Didn't you find it?"

She presented me the page in a sealed plastic bag. "That piece was proven to be part of a student's work project. It showed no links to MK-Ultra aside from this line." She pointed to a sentence. "It was from a boy's short story. It wasn't real."

I looked down at my feet and sat back in my chair. "I-I don't

216

understand..."

The detective gathered up her papers and folded her arms, leaning on them against the desk. "Mr Coleman?"

I glanced up at her.

"Have you had these kind of blackouts happen to you before?"

"What?"

"Have you ever experienced being in one place only to blink for a second and realise you're somewhere new?"

I shook my head. "Not until recently when all of this happened."

"I see." She leant back and scribbled on one of her papers.

I inhaled and leant forwards again. "Look. I'm not crazy, alright? I don't have some kind of problem or whatever. I know what happened to me."

"Mr Coleman, the more you go on about this MK-Ultra business, the more you sound crazy." She stood up. "Look. We're going to give you another psychiatric test and if you pass it then we'll continue this conversation, yes?"

I looked away. "Yeah..."

"You're being charged for attempted murder, Noah. I'd suggest getting that into your head before you do anything else."

I remained silent as the detective swung herself around to the door and stepped back out to the hallway.

I was cleared by each of the psychologists as sane, only with a few delirious thoughts from what they assumed were from the aftermath of the LSD. Weeks later, it was time for my official court hearing to start, and ever since I came back from the Other Side, I had a constant fog in my head. I managed to ignore it for the most part, until the day of court came.

Beforehand, I was given a five minute visitation with Aaron and a quick meal an hour before that. It wasn't exactly five stars, but it was better than nothing. A few moments after finishing my food, the weariness became overwhelming, and a growing pain settled at the side of my head. It started weak and I could ignore it for the most part. Followed by that, I had the familiar nauseous feeling I had when confronted with Ryan in the canteen. It curdled up in my stomach and started rising up my throat, and so I rushed over to the toilet and crouched down beside it before throwing up. I fell back against my wall and closed my eyes as my body was drained.

"Oh, God..." I groaned as I leant my head against my hand. I shuffled my other hand across the metal and flushed the chain as I heard the bolts on my door unlocking.

"Five minutes," a man said as Aaron stepped into my cell, the door locking behind him.

"Hey," he said as he approached me.

I pulled myself up from the floor and wiped my mouth on the towel. "Hey."

"You don't look so good."

I shrugged and sat down on my bed. "I'm fine, I just... I'm not exactly feeling great."

He took a seat beside me, and I rested my head on his shoulder. "If it helps, I believe you."

I chuckled softly. "Thanks, but I don't think that'll change the jury's minds."

He rubbed my back. "It's gonna be fine."

"I think that's the lie of the century."

We both chuckled until I was shot with another searing pain in my head. I leant forwards, clutching at the area and winced.

Aaron watched me in concern. "Are you sure you're okay?"

I shook my head. "I dunno. I just don't feel well."

"Have you told anyone?"

I leant back again. "It only just started. It's probably just nerves... and... bad karma." I stared up at the ceiling as I fell onto my back and felt my body start to detach from itself. I was suddenly lost in the sea of swirls on the ceiling that meshed together as one. My blinking began to slow, and Aaron's voice turned to a murmur. I shook myself back to my body and faced him. "What did you say?"

"I said 'Karma comes around to everyone, she doesn't loiter about'."

I stared at him blankly. "I don't know what we're talking about."

He stared back at me, this time his face full of worry. "Noah, what's wrong?"

I shook my head and stepped away. "I'm fine."

Aaron rose from the bed and stepped over to me, feeling across my forehead and holding my shoulders. "Noah, you're *really* warm. What's the matter?"

We both turned to the door as we heard the locks grinding and watched as my lawyer stepped in.

"Are we ready for this?"

"Yeah…" I said drowsily as I went to follow her, but Aaron pulled me back.

"Noah, there's something really wrong with you. I don't think it's exactly wise for you to give your statement like this."

"What's the problem?" my lawyer asked.

"Nothing, nothing," I replied, my body draining further.

"No, he's burning up, he forgot what we were talking about, and he feels sick," Aaron explained.

"I didn't know you were a doctor," I said to him as I rubbed my eyes, the pressure building up at the back of my head.

"Is this true, Noah?"

"Yeah, but I'm fine."

"He can't go out there like this."

"Well, there's not exactly much we can do about it. This case has already been delayed for the psych tests."

They bickered some more, but I couldn't understand what they were saying. Their language almost seemed foreign. My eye line drifted to the concrete on the floor and a thick fog began working its way through my head. We had no time to discuss the problem further as the officers were ready and waiting to escort me to the trial room. They cuffed my hands together and we stepped outside.

Aaron ran his hand across my back. "I'll be in the gallery."

"Okay…" I replied quietly.

"I love you," he said as he was separated from me.

I took in a breath and held it as the court doors swung open. I was seated at a table with my hands still cuffed and an officer either side of me. Throughout the beginning of the trial, I was fine, I was steady. That was until the problem spiked. Without warning, the feeling struck again. My whole body was trembling, and I had a pounding in my head that was growing worse with every noise I heard. I kept my eyes fixed on the wooden half-wall that surrounded me, trying to calm myself down and gather my thoughts. But I couldn't keep any. They all overlapped each other, a constant screaming. I felt sick, dizzy, with a stabbing in my chest that shot through my veins like at any moment my body was going to tear apart from the inside out.

"Noah?" called a woman's voice.

I twitched my head about then caught eyes with my lawyer who had suddenly appeared in front of me.

"It's time for you to make your statement. You ready?"

I nodded friskily. "Y-Yeah."

"Come on," she said softly.

I scratched my head then slowly drifted my arm down again when I realised my wrists were no longer restrained. I then noticed that I wasn't sat down anymore either. I was stood up. On the other side of the table. I swallowed nervously and stepped back in confusion, my heart rate beginning to rise.

"Noah? Are you okay?" she asked me, placing her hand on my shoulder.

"Uh-huh. I'm… I'm fine."

"Alright, let's do it. This way."

I nodded then glanced behind at the rows of people staring at me and stumbled back. I caught eyes with Aaron, and he smiled reassuringly at me as the court officer grabbed my arm and directed me towards the witness box. He sat me down then watched me closely from my side. Suddenly, my mind was filled with that same foggy haze and my eyes fell heavy. I rubbed them and tried to focus.

My lawyer leaned in towards me and whispered. "Remember what we rehearsed."

What?

My breathing began to stagger, and I clawed at the wooden surface in front of me as I watched my lawyer step back and mutter up to the judge, seeming to ask a question but I couldn't make it out. I swayed back and forth as she stopped across from me. I looked around me fearfully, everyone in the room glaring in my direction. I stared down at my hands and picked at my nails, my hands trembling more and more.

"Mr Coleman?" the woman asked.

"Huh?" I looked back up, glancing over at the jury and seeing them murmur to each other, keeping their eyes fixed on me.

"You were saying about Mr Hayes?"

Oh, my God.

"I didn't say anything. I just sat down".

A swarm of whispers cast across the room then quickly settled as the judge called down to the people below.

My counsellor gave an anxious chuckle. "Mr Coleman, you've been here for several minutes now telling the court your side."

I felt sweat drip down my back, and I started to lose control of myself. It happened slowly. My fingers numbing. My chest swelling. My throat drying. My eyes twitched rapidly as I tried to cast myself back to the last thing I could remember. But I couldn't. Within that very moment, I felt my mind shatter. Every little part of me began to get stripped away.

Thought by thought. Memory. By. Memory.

I closed my eyes and leant my head down, trying with every shred of me to hold onto what I had left. I spoke softly, almost in a whisper. Fear winning control.

"I don't remember…"

I heard my counsellor step towards me, her heels echoing throughout the room. "I'm sorry?"

I lifted my head, a single tear falling from my left eye. I spoke again. "I don't remember."

She leant in to me and lowered her voice. "Noah? Are you okay?"

"I don't remember."

I shot up from my seat and gripped my nails at the wooden surface, taking in short, uncontrolled breaths. The officers around me jumped at my quick movements, as did most of the jury.

"Mr Coleman, please sit down," a voice ordered.

But I was too scared to obey. My panting grew louder, and I felt more tears rolling down my cheeks.

"I can't remember. I can't remember!" I took a step back and gripped tightly at my hair, repeating the sentence over and over, each time gaining greater attention. I then fell against the wall and trembled on the floor.

By now the whole of the courtroom was on its feet, each person clambering over one another to get a glimpse of the action. There was so much noise. It tore at me. The judge banged his gavel. The gallery screamed. The officers yelled orders louder than I could process.

They dragged me up from the carpet and yanked me across the room, my arms an inch from being separated from their sockets. I shrieked. I shouted. I screamed for anyone to help me. Just a single person. But they merely forced me to the ground.

I fought back against the hoard of towering men and women who jumped me, breaking free for a fraction of a second before getting dragged down again. My head was pinned on its side. My eye line just free enough to watch as Aaron dug away from the crowd and leapt over the barricade. He slipped past the guards, and I managed to crawl out from under mine. I ran to him and fell to my knees sobbing. He dropped to my level and held my head in his hands, keeping his eyes locked on mine.

"Look at me, alright? Just look at me. It's okay. You're gonna be okay."

"I don't know what's happening! I'm so scared, Aaron, please! I can't remember anything! It's all going! Everything!"

"Shh, shh, shh. Don't panic. Just look at me. Look at me. Breathe. Okay?"

I crumbled into his lap, soaking his shirt with tears. He rubbed my back before I was pulled away once again.

"No!" I screamed as the officers picked me up and carried me back towards the cells.

Aaron ran after us, dodging the guards the best he could. "Stop! He needs help!" He grabbed my hand as he chased after me before getting taken down by the court officers.

I watched through blurred eyes as he was pulled away and we were separated by the swinging doors. Before getting locked in my cell, I was sedated. Kept under close watch by the camera in the corner. I was laid down on the bed pad and left alone. I wasn't sure how long I was under for, but once I started to wake, I felt empty. Everything wiped clean. I opened my eyes as I heard voices coming from behind the cell door, seeming to be a man and a woman.

"He wasn't faking it. His reaction was genuine. For whatever reason, he's completely lost his memory," the woman began.

"Well, have you tested him?" replied the man.

"Yes, several times. He has no recollection of anything, apart from a few odd things and his partner."

"His partner?"

"Yes. He's the only person he can recall."

"Seriously?"

I took in a rather broken breath as they went on, wheezing each time I inhaled. I brought my hand out from under the scratchy blanket and stared at it then closed my eyes again and went limp, continuing to listen to the conversation.

"He has no idea why he's here, what he did, or why he can't leave. He's insane."

"Hold on. What?"

"He is in no condition to be sent to a prison. He needs real help."

"Listen Heather, we can't just be sending criminals to psych units just because they say they don't remember things. Heck, I forget things sometimes and I don't need to be institutionalised."

"I know, Jac. But this is serious. He doesn't remember how to be a functioning person! Sure, he can do normal things, act normal, but he doesn't know why he can do it."

The man sighed.

"Look, Jac... If you don't believe me then you can talk to him yourself."

"Why should I? He's just like any other criminal in this building."

"He's your brother, for Christ's sake!"

"I don't care!"

They went silent.

"I'm sorry. But if he won't accept what he is then I don't want to see him again. Send him wherever you like. Just don't tell me where he is." The sound of his footsteps faded down the corridor.

I felt a dampness on my pillow and looked around to see where it had come from. It was my eyes. I was crying.

The next week was my final day in court. It wasn't meant to be, but after what happened, I think everyone decided it was for the best. I couldn't move my body. I could barely form a sentence. They had me strapped tightly to a wheelchair with my arms fastened around me by a straitjacket. I was surrounded. My only view was of the judge sitting at his bench glaring down at me as he gave my sentence.

My eyes were still wet from tears, and I could barely retain my attention to him. I kept finding something new around me to investigate, even if it was something that I had already looked at, my brain kept resetting to see it again for the first time. The court officers repeatedly made me return my attention to the judge as he spoke. His voice was calm and thoughtful. He almost sounded sorry for me. I don't know why he would be. I tried to kill someone, why would that need sympathy?

"Noah James Coleman, you were found guilty of attempted murder through reason of insanity. Usually, I'd express little towards someone with such a crime, but from what we all saw, there is proof that you require help for your mental state. I have found you a facility that focusses all of their resources to help people like you. The Ocean Cliff Psychiatric Hospital. They have accepted to take you into their care and have agreed to keep you there until you are recovered, and we can reassess this case. If you are not to improve, it has been decided to keep you there indefinitely."

I heard muttering coming from the gallery and I checked to see what it was. Along the front row was Aaron comforting an older woman who was tearfully clutching at his side. As well as that, there was another man to her left who was also holding her hand, seeming to find a way to hide his glassy eyes. Then I was turned to face the judge again as he delivered his final lines.

"You seem like a troubled young man, Mr Coleman, and I am truly sorry for all that has caused you to be like this. In the nicest of ways, I wish to see you here again. I hope you understand what I mean by that." He nodded at the officers. "Take him."

The officer behind me rolled me across the carpet and I twitched my head around, trying to understand how I was moving. I glanced back at the gallery and spotted Ryan and his family on the opposite side to Aaron's. They were holding their son tightly as I caught eyes with them. I tilted my head as Ryan looked away and I returned forwards as I was wheeled back out to the corridor.

My emotions swayed from one extreme to the other. With every second that passed, I became more paranoid. My manner fell frisky, and a deep distrust took its home in me. These feelings became a part of who I was, and it didn't convince the doctors who arrived at the courthouse of my sanity. It took two hours for the bus to come. Two extremely long hours. There was said to be heavy rainfall and flooding across the roads which slowed my transfer. Through my fearful wait, I had Aaron by my side. He wasn't allowed to touch me, and I'm sure if I weren't restrained, I wouldn't have been allowed to touch him either.

Then finally, the transfer van arrived. The staff tried to keep me calm by talking softly and giving me reassuring gestures, but once I caught a glimpse of the vehicle, I freaked. I had to be taken out of my wheelchair to get me outside, so as my panic rose, I dug my heels into the ground and pushed back against the escorting officers. I shook back and forth as I tried to break free but was swiftly hoisted off of the ground and pinned down on the bed. I was strapped in by the doctors and allowed Aaron one last

224

goodbye before they secured the doors. I felt the engine tremble as the woman standing beside me secured a sedative needle. As she injected it into me I heard the screams from a woman outside.

"No, wait! Please, let me see him! I didn't say goodbye to him! Please!"

Then as we pulled away, my senses faded.

And that was it. My new story started there, and as I fitted the last page into my life, a betrayed buzz shuddered over me.

"They drugged me…" My breath was shallow, the words barely even making it from my mouth.

Dr Olsen edged forwards. "What was that?"

I felt the inside of my throat shrivel up as I repeated my sentence. "They drugged me."

He leant back in concern. "What?"

I shot up from the chair and fell heavily against the wall, keeping my whole body fixed to it as the strings of my memories connected. Each one linking with the rest. "They drugged me." My breathing became short and staggered as tears seeped down my cheeks. "They drugged me."

Dr Olsen cautiously rose from his chair, his hands raised in the same manner. "Noah. Noah, listen to me. Calm yourself. Close your eyes and take in a breath. You're safe, okay?"

I wanted to listen to him, but everything in my body was fighting against him. My head shook back and forth as I started to hyperventilate.

"It's just you and me in here, Noah. No one else. Just us. I'm not going to hurt you."

My vision blurred and I ran my hand across my neck again. "They tried to… They knocked me out and…"

Dr Olsen took another step closer as I fell further into delirium. "Noah, please, just look at me. Look at me."

"They, they made me kill Ryan. They took control of me. I-I couldn't do anything. I was strapped down and I…" From then, I couldn't let another syllable out. The flood of my memories consuming me. Strangling me. Drowning me. In every way they could to stop me from fighting for my side.

Dr Olsen took my head in his hands and spoke in a clear and calming tone. "Noah, it's okay. It's okay. Please, just take a minute. You're safe. You're with me. Please." There was a pounding on the door and the shuffle of feet. "Ignore it. Keep your eyes on me."

I gripped at his wrists. "No, no, no, no, no! You don't understand! They used me! They're trying to take me back! They made me kill Dr Wilks! They're gonna make me do it again!"

The pounding outside grew louder and layers of voices formed, calling Dr Olsen's name.

He wiped the tears from under my eyes. "No, they won't. I won't let them."

"You can't stop them! They'll get to me! They won't stop! He's gonna take me!"

The door started bending in as the gathering outside grew frantic.

"Who, Noah? Who is it?"

"CALEB! BLAKE IS CALEB!"

I heard the lock on the door snap off, the metal flinging against the table beside us. I shrieked and pushed Dr Olsen back just as the other doctors and security broke in. I clambered to his back wall, holding my hand out to them to stop them from approaching.

Dr Olsen stumbled back up straight and tried to hold the guards back, but they were too large for his small figure. "No! Stop! You'll make him worse!"

"This is the last straw, doctor! He's too unstable for Riptide!" bellowed an unknown, husky voice. "He's going back to Sector 1."

"Please, he just needs to talk to me!" Dr Olsen pleaded as he was brushed aside.

I cowered to the floor as the officers forced their way to me. "PLEASE! I CAN'T GO BACK THERE!" I was gripped tightly under the arms and hoisted up from the carpet, my legs crumbling and being unable to support my weight. "PLEASE!" They dragged my body effortlessly across the bricks, my face scratching against the rough surface as they yanked my arms backwards. "PLEASE!"

From the familiar feeling, I knew they were cuffing me. I pleaded desperately as I kicked and angled my body to even gain a chance of winning the battle I knew I couldn't. I was forced to the floor and pressed down as they pierced my skin with a needle. My cries faded as my eyes drifted shut and my body loosened until I was perfectly still.

I was out for what seemed a fraction of a second. As soon as my head hit the floor, I began to resurface. I couldn't move my body. I couldn't see.

226

I could barely breathe. I had so much pressure being forced down on me, it felt like my bones were about to snap. I tried my hardest to move even the smallest part of me, but it was useless. My hearing seemed slanted too. I could hear voices moving around me, fading in and out, followed by metal clattering and screeching. I knew I was moving – someone was moving me. We were going very slowly, so slowly that it almost didn't seem like we were moving at all.

I managed to twitch my finger. Then my hand. Then my eyes. They were so heavy, I couldn't keep them open for very long. I scanned around me. I was in my room. Laying down. Halfway to the door. The room had been stripped bare. My belongings that were once all around had been tossed into the cardboard boxes and stacked high across my desk. My head flopped onto its side and my eyes jolted opened as I realised what was happening. My adrenaline surged and my senses came back. I shot forwards, the force that was keeping me down previously was found to be thick leather and metal restraints that were wrapped around my ankles, wrists and stomach.

"No! Please, wait!" I screamed as I was wheeled towards the door on my bed.

The doctors forced me back again, pushing against my chest and pinning me down. They kept a grip on me as they called for another dose of sedative. As the doctors struggled to keep me down, I heard Dr Olsen's voice approach.

"Let go of him! Let him go." He skidded to a stop beside me, and I tried to reach my hand out to him.

The doctors continued to pin me harder as he tried to explain. "Let him go? He's having a psychotic break. It's in the policy to keep the patient sedated when they are transferred."

"Please, don't take me back down there! I can change! I can!" I pleaded to them.

Dr Olsen pulled their arms away and I pulled myself back up again. "I'm the head doctor here. You listen to what I tell you!" He held my hand and directed me calmly onto my back again. "Noah, lie down. Don't struggle against the restraints, you'll hurt yourself. Take in a deep breath."

I shook my head back and forth and teared up as I rested my head down on the pillow. "No, no, no, no, no! I can't go back down there! Please! Don't make me go back down there!"

He stroked his hand across my head. "I don't want you to go back down there either, Noah, but it's out of my hands."

"Please!" My voice was desperate and began to fade away under the chaos.

Dr Olsen stuttered and shook his head before being pushed back by the other doctors. His hand slipped from mine, and I started to panic.

"It's Dr Hawthorn's orders! We don't have the resources up here to control him."

I shook back and forth and kicked my feet the best I could against the bars beside me.

"Get him down. He's gonna break the bloody bed again if he's awake any longer. Only just fixed the damn thing."

"No! Don't touch me!"

Another man forced my head to the side and revealed my neck and shoulder. I had flashbacks to that day, and I ripped my hand out of one of the restraints and smacked the needle out of the man's hands. He stumbled back in shock and the rest of the doctors leapt to my side and each one pinned a part of my body in position as they readied another sedation needle.

I heard Dr Olsen scream over and over to stop them, but he was ignored. The doctors with me were not from Sector 3. They were dressed head to toe in a grey and mint uniform, and I knew where they had come from. I remember the colours from underground. They're the Sector 1 doctors. They had power over all the staff here in Sector 3, even Dr Olsen. He couldn't save me.

They pressured down on me as the needle drew closer to my skin. I felt my tears flood onto the pillow as the sedative was injected. The tension in me loosened and my eyes fluttered shut again.

Like a never-ending loop, the sleep was as instant as the awakening. The feeling repeated. The pain remained. My sight was blurred but I noticed my change of clothes. They were black. I pushed my limp body up with my trembling arms and placed one hand on the padded wall beside me. After feeling the softness of the cushion I took my hand away, staring at in awe as I became more aware of the situation. I looked back down at my clothes, jolting forwards as it finally clicked in my mind. I was dressed in black. The walls were padded. The bed was by said padded wall.

I took in a sharp breath as I checked my surroundings. "No…" I slid off of the sheets and stumbled across the matching cushioned floor. "No." I attempted a run towards the large metal plates that lined the opposite end of the wide, empty room, but collapsed to the ground as my energy reached its limits. "No!"

I pulled my body along the floor, crawling towards the steel – only to realise that there were several inches of glass before it. I pounded against it, screaming, until I heard the build-up of electricity in the air and a surge shock through the hidden components in the pane and straight through my fingertips and the rest of my body. I curled up in pain, holding my hands to my chest as I rolled back and forth in tears.

Chapter 8

Riptide Runner

So… here we are. Sector 1. Back again. I should've seen it coming, really. It was only a matter of time before I went back dark down. I lost everything. I should've just stayed quiet. Followed the rules. Remained compliant. But I didn't. I had to go and dig up what was buried. I guess Blake was right – or maybe I should say Caleb – I am too curious for my own good. I was too trusting. I fell in his trap. He's the whole reason I'm here.

Now, I'm stuck in this same room for twenty-four hours a day – for the most part. For an hour, every week I get to sit in a concrete box with a cage above it to tease me with the sky I won't ever see again, then some other time for tests. At least I think it's every week. I can't tell any more. There isn't a window in sight. I can't tell when it's dark and when it's light. The only chance I get to re-establish my timings is when I see that blocked off sky. I could see it every day, I could see it every month, I have no clue.

Every meal I get is the same, so I can't tell which is dinner or which is breakfast. There's no lunch. Just breakfast and dinner the same time apart. In a plain room. All that's with you is a bed, a table, a single stool, and a cabinet. All of the furniture is immobile. The cabinet's built into the wall with its doors covered with the same cushioned material as the rest of the room. The table is more of a slab – it's fixed to the wall – the stool hooked onto it. No movement. Some hospital.

You can't do anything. Just wait. Wait until something happens. You could scream. You could bang against the glass. You could tell everyone that dares come near your cell that you're sane. But what's the use? If you do anything that comes across aggressive – even if it's just responding to a question – they'll shoot you. It's not like Riptide. The staff don't take any kind of nonsense down here. They'll load up a tranquiliser gun and shoot you with it. If they miss, they try again until they hit you. If that's not on the table of available options, then they result to shocking. The glass connected to the viewing area is fixed with electric wires across it. You can't even see them. That's the trick of it. If you get too near the pane then they'll tease you with the noise. The crackling. The whirring. Whichever method they use doesn't matter though, they all make you want to shrivel up and die on the spot. It's almost like the crackling gets taken from the glass and engraved under your skin.

As for the sedative? You can't move. You can't speak. You can't think. Wherever you get hit, that's where you get left. The doctors don't even have the liberty to move you to your bed. The floor's just as good according to them. How do I know this? It's happened to me every time I've opened my eyes. Apparently I can't even get out of bed without threatening someone – that's probably how they see it so why not shoot me?

The staff took advantage of me whilst in such a state. With the knowledge that I was incapacitated, I'd be taken from my room and dragged down with every kind of restraint they had on hand. They'd sit me in a room with a woman – the room was also void of outside life. She'd sit opposite with a light beside her. She'd talk to me. She'd talk to me in a manner that seemed innocent to an ignorant eye, but every word she said was of no truth. Her tone would then be drowned out as the light was switched on. It would flash rhythmically in the same repeated sequence each time. They were wiping any thoughts of MK-Ultra from me. Undoing what was done.

It's not real. It never was. It's a work of fiction. It's a story formed from a delusional mind to deter from the fact that I'm not strong enough to accept what I am.

I know what I am, I just wonder if they know too. They say what they say, and I end up agreeing. I have no strength to retaliate. I refuse to believe them, but when they question me, it's best for me to do what they want to see. After I figured this out, they eased off of me. But only slightly.

Nights after I'd been subdued, I watched from my bed as the metal of my door slid across into the wall. A group of armed staff marched in – sedative firmly in hand. I sluggishly pushed myself into a seated position.

"What's going on?" I said as I rubbed the clumps of sleep out of my eyes.

A man gripped my underarm and hoisted me to my feet. "You've got visitors."

I tripped several times as my feet scuffed the ground from the aggressive tugging of the guards. "What? Who?"

231

He scowled at me. "You'll see."

I was taken out to the hallway, a thick, darkened strip with mint coloured wall pads that were the only splash of colour in the unit. To my left was simply an endless run of other cells, whilst to my right, the doors to the staircase. With Dark Down being the smallest of the sectors, there really wasn't that much need to spread it out – it *is* underground, where are we to go? I could run – I could make it those few metres – but I'd never make it, not with the aim these guys have.

We headed through a hidden door, and I was quickly strapped up with a chain or two. Ahead was another door. I squinted my eyes, trying desperately to peer at what might be on the other side. The guard pinned the needle up against my back and a shiver skimmed across my skin.

"Move it."

I swallowed and was pushed through to the visiting room, the chains around me tangling me up. The room was small. The room was bare. The room was somehow chilling even though there was warmth in the air. I was thumped into a red, plastic chair that was facing the large black window. At first, all that could be seen was me. My reflection. I could see the cuts and bruises of my many affairs, my eyes sunken and skeleton almost breaking through my cracked skin. Then once the airlock sealed both me and the guards in, the black abyss ahead turned out to be curtain. It was shakily drawn across and several faces were revealed. I remembered two. Two girls.

One was short with ash blonde hair that flowed way past her shoulders. It was parted slightly off centre, a few stray strands casting over her mole-covered face. The other girl was taller, brown hair that stopped just past her ears and held a much more tensed expression. River and Tess. Students from Layset, the best friends of Ryan. They used to have lessons in the library a lot and they always ended up at the tables next to my desk. That trio was mischievous, but their kindness could sure melt your heart. Sadly, a lot of the time they were overlooked because of this. They could shower their teachers with love and gifts for years to come, but only those that cause trouble are the ones that people ever took notice of.

My throat shrivelled upon the sight of them. They seemed fearful. Why wouldn't they? There may have been inches of glass between us, but that doesn't change the fact I nearly killed their best friend – even if it was under someone else's command. That's probably what makes it worse.

I wasn't sure of the others in the room, but I did notice Dr Olsen leaning against the wall in the corner, his arms folded and looking glum in appearance. He caught eyes with me, and I cowered away. The awkward silence was then broken by his voice.

"Noah? Can you hear me, mate?"

I gently glanced up and down to signal that I could. "Yeah..."

He didn't react when I spoke, but he carried on just the same. "Noah, these girls have come to see you. They're friends of Ryan."

I shuddered and looked away then noticed the confused looks upon the guard's faces as I did. "I know who they are..." I muttered under my breath.

"It's okay, mate. They're not here to hurt you."

I took in a breath. "Are you sure?"

The message didn't get through. The group behind the glass murmured to themselves as I watched the guards anxiously step closer towards me. Then from the other side came a voice.

"The microphone isn't on."

Dr Olsen whispered back. "If the mic isn't on then how can he hear us?"

I wondered just the same. I thought maybe the mic was on one way or something, but the guards couldn't hear either. Then came another sound of feedback and I shuddered once more.

"Noah?"

I turned back.

"Can you hear me?"

I nodded.

"This is Tess and River. They came to talk to you about Ryan."

I caught eyes with one of them and they gave me a nervous smile.

"Are you okay with that, Noah?"

"Yeah..."

"Okay." He gestured to the other figures. "These other people are investigators. They're looking into Ryan's case, as are the girls."

"Why are the girls here? It's dangerous," I said quietly.

"Indeed, it is. But they insisted that they see you. They're desperate for your help."

"Help with what?"

"Mr Coleman?" started an investigator. "We need you to help us with Ryan."

I clenched my jaw and hung my head.

"Since your case has been taking over the news lately, quite a few people learned about your incident with Mr Axel, and they now believe that you may have knowledge on the situation."

I didn't reply.

River cleared her throat and shuffled forwards. "Um, N-Noah?"

I drifted my eyes to her considerate ones.

"Hello."

"Hi…"

She gave an awkward chuckle. "I still can't get around your real name. It's nice – I like it – but only knowing you by another makes this a bit confusing."

"I'm surprised people bought it…" I mumbled. "Phoenix Close. He sounds like a right tosser."

She pulled at her sleeves, unsure on how to react. "Noah, um… you were always nice to us, always. You never cared when we jammed the printer or used books as dominoes – you even joined in sometimes."

A smile flickered across my face, memories flashing behind it.

"Our year loved you, but I'll say we were all shocked the day you… well…"

"Snapped?" I replied slyly.

"I wasn't sure if that was the right word…"

I scoffed. "You'd snap too if someone tried to steal your mind." I glanced over at Olsen in the corner. He gave a disappointed sigh. "No one ever believes you, either."

"Anyway," Tess continued, holding her friend's hand. "The thing is… Ryan's missing."

My head shot back to them. "What?"

The investigators edged them to the side. "Mr Coleman, we're here to ask what you know about his disappearance."

I took another look at Olsen. "Doctor?"

He gave a smile. "Hey, mate."

I adjusted the chain around my waist. "I… I don't…"

"It's okay, mate. Just tell them what you feel comfortable with. You can say anything."

"Anything?" I said shyly.

He chuckled. "Maybe not *anything* but whatever you think could be a link to this case."

"So you believe me? "

His smile faded and he adjusted his stance. "I wish I could, Noah, but I can't. I'm just here to do my job."

I slumped back in my seat.

"Noah?" said River kindly.

I nodded at her.

"Please. We just want to find him. We just want him to be okay."

"I don't know what you want me to believe. I don't know anything anymore. It's just a mess…"

She locked her eyes tight on me. "Please."

I took an inhale and straightened out. I fiddled with my right handcuff as I spoke. "If you came here for my views then that's all I can give you." I glanced over my shoulder at the guards. "You can't make me change." I turned back, speaking only to the girls. "I don't know anything about where he could be, but I can help if you tell me what he was doing when he was taken."

"Taken?" Tess questioned fearfully.

"Taken, missing, lost, whatever word you like to use. What happened?"

The girls faced each other as they tried to piece the puzzle.

"I don't remember how long ago it started, but he started going crazy with what happened to him," River explained. "I don't actually blame you, neither does he, but he was looking into everything you said in the school and what you said to the police. About the ACC, about Mr Hayes—"

"You mean Caleb? "

She stuttered. "I-I don't know who that is."

"They're the same person. He's the one that—"

Olsen stepped forwards and whispered to them. "That's not true. They look the same, but they're different people."

"No, they're not! It's my memory, I lived through it, I saw him. He drugged me!"

"What did he drug you with, Mr Coleman?" asked an investigator.

"LSD or something. He called it Otherdoxersiderin. The Other Side. He made with The ACC! They're making people compliant!"

"Who are they making compliant?" River asked desperately.

"Criminals. Anyone who's ever broken the law, been to prison, anything! They're trying to make a drug that mind controls them!"

The investigators glanced at each other. They didn't seem shocked by my comments, in fact, they almost seemed to know exactly what I was to say. Perhaps the staff told them what's been running in my head.

"Do you think they could have taken Ryan?" asked Tess.

"Ryan's never broken the law," River replied. "Why would they take him if he wasn't a criminal?"

I gently settled back in the chair I had since been rising from. "You say he was looking into what I said?"

"Yeah."

"Then he was onto something. They're obviously not ready for people to know yet, so anyone who finds something out is a threat. Find his work, find out what he's been doing, it'll tell you—"

The microphone was shut off. I was the only one who could still hear what was beyond the glass once the curtain was shut.

"I knew we shouldn't have come here. It was a waste of time," said Tess.

"No, I believe him. He was always there for us at school, nobody snaps the way he did," replied River.

"Some people do," said Dr Olsen.

"No. I knew him, and I knew Ryan. I know that Noah said some things about Mr Hayes, but I kind of believe him. Nobody gets a theory from nowhere. Even if they're deluded."

"I'm aware. I've studied Noah's behaviour for a year and he's quite the mystery of a patient, but we treat him like we do the others. At least we did in Sector 3, I don't know about here. Delusional disorders can be tricky, but he's also schizophrenic, bipolar and paranoid, anything can trigger an outburst even if it's just a sentence in a book."

The conversation continued as I was dragged back out to the corridor, chains clattering as I wobbled shamefully away. The doctors had their sedative guns at the ready and kept them on me as we returned to my cell. As we did, I inspected my surroundings once more.

I knew the way back upstairs. The floor lines taught me as much. If I could get through the maze by the stairs then I could get to Riptide.

What was I even thinking? They'd shoot me down before I even wriggled from their grasps. I kept my eyes shut tight as I was pinned to the floor of my cell and had my restraints removed. I fought against any reflexes that showed signs of surfacing, and through the process, they had the gun pointed for me.

I think they were surprised by my lack of reacting. They were probably hoping they'd broke me, but that little ramble in that interrogation probably broke their hopes. If that's what they wanted, that's what I'd give them. As the group headed for the door, I remained on the floor with my arms folded under my head. I heard the door shut, and I closed my eyes again. I focused on listening. I tapped my fingers on the cushion, focusing on the sound before I heard the voices through the wall.

"He's becoming submissive."

"That happened last time. He could be faking. Then we'll end up in the same old loop."

"If he's becoming submissive then we could easily take him where we want."

"He's still delusional. The first time he was here he wasn't."

"We could try out Sector 2 on him."

"Sector 2 isn't for patients like him."

"We need to talk to what's-his-name. Joel."

There was another sound of sliding metal and the voices disappeared. I sat up and rested on my knees before I glanced up at the camera. I watched as the lens behind it zoomed in and out, and I wandered over to my bed and burrowed underneath the sheet.

I remained crumpled in the corner for the hours I wasn't needed. I didn't move an inch. Why would I need to? There's nowhere to go. The atmosphere was empty, everything perfectly still. What felt like days passed. My meals were balanced in the opening, the staff yelling for my attention, before they'd give up and shove it to the floor.

For each doctor that came for me, I'd give the same response. Nothing. They'd parade in with their sedation guns, practically an army of them to surround me, ready to shoot at the first sign of aggression. Then I'd be strapped in place, hypnotised, and put to sleep. I didn't take a step out of line. This obviously did something, I wasn't sure what at the time, but it obviously convinced the staff to make the call.

They barged into my cell as the routine goes, guns locked and loaded, but someone stood out amongst the sea of grey and green. He stepped forwards. Slowly. His familiar frayed coat curving around him. I dragged my head out of the darkness and followed his figure upwards. Slender, pale, and a fixed care in his eyes. Gripped in his hands was a book. Thick, crumpled, and covered in a collection of markings.

I fixed my eyes on his. "Hi…"

He smiled back at me. "Hey, mate." He presented the book to me. "I thought you might want this back."

I reached my hand out for it, retracting it quickly as the doctors twitched their fingers across the trigger.

"It's alright," he said again, waving the book up and down.

I tried once more, snatching it from the doctor's hand and consoling it tightly against my chest. "Did you read it?"

"I had to. We needed to see what was going on."

I trembled. "Are you here to say I'm crazy?"

Olsen crouched to my level. "No, no, of course not." He gently scratched the side of my arm. "We're taking you back to Sector 3."

I jolted my head up. "What?"

He smiled. "That's right. The staff down here say that you've been well behaved, that your psychosis is slowly calming down, and that you'll be safe to transfer upstairs again."

"I'm going now?"

"Yep. Is there anything you want to take up with you?"

I gazed around the cell. "There's nothing here."

He chuckled and followed my eyeline. "Yeah, you're right. There will be upstairs though."

I let my body fall into his arms, gripping at his coat as he took my hand. "Thank you."

"It's okay." He lowered me onto my back. "We've gotta sedate you to take you up, okay?"

I nodded gently and the doctor turned me to my front. I waited patiently for the injection, jerking slightly as I felt the needle hit my skin. I dug my nails at the cover of my journal as the pain lingered.

I heard Olsen's calming voice as he lowered my top again. "Well done, mate."

I curled up as the sedative slipped in, my surroundings echoing and fading until my eyes flickered shut. A few hours later, I was back. Back in the same old room with the same old walls and the same old window. I slipped from the bed. I was still donning the Dark Down uniform, but the doctors had neatly folded up my new one on my desk. There was a small welcome crate beside it. I tore the Post-It note from the plastic.

'Welcome back. Here's your basics.'

I lowered the note, and one-by-one removed each piece from the box. Shampoo, shower gel, toothbrush, toothpaste, a comb, a towel, paper, pens and my journal. I left them scattered across the desk then crawled up to the window. I stared out at the sky. The beautiful, bliss, blue sky. Not a cloud cast over us.

I leant against the casing surrounding the window, only for it to snap when I rested my weight on it. I fell flat across the desk, the comb digging into me and was somehow still hooked onto me once I sat up. I pulled it out from my top and held the piece of broken casing in my hand. I sighed and chucked it in front of me.

"Well, that's a good start."

As I sat back, I noticed what was behind it. The few items the staff had missed in their clear out. My letters, a few pins, a blunt screwdriver, and a note. I lifted the small piece of paper, excitement filling as I found a way to contact him. Aaron's number. I stashed that, my journal, a pen and the screwdriver in my pockets and rushed out of the room. I shuffled about, ignoring the other patients whose glares drove through me. I dodged each doctor as I ran for the phones, slamming myself against the wall as I forgot to slow down. I scrambled the number into the keypad and brought the phone to my ear. The rings stretched out for so long I didn't think I'd catch him until...

"Hello?"

"Aaron? Aaron, it's Noah."

He gave a shudder of relief and he almost appeared to be crying. *"Oh, my God, Noah. You don't know how happy I am to hear you."*

"I'm glad to hear you too," I said, tearing up. "I don't think I have a lot of time to talk, but I needed to let you know I'm okay."

"I'm so glad! I'm so glad! I've been so scared, Noah. I don't know what to do!"

I gripped at the phone. "What? Why? What's happened?"

"I don't know! It's Wyegate!"

"What about Wyegate?"

"It's empty, Noah! The prison's empty!"

"What? What do you mean empty?"

"I mean, it's empty! Every single inmate is gone. Anyone that has ever stepped foot in that place is gone. I'm the only one left."

I shuddered. "Aaron, where are you now? Are you safe?"

239

"I'm at home. I haven't left the house. I've just been in here hiding, and I know that the court has my address and everything. God! I can't do anything!"

I panted and scanned around me in a panic. "I've got a plan. It's crazy but so am I. I'm gonna come to you."

"W-What? How? Noah, please, don't do anything! You're in enough trouble as it is!"

"I don't care. I'm gonna find you. Just get some stuff together, whatever you think we'll need. I'm gonna find a way to—"

The phone cut out. I tapped on the plastic, calling his name, but there was no answer. I spun to face the machine and met with Dr Phillipson holding her hand against the 'end call' lever.

She laid her hand out. "Two hours in and you're already causing trouble." She gave a smile. "Come on, give me the phone and I'll take you back to your room. You need to get changed before you go running around Riptide."

I dropped the phone into her palm, and she rested it back on its stand.

"Good boy. Let's go."

I backed away from her. "No."

"Come on, Noah. There's no point in making waves on your first day back."

I shook my head and continued backing down the hall. "No."

She followed. "Noah, I'll have to call someone else if you don't cooperate."

I quickly leapt around the corner and barrelled down the recreation corridor. I skimmed past the common room and swung into the medical area, walls lined with doors that opened to many very different rooms. I skidded at a crossroad, flicking between the signs on the walls.

'Psych Test 1'

'Exam Room 3'

'Medical Store – No Patient Access'

'Guards' Watch Room – No Patient Access'

'Staff Wing – No Patient Access'

Before I could make a choice, I spun into Toby.

"Coleman? Are you alright? What you doin' out here?"

I shoved past him and headed down to the offices, running into another doctor as the rest closed in.

240

"Noah, mate. It's alright, calm down. What's the matter?"

I stared at Dr Olsen, shaking as I dreaded what I had to do. "I'm so sorry."

"What?"

I launched for him, taking the screwdriver from my waist, and wrapping my arms around the doctor's neck. The staff all pounced towards us, but all skidded to a stop as I tightened my grip on the weapon and held it against Olsen's skin. Little did they know that he was a lot stronger than me, the only reason he didn't fight back was because that's not the kind of person he is. I, on the other hand, have been proven to be the opposite, the staff didn't want to risk what I would do to the poor guy.

"Don't any of you come a step closer to me!" I shouted, shuffling in the direction of a storage room

Dr Olsen gripped at my arm. "Noah, please…" he said breathlessly.

I forced myself to ignore him to maintain the composure I was already struggling to keep. "If anyone touches me, I'll kill him!"

One woman went against my demand, raising her hands as she spoke in a monotone voice. "Noah. Let him go and this won't escalate. We'll take you back to your room and calm you down."

I almost fell through with the plan as I felt Dr Olsen's grip start to loosen and his breathing become staggered but replied sharply as I was almost grabbed from behind. "I said stay away from me! I'm not doing anything you say! I can't stand taking orders anymore! I'm done with being nothing but a complier to all of you!" I reached the room. "OPEN THE DOOR!"

Nobody moved.

"Open the door! NOW!"

The woman nodded at another younger doctor, and they shakily jammed their keys into the lock. I scrambled in, and not too long after that, the guards were about, and the emergency alarm was engaged. It deafened all who walked the halls. I stumbled as I was stunned by the racket but managed to snatch Olsen's keys from his belt to lock us in together. I released my grasp on him and he fell to the floor. He gasped desperately and lifted his trembling hand to his throat and rubbed it back and forth.

"Noah…" he said raspily. "Please."

"I'm sorry," I replied as I spotted the window. "But it's all I have left to try. I never wanted to have to do that to you."

I took the handcuffs from his belt and cuffed his hand to one of the metal shelving units. He gripped at my clothes, helplessly trying to force me back as the staff clattered against the door. I rifled through the different boxes, flinging cardboard and contraband wherever it deemed necessary. I swung back to the door as it started curving in, the keys I had left in the lock blocking the staff from using theirs. I rushed to another shelf and heaved my weight against it. It barely moved an inch, I was too weak to even block the door. I returned to the window, screwdriver firmly in hand, then stabbed frantically at the glass.

Now with his voice back, Olsen yelled, "Noah, stop!"

I continued battering it. Whatever I had, I used. With each pound came a cracking. Cracking. Cracking. Cracking. Soon enough, the window burst into a cascade of shards. I cowered back as they scattered before jumping forwards and diving onto the bars that blocked the exit. Olsen continued to plea.

They were fixed on tightly. I pulled at them, thinking that if I had a will strong enough my twig arms would be able to bend them. In anger, I kicked at the bolts, causing the metal to shake. I scanned what was with me in the dust-covered room and noticed the pipe running up the wall. I grabbed it, forced it back and forth until it gave out and hissed as the gas escaped. I fell back and returned to the window as the doctors pounded on the door, the panicked jangling of keys vibrating through it.

I struck the broken pipe against the bars then forced it between the end one and the wall. The concrete around the bolts chipped, and eventually started to come loose. I kept at it until the bottom hook pinged from the wall. I turned as the door was broken through. They freed Olsen and the group pounced.

"Noah, stop!"

They were too late. I fell through the gap. I hurtled down until my fall was broken by another set of bars that covered the Sector 2 windows. My fingers hooked onto the top and I slipped down the slant, falling into the deep sludge that lined the wall. I was stunned for several seconds, frozen stiff as I sunk into the mud. I had a stream of blood dripping down my face. It was warm and contrasted with the bitter ground. I pushed on my arms to bring me up, and I looked back at the window to see the doctors staring out at me. They quickly turned and spoke into their radios, Dr Olsen remaining still as he gripped his hands over the edge.

I stumbled to my feet, almost collapsing as I straightened out. Then, in an attempt at a run, I headed for the gate. It wasn't like the rest of the outer wall, it was constructed out of wire, but it still had the lines of barbs looped across the top fixed to the gate rail. I reached the road and stared through at the bright and swaying grass. With one last look at the hospital, I jumped up and grabbed onto the fence. I heard the voices scream.

"STOP! STOP HIM!"

I hoisted myself up each inch, slipping my feet into the gaps. As I scaled higher, the wind blew stronger, and for the first time I felt the burning rays of the sun against my skin. I made it up to the barbs and hung off the side as I tried to find a solution, but after that fall from the second story, I think my logic nodes had been smashed.

As I heard the calls and shouts from the guards that were stuck behind the reception doors, I powered through it. It slashed at my clothes and sliced deep into my uncovered flesh. I cried out as it cut through to my already beaten legs, and then swung onto the other side. I let myself drop, whilst keeping my fingertips skimming on the fence to catch me before I hit the ground. I whimpered as I was forced to place weight on my injuries but used my speeding adrenaline to keep moving.

I limped into the dry, waist-high grass as the hospital's outside siren sounded. My blood stained the blades, as it did my outfit, but the black colouring hid most of it. Ahead of me were the pine woods. It separated the hospital from the rest of the world. With an ocean on one side and that on the other, I had no choice but to go through it. I ran. I was forced to embrace the pain until daylight came through again.

The woodland stretched far. They couldn't build a place like Ocean Cliff in the town centre. It needed seclusion. It needed isolation. That didn't stop people finding the place though, did it? I was just thankful that today seemed to be a rest day for the justice seekers. There was no rest for the wicked though. I smashed past each leafy tree until I slammed against a small, waist-high fence. It was made out of wooden strips, and just behind it was a cracked concrete path.

The sun was still high and shining down on the houses across the green. I panted deeply and used my limp limbs to crawl underneath the gap. I could still hear the siren in the distance, but it was more faded than frightening. I checked up and down the path and was thankful to be alone. My handprint was left on the wooden beam as I pushed off against it and dashed over to

243

the back of the houses. I slid down the slats of one's garden fence and wheezed as I reached up for the gate handle. I twisted the loop and felt the gate slowly swing inwards. I exhaled in relief and crawled through. I pulled myself across the dotted steppingstones, passing the different flower beds and the several small toys that were strewn randomly over the grass, some floating in a small paddling pool.

I reached the ridge of some decking and tapped on the glass door. I kept hitting it, but nobody seemed to be home. I sobbed and slid my palm down the glass, leaving a smear of scarlet across it. I curled up as the pain I tried to ignore built up, and the slashes consumed me as my blood leaked out onto the porch. I was left collapsed in my liquids until I felt around me for something to use. I rolled over and dragged a large rock towards me. With a staggered breath, I used my remaining strength to smash it through the glass. The door shattered, and I covered my eyes as the shards fell. I reached my foot inside and held in my scream as I lunged my legs. The glass crunched underneath me as I made it to the centre of the kitchen.

"Hello?" I called, holding my weight up with the countertop.

There was no reply.

"Okay… Okay…"

I turned to face the cupboards then reached up to open them. I raided each one on a search for a first aid kit. I failed to find one on the first side, so stumbled to the other and raided them the same. I found the kit tucked behind a pen pot and flicked it open. I tossed each item onto the surface until I found a bandage. I took it and slid down the lower cupboards then rolled up my soaked trouser legs to see my once white skin covered in crimson. I pulled a tea towel from the drawer and used it to clean up the excess blood before wrapping up the hoard of cuts. I moved onto my arms – they were less damaged – but what was most hurt was my hand. I cleaned it and revealed the depth of the injury before wrapping it up too. I ended up using the entire roll before bringing myself to move to the other materials. I took apart the plasters and hesitantly swallowed the painkillers. I then turned my attention to other areas.

I took a glass from the cupboard and ran the tap. I drunk at least three glasses just to help me feel normal again before I placed it on the draining board and splashed my face. I'd come this far, I might as well go further. I left the kitchen and ventured upstairs. I followed the slim staircase onto the landing and checked in the first room I saw. It was the bedroom. It was incredibly tidy, and I was about to ruin that – not that the shattered door and blood-soaked kitchen didn't ruin anything. I sat down at the dressing table and stared at my grim face in the mirror.

"Oh, God," I groaned as I ran my fingers through my now damp hair.

I glanced to the side at the wardrobe and proceeded to scavenge through it for an outfit. It didn't matter what it was, I just needed to look normal and… not me. I made sure the curtains were shut before removing my old uniform to replace it with a pair of black jeans, a white top, and a red-check shirt hanging just over it. I had to change slowly as to not add to injury, but I managed to do it within a few minutes.

I then found a small drawstring bag which I used for my supplies. In the bedroom itself was quite the lot already. The first thing I stuck in the bag was my journal. I'm surprised it's made it this far. It should probably be disintegrated by now. Along with that were a few coins and a note in cash, a few water bottles, the least bulky food that was in the kitchen which happened to be a box of breakfast bars, then I added a blanket, the rest of the painkillers, and a torch. I didn't know what to do. I've never been on the run before, and now the fear of my withdrawals was kicking in. I had about two days to get as far as I can without my brain turning on me, and there was only one person who would be able to keep me safe. Aaron.

I needed to contact him, but I had no clue of how. I didn't have a phone, only a number. I don't know where he lives, or how far away he even is. It was hopeless. Whilst I scrambled for ideas in my head, I wandered into the bathroom for a final makeover. I opened the cabinet on the side and pulled out a pair of scissors and returned to the sink. I lifted my sleeve and hovered the blades over my I.D. band, but before I could snip it off, I heard a car, and it was pulling up on the driveway. I couldn't see out of the bathroom mirror, so returned to the bedroom and peeked out from behind the curtain.

There *was* a car. In the front seats were two people – a man and a woman. I ducked back before I was caught and made a break for the stairs to escape out the back, but as I got halfway down, I saw them opening the front door. I was forced back up, my heart pounded as I heard the creak of the hinges. I dived beneath the bed, pulling the bedsheet to cover the gap. I gripped at the scissors in my hands and shook with tears in my eyes as I heard their distraught voices.

"Oh, my God, Sarah!"

"Oh, my G—What—Who—"

"The place is wrecked."

"I'll check upstairs with Bruno."

I tensed up as I heard the unbearably slow footsteps coming up the stairs. Along with it was a patter. Two heavy steps and a light patter. I gripped my nose with my hand as I held onto my breath, forcing the blade of the scissors into the crisp carpet with the other. The bedroom door creeped open. Behind it were two feet. Behind those, four paws. Together they scoped the radius of the room. A large snout dropped to the carpet as it followed the feet. It gained a trail. The trail led it to a red mark on the carpet. It barked, and the figure knelt down.

"Good job, boy," spoke a woman in a quiet tone.

I caught sight of her bag that was strung across her shoulder. From it, she pulled a small canister. Across it, the words 'Police issued mace.' I pulled the scissors from the carpet and held them in my hands as if in prayer as the snout of the dog continued its search. The woman rose. The dog kept down. It checked at the wardrobe. It checked at the window. It checked at the dressing table. Until…

I let out a cry as the creature snapped its jaw onto my ankle. I was forced out from under the bed as the dog kept a grip on me. The woman shot the spray in my direction, but I managed to block it with my arm. She pounced on me, pinning me in position as she tried to bat the weapon out of my hand. I continued to yell as she pressured down on my slashed skin, but somehow I had the power to dislodge her and force her to the floor. I kicked my free leg at the German Shepheard's face, which caused it to whimper and release me. I stumbled back up but was quickly beat down again by the woman. She readied the canister again, and this time, I attacked her. I slit the blade across her wrist, and she let out an ear-piercing scream as she fell back.

The dog jumped me again, going straight for my arm. He missed the first shot, but by the second, he had taken me down. I fell onto the landing and the hound gripped his teeth into me. I hated what I was forced to do to defend myself. I stretched the blades into a slither and sliced it across its leg. It whimpered once again but fought on to defend its owners. I took at it again and this time sliced across it's back. That was when it fell. I scrambled up as from the stairs came a man. His face was mortified, and he instantly came for me too. He wasn't as strong as the woman. He was a similar size to me, and I quickly forced him over the banister to see him land on his front with a crack. He didn't wake up.

I returned to the bedroom to see the woman wrapping her wrist in a T-shirt. She swiftly brushed her hand up and finally landed a hit on me with the pepper spray. I stumbled back against the wall, rubbing my eyes wildly as the burning sensation overtook me. The scissors fell from my fingers, and I cowered in the corner, the woman closing in as I screamed my throat out. She grabbed my shirt and forced me onto my front.

"Don't you move one more inch."

She twisted my leg onto my back and brought my arms with it. I heard the sound of handcuffs, but she didn't put them on me. I was still crying, so I couldn't see a thing, but I felt what she was doing. She lifted my sleeve and pulled my wristband around.

Her breath staggered. "Patient?" She spoke in a whisper. "You're from Ocean Cliff?"

Whilst she was distracted, I was able to roll back around and strike her down. I brought my hands upwards and fixed them tightly around her neck. Her eyes widened and she kept them fixed on mine as she pleaded.

"Please... Please, I..." Her face was slowly fading blue. "Don't do this..."

I kept a grip on her, and she began to jolt up and down. All the while, she continued to plea. I let out a cry and clenched my eyes closed before releasing my grasp and holding myself against the line of drawers. The woman gasped and backed away, gripping at her still bleeding hand. I looked over at her as she tried to hide her fear.

"I-I-I'm... s-s-sorry," I trembled.

She nodded. "It's okay." Her tone said otherwise.

"Do you have a phone?" I asked sheepishly.

She nodded again and pointed to her bag. "It's in there."

I scampered over to it and reached inside. I pulled it out and tried to access it, but the screen displayed 'locked'. I looked back up at the woman who had now fallen to her side.

"What's the code?" I questioned.

"Five... Three... Seven... Two..." she answered.

I inputted the digits, and the device was unlocked. I smiled and looked back up at her only to see that she had fallen unconscious. I scurried over and turned her onto her back in a panic. I rested my ear against her chest to hear for movement. I was relieved when there was.

With the scene over, I quickly yanked another outfit from the wardrobe, picked up the scissors and marched down the stairs. I carefully stepped over the man's motionless body and headed for the front door but froze as I heard another voice.

"Hello?" The voice was young, complete in innocence. If they were to venture upstairs that innocence would soon fade.

I turned with my throat shrivelling dry to see a young boy waiting in the living room doorway, freckles covering his tiny face. "Hello," I replied in shock.

He picked at the paint. "Can I come out now?"

I stuttered and hid the scissors in my pocket. "Um… come with me." I reached my hand out and the boy crept forwards.

I led him towards a small room by the side of the kitchen, without revealing the mess on the other side of the door, then sat the boy in what turned out to be another bathroom.

"Stay in here. Help'll come soon, okay? I promise." I slammed the door then reached for the broom beside me, sticking it under the handle and fixing it against the wall.

I didn't stick around a second longer. I darted out of the house and down the neighbourhood. I caught different faces peeking from behind their curtains with phones to their ears. I followed the road then disappeared down an alley that was lined with crumbling brick work. I took out the woman's phone, unlocked it once again, then typed Aaron's number into the keypad.

He didn't answer. I tried again. No answer. I then heard footsteps coming from around the corner and I scrambled into the bushes, ducking down and shrinking myself as small as I could. I bit the tip of the phone as the group passed, their voices echoing as they grew further away. I tried the number again, this time Aaron picked up.

"Hello?"

"Aaron? I-It's Noah!" I stammered.

"What? Noah, are you okay? What was that about earlier—"

"I-I escaped. I j-just b-broke into someone's house, and—Aaron I-I think I killed them," I said hysterically.

Though in confusion and worry, he calmed me down. *"Okay, Noah. It's gonna be fine,"* he began. *"Tell me what happened."*

I shook my head. "No, no, I can't. Not now. There's too many people.

The staff watched me jump out the window and get over the fence, they'll be on the way."

"Wait, what? Are you okay?"

"No," I said as my voice broke. "E-Everything hurts. Every part of me."

"It's okay. It's okay. I'll come to you. Don't worry."

"Thank you, thank you," I replied as I wiped my face with my sleeve. "Meet me at Shenfield Station."

"Wait, wait—"

"Please, just be there!"

Chapter 9

The Eye of the Storm

I followed the overgrown path towards the train station, the branches from trees entwining together above me. I adjusted my hood as I heard twigs snapping from behind. I glanced over my shoulder, expecting the worse, but I was alone. I turned back and quickly picked up my pace, on the edge of breaking into a run. Another snap occurred and I flinched. I kept moving, keeping my eyes on the bright light ahead. My breathing became heavier as my fear led the day. I flinched once more as a bird flew out from the bush beside me onto another branch. I launched down the path, gripping tightly to the string on my bag.

I reached the light and came to a stop, staring up in awe at the modern buildings and the bustling park in the distance. My throat dried and quivered shortly before clenching my eyes tightly and swallowing, forcing any emotion I had near the surface to the back of my fading mind. I bit my lip as I came back to reality, taking a breath as I followed the signs to my destination.

I managed to keep on my original path, but after a while I had to cross the road (something I'd been desperately avoiding). Cars sped past me in a flash, the wind shooting through me as each one passed at unbearable velocities. I managed to locate a crossing at the same time as a young family. I kept close behind them as we made our way to the other side. My pace was a lot faster than the woman's, however, and I noticed her glance at me with suspicion as I kept close behind her two children that were running in front.

We reached the path and I sighed with relief, my heart feeling like it could finally beat again, although that feeling was only short-lived. I watched as the woman wheeled her pram faster and grabbed a hold of her child's hand then telling the other to hold onto their sibling's, all whilst keeping her firm eyes on me. I looked away. I knew exactly what she was thinking. I knew what I looked like. I had to trash the old outfit after the attack at the house for an equally battered new one. She could have known who I was. She could have screamed. I could be going back to Ocean Cliff at any minute.

Shut up, Noah.. Keep focused.

I inhaled deeply then followed the path down the hill. It wasn't too steep, it was more like a slope really, but it was one heck of a long one. Thankfully, I made it all the way down without passing another person. The pavement was only thin, so I don't know what I would have done if someone *had* passed by me.

Upon reaching level ground again, I glanced from building to building. There were people everywhere, I couldn't hide from them. Around every corner there was a new group. I didn't dare ask anyone where the station was. I had got to where I was so far by using an online map. I near chucked it when it asked to use my location, but I kept telling myself that it was unlikely for many people to know of my disappearance.

I circled the area several times before I found the entrance to the station. It was hidden by a few trees and bushes. I followed the path down and reached the car park. I cautiously made my way up the steps and approached the outside machine. I reached into my pocket and pulled out the stolen cash. My hand shook, rattling the very little coins I had then peered over the shoulder of the man in front to see what he was doing. I couldn't see anything, the sun was too bright and was just making the screen appear black. I pulled at my sleeves as he took his ticket and stepped away. I took a look at the growing queue behind me and shuffled forwards. I inhaled deeply as I randomly tapped my finger on the monitor, a sound playing each time I chose an option. I kept hearing impatient movements from behind which rattled me further into a spiralling mess. But eventually, the ticket printed. I yanked it from the slot and dashed into the reception, leaving the annoyed group.

I stumbled in and I felt what remaining blood I had drain as I saw how many people there were. There were only two platforms, but everywhere in between was packed. I joined the crowd that waited below the digital board to see why the place was as it was. There had been a delay. On Platform 1. I overheard what was being said.

"The train broke down."

I bent my ticket back and forth, scanning across it, praying that that wasn't my train.

'One-way, Adult Ticket, Shenfield Station – Platform 2'

I gave an exaggerated sigh, which led to me catching eyes with the large security guard who was stood by the ticket gate, arms crossed. With my body still shivering, I jumped back and headed into one of the shops along the side. I felt the guard's eyes on me as I stepped through the detectors. I slipped my ticket into my pocket and returned my attention to the left over cash. £3.50. It couldn't get me much. I'd used one of my water bottles already. The breakfast bars were still with me, but I tried one and almost spat it out again. It tasted like cardboard. I didn't throw them away, though. I left them as a last resort.

I weaved sluggishly through each aisle, the pain from the dog bite flaring up. I lifted the bottom of my trouser to check the damage and saw a dark tint underneath the bandage that I had pulled down from the other cut on my leg. I lowered my trouser again then limped my way to a shelf. I glanced at each of the prices, debating over what I'd need more. I had to believe that Aaron would have something with him, so I took the chance and chose the bandage box over any food. I rubbed my eyes and stepped over to the counter.

The cashier scanned my item and tapped across his monitor. "£2.99, please."

I shakily dropped the coins in his hand. He took a glance at the one wrapped around my hand already and flashed an uncomfortable smile. I snatched the box and turned to leave but froze as I was called back.

"Um, do you not want your change?"

I stuttered. "Uh, um, keep it."

I swung out the door and opened my bag to drop the box inside. I didn't get further than a few steps before the security guard stopped me. I gasped and covered my face with the side of my hood on instinct.

"Excuse me, but can I check inside your bag, sir?" he said gruffly. "It's just for security."

I stared up at him, my chest tingling and throat constricting as the bag strap slid onto his hand. I didn't say a word, I couldn't move. I was fused to the floor, my weight draining to my feet. The moment was drained, the world around me throbbing, and through the corners of my eyes, the crowd became a blur, as did the guard. He stuck the tips of his fingers into the top, dragged them outwards, and dug into the material. He rummaged through

252

the items, pulling each one to the surface to inspect them before letting them go. I was hoping he'd stop before he'd go any further, but he eventually found the pair of scissors. The blade gleamed as the lights reflected off of it, the inside of it still dyed a dark red.

"What are these for?" he questioned.

I guiltily pulled my hood down. "The bandages," I replied. "I had an accident before I left the house and just took them with me." I pulled up my trouser leg. "See?"

He bent over slightly to gain a closer look. "That looks pretty deep. What happened?"

"It was nothing… Just an accident with a dog. I tried to cover it up, but ran out of bandages, so I bought some here since I was coming anyway."

"You didn't call an ambulance? Dog bites can be serious." He lowered the scissors into the bag again.

"No," I said bluntly. "I'm fine." I took the bag from his hands and yanked it shut.

He pulled me back by the arm. "I'm sorry about what happened, but I don't know if I can let you get on the train like this, especially with the scissors. It's for health and safety."

I continued backing into the growing crowd. "I'm fine!"

He tightened his grip. "Look, mate. I don't want to make a scene here, alright? Enough has already happened today, I don't want you to cause anything more."

I glanced at the platform board. My train was arriving any second. "Listen, I need to get that train. I'm sorry." I twisted my arm out of his grip and hid amongst the hoard behind me.

The guard yelled for me as he pushed through the group, but I lost him once I dashed up the stairs to my platform. The train was beginning to slow, the mechanics whirring as it strained and hissed at those on the platform. There were a sequence of beeps and the doors slid across with the passengers on board jumping off, pushing past those on the platform. In a panicked scramble, I gripped at the side of the train and hoisted myself over the gap into the cabin. I swung around a pole that was fixed inside and collapsed into a seat beside the window just as drops of rain began to spit down. I yanked the hood of my jumper down and panted, inhaling deeply. The train sounded another series of beeps before the doors scraped across and sealed shut.

With a starting jolt from the train, a voice came from overhead. *"Welcome aboard the Greater Anglia service to Stratford. This train will be stopping at Chelmsford, Ingatestone, Shenfield, Romford, and Stratford. This train has six carriages."*

I gripped tightly at my bag as I watched through the window at the passing station. I ran my fingers through my hair and leant back in relief. I took a look around the compartment and was surprised by how little people there were. With the pack that was at the station, I suspected mayhem on here. Each person was sat at their own table, all with another space to spread out. With the realisation that I had actually made it this far, an overwhelming tiredness joined. I opened the drawstring bag and pulled out my journal. I flicked through each page, reading over my own oblivious words.

Moments later, we pulled away from another station. The carriage was now full, with the chairs around my table now taken by two young children and a woman beside me. The book had fallen from my hands and disappeared. In a surge of panic, I jerked forwards, causing the boy and girl to flinch.

The woman jumped too. "I'm so sorry, I didn't mean to wake you."

I stuttered as I spotted my journal on the floor. "W-What?"

"You were asleep. I'm sorry if I woke you," she repeated calmly.

I fumbled for the book. "N-No, don't worry, um... I d-didn't even realise I fell asleep. I'm very... out of it these days."

She smiled. "That's alright. We all have days like that."

I nodded with a rash look on my face as the voiceover sounded again. It read the same message, only with a slight difference.

"The next station is Shenfield."

I exhaled in relief and slipped my journal back in my bag then pulled out the phone. That's when another storm of chaotic bewilderment consumed me. I hadn't even noticed until now, even though it must had been in plain sight the whole time but...

The date on the phone read the 21st of June. June. I was taken to Sector 1 in March. There's no way it was that long. There's no way.

I quickly shut the phone down and bit the top in shock. I swung my head to the window and stared out at the fully blossomed flora that lined the track, some of it was even dangling over the edge of the metal fence that separated the town from the train mechanics. I quickly turned to the woman next to me.

"Sorry, is it okay if I get by?"

"Sure," she replied and shuffled off the seat.

I shimmied into the aisle, slinging my bag over my shoulders as I turned around. "Thank you."

She gave another gentle grin as I wobbled towards the doors. I held onto the pole beside me as the train skidded along the tracks to a stop beside the station's platform. With a few beeps beforehand, the doors slid across and I hopped down to the concrete along with several other people, all of us becoming splashed by the heavy rain that was ricocheting from the train. I stayed with the group as we scampered down the stairs to reach the main station. I kept an eye out for Aaron. I had no clue where he'd actually be, or if he'd even show up at all, so after the ticket gate claimed my ticket I took the phone out once more and called his number.

He picked up straight away. "*Noah?*" The line was crackled.

"Aaron, I'm here."

"*What?*"

"I'm here. I'm at the station, where are you?"

"*I'm by the entrance.*"

"Okay, I'm coming up." I lowered the phone and rushed towards the next staircase.

It led me to the larger reception area where another swarm of people were hiding from the growing storm outside. I waded through to the centre, spinning and searching for Aaron's face. As I went to call again, I lurched forwards as a hand touched my shoulder. I faced the figure and had tears build in my eyes to see Aaron's drenched face.

He chuckled. "Taxi for Noah Coleman?"

I sighed and embraced him. "Oh, Aaron."

He hugged me back. "Noah, mate, what are you doing?"

"I needed to get out of that place. They were… They were breaking my mind."

We separated.

"We've gotta get you outta here. Come on, my car's outside."

"Okay."

He took my hand and we sped out to the car park. He took out his keys, unlocked the doors, and we both sat down.

"So, tell me exactly what's going through your head right now." He turned the keys in the ignition. "Because I don't think I'm up to date."

The engine rumbled as we reversed out.

"Okay, so these people, that doctor, Caleb, they're planning something. Some kind of project."

"What's the project?" he asked as we pulled onto the main road.

"Something like 'The Other Side Project'. It's a mind control project. They're taking anyone ever convicted of a crime and using them for mind control."

I caught sight of his doubtful glance.

"I know it sounds farfetched but think about it. Everyone who was in Wyegate have gone! No one can find them, right?"

"It's all over the news," he replied. "It's not just Wyegate, either. Another prison's been emptied too."

"Which one?" I asked.

He shrugged. "I don't remember the name. It was a women's prison."

"Okay, so do you agree that something must be happening for them to all be disappearing without a trace?"

"I do."

The rain fell harder.

"Do you remember when I was arrested after I attacked Ryan? What I said?"

"Yeah."

"There was a page. The detective said it was from a student's story, I could accept that, but then there was a USB. On that USB it had everything mapped out about the project, which connected to the story."

"Was it a part of the story?"

"The USB had one of the *teacher's* names on it. Then after I told Caleb I had found it, I was knocked out and given the drug in the lab."

"Noah, the report said you were on LSD. You sure it wasn't a bad trip?"

"You know me, you saw me before work, I never took anything."

He nodded as we turned down a lane. "I do know you, that's why I said in my statement that you were clean, but that didn't match with the evidence they had."

"Either way, something happened. I haven't quite figured it out yet, but when I was down in that lab, I was told a phrase. Over and over again. 'Monarch's fly in the rain'." Even saying it myself made me feel dizzy and disorientated.

"As in the butterflies?"

"Yeah. They said it on the news, and I heard, which made me black out. That's what caused me to kill that doctor. Another patient said that's what they wanted to do, and it stuck with me. It was the same thing that I had with Ryan." I leant my head against the window as I flashed back to each scene, the pain of the phrase flickering in my head which caused me to wince. "We can't ever say it again."

Aaron obviously noticed the pain I was in and rubbed my shoulder. "It's alright. Let's just take a break from all this stuff. I'm taking us to a hotel. I already booked the room."

I chuckled weakly. "That's eager."

"I needed a holiday," he replied with a smile.

I gestured at the flooding appearing on the road. "It's not exactly picturesque."

We both laughed.

"Please tell me you have dinner."

He pointed to the back seat. "No, but I got money, plus I brought some stuff I thought we might need."

I glanced over to see a small suitcase and a plastic bag with what seemed to have toiletries inside. "You really are prepared," I said.

"I've learnt to be prepared after seeing into your life."

I sat back and laughed sarcastically before closing my eyes and falling asleep again. Aaron later woke me, and I peered through the rain-covered windscreen to see the hotel. He patted my leg to get my attention.

"Hey, we're here."

"Where?" I questioned.

"We're just off the M25."

"How long was I asleep for?"

"Not long," he said as he took the keys from the ignition. "About five minutes."

"Was that it?" I questioned again.

"We didn't go very far. I wasn't sure where you wanted us to go." He patted me again. "Come on, let's get inside before we get flooded."

I nodded then stepped out of the car and onto the soaked pavement. I turned to Aaron as he hoisted the suitcase from the backseat and began wheeling it towards reception.

"Let's go." He clicked the button on his keys and the car flashed locked.

Together, we hurried inside. I kept my hood up to cover my face as we approached the man behind the counter. Thankfully, the rain had given me an excuse as to leave it up.

The receptionist smiled as Aaron pulled his phone from his pocket. "Hello. You alright?"

"Yeah, yeah," Aaron replied. "It's a bit wet."

The man nodded and glanced out the large window beside him that overlooked the car park. "It is a bit." He turned back. "Are you here for a room?"

"I am, yes." Aaron showed him the information on his phone. "It should be under 'East'."

"East…" He typed across his keyboard, the clattering echoing across the almost empty room. "Ah, here it is."

The two continued their transaction and I glanced over my shoulder at the sofas in the waiting area. There was a family, similar to the one I broke into. They had a son who was joyfully climbing across his parents who were busy seeming to try to find the correct direction to their destination. I closed my eyes and turned away. They looked exactly like them. I felt the tingle across my back and the weight grow on my shoulders.

They're fine. They're fine. The doctors were right behind me, the people in the other houses saw me, help would have come. They're fine.

I heard footsteps grow closer to me and I opened my eyes again.

"I got the key card," Aaron said. "Room 52. I also got a menu."

I couldn't bring myself to form any words, so all I could manage was a frisky nod.

"Okay." He placed his hand on my back and directed me towards the stairwell. Halfway up, he whispered to me. "If anyone asks, my name's Rob East."

I chuckled. "Okay."

We looped up several flights before we found the sign on the wall that read where our room was. I kept close to Aaron as we searched for the door, passing several people as we did, all of whom saw my face. It's been hours since I got out of Ocean Cliff, it's bound to end up on the news at some point. We had to turn back a few times, and almost tried to open Room 62. I wasn't really helping find the room, so I left it down to Aaron, but his glasses were swamped with rain and blurred most of his already poor vision.

258

Eventually, we found ours, and with my first moment to relax, I collapsed front first onto the mountain-high bed.

Aaron laughed as he laid the suitcase down and approached the curtains. "And relax." He glanced out of the window at the setting sun.

I rolled onto my back then sat up. "I haven't been on a real bed in over a year. You don't get to judge me." I kicked off my shoes then winced loudly as I caught the broken skin around my ankle.

Aaron quickly rushed over and stood beside me. "Are you okay?"

I shook my head and carefully rolled up both of my trouser legs. I unravelled the destroyed bandages and revealed the deep, dark patches on my skin.

Aaron bit at his lip as he saw the state of me. "Noah, what-"

I then removed my damp clothes to reveal similar slashes across my arms.

"How did that happen?" he questioned as he knelt on the floor to examine my legs.

I pointed at different parts. "Dog, dog, barbed wire, barbed wire." I passed him my bag. "There's bandages and scissors in there."

He swiftly took the bag from me and emptied it out across the carpet. "Jesus, Noah." He scrambled to open the box then yanked one of the rolls from it. "What did you do?"

"I had to crawl through razor wire to get over the fence in the hospital, I didn't know it could go that deep." I explained as he rushed into the bathroom with the bloodied scissors.

"You do know that's the reason they put it on prisons, right?" he called with a gush of the tap.

"I know," I said as he returned with a damp towel and the clean equipment.

"What happened with the dog then?" he asked as he dabbed the areas around my injuries clean.

"Um…" I took a pause as I watched Aaron carefully conceal my left leg with the cotton. "I ran to someone's house for help, but no one was in when I got there. So, I broke in and looked for something to help then the family came home, the dog found me and bit me."

He glanced up at me with worry in his eyes.

"The dog was a police dog, and the woman was an officer. The dog kept at me until I… um… dealt with it."

259

He moved on to my arms. "You said on the phone that… you thought you'd killed them. What happened to them?"

My lip quivered. "I… I hid. I heard them come home and I hid. After the dog attacked, I cut the woman's wrist and threw the man over the banister. The woman came back, and pepper sprayed me, and then I… tried to choke her."

"Tried to?" He gently tugged at the wrapping.

"I stopped myself, but after I let go she passed out. She was still breathing when I left."

Aaron wrapped up my final cut. "Well, then. I think there's a chance they're okay." He rubbed my back and stepped over to the table where the menu was laying. "Are you hungry?"

I nodded.

"I'm gonna go order something. You'll be okay on your own, right?"

"Y-Yeah. I'll be fine."

He smiled then headed back out to the corridor.

I sighed deeply then glanced down at my wrist. I swerved my I.D. band around with my fingertips then rose from the bed, shivering from the lack of layers covering my body. I reached for the scissors and stepped into the bathroom. I switched the light on and leant against the sink, staring at my reflection in the mirror. I widened the blades then snapped the plastic band off of my wrist. It fell onto the surface surrounding the sink as I looked back up at my reflection then took the scissors to my hair. I snipped at the top and snapped chunks from the bottom. The clumps of hair floated down into the porcelain until I was satisfied with my new look. I dropped the scissors and ruffled my fringe to the side. I ran the tap, the hair in the sink getting washed away, and I splashed my face with my hands. It ran down my cheeks as I gave in to my guilt and burst into tears. I gasped in and out heavily as I tried to breathe until I chose to return to the bedroom and lay down.

I curled up underneath the thin sheet. I didn't mean to, but the moment my eyes closed, I fell asleep. When I awoke, it was much later. The sun had gone down, and the outside was dark. The only light on in the room was the bedside lamp. I rolled over and saw Aaron stood by the table below the television, which was playing a run of adverts.

"Aaron?"

He glanced over his shoulder and smiled. "Hey. I was worried you were never gonna wake up again."

I pushed myself up and leant against the backboard. "What're you doing?"

He stepped to the side and revealed to me a pizza box and a large bottle of lemonade. "Making dinner." He brought the box over and placed it beside me.

I lifted the lid and stared at the slices.

"What made you choose this?" I said with a smile.

"I thought it was the nicest thing for you to eat." He placed the bottle on the set of drawers beside him and hoisted himself onto the bed. "Nice hairdo."

I chuckled as I lifted a pizza slice. "I don't even remember if I like pizza or not."

"Everyone likes pizza. Unless there's pineapple on it."

"What's wrong with pineapple?" I asked as I bit into the slice.

"You don't put fruit on a pizza, mate. It's just wrong."

"Agree to disagree."

We both smiled at each other, and Aaron kissed my forehead. "I've missed you so much."

"I missed you too."

He leant his head against my shoulder.

"Until you bashed my pizza choices."

He shot up and jokingly hit me with his pillow. "Oh, you piece of... peperoni!"

"Did you mean *pizza* peperoni?"

We both laughed loudly, almost knocking the box onto the floor.

We went quiet. "Was this what I was like before?" I asked.

"You certainly had a cheek on you, that's for sure."

I giggled and nuzzled my head into him. He leant his head against mine and my smile faded.

"Let's hope I wake up knowing that tomorrow."

Aaron stroked his finger across my hand. "Is it that bad? Your amnesia? I know what you've got is really rare, but there's not much else I know about it."

"I don't know much either," I replied. "But my memory usually messes up overnight, but it's only past memories that have gone. Most came back when I remembered getting drugged, but it's all fading again."

"So how do you remember?"

"I write it down," I said as I pulled my journal out. "If I write it then it seems to stay." I skimmed my fingers through the pages.

Aaron scoffed. "That's a lot of memories."

"You're telling me," I returned with a smile.

"What happens if you don't write in it?"

"I forget. Of course, sometimes I forget anyway." I placed the book back and continued eating.

After we finished dinner, Aaron unzipped the suitcase and pulled out two pairs of pyjamas. I took one pair and changed into them whilst I watched him change from the bed. I made my body smaller, bringing my knees up and hiding them underneath my top as Aaron stepped out of the bathroom. I gazed over him as he pulled his pyjama top down his chest and carefully hooked his glasses over his ears, brushing the spare waves of hair that drooped down from his already unkempt blonde mess. As he straightened out, he caught sight of me staring, a glimmer of the amber light shimmering against the silver metal frame of his glasses. He smirked in a devilish way.

"What?" he chuckled.

I turned away in embarrassment, my cheeks becoming blushed as I chuckled with him. "Nothing," I said with a shrug.

I looked back up and watched happily as Aaron scampered across the carpet and crawled onto the bed. He edged closer to me, nuzzling his head against mine as we both grinned. I began to loosen my position, slowly stretching my legs out and resting my hand on his neck as I brought him closer. Aaron kissed my cheek gently, remaining cautious of how fragile a state the rest of my body was in. I let my hand slip down his arm until I found his fingers, letting mine rest there as we continued to nuzzle our heads against each other.

"Why did you stay?" I questioned softly. "You could have just left me the day after I went to Ocean Cliff, but you didn't. Why?"

We separated, a sense of pain growing behind his eyes.

He sighed. "Honestly... I don't know. I know I could have left, I know I could have never even said goodbye to you, but it wasn't like I had much else going on in my life."

"But I was meant to be there for good. I wasn't going to get out. It was all fixed."

"I know," he continued, looking away as he spoke. "I guess I just had hope that I'd get a call one day saying that you could come home. I thought that if I just waited one more day... then I'd get one." He chuckled half-heartedly. "Instead, I got a call from you." He turned back to face me.

"But still..." I picked at my nails. "You know what I've done. I killed someone, I probably killed those people in that house!" My voice fell shaky. "I'm not a good person."

Aaron lightly scratched the top of my hand. "Neither am I..."

I lifted myself onto my knees and stared at him in concern. "What do you mean?"

He shuffled and brought his knees to his chest. "In Wyegate, before you came, I had a different roommate. He wasn't the nicest – when comparing to the types of people in Wyegate."

I flashed a smile. There certainly was quite an array of people in there.

"He told rumours about a fair few people," he continued. "Including me."

"What did he say?"

He shrugged. "He told everyone I was gay. He seemed to realise before I did."

"How'd he figure it out?"

A smirk grew across his face as he glanced up at me. "Not a lot of straight guys in prison sit around knitting blankets, do they?"

We both laughed and I nodded in agreement. "That is true. I mean, some of them seemed a little bit... you know?"

"Oh for sure," he replied. "The guys in Cell 78 definitely had some kind of thing going on."

We both smiled gleefully at each other before both of us fell into a sense of sorrow.

"What happened after that guy... you know?"

He picked at the wood on the bedside table. "Not a lot. Y'know, just the usual homophobic responses. Shouting slurs, threatening me, the so-called Christians trying to 'save me'."

I felt a surge of pain rush through me. That's just what happened to me in there. I was obviously a bit more queer in appearance than Aaron was. Those same apparent 'Christians' yelling at me, reciting the same passage over and over again, explaining in vivid detail what was going to happen to me in Hell. It hurt for sure, but it wasn't every Christian that did this. The majority didn't care as long as I stayed out of their business.

There was one guy – he was Muslim – and he's the one who helped me through some of the rougher days. Him and his wife. I met her in visitation whilst my brother came to see me, and although her figure and face was wrapped in coverings, her gentle nature shone through. The both of them gave me support – Aaron too. The reason as to why they helped. His wife was a lesbian, but they married to keep the family at peace when partnership was necessary. When it wasn't, she could run back to her true love. She got lucky when the husband got arrested.

It was helpful since I actually hadn't come out to my family yet. It was nice to have some parental figure to fall back on for support. If only I could remember their names, but sadly, that bit of information wasn't there to stay.

"It died down over time," Aaron said, continuing his story. "Most of the men got transferred or just started ignoring me, but when that guy started stirring things up again, I think a few of us snapped."

I edged closer. "Aaron, what—"

His eyes became glassy. "We didn't plan it to end the way it did, we just wanted to get him to stop, but…" He looked to the ceiling, a scene playing over in his head. "I messed up the pills we were gonna give him and he… overdosed. He died because of me."

I felt a stab in my chest and a crawling across my skin. "What? I-I don't really—What happened to you?"

"Nothing. The guards thought it was an accident, which it was but…he did a fair few drugs himself, so it was no surprise. I didn't sleep for a week after. I hated myself."

"Oh, Aaron." I fell against him, wrapping my arms around him and embracing him as he let out a scoff.

"The next month, you turned up." We separated slightly. "And… well…" He smirked. "Do you remember what happened then?"

"Yeah." I flashed him a tearful grin. "Why didn't you tell me?"

He shook his head. "I don't know." He broke into tears. "I don't know!"

I pulled him towards me, and he sobbed into my shoulder. I rocked him back and forth, cradling his head against me.

"It's okay," I said quietly. "It's okay."

His body trembled as did his voice. "I'm so sorry, Noah. I'm so sorry, I should have told you."

"It's fine. I know now. It happened and you can't change that." I lifted him up. "You can just make sure it doesn't happen again, right?"

He shook his head and removed his glasses to wipe his eyes. "Right…" He glanced up at me, darting his eyes around as he tried to see what was actually me.

I chuckled and took his glasses from his hands. I cleaned the lenses then slung them over my eyes, straining at how blurred the world became. "Whoa…"

I heard Aaron sniffle and giggle. "You know I can't tell what you look like, right?"

"You are horrifically blind."

"I know. I'm sure you look fabulous, though."

I slid them off and returned them to him. "You look a lot better than me."

He scoffed as he hooked them back over his ears, although he took them off again soon after. "Thanks."

I smiled. "I like you with them on."

We rested our foreheads together and nuzzled some more. Aaron lifted his hand and gently placed it on my neck, bringing me towards him. He kissed down my cheek as I cuddled against him. We slowly drifted onto our backs and buried ourselves beneath the sheets.

Aaron wrapped his arm around me and spoke softly. "I love you."

I blissfully closed my eyes as the words settled into me. "I love you too."

He switched the lamp off, the room falling dark as we both became overcome with the day. His arm stretched back over me, and I held his hand against my chest.

The morning quickly came. I rolled across the empty mattress as I began to awake then opened my eyes to see Aaron stood at the table below the window. The curtains were slightly drawn, allowing the grey daylight to spill in with the heavy rain slamming against the window. I groaned as I rubbed my eyes, and Aaron glanced over his shoulder.

"Morning," he said quietly.

"Morning," I replied as I kept my head rested on the sunken pillow.

"You feeling okay?"

"I am in… immense pain," I said nonchalantly.

Aaron gave a quick smirk then stepped over with a travel mug in his hands. He crawled back onto the bed and sat beside me. I pulled myself up, straining from the aches over my body, then leant against the backboard.

"I would've made you one, but I wasn't sure when you were gonna wake up," he said as he held the cup in his hands.

"It's okay," I replied. "What is it?"

He peeled the silicone lid off the top and showed me the drink inside, steam escaping into the air. "Tea."

"What does it taste like?" I questioned.

He paused. "Leaves, milk, and hot water."

"Ew."

He chuckled. "I didn't think you'd approve."

I smiled as he looked down at me.

"What's the plan then?" he continued.

I shook my head and sighed. "I don't know."

"We need to leave as quick as we can. After you fell asleep last night, your story was on the news."

"What did it say?" I asked in urgency.

"About how you had escaped, and about how you broke into that house."

I ran my hand through my fringe and leant my head back, closing my eyes. "Oh, God… We need to get out of here." I scrambled forwards, but quickly collapsed onto my front wincing as I put pressure on my cuts.

Aaron lowered his drink onto the side table and lurched over to keep me down. "Hey, you alright?"

I nodded through gritted teeth as I swung my legs over the side of the bed and sat up. "I'm fine."

He rubbed his hand on my back. "I know we need to leave, but we need to do it carefully. At the minute, no one knows we're here. We need to keep it that way."

"But what if someone recognises me around the hotel? What about the receptionist?"

"You never spoke to the receptionist. He never saw your face, he only saw mine. I wasn't on the news, I'll just seem like any other visitor here."

I faced him. "Well, what do we do? I can't live here my whole life."

"I know," he returned with another rub of my back. "We're gonna have to drive through that somewhere." He gestured to outside. "The rain should keep us out of view."

"Still. Where do we go?"

He sighed deeply. "I don't know… It'll be impossible to get out of the

266

country now. We don't have enough money to get petrol for too long a journey, the friends who got us the fake identities before are missing, we can't go home – they're probably tearing it apart as we speak."

I drew my gaze to the carpet, gripping at the bedsheet in thought. "Are you sure there's no one left that could help us?"

Aaron shrugged. "Not from Wyegate but…" His eyes lit up. "There is someone."

With no other choice, we swiftly gathered our belongings, stuffing whatever we could from the hotel into our bags. Aaron gave me a new outfit to wear. I changed into it as he changed into his. He re-examined my wounds before we snuck out of our room. It was still very early morning. Everyone else in the hotel was still fast asleep, so we managed to get down to the lobby without raising anyone's suspicions. I kept my several hoods firmly up as Aaron dropped the key card into the deposit box.

"Alright, let's go," he said as we pushed through the spinning doors to the outside.

I shuddered at the thundering flood that poured from the black clouds above as we dashed for the car. Aaron swung the suitcase into the back seats as I took my place in the passenger's. He clambered into the driver's side and jammed the keys into the ignition. The car rumbled and the radio crackled as Aaron pulled out of the car park. We splashed against the rain on the road as we made our way into the storm.

"Are you sure this guy can help us?"

"I'm sure. He's helped me before."

"What did he do?"

"Well, remember I was arrested for all of those diamond thefts?"

"And other thefts," I said with a smile.

He waved his hand jokingly. "One crime at a time. Anyway, he helped me stash the stuff they never found. He even sold a few to get me some money."

"Was that where the money for the house came from?"

He darted his eyes around and grinned.

I chuckled. "I thought you never wanted to sell your stash?"

"I didn't, but desperate times call for desperate measures, and this is one of those desperate times."

After about half an hour of driving, we rolled up in some raggedy street.

Graffiti and rubbish seemed to have taken over, whilst feral cats hissed at one another for the last scrap of meat. The people seemed to match the area, although there was barely any of them about. Just the parents rushing to get their kids into the car for school, whilst the drunks were just coming home from the night before.

I turned to Aaron. "Lovely spot."

"I know. It used to be nice around here, but then there was some big council scandal, and everything went downhill. I guess that's why Marco lives here, nobody wants to come down this way and it's not too much of a threat for the police to be around. It gets a lot nicer around the corner."

"So how do you know this Marco? How'd you meet?"

"I tried to rob his daughter. She caught me and I thought that I was going down, but then she introduced me to her dad. He's like this underground, go-to guy. He's nice enough, but you'll know if you're not in his good books."

We turned down an alley, hiding the car in a small archway as to keep it out of sight of the roads. We stepped onto the pavement and scampered through the mud and puddles to a door that was hidden behind a piece of fabric that draped down from the balcony above.

Aaron knocked on the door then whispered to me. "Just a heads up, he's not so good at English so it can get a bit confusing sometimes."

"Oh. Where's he from?"

"Italy."

The door then swung inwards and revealed a towering build of a man. The mere sight of him sent a surge of unease through me, knowing that he could probably break my legs just by tapping them. His square face was covered by a thick beard, but through it I could see a smile form at the sight of Aaron.

"A Ron!" he said with a booming voice.

"Hey, Marco," Aaron replied sheepishly. "Listen, um, we're in need of your assistance."

He opened his arms out wide. "No problem, no problem! Come in, come in! Lousy British weather out there." He took him by the arm and pulled him inside.

I trailed along anxiously behind them, staring at the dark room we entered. It was overwhelmingly bare. Just a sofa and a rickety dining table was there to fill it whilst an orange lightbulb swung about to bring the room aglow. Aaron was released from Marco and joined my side, kissing my cheek.

"It's gonna be fine," he said quietly. "He can hide us until we find a plan. Okay?"

I held his hand. "Okay."

Marco zipped back to us. "Who is your friend, A Ron?"

I let my grasp go quickly but Aaron swooped it back, holding onto me tightly. "This is Noah, my boyfriend. He's in some trouble which is why I thought to come to you."

"Oh! Boyfriend, boyfriend. *Mie scuse*. What is the problem you have? Does boyfriend have the problem? Did you give him problem?"

Aaron waved his hands and chuckled. "Oh, no, no. It's nothing to do with boyfriend stuff, it's the law we need help with."

He laughed. "Oh, I see. I thought you been a naughty boy, A Ron. Now I understand. Crime is much easier to fix. Follow, follow." He marched towards another door that he barely managed to fit through as Aaron fought to contain his embarrassment.

"What did he mean about you giving me a problem?" I whispered to him.

Aaron held me close as we headed through the strange building. "Oh, nothing, nothing. It's just… I came here with… a problem of that nature before."

"Oh."

We entered a side room. It was much more appealing to the other one, it's walls newly painted but it's floorboards still creaked. We settled together on a sofa whilst Marco stepped into the kitchen.

"You want drinks?"

"We're good for now, thanks."

He wandered back out and sat on the opposite sofa. "So, what is the problem?"

Aaron cleared his throat. "We need a place to stay. We're… in a lot of trouble."

"You are always welcome, A Ron. I can clear the room upstairs for you. Do you know how long you'll be here for?"

"We don't know."

"That's okay, I can tell you when I can't keep you." He stood up. "Is there anything else you need?"

269

Aaron rose too. "No, no, we just need a place to stay."

Marco patted his back. "I can do that. Do you have bags?"

"Yeah, in the car out back."

"How many?"

"Just one."

"Alright, that's good. I will go do your room." He smiled at us both and rushed out to the staircase.

I quickly shuffled over to Aaron. "I don't know if I can stay here," I whispered. "It doesn't feel right."

"I know, I know. But this is the only choice we have." He stepped closer and wrapped his arms around me. "It's just until we figure things out." He kissed my cheek. "I'm gonna get the suitcase. I love you."

I watched as he headed back to the alley. "I love you too."

It's nightfall now. I'm the only one awake. Aaron's tucked into the rickety old bed of the spare room whilst I'm stood here by the mouldy window as rain poured outside. They say that scientists are unsure on why the weather was being so erratic, and they still couldn't figure the mysteries of the monarchs. Even after months. This meant that whatever The O.S. Project is, hasn't been put into full effect yet.

There wasn't much me and Aaron could do, we just sat out the day, trying to distract ourselves from the madness of our lives. This was done mostly through the power of television. Although, that didn't help either. Every time we'd change a channel, the news would flash up with the words 'Breaking News' and my name below it.

The main footage they used was from the house raid, showing what monstrosities I caused after being out for less than an hour, but as well as this they'd show Ocean Cliff and the reports on Dr Wilks. Each time they persisted on how dangerous I was, and that under no circumstances should I be engaged with by anyone. They even insisted to not engage with Aaron. He's not even the fugitive. Well... I guess he is now. The police don't know that, but since he's not around to be questioned, they assume he's with me, and so guilty by association.

By the time the sun had set, Marco was kind enough to prepare dinner for us. It wasn't much, but I was thankful for anything. We sat together at the table, eating in an awkward silence. After, Aaron assisted in clearing up whilst I cowered away in the bedroom alone, and that's where I stayed until now. I was tossing and turning, pain and burning searing through my bandages each time it pressed against the rough sheets. The hotel had spoiled us. Going from crisp sheets that were remade every day to crusty, ripped ones was quite the turn off. But I'm not complaining. We're safe. We're together.

The rain dripped down the window pane, curling in different directions and merging with itself until it gathered together on the mossy ledge. As the clock ticked over to twelve, there was a flash of neon outside. I jumped and stared out at the road. It's sirens were loud, and its lights were blinding. I shuddered as I read 'POLICE' across its doors then stepped into the darkness as it sped away.

I adjusted the sleeves of my pyjamas then crawled back beside Aaron. I ran my hands through my fringe and rested my elbows on my knees. I glanced at him. He was peacefully snuggled up in the duvet. I turned back and sighed. I know Aaron's scared of what's happening around him – every single friend he's ever had was missing. Most were living their honest lives, just as we were, but then I went. Then a year later, his friends went. At least I couldn't remember who I'd lost to this project. He could.

Then it was like my thoughts had awoken him. He shuffled and stretched his legs out then reached for his glasses upon seeing me upright.

"Noah?" he whispered. "Are you alright?"

"I'm fine. I didn't mean to wake you."

He sat up. "Nah, it's fine. What's up?"

I shrugged. "Can't sleep."

"What's on your mind?"

I sighed. "I can't stop thinking about that house. Those people. What I did to them. They were innocent people who had their lives ruined because of me. The news says they all survived, but what if that's made it worse? They've gotta live with what I did to them. And the boy, God! He's probably scarred for life."

Aaron rubbed my back. "Hey, hey, it's alright. They're gonna be alright."

"But how do you know that?"

He sighed. "I don't. But you had no choice. You could have died, Noah."

I chuckled as a tear rolled down my cheek. "I wish I did."

Aaron shuffled onto his knees and hugged me tightly. We fell back against the wall as I sobbed against his shoulder, and he rocked me from side to side.

"Oh, Noah."

"I'm so sorry, Aaron. I'm sorry I wrapped you up in this."

"No, no, no. It's not your fault. It's those people. They've done this. What are they called? The ACC."

I sniffled and sat back. "Yeah... I don't even know who they are."

"Me neither. It was just in your old statement, and I thought it could help you remember if you saw the name again."

I scoffed. "Nobody else wanted me to."

We both slid onto our backs, cuddling against each other as we stared up at the peeling ceiling.

"It's crazy, right?" said Aaron. "What's happening?"

"Mm. You wouldn't think it were true, would you?"

"Do you think we'll be able to get away? Do you really think we'll make it without getting taken?"

I sighed. "I don't know... It's like they're everywhere. When I was in Sector 1, these investigators came to question me with River and Tess. You know, the girls from Layset. It was almost like they knew everything I was gonna tell them... Like they already knew about the project."

Aaron rested on his elbow and turned to me. "Are you saying that other people know about it? Even the police?"

"It would make sense, wouldn't it? Not one person is searching for the missing criminals. No one. The only time when they cared was when they found out Ryan was missing."

"Do you think they took him?"

"I do, and I think the investigators already knew that."

"Jeez..." He rolled onto his back again.

I gazed over at the window, watching the drops curve against the glass. "If we can't get on a plane then we're gonna have to find some other way out of the country."

"What do you suggest?"

"Does Marco still have your stash?"

Chapter 10

Only Chance

In the early morning, we jumped to Marco with our plan.

"You want a boat?"

"Please, Marco," Aaron replied. "It's our only chance to get away."

Marco sat back in his chair, locking his fingers together in thought and resting them on his stomach. "I do know a boat smuggler, I can get a meeting for you, but he is not so nice. To get two men across would require a lot of money."

"That's why we hoped you still had some of my stash left. I know I said that it was yours, but we could really use it."

The wood of the chair creaked as he slowly jogged his leg up and down. "I may have ruby left. The rest has been spent."

"The ruby should be fine," said Aaron desperately. "We'll take anything."

He rose from the dining table with a strain. "I can get you the ruby. It is yours, A Ron. You kept me in business when you in prison." He gave a booming laugh as he headed for the stairs.

Aaron turned to me with a sigh of relief before he noticed my manner. "Hey, it's gonna be alright. Marco knows a lot of people – more than I do. Trust me."

I shook my head. "It's not that," I said breathlessly. "It's me."

He rested his arm over the back of the chair. "What's wrong?"

I presented him my scratched and shaking hand. "It's my meds." I took it back and pulled my sleeves down. "The hospital gave me pills on a daily basis, and I think I'm withdrawing."

Aaron had a sense of uncertainty as he shuffled about to face me. "Do you know what they gave you? Maybe I could get some for you."

"I don't know, I don't remember the names. All I know is that last time I went off them, I was complied, but when I'm on them I barely know what's going on. It's safer if I just power through this."

Aaron nodded. "Okay, but if you feel ill then tell me. I'll help."

"Thanks."

He sat back as Marco clambered down the stairs, another set of footsteps behind him. He held a small box with wrappings flowing through its cracks. He placed it down on the table in front of us then gestured to the figure behind him.

"This is my daughter. She can help find Denzel – he's the smuggler."

"Hi. I'm Bella." She gave a wave of her hand then stood proudly with her arms crossed over her lilac crop top. She was the spitting image of her father. Tall, curved and had thick black hair that curled over itself and onto her light tan skin.

"Hi," Aaron replied. "Thanks for the help."

"No problem. Anythin' for you." She winked. Although she looked like her father, she didn't sound anything like him. It was clear she'd grown up in Britain over Italy. Her accent was full Londoner. She nodded at me. "Who's your friend?"

"He boyfriend, Bella," said Marco as he began opening the box.

"Ah, right. So what's yah name?"

"Noah," I replied meekly.

"Cool. Nice to meet yah."

"You too."

Marco lifted the lid from the box, pulling out the precious gem and holding it amongst its wrappings. "This is it."

Aaron quickly leant close, staring at the ruby in awe. "God, I've missed you." He took it from his hands and cradled it against him.

Marco chuckled. "You remember the worth of it?"

"This one?" He measured it in his palm. "Is this the eight grand one?"

"You've still got your skills, huh, A Ron?"

"Eight thousand pounds? " I questioned.

"Yeah," Aaron replied, showing off his steal to me. "Maybe I should have sold more. I could have been rich."

"You'd still be in prison," remarked Bella. "Stealing them is one thing, but if they knew you sold 'em? Hah, you'd be gone, mate."

"Maybe that wouldn't have been so bad," he said placing the jewel back in its box.

The room fell into silence. It was as if we were mourning people we

274

didn't know.

Bella turned to her father. "Should I meet with Denzel, then?"

"*Si*," he replied. "The sooner the better."

"I'll head out now." She spun herself around the banister but slowed her momentum as Marco called out.

"Be careful, beauty. You are on criminal list! You could get taken next!"

"I'll be careful, *papà*." She then disappeared upstairs.

Marco sighed. "*Mia* Bella. She is in danger as you two are. She had to be taken to the Rilestone."

"Rilestone?" said Aaron. "You mean the prison? HMP Rilestone?"

"Yes. She was away for two years. She got caught helping with a job."

"Rilestone's one of the emptied prisons, ain't it?"

"*Si*... This is why I worry. I am safe, I am never in prison, but she was. We have been watching your case, Noah."

I glanced up at him.

"They call you crazy. You are not crazy. You know the truth of what is happening to the world. Crime is going. Every day I lose a customer, everyday someone comes to me for safety. They are scared. But the public? They are happier. They can go outside happy. The government has had plan for many days. You knew too early, so they send you to that place, and now—"

"The project's started..." I muttered.

"Indeed. You must get on this boat. You must get away."

"What about you two?" asked Aaron. "Why haven't you gone away?"

"We stay to help others like you. We cannot run when people need our help."

Bella returned from the bedrooms with a small backpack hanging from her shoulders. She kissed her father's head and gave us a wave. "*Ciao, papà*. See yah, boys." She then dashed through the back door and out into the alley.

"Goodbye, my beauty." Marco turned back to us. "All that's left for you is to find supplies. I'd give you some, but we have little."

Aaron rose from the table. "It's okay, Marco. You've done plenty for us. We can find some stuff for ourselves." He patted my shoulder and took the ruby. "Come on, Noah."

I followed his lead upstairs and watched him from the doorway as he packed up the small drawstring bag with money then buried the gem beneath his pillow.

"What are we doing?" I asked.

Aaron slung the bag over his shoulder and hooked a cap onto his head. "You don't have to come if you don't want to but I'm going to get us some things to take with us for the boat."

"I'm not letting you go out by yourself. Your face is on the news, you know?"

"Not as much as yours is." He stepped up to the doorway. "If we're alone then we're not as noticeable and we can get away if there's any trouble." He tried to pass me, but I kept my arm stretched out.

"Aaron, I don't want you going out alone."

He sighed. "Fine. We'll stick together, but you'll need to find something to cover your face."

I flicked my hood up. "Okay."

He yanked it back down again. "Noah, everyone looks suspicious in a hoodie. People call the police when you haven't even done anything. Here." He placed a pair of sunglasses in my hand. "Let's go."

I kept close beside Aaron as we strode down the back street of the town centre. Although the sky was grey, I kept the glasses fixed to my face. Thankfully, not too many people were out at this time, but honestly, a crowd might have been useful. In a crowd there are so many faces that you could never focus on just one. When a space is empty, you could stare at every single person and never lose any of them.

Aaron was leading the way, he seemed to know what was needed. He took us into a large store that was lined with shelves of clutter. Not one section was organised, but it seemed to be a popular shop.

I whispered over his shoulder. "What exactly are we looking for?"

He lifted up a metal basket. "Whatever you like. We won't be coming back, and we'll be on that boat a long time." He picked up a bottle of sun cream. "Of course, we don't have much cash left, so try to find basic stuff to keep us alive." He shook the bottle. "Like so. Skin cancer is no joke. Plus, we can't risk going to a doctor's surgery."

We scoped around the store, glancing at different items, tossing some aside and some into the basket. The funny thing is the part I got most excited about was getting a toothbrush. I haven't brushed my teeth in days, and I was looking forward to fresh breath again.

276

With the basket filling to the brim, I found myself in the kitchen section. I gazed over each pot and pan until I fixed my eyes on the pair of scissors that was hanging from its display rail. I shuddered and glanced at the slices on my arm, thinking back to the house once more. I covered my mouth with my hood as an older lady passed me with a bright smile. She came to a stop beside me and began straining to reach the egg cups on the bottom shelf. After a while, she started to wince, and so I quickly bent down and grabbed the item for her.

"Here." I placed them into her trolley and flashed a quick smile.

"Oh, thank you." She gave a quaint chuckle. "It's not often people help me out. Especially ones so young."

"I'm happy to help," I said, edging away until I backed into another shopper and had my glasses slip from my face.

"Sorry, mate," the man said as I scrambled to pick up the now shattered glasses.

In a panic, I slung my hood back up and dashed away to find Aaron. He was searching through the craft aisle, blissfully stroking wool fibres as if this were any other day. I skidded to stop beside him, panting and shaking.

He glanced up at me. "Noah, I told you about the hood—where are your glasses?"

I presented the broken mess. "They fell off, shattered, people saw my face, but I don't think they know who I am."

He dropped the wool back on the shelf. "Okay, well don't panic. Panicking will only bring attention to us."

"I know that, it's just—I'm kinda freaking out here, Aaron. Every person I see is looking at me."

He sighed and pushed me around by my shoulder. "Alright, we better go. I found the most important things. I got a bit carried away in this shop." He chuckled and hurried me towards the checkout before he was pulled back by a curly-haired woman. He jumped and turned to her. "Yes?"

She smiled. "Sorry, it's just, I saw this fall out of your pocket." She presented a thick leather wallet.

Aaron hesitantly took it from her hand and gave a smile. "Thanks."

She returned to her shopping. "You're welcome."

He slipped the wallet back into his pocket and we joined the queue.

"Seriously?" I said quietly. "Pickpocketing?"

"I'm sorry," he replied. "It's a habit, but one we could do with right

277

about now." He gestured to the front doors. "Wait outside. There's not so many people out there."

I nodded and friskily shuffled out of the shop, holding my breath as I passed the detectors. I glanced up and down the centre and briefly leant against the window of the shop before jolting forwards at the sight of neon in the distance. There were two officers marching down an alley towards the town. Although they were too far to make me out, I still spun to face the store, keeping my head against the glass and my hood firmly up.

The heat from the summer sun was blaring down on me, but I barely felt the warmth. It was as though the coldness inside me was freezing over everything else. I pulled up my stolen phone and flicked to the search bar. I typed in my name and gripped at the plastic case as several articles popped up, one marked: 'Latest Sighting'.

'After simply fifteen minutes of his escape, Noah Coleman was spotted by several witnesses of him breaking into a home near the perimeter of the hospital. Witnesses quickly called the police, but they were not soon enough for when the family arrived home to find out a murderer was hidden in their house.

Once discovered by the family, Coleman instantly attacked both the mother and father – and family police dog – before trapping their son in a downstairs toilet. All survived this attack but suffered many injuries, including major blood loss on the mother's part.

Coleman was not once spotted by officials and managed to sly away undetected until Witham train station. Although not identified, security regarded him as suspicious and unruly. They attempted detainment but Coleman stowed away on a train where CCTV footage shows him meeting with his boyfriend, Aaron Wickers, at Shenfield station.

Police have stated to those living in the vicinity to be extremely cautious, and if anyone spots either men at any point, do not engage with them. Get to a safe place and call 999.'

I reached the bottom of the page and saw both mine and Aaron's mugshots. Mine was more recent – from Ocean Cliff – whereas Aaron's was from our Wyegate era. He still looked like a child. I'd actually never seen Aaron's mugshot before. His glasses were wonky, his skin slightly burnt, and his hair was matted with sweat, probably due to the fact he had only just got home from holiday at the time. The two of us together made us look like methed-out psychopaths.

"You alright, mate?" came a voice from behind me.

I clenched the phone in my hand and glanced at the reflection in the window. Neon yellow. I shuddered and pulled down on my hoodie strings.

"Hey," said another voice as they tapped my shoulder firmly.

I hesitantly glanced over my shoulder to see the two officers staring at me in concern. "Hello," I muttered.

"You okay?" asked the woman.

I nodded and turned back.

"What you doing out today, then?" said the man.

I shrugged. "Shopping…"

"You don't seem to have bought anything."

"I'm… checking something."

"What are you checking?"

I quickly flashed them the phone in my hands.

"Right." The woman placed her hands on her belt. "Well, I'm afraid you'll have to move from this spot."

"Why?"

"Because the owners of this store have a policy against people loitering outside their windows."

I bit my lip and shuffled back towards the shop doors before the man stopped me.

"One more thing—" As he reached out for me, his fingers caught a fold in my hood and pulled it from my head. It dragged my head into their view, and they jumped back. "Shit."

The man quickly grabbed my sleeve and dragged me back out into the daylight. He dug his fingers into my wounds, and I cried out at each angle my weight was thrown. Witnesses grew in the distance as the female officer frantically rambled into her radio.

"We need a secure transfer vehicle at Ridendale Town centre, immediately. We have found Noah Coleman. Repeat, we have found Noah Coleman, over."

I flailed my arms about as the two officers battled to restrain me between calling for backup. "Let go of me!" I yelled as I was briefly lifted from my feet.

The man then slammed my body against the gravel, pinning me down with his weight as he reached for his handcuffs. "Don't move," he ordered. "You'll only hurt yourself."

279

"A team's on their way," said the woman, scanning the area.

"Good. The sooner we get him back, the—"

Suddenly, the officer slumped to my side, lifting the restraint he had on me as he cried out in pain. I scrambled onto my back and spotted a shaking Aaron stood above his body with a thick wooden plank.

The other officer instantly leapt for him, the two brawling as they fought to take the wood from the other. As I stumbled to my feet, the woman slammed her heel into Aaron's shin, causing him to crumble. The beam was cast aside, and Aaron pushed to the floor. Before she could touch him, I pounced onto her back and fixed my arm around her neck. She swung back and forth as she tried to free herself – even reaching out to her unconscious partner who was sprawled out on the concrete, blood leaking out from his head and seeping into the cracks.

The woman began to gasp, almost retching as her throat slowly clamped. I watched Aaron regain his balance before shoving her beside the other officer.

"Come on!" he yelled, lunging into a sprint.

I followed his lead, not giving a second to allow time for guilt to sear into our souls. I couldn't bear to glance back, but I caught speeding glimpses of the small crowd as they shouted and snapped our image with their phones.

"Where are we going?" I questioned, panting wildly.

"This way!"

We skidded down an alleyway, slamming into a wire fence. My fingers clung to the chain links, shaking it in frustration as more neon cars swerved towards the centre in the distance. I swung to Aaron.

"What do we—"

He groaned as he heaved one of the bins towards the fence, the wheels scraping up the broken bottles below. "Up, up, come on!"

He hoisted me onto the bin, and I leapt to the filthy rubble below before looking up to see him jump after me. He stumbled upon landing, grazing his arm on the bricks and leaking drops of blood onto the concrete.

I quickly cradled him. "Are you alright?"

He pushed me back. "I'm fine," he said, consoling his arm. "We've gotta go."

We sprinted out across the bus lane, dodging each towering vehicle as they barrelled in our direction until we bounced off of the wooden fence that lined the large river.

"Where's the car?" I said breathlessly.

"We can't... we can't go back to the car. It's too close to that lot."

"So we keep running?"

He nodded. "Yeah."

Although it was a short break, we had managed to regain some ounce of strength to dash up the woodland bank. It was still bogged down with rainwater and every step resulted in us sinking halfway into the ground. Before we got too far, I could still hear the faint calls and sirens in the distance. Two voices were very distinct to me, I'd heard them enough times. I came to a stop and ducked behind a tree trunk to peer at the group.

Aaron noticed my absence and waded back over to me, speaking in a hushed but urgent tone. "Noah, man, what are you doing? We've got to go!"

I ignored his demand, even though he was quite right. I stared out at the road we had just run from and spotted a large box van. Across its side were the words 'Ocean Cliff Psych Transfer'. I gripped my nails across the bark of the mossy tree and then spotted the figures who the voices belonged to.

Dr Olsen was rushing from officer to officer as they rambled through the situation to him. At first he seemed relieved, but as he gained more of the story, he became distressed. He paced back and forth in annoyance, running his fingers through his dark hair and returning to the van. He opened the door and shuffled next to his silver-haired colleague.

"Caleb," I said angrily.

"What?" Aaron replied, still pleading for me to follow him.

I pointed at the van. "He's there. He came to get me. He came to bloody take us!" In frustration, I took a heavy step back to the road before a soggy log split below my feet.

"Noah!" Aaron dived after me, hiding the two of us out of sight.

We crouched down low and stared through the branches of a thick shrub at the gathering, Aaron keeping his arms around my waist to keep me down.

"Look," I began. "The one in the van with the grey hair. He's the one. He's the one who complied me."

"Really?"

"Yes. There's like a hundred doctors at that place, and out of all of them, he chooses to come!"

Then something swooped across their windscreen. The bright orange glow of a butterfly. They both stared at it, following its trail until it lifted into the sky.

Aaron's attention seemed to differ from mine. He quickly jumped into a crouched position as he spotted several dogs jump from the back of a police car. "Shit. Dog unit." He glanced down at his bleeding arm. "They're gonna be able to track us. We've gotta move." He scampered around the back of a tree. "Noah!"

I stepped to follow him, only for us to flinch as the monarch darted through the branches and swerved frantically around me. I swatted at it the best I could, but this only revealed my position.

"He's there!" cried Caleb's voice. "He's in the woods!"

Aaron grabbed my hand and yanked me to my feet. "Come on! NOW!"

He dragged me through the shrubbery and bark that formed with the moss and bluebells to create the woodland carpet. We dragged one another left and right, working together to lose the pursuers but not each other. Calling out above the others was Olsen. I took a quick glance back to notice that he was well ahead of the group and seemingly faster than either of us.

"Noah!" he yelled. "Noah, stop!"

I couldn't help but check for him over and over, a part of me willing to follow his command so much that my pace was beginning to drop. My chest was burning, and my coughing was as if I were spitting up the embers of the devil himself. Then, as I took in one long breath, my toes hooked beneath an exposed root, sending me tumbling down a small valley and into the murky stream at its depth. There seemed to be more mud than river.

I spat out the dirt that piled into my mouth and ran towards the other bank, only my shoes had no grip on the loose terrain, and I slipped back down to the water again. Before I could call out to Aaron, Dr Olsen had already caught up to me.

He gently stepped down to reach me and raised his hands in a calm manner. "Hey, mate."

I continued to scramble and slide across the bank, releasing cries of frustration and pain.

"It's alright! It's alright! I'm not gonna hurt you, Noah. You know that."

I backed away, following the valley of the stream to search for a less steep incline.

This didn't stop the doctor from following. "Noah, Noah. Look at me.

Stay calm."

I gave an annoyed growl and kicked a stone into the growing flood beside me. "Stop! Stop it, alright? I'm not a child!"

"I know that, Noah—"

"Then why do you treat me like one? I'm normal! There's nothing wrong with me! I'm not crazy and I'm not the lunatic the news calls me! Just let me go!"

"Noah, you hurt someone. I can't let you go. You were at Ocean Cliff to serve your time in a way that benefits you. Now that you've escaped, you'll have to stay longer. You were too unstable for prison the first time, and you still are."

"I'M NOT UNSTABLE! I'm just losing it because nobody believes a damn word I say!" A shuffling came from the distance, and I quickly waded through the bog to reach the curved tree roots that allowed me access to the upper bank.

Dr Olsen chased after me, shimmying past the river and grabbing my ankle as I made it to the top. "Noah, please. Stop this. I'm trying to help you."

I caught sight of the officers nearing us and glared down at the doctor. "Let go of me."

"I can't, mate. I'm sorry."

The officers spotted me, shouting and pointing my way.

"Let go of me!" I pulled the old screwdriver from my left pocket – where I had been storing it for a moment I needed it – then pressed the pointed tip against the underside of Olsen's chin.

He clenched his teeth and slowly released his grip, raising his hands and keeping his head up as his breath became shaky.

"Good." I pulled my legs up. "I'm not letting him take me."

With one final glance at the officers, I swiftly sprinted to catch up with Aaron, shoving the screwdriver back into my pocket. I kept running, refusing to look back until I reached the outskirts of the road. I gripped at the branches of a tree and scanned the area.

"AARON!"

The place was bare. There was no sight of him. I slid down to the road and darted right, leaving a trail of muddy footprints behind me. I followed the lane towards a car park, where I met with an open field. By now the mud had been scraped from my shoes, meaning the trail stopped halfway. I scanned the area, only a few cars were around, but from one came a small noise. It rattled across the concrete and rolled up to my feet. It was a pebble. I glanced from the direction it scattered from and saw a figure hiding in the shadows of a van. I scampered back but they quickly jumped out, revealing their face to me.

They were white skinned, scarred and holding a fixed glare in their eyes. The short hair and thin stubble revealed the tattoos that wound up his neck, meeting with an ink tear drop under his eye.

"Get in the van," he ordered.

I stumbled against one of the parked cars before tumbling into the arms of Bella.

She pushed me forwards. "Come on. Get in!"

The man yanked me into the navy van and sealed me in the back, along with stacks of cardboard boxes which towered over me and were fixed together with large plastic straps. I banged against the back doors of the van, shaking them violently before the other two jumped into the front seats and pulled out of the car park.

"Wait! What's going on? " I yelled as I stumbled back and forth through the bumpy van.

"Shut it!" the man replied, swerving the steering wheel from left to right.

Bella peered over the passenger seat. "Noah, keep down. We're getting you out of here."

I crawled in between two towers. "What—How did you know where I—"

She presented a radio to me. "Denzel's hooked up with the police chatter. We just met to discuss getting you and Aaron on a boat and we heard that they'd found you, so we were waiting to see what happened. That's when you came barrelling down the road."

"Where is Aaron?" I panted.

She placed the radio down. "We ain't seen him."

"We've gotta find him!"

"No," Denzel said bluntly.

"Why not?"

"If we stop, we get caught and we get taken."

"But what about Aaron? They could take him."

"Sorry, mate, but we can't go all 'round the place looking for your

284

friend. There ain't time."

I cowered against the cardboard with my knees tight in as I was tossed about, praying that Aaron could make it somewhere safe. This is my fault. I shouldn't have stopped. We wouldn't have gotten separated if I'd have just listened to him. My body was still shaking, I'm not sure what the cause even was at this point. Withdrawal, the van, or the fact I had just threatened the man who's been nothing but kind to me. I scratched harshly at my forearms, the skin being whittled at so much that flakes carpeted where I was sat. I then turned to my hair. The roots were burning and a searing urge to dig at the scalp took over me. I clawed at it for several moments until a clump of strands floated from my hand.

There was no time to dwell on my decaying state as the van had suddenly jolted to a stop. I scrambled myself tight together and heard as one of the van's windows rolled down.

"Hey," Bella said kindly. "Is there a problem?"

"There is," replied a stern voice, followed by the ruffling of paper. "Have you seen either of these men?"

"Um... No, I don't think so. Why?"

"They're fugitives. They were seen heading this way."

"Oh, God." Bella was making herself seem quite flustered. "W-What did they do?"

"They're extremely violent and have been seen attacking several people, breaking into their houses and robbing them."

"Oh, my—Did you say they were near here? We, we live close, my daughter, she's home alone! Oh, God! We only came out to pick up the van, didn't we?" She turned to Denzel.

He acted just the same. He placed his arm onto her shoulder in a caring manner. "It's alright, baby. Chloe will be fine. They'll catch 'em."

Bella began to pant and wave at the officer. ""Sorry, sorry. It's just... you know, being parents, all you do is worry about your kids."

"I know, I'm the same, which is why we're so focused on finding these two. Would you mind if we just check your van? It's just a precaution."

I clenched my eyes shut and covered my mouth with my hand.

"Oh, I doubt they'll be back there. We only just got in ourselves."

"These two are tricky. There's a high chance they could have snuck in without you noticing."

"Well, I—"

"It's just for safety."

She sighed. "Go ahead."

I heard the officer as they ambled around to the back of the van. I remained still, taking in sharp, rapid breaths as the metal latch began to lift. It creaked slowly and a slim bar of daylight crept through, shining against one of the stacks of boxes.

Then another voice called. "They've caught the scent! They're on it!"

The door remained at its thin state as the officer called back to them. "Where are they headed?"

"Back into town! The dogs are on them!"

The streak of light became dark again, and I let out my relief as the metal sealed me inside. A scatter of footsteps occurred outside until the officer appeared beside the window.

"You can go. Just be safe, alright?"

"We will!" Bella replied. "Thank you."

Denzel slowly edged the van away from the crisis before driving up the pace and returning to his original urgency. "Damn it, Bells. One day back with you and I'm already on the edge of getting arrested!"

She chuckled gleefully. "Oh, you love it!"

Denzel rolled his eyes.

"Did you see us, though? Ten outta ten acting right there!" She bounced her arms back and forth in a dancing motion. "I could get me an Oscar!"

I wobbled back onto my feet and approached the front seats. I gripped to the headrest and balanced my knees atop a large metal box. "Guys, please! We need to help Aaron!"

"I told you," said Denzel. "It's not in my interest to go on a wild goose chase looking for fugitives. I only ship then from A to B. If they don't show, that's their problem."

"I don't care! He's my boyfriend! I'm not leaving him!"

"Shut it, alright! Or I'll dump you on the side of the road."

I gritted my teeth. "Fine."

Bella swung to face me. "What?"

"Let me out. I'll go."

"Noah, you can't. They'll catch you."

"I don't care. I'm not leaving without him."

Bella sighed and Denzel slowed the van, pulling into an escape zone and unlocking the back doors. I clambered onto the pavement and stepped

286

towards the woods. As the two of them jumped back into the front, I called to them.

"Thank you."

Bella smiled. "I hope we can see each other again some time."

I nodded. "I hope so too."

Then as the van pulled back out to the road, I ventured back out into the overgrown woodland.

Chapter 11

No More Choices

I wasn't sure what drove me to this, but really, there's no other choice. I could be gone, I could have been away from all of this, but knowing that Aaron would be left here just didn't seem right. I couldn't be sure where he was – I couldn't be sure where I was, honestly.

I'd trapsed in circles for the past half an hour just running through thoughts and emotions in my head. Every way I turned seemed like a mirror image of itself and the sounds of the wind rustling just threw off my sense of direction. It wasn't for at least ten minutes until I found a small treeless opening. The woods still enclosed the area, but there was no sign of wildlife for this one small section, all except for a single oak tree with one of its thick branches being used as a support for a small rope swing.

I approached it cautiously before gently running my hand down one of the tatty blue ropes. There were two, both elevating a small branch that seemed to have been worn down from varying weights. I gently edged myself onto it, letting my feet have a moment of freedom before having to continue the trek. I gripped to the strings and slowly began rocking back and forth, the branch above creaking as my momentum grew. I let my body relax and allowed the swing to drift to a stop.

I sighed and pulled the phone from my bag. It was slightly scratched, and the battery was nearing shut down. I tapped through different screens until I found the call page. I found Aaron's number and waited for it to ring out, but it simply disconnected. I tried again, the same result. I took the phone away and rested my head against the rope, stifling my cries to stop myself from breaking down.

The breeze ruffled my hair in a familiar way, bringing me back to a time that seemed of no importance to most. It was the early morning outside the gates of Layset, the sun barely making it over the horizon, that same sensation of the bitter wind brushing my face. To my right was the crowd of equally exhausted students, balancing on suitcases, each of them desperate to get inside the warmth of the locked coach beside them.

I glanced to my left and spotted Ashton, the old Science teacher, approaching me. "Hey, Phoenix," he began.

"Hey," I replied through several shivers.

He kept a cautious distance from me, presenting a clipboard in his hand. "You need to register the sixth formers. They're the smallest group."

"Alright." I took the paper from him and watched as he shuffled back to Caleb who was stood beside the bus driver. I turned towards the students and fumbled with the pen that was dangling from the clipboard on an old string. "Okay, guys, we've gotta register you before you can get on."

There were several groans.

"Sir, please, can't we get on the coach first?" one boy pleaded.

"I don't make the rules, I just follow 'em. Anyway, I'll call your name and you reply, however. You all know how to register. Ruth Andrews?"

"Here."

"Finley Bucket?"

There was silence.

"Finley, I saw you two minutes ago."

"If you saw me then why ask if I'm here?"

I sighed and lowered the paper. "I dunno, knowing you, you probably would ran off and graffitied the bike shed. Now, come on, guys. We can get on the bus sooner if you listen to me."

A hand rose and River's noticeable face peered over the shoulders of her classmates. "Sir, are you okay?"

"I'm fine," I replied bluntly, keeping my head down.

"It's because it's early, isn't?"

"Let's go with that." I caught sight of Ryan through the crowd and noticed his sceptical face as I called out each person on the list.

As I reached the end, Caleb ushered the students towards the coach, the line briskly skipping across the path. I gazed back at the trees that lined the outer fence, double-taking one as a blur wafted past it. I glanced between the tree and the class before making out a figure. His silver glasses were glowing from the streetlamp above, as was the glittery bag that was swinging in his hand.

I quickly dashed for him, and he took me in his arms, swinging me around and hiding me behind the large trunk of the tree. "What the hell are you doing here?" I whispered gleefully. "It's four in the morning!"

He chuckled and gave me a kiss. "I know, but I couldn't miss today, could I?"

I scoffed. "It's nothing to be celebrated. It's the day that made my family miserable – if they weren't already."

"Aha! But what you fail to see is that today is the anniversary of our meeting. If you didn't go out on an angry, late-night bender, we'd have never 've met." He presented the bag to me as my face reddened in embarrassment.

"What is this?" I asked as I inspected the wrappings.

"Happy incarceration day!"

I laughed as I dug my hand into the paper and felt around inside. I gripped an oddly shaped piece of plastic and lifted it out, the light revealing a pair of toy handcuffs. I glared up at Aaron with a smirk. "What exactly are these for?"

"That's for when you get home," he said seductively before straightening out and glancing at the coach. "I didn't mean for you to pull the skimpy item out first, it's just, everything fell out in the car, and I had to stuff it all back in."

I continued to laugh as I rifled through the other items, pulling out a bag of sweets, a new set of sketching pencils and a hand-knitted scarf. I wrapped the scarf around me and leant forwards into Aaron's embrace.

"Thanks," I said quietly as we both shivered against the January cold.

We tossed from side to side, smiling.

"I'm gonna miss you," he said.

"I'm gonna miss you."

"How long's the trip again?"

"Just the week. Stupid reward trips. I was never invited on a reward trip."

Aaron chuckled and nuzzled against my neck. "That's because you were a bad boy."

"Yeah, but I wasn't the only 'bad boy'. There were literally guys who would go around half naked, trying to spit into girls' mouths, then literally fight the teachers, and they would still get invited." I scoffed. "Bloody favourites game. The teachers never admitted it, but God did they play it. 'We treat you all the same'," I continued, imitating the old staff. "Yeah you'll let old Bradley run around harassing ten-year-olds, but when little

290

old Noah is collapsed on the ground in rugby, bleeding from his mouth, pfft, he's just a lazy brat."

"Did that actually happen?" Aaron questioned with a tone of scepticism.

"Yeah! I was too light so the other guys could pick me up and lob me over their heads. I landed on my chin and bit through my lip. I was laying there, bleeding all over the joint, and the PE teacher was just yelling at me for not fighting for the ball." I went to step away, but Aaron took my hand and pulled me back towards him.

He brushed the tip of my fringe behind my ear. "Well, now you can be the one that yells at dying children."

I smiled as he kissed my cheek. "Very funny."

"Phoenix!" yelled a voice, causing the two of us to quickly separate.

I passed the bag back to him and waved. "I'm so sorry, I've gotta go. I love you."

"I love you too."

I jogged towards the caller, presenting the clipboard to them, and hiding my chin inside the scarf.

It was Caleb. He took the register and glanced over it. "Who was that?" he asked.

I glanced over my shoulder at Aaron who was rushing back to his car. "No one. Just a friend."

"Right." He nodded towards the coach. "You better get on."

I nodded back to him and hurried up the steps of the vehicle. I settled at the front, watching through the gap in the chairs as each student fought for the power of the backseats. All except that famous trio. They wandered up and down the aisle, searching for a seat for the three of them, but couldn't seem to settle. I noticed a spare two behind me with another free seat to my right.

"You three can sit up front, if you like."

They glanced to each other, seeming to telepathically decide on how to answer, until River replied. "Thanks." She turned to her friends. "Who's sitting where?"

"I need the window, remember?" said Tess as she immediately slumped herself in the behind seat.

"What about you?" River asked Ryan.

He shrugged. "I don't mind... You know how to help Tess on journeys so…"

"Are you sure?"

He smiled before taking his seat beside me, River taking hers beside Tess. We awkwardly smiled to each other before Ryan pulled out his phone. He tapped across it, only for it to shut down shortly after. He gave a sort of whimper and rested his head back.

I reached into the rucksack by my feet and pulled out my charging bank. "Here." I passed him the device.

He smiled. "Thank you." He quickly fumbled for his charger and plugged it into his phone, placing the two items onto the tray table in front of him. "I swear it was on charge this morning, unless I didn't turn the plug on."

"Don't worry, I do that all the time."

We both turned to Caleb as he called down the aisle to the students. "Alright, everyone! The coach is going to drive us straight down to the New Forest, when we get there you are expected to stick with your year group. Year 11s will be with Mrs Whittle, Year 12s with Mr Close—"

We heard the back of the bus clamber with excited yells.

"Yes, Year 12, you get Mr Close, and Year 13s, you will be with me. The other coach will meet us there and we will go over everything once we make it to the camp. Try to keep the noise down, and please, don't leave your rubbish on the coach."

"Sir? " called one of the boys.

"Yes, Uzair?"

"How long's the journey?"

"No more than three hours."

"What? " clambered the majority.

"Hey! I said, 'no more than'. We can stop if anyone needs to." He turned to Tess. "Tess, have you got your travel sickness tablets?"

She presented the packet and shook them.

"Great." He glanced back at the driver who gave a thumbs up. "Alright, seatbelts on." He settled in the chair opposite Ashton just as the coach began to move, followed by the clicking of seatbelts.

I slipped mine over me and watched through the window as we pulled away from the school gates, seeing the street sign pass; 'Albridge Street', so called because of the large bridge that stretched across Lake Layset – the bridge we soon crossed, and the lake that our school was named after.

"Mr Hayes?" said River through the crack in the chairs.

"Yeah?" Caleb replied.

"Is it bad that I need the toilet?"

He chuckled. "Seriously, River? God, don't you take after your name."

"It's not my fault! I couldn't go this morning!"

He sighed and pointed down the aisle. "There's a toilet just down the stairs over there. You better use it before the lot at the back do. They'll bloody destroy the thing."

River quickly fumbled her seatbelt off and wobbled towards the cubicle. "Thank you!"

Tess chased after her. "I think I need to go too."

Me and Ryan glanced at each other and laughed.

"The amount-a times I've been abandoned by them because they've needed a wee is astounding," he said.

"When I was at school, I'd fake needing a wee just to get away from everyone. I'm surprised nobody thought I had a bladder problem."

We both chuckled and stared out at the lake as the sunrise cast over it, sending the rays blinding through the windows. A few moments passed until the students had either fallen asleep or had woken right up, the Back-seat Boys seeming to be performing one of their best shows as they all burst out singing. Honestly, I never saw the appeal of the back of the bus. A bunch of screaming kids with milkshakes flying from left to right, no thank you. I was much more interested in the gossip upfront, not that anyone was ever interested in me. It's why I tried so hard to make an effort at Layset. If I can be the person I needed to someone else then that's fine by me.

Whilst I was busy lost in thought, Ryan spoke, keeping his voice low. "Um… Mr Close?"

"Yeah?"

He glanced back at River and Tess, who were now fast asleep over each other – earphones dangling between the two of them as music leaked out. "I didn't mean to nose, but I was at the back of the line earlier, and I saw you with that guy…"

I shuffled awkwardly. "Oh, yeah?"

"Yeah… I'm sorry, don't worry." He turned away in embarrassment.

I sighed. "Yeah, you caught me. I am a *homosexual*."

A glimpse of a smile flickered across Ryan's face as he picked at his nails. "I'm sorry, I really didn't—"

"Oh, it's fine. I'm surprised I made it this long without anyone noticing, to be honest."

"I mean, some of the guys in PE say things about you, but that's about it…"

I leant my head back. "Story of my life, mate."

Ryan nodded and checked the percentage on his phone.

"Did it make you uncomfortable?"

He slipped his phone away again. "No, no… It just felt weird to see one of the teachers kissing someone, but not because it was a guy…"

"Well, that's good." I fiddled with Aaron's scarf.

Ryan shuffled anxiously and continued to keep his voice down. "There's a reason I wanted to ask though."

"Go ahead."

He pulled his sleeves down. "How long did you know that you were… you know…"

I sat in thought as I traced the days back. "I couldn't tell yah. My life seems to have blurred together these past few years."

He nodded and lowered his head. "Right…"

I noticed his sorrow slowly forming and knew immediately what position he felt in. "But I will say, a part of me always knew something was different – whether I realised it or not. Even as a kid, whilst all the other guys were busy playing kiss chase with the girls, I was busy trying to understand why I was chasing the Liams instead of the Lisas."

Ryan gave a chuckle. "I was just asking 'cause… I didn't start noticing these things until last year. I always thought that, I dunno, maybe I didn't like anyone, but…" He smiled. "There was this guy I met at work, and he's… amazing."

I began smiling with him. "Is he cute?"

He shied away, but his grin shone through. "Kinda, yeah."

"Have you spoke to him at all?"

"Yeah… we're good friends, but it wasn't until I actually got to know him that I… maybe liked him." He finally made eye contact with me. "It's just… I'd never felt attracted to anyone before I met him, and I don't even think I like girls…"

"That's okay. Just don't let it drag you down too much. I've been in that place. I only came out to my family last September. They didn't even know I had any friends let alone a boyfriend. But honestly, it was the best

294

thing I ever did. This weight I'd been dragging around for over twenty-five years was suddenly gone, and now me and my partner are happier than we've ever been."

"I still don't get how you're twenty-five," he chuckled. "You look like you could be in our class."

I yanked my sleeves down and forced a laugh. "Yeah, well, using moisturiser every day will do that to yah."

Ryan brushed his hair back with his fingers. "So... when you were my age, did you *know* you were gay?"

"At your age, mostly, yeah. But I still couldn't be sure. It wasn't until I met Aaron that I really knew." My chest jumped slightly as I realised I gave his true name. "I, um... we got together in about 2019. We met the year before and once we got to know each other, we realised that we were more than friends, and even though we had to keep it a secret to most people, it was still worth it."

He nodded.

"Just take your time. Nobody knows who they are in a day. They may *think* they do, but trust me..." I lowered my voice and glanced to the back of the coach. "Half of them probably go home after a late night with the boys and for a slight second they'll question their whole lives because they thought their best mate looked attractive. But to me, there's a big difference between thinking someone's attractive and being attracted to them. That's how I finally figured it out. I knew which people seemed attractive, but I wasn't *attracted* to a single woman. You'll figure it out one day, and if you don't, don't worry. You can *never* predict the future, no matter how hard some people try. It's best to just accept what comes to you."

Another breeze ruffled the leaves, causing the oak to shed and cast a waterfall of green shapes down to me. One fell into the palm of my opened hand, and I stroked across it with the tip of my thumb. 'Accept what comes to you'. Easier said than done. I let the final leaf twirl to the bark below then glanced up as another gust drifted the glow of orange to my feet. I scoffed.

"Here to rat me out?"

The monarch flapped its wings.

"I don't s'pose anyone's gonna believe me now, huh?"

The creature fluttered up and balanced on my knee. I cautiously edged my finger towards it, its wings beginning to move faster until it hopped into the air and gripped its legs onto me. I chuckled as its twig-sized body was fighting for balance against its giant wings. I began to inspect it, running my other hand across its scales until I retracted it as I connected with its coldness. Actually, they barely seemed like scales. They were silky yet metallic with its antennae appearing to be smooth and fixed in my direction.

"You're a strange little guy, aren't yah?"

It gave a flutter of its wings again before leaving them stretched out firmly. I stroked its soft back before pulling up my phone again, the monarch quickly making its way to the side of my neck. I tapped across the keyboard, selecting one of the options from the search bar, and pulled up the news on Layset.

'Ryan Axel still missing. Although advised not to, his two friends, Tess Colton and River Snow, are on a desperate search for any clues to his whereabouts. The two even joined the case detectives in questioning the main suspect Noah Coleman shortly before his escape from the Ocean Cliff Psychiatric Hospital. Although hospitalised at the time, police are led to believe that this is a part of a much larger case, possibly involving multiple people from Coleman's life – including his known friend Aaron Wickers.

Both Tess and River have been informed thoroughly about Coleman's escape and are warned of the dangers he presents to them, however, the duo refuse to give up on their search for their lost friend.

Before his disappearance, Axel was said to be looking deeply into his attack, seeking out the truth behind why his old teacher was set on killing him. After his disappearance, the police searched his home and found a sheet of paper with a symbol scribbled across it.'

Attached below was that same multi-coloured symbol. A red, a blue and a grey oval, each overlapping. Beside it; The A.C.C. This place has got to be it. I rapidly typed across my phone, desperate to find the truth of this hidden place, when suddenly, the screen shut off. I jumped back in confusion, tapping violently across it as a spinning spiral appeared in the centre.

"No, no, NO!"

I groaned and lobbed the device at the tree in anger, watching as it shattered into several pieces, before staggering towards it in realisation of what I had done. I frantically attempted to push each piece back together, but it was hopeless. My only way of communication with Aaron was gone.

I couldn't remember his number, not now. It was saved onto the phone. I sobbed as I held a piece in each hand before the monarch drifted to my side and flowed through the breeze towards a hidden walkway, the dirt grinded down by the many feet that had trampled over it.

I left the phone and dashed for the opening, the butterfly chasing close behind as I grew closer and closer to a field. My pace grew until I finally slumped against a short wooden fence that lined the large park. I hid behind an overgrown blackberry bush and glanced at the monarch.

"If Aaron's gone, then there's only two people left who will believe me," I said breathlessly. "I need to get to that school. Tess and River can get to Ryan, and I can get to Aaron. They must have found him. Oh, God, they've got him." I peered out at the several families running across the fresh grass, dogs chasing their owners, and parents chasing their kids who had run after their dogs. "The question is how I get there." I fumbled around in my pocket and felt the handle of the screwdriver. I gripped it tightly and took in a breath. "I've got no choice…"

With my mud-covered clothes and worn-out body, I marched out into the light of summer. I batted the monarch away from me, sending it soaring into the sky. I circled each family from a distance, analysing who would be the easiest to take on, but compared to me, even the babies could probably tackle me. I turned away from the groups and stared out at the car park. I thought about stealing one of the vehicles, but what was the use in that? I can't drive, and I can't exactly call a taxi either.

Then, just as my short-lived plan was losing hope, I spotted one of the cars in the distance. The model, the colour, the size, it was all familiar. I'd seen it before. Medium-sized, silver, curved. I'd seen that exact car in the staff car park back at the hospital. Jaiden.

I shot my head from group to group, in shock that this luck could fall my way. At this point, I wasn't sure if it was good or bad, but what else have I got left. I glanced around some more then spotted her. She was sat at one of the old benches, donning a bright summers dress over her grown stomach.

I hobbled towards her, my shoes scraping up the dried dirt. She seemed so happy, the grin on her face beaming as she watched her family run around in the distance. I remained silent as I approached, only clearing my throat once behind her.

"Jaiden?"

She gasped loudly and swung her head to face me. Utter disbelief filled her demeanour. "N-Noah! What—How—"

I gently perched beside her on the bench, being weary to keep my distance from her. "Jaiden, I... I need your help. Please. I don't have anybody left. They took Ryan. They took Aaron. I need to find them."

She continued swinging her head, shaking it and scrambling her hands over her belongings. She kept her voice low as she spoke. "Noah, you really shouldn't have done this. This is really serious!"

"I know..."

"I've seen the news. I know what's been happening, and I'm sorry I couldn't be there when you needed help, but I couldn't stay at the hospital like this." She gestured towards the bump on her stomach.

"I didn't expect you to. I'm not an idiot – I know everyone thinks I am."

"That's not true, Noah. You're very smart, which is why I thought you'd understand that you can't be on the run! It's dangerous for you."

"I can't go back there. They'll get me."

"Does anyone know where you are?"

I shrugged. "Not anymore."

She quickly turned to her bag, which was sat to her right, and rifled through the many compartments. "I'm sorry, Noah, but I need to call someone. I can't let you go on like this. You need to go back."

"No," I demanded. "Stop it."

She unzipped the final section. "I'm sorry. You can't do this. I'm gonna call Dr Olsen."

I clenched at the handle to the screwdriver, speaking through gritted teeth. "Stop. It."

She took the phone from the bag. "Noah, you need help! I'm not just gonna let you go out and—"

I swiftly flicked the weapon out, pressing the tip against Jaiden's stomach. She stammered and slowly gazed down at the metal creasing her dress before lowering the phone and looking up at me with heartbreak in her eyes.

My hands were shaky as I fought not to hurt her. "Put the phone away."

"Noah..." She was breathless. "Please... Please, don't."

"Put it away."

She stifled a cry and gently tucked the device back into the bag.

298

"Good. Now, tell me. How do I get to Layset?"

She shook her head, her hands raised just enough for me to see them and just enough to protect herself. "Please, Noah. Think about this."

"How do I get to Layset? Tell me." I pinned the screwdriver down more and she flinched.

"I don't know."

"Where is it?"

"I swear to you, Noah, I don't know!"

"Tell me or I'll—"

A girl's voice cut me off. "Noah!"

We both glanced at the field as Olivia was dashing towards me. I quickly muttered to Jaiden. "I won't hurt them if you help me."

She swallowed and nodded. "Okay, I will. Just don't touch them."

I snapped the weapon back into my pocket just as the young girl reached the table. She leapt onto the bench and hugged my side.

"I've missed you, Noah!"

I hesitantly hugged her back. "I've missed you too, Olivia."

She nestled her head against my jumper. "Are you still sick?"

I felt Jaiden's glare of panic. "No," I replied. "I'm all better now."

She looked up with happiness. "Really?"

"Yeah. Me and your mum were just talking."

"What were you talking about?"

"She's gonna help me, aren't you?" I turned to her with a glare of my own.

She gave her best smile. "Y-Yeah."

Olivia grinned brightly. "Can I help?"

I stuttered. "Um, I'd like you to but, um…"

"It's a secret, honey," replied Jaiden. "We can't tell anyone."

She tugged at my sleeve with a glum look. "But I want to help…"

"You can help next time, sweetie. Go back to daddy."

"But—"

"Please!" Jaiden adjusted her position and cleared her throat. "Please, Olivia."

She turned to me. "Noah wants me to help!"

"I do," I replied. "But the thing is…" I lowered my voice and leant closer to her. "If I tell you a secret, you promise not to tell?"

She nodded happily. "Uh-huh!"

"Okay. The thing is, I'm on a special mission. I've been sent to find someone so I can stop the bad people. Nobody's allowed to know, so you and mummy have to stay quiet about it, alright?"

She bounced up and down excitedly. "You're like a secret agent? "

"Yeah, yeah. I am."

She squealed. "That's so cool!"

"It is, but remember, if you tell anyone, then the bad guys will catch me, so shh."

She mimicked my action with a smile. "Shh."

"Okay, go back to daddy. Go have some fun."

Olivia nuzzled against me with her arms wrapped tightly around me. "I hope you beat the bad guys."

My lip quivered slightly. "Me too…"

Olivia then dashed back over to the others, and I glanced back at Jaiden, who was sat with her head hung and her hands in a praying position on the table.

"Take me to Layset," I ordered a final time as I moved away from the bench.

With a shaky inhale, she rose too and called to her husband. "I'm just gonna take my friend somewhere. You can keep an eye on the girls, right?"

Tom shuffled forwards, Olivia swinging from his arm. "Are you sure? I can take him if you want—"

"No! No, it's fine. I'll take him. Just stay with the kids." She hesitantly stepped towards me.

"Honey, are you sure? You shouldn't really be driving."

"I'm fine, I'm fine. Just stay with them." She quickly approached her car, reaching into her bag for her keys as I trailed close behind her.

She fumbled them in her hands, shaking as she flicked through each one before tightly gripping her biggest one.

"You alright?" I said, silently swapping sides as she positioned them into a dagger position.

She swiftly raised her hand into the air and swung the key to where I had been standing. She staggered in confusion before I clasped my hand around her mouth and pinned the screwdriver to her stomach again. She whimpered and gently lowered her arm to her side.

"I told you." I glanced over at Tom. He was sat playing with the girls. "Take me to Layset, and I won't hurt anyone."

She quickly swatted my hand away and went to jam the keys against my thigh, only the jagged metal pushed right back through her fist. I pinned the weapon closer to her.

"I take it you were only taught basic self-defence. Wyegate taught me that keys in a poor grip will only send them the other way. You can't do a thing with 'em when you actually get attacked." I yanked the keys from her and unlocked the car. "Get in."

She quickly clambered into the driver's seat, adjusting herself and rubbing her stomach as I slid around to the other side. I slammed the door and placed the keys into her hand. She cowered back and cried as she repeatedly tried to fit the them into her ignition. Eventually, the engine revved and she pulled away from the park, joining a road and reaching for her phone that she had managed to tuck in her pocket.

"What are you doing?" I asked.

She jumped and pulled the phone out again. "S-Sat Nav. I didn't wanna get l-lost."

I held out my palm. "Give it."

She kept her eyes on the road, biting her lip and swaying her head from side to side.

I threatened her once more. "Give it to me."

She sighed and forced the device over.

"Thank you." I tucked it away. "If you take me anywhere but this school, I will ram this thing through you. Got it?"

Jaiden stuttered and glanced from me to the road. "Please, Noah. I know you're not like this. You're just scared and confused. What you're doing it's... it's not right—"

I pinned the tip of the metal against her neck. "You think I don't know that? You think I'm enjoying this? I've had to become exactly what everyone thinks I am just to stay out of that fucking place!"

Jaiden trembled again, tears seeping down her cheeks – one even rolling down the screwdriver and meeting with the plastic handle. "We—were—trying—to—help—you," she said breathlessly.

I dragged the metal down her arm before rapidly taking it away and resting my head against the window. "I know..."

We drove silently for the rest of the way, Jaiden constantly keeping a free hand over herself whenever she could. I simply watched as the town became country fields and as the miles dropped from the petrol metre. I reached into my battered bag and pulled out my journal. It was in the same torn up state the bag was, but every word was still readable.

I caught Jaiden as she gave a brief smile. "You still have it."

I nodded. "Yeah, I… can't seem to forget about it." I slung it back into the bag. "It's stupid."

"I don't think so," she replied. "It means something to you. It's good to keep things like that."

I rested back against the window, another ten minutes passing before we reached a sign of civilisation again. We drove past several streets, curving across roundabouts and eventually rolling up to the gates of the school. I stared at the large bars and swallowed.

"I'm so sorry…" I quickly slung my bag over my shoulder and stumbled away from the car.

I heard as she quickly sped away, probably leaving me only a few minutes until backup arrived. I approached the main gate, the metal seeming a lot more rustier than it was before. I ran my fingers over the peeling paint, following each flake as it drifted to the floor – some even landing on the main lock. I gripped the handle of the bar and hoisted it out of the hole in the pavement. I slammed my weight against the rest of it and fell through to the grounds of the school, the metal creaking loudly.

I stumbled across the cobbles and hid amongst the line of trees that were flooding the grass bank. It followed the path downwards, leading towards the main building. I glanced back and forth between the sudden noises around me. The sound of students. The sound of teachers. The sound of students getting yelled at by teachers. The place was just as I left it.

I checked the time on Jaiden's phone. It was nearing lunch. I headed towards the sixth form block, keeping hidden behind the large mass of greenery. I slid down to a crouch and waited several moments until a large group of teens bustled through the tiny doors, each one spreading out and dashing off in separate directions.

I froze as the girls crossed over the bank, only a few feet away from me, to continue on a different path on the other side. They were the last out. There wasn't a soul to see. Everyone had ran from the block. I shortly searched around me then lifted a pebble from the matted grass and threw it gently in their direction. They stopped and looked around, analysing what the sound was. They took a few more steps before I threw another.

"What the hell?"

They faced my direction but didn't appear to notice me.

"If that's you Tony, I swear to God," Tess yelled before returning her nose to her phone.

I threw another pebble, which triggered Tess to give in and march over to me, River following behind her.

"That's it, you little—" Her words crumpled as she stepped into the shadows of the overgrowth. "Oh, my God…"

"Shh," I said quietly. "I'm not here to hurt anyone. I just need your help."

"Mr Close—Coleman?" River replied in shock as she joined the shade.

"Please… this is important. It's about Ryan."

They edged closer.

"You know where he is?" River questioned.

"Not yet…" I replied. "But I know the name. The A—"

"The ACC?" she interrupted.

"Yes! And I need your help to track the place down. Do you guys have phones? I can't unlock the one I have."

River reached into her pocket.

"You know the school's on high alert, right?" said Tess. "Because of you and Ryan. First you attack him, then he goes missing, then a few months later you're back. Do you understand that we shouldn't even be at school? We're both meant to be at home because of you."

"I'd expect nothing less." I turned to the other student as she tapped across her screen.

"What do you want me to do?" asked River.

"The ACC, look it up." I ducked behind another tree trunk as one of the staff passed.

"Alright, girls?" he said.

They both nodded. "Yeah!"

"Good." He then entered the block opposite.

River scrolled through each website, shaking her head. "I mean, we've already checked this before. It hasn't changed. It's just articles and articles about you and Ryan." She presented the screen to me. "See?"

I groaned. "Damn. Alright, what evidence have you found?"

"Nothing. Well, close to nothing. Nobody is telling us anything. It's why we came to see you at the hospital. You were our only chance at getting somewhere, and you've been the only one that seems to make sense!"

I edged them closer into the bushes. "Okay, one more question. Do you guys remember a teacher called Blake Hayes?"

"Yeah," replied Tess. "He was the old science teacher. We went on that reward trip with him."

"So you *do* remember him? " I pushed on.

They were becoming more startled at my movements.

"Yeah. You said last year that he tried to control you and that's why you got taken away."

River tossed her head between us in concern. "D'you think that's why they took Ryan? Because he knew about the project?"

"So do we," added Tess. "We're probably next on the hit list. I'm gonna go sign a will."

"Stop it!" River shoved her. "I'm serious! This isn't a joke. Kidnapping isn't a joke!"

"Look, River, I'm sorry, it's just, I'm struggling to process this all at the minute! We're standing here with a bloody murderer in a bloody bush, and I'm the only one that seems to be uncomfortable with it!"

"Shut up!" I yelled, drawing the attention of another teacher.

They began stepping towards us, keys jangling from their neck ID as they called up to the girls. "What are you two doing in there?"

"Um, nothing!" Tess called back.

River whispered aggressively to me. "Look, sir, I want more than anything to get my friend back, I would search till the ends of the earth for him, but we have nothing! Literally nothing! All we have is a stupid acronym." She took a breath. "If this project is really out there then I want to stop it. I believe that people can change. Stealing their minds because they made a mistake or two isn't fair, especially when the innocent are starting to be taken."

The teacher grew more curious. "Tess is River with you in there? I thought I saw her."

I shook my head as River began stepping away, before our whole group jumped at the sound of a mass of sirens hurtling the school's way.

The teacher glanced towards the noise. "What the hell?"

With little time to think, I reached out and grabbed River's wrist. I yanked her towards me and hoisted her over my shoulder. She screamed loudly and flailed each part of her around, hoping that enough movement would set her free. The teacher lunged onto the bank as I stumbled onto the path. I sprinted back up to the gate, Tess keeping close by me as she reached her arm out for her friend. She tried tripping me up, she also tried kicking me. Every pain was burning, everything hurt, but my adrenaline and desperation to prove a point was forcing me through it. And somehow, I kept going, but as I reached the path to the gate, I skidded to a stop.

The road became overrun with the siren-sounding cars, each desperately trying to pry onto school grounds through the slow opening bars. With me distracted, River was able to wriggle free. She bent my arm out of place, causing me to give a shout as she smacked against the concrete. I gripped at the skin around my temples as the piercing cerulean lights casted dark blotches across my vision, joining with a sharp whistling caused from the sirens. I crumpled against a car as Tess cradled her friend's body on the ground.

"RIVER! RIVER, PLEASE!" she cried as the drizzle in the atmosphere became a slow downpour.

I adjusted my balance and stared at the two girls. "Oh, God. I'm so… I'm so sorry…" I twitched around as the vehicles sliced through the forming puddles.

I took one last look at the duo before I sprinted down the large hill towards the main courtyard of the school. The staff were blocking each door, each with their own weapon in the form of school supplies. They yelled into their handheld radios as I passed them, heading straight for the large open playing field.

The convoy of cars was covering the south side of the school. Then the north. Then the west. The only clear option left was east, the direction of the furthest car park, and the direction of the last gate – the one that connected to Layset Lake. I hurtled for it, knowing no car could ever touch the swampy banks and make it through. It was like tunnel vision, all that was in focus was the gate. But through the specks of rain, I spotted another figure. He was clambering out of the door of a van. I slowed my pace as I recognised the make of it. The figure then spotted me. He pointed my way and yelled.

"Noah! Stop!" the doctor cried as he thundered down the muddy bank towards me.

I dug my heels down, sliding across the damp grass as I bolted back the way I came. My surroundings were enclosing, the perimeter shrinking, each possible exit covered. As I sprinted, Olsen's voice called again.

"NOAH!"

I glanced back at him, my pulse rising higher as the doctor bounded closer. He had ran half of the field already, he was only a metre or so away. I could have made it, but my shoe slipped. It got caught in the soil and my body slammed to the ground. Yells and orders pursued, the rain fell heavier, and my body was numb. But with whatever I had left in me, I scrambled up, taking a single step before I was tackled down. By now, I was too battered to feel the collision, only dizziness was left to confuse me.

I felt as the attacker pressed their weight on me, pinning harshly into a restrained position. I writhed from side to side, using all I had left to make one last break for freedom.

"Noah, mate, please," Dr Olsen said as he gripped at my clothes tightly. "It's me. I'm not gonna hurt you."

I inhaled sharply, releasing a shriek as I dug at the dirt. "BUT *THEY* WILL!"

"I won't let them, Noah," he replied sincerely. "I won't let them."

I had no choice. It was over. There wasn't a thing I could do to get out. To get away. Just accept what's to come. With this – my only thoughts – I loosened my figure, closed my eyes, and let my tears get stolen by the raindrops that cascaded across my skin.

"I can't go back there…" I muttered. "I can't…"

Dr Olsen sighed deeply, running his hands up and down my back as he tried his best to comfort me. "You have to, mate. You have to."

My breath shuddered. "I'm so sorry. I-I'm s-so SORRY!"

"I know, mate," he replied. "I know."

I tossed my head to the side, watching as the flashing vehicles circled, the officers dashing out of them. From above came the roar of the helicopter. It's propellors sliced through the storm with its blinding spotlight fixing to my location. As the figures approached, Dr Olsen called to them.

"I've got him! I've got him."

He held his hand out to a woman behind him and she placed the thick handcuffs into his palm. Olsen turned back and gently lifted my tiny arms onto my back. The right cuff clicked into place, my sleeve saving my skin from the grind of the metal.

"Good boy. It's okay," the doctor said as he continued to comfort me. As he pulled my second arm, he caught sight of the layers of bandages and carefully hovered his finger across them before he quickly slid off my body. "Oh, God, Noah. What happened to you?"

I whimpered again as he fixed my other arm into place.

"Alright," he continued. "It's alright." With a gentle manner, he dug his arms underneath my shoulders and hoisted me from the ground. "Come on. Let's get you out of here."

I stumbled and limped across the uneven grass, keeping tight to Olsen all the way. Through swollen eyes, I gazed back over my shoulder at the school skyline. The clouds were thick and grey, casting shadows across the large blocks and swaying trees. The students were desperately tearing at the blinds covering the windows to watch as I was escorted from the premises. The place was on lockdown. A part of me felt relief that the school even had that procedure, but then I realised that the only reason this had to be brought into effect was because of me. It was never in place when I worked here. Not until after I attacked Ryan. It's my fault.

Before my thoughts drew darker, I turned away. I kept my gaze down, my movements slim, and never dared to do anything else. I saw no point. I didn't realise it then, but I was beyond exhausted. It wasn't until I was laid in the transfer van when my adrenaline began to fade. The true extent of the aching and weeping of my injuries had finally come to light. Each bandaged wound was searing, every muscle was torn, and each speck of blood was fiery. I'd say what happened, but I don't know. There was a pinch in my arm and suddenly I was out.

Chapter 12

The One for the Many

I woke up in a cell, Dr Olsen and half of the police unit surrounding me. I was laying on the floor, no mattress or anything, just on the concrete. Cradling my head was Olsen. He had his considerate smile across his face each time my eyes fluttered open. I rolled slowly from side to side, Olsen's voice becoming clearer.

"Come on, Noah. Come on."

I tossed back to face him and gripped loosely at his jacket as I tried to sit up.

"That's it, mate."

I whimpered and swung my head about to analyse the room. The officers were dotted around the cell, each one glaring at me with spite. I trembled at the sight of each of them, attempting to shuffle to the wall only to get pushed back by Olsen. He had my hand held in his as he lowered me to my back once again. He continued to comfort me, his voice echoing as I struggled to stay conscious. I closed my eyes as I gripped the edge of the doctor's coat, listening to the conversation that ensued.

There was the buzz of a radio, followed by a woman's voice. "We need a medical kit in containment room 2. We'll need one of the paramedics too."

"No," Dr Olsen said quickly. "I'll do it." He leant forwards, whispering quietly. "You will not get a paramedic within three feet of him. Let me do it. I'm a trained doctor. I'm *his* doctor. He trusts me."

My eyes fluttered open again and I caught sight of one of the officers approaching me again, causing me to jolt upwards. "Don't!" I buried my head in my knees.

Olsen crawled closer to my side and glared up at the officer.

She sighed and buzzed her radio. "Forget the paramedic. Just bring the kit."

"Are you sure?" came the voice from the other end.

308

She clenched her jaw. "Yes."

We waited in silence, the only sound in the room coming through the form of my restless breathing. Of course when the pound on the door came, I shrieked and covered my ears, causing the gathering to jump. Through the door came a large, green medical bag. The woman slid it over to Dr Olsen and he unzipped the top.

"I think it's best if you give us some space here," he said.

The group glanced at their captain. She nodded stiffly and gave a wave of her hand to the others.

"Are you sure?" I heard one mutter.

"Everybody out," she replied, sliding the door across.

Slowly and sceptically, they all left, leaving me and the doctor alone. The door sealed with a loud slam, and I jolted again.

"It's alright," Olsen said softly, rubbing his hand on my back. "You're gonna be okay."

He carefully rolled up my sleeve to reach the cuts, but I winced each time the bandage caught against my skin.

"I'm sorry, mate." He took his hands back and looked up at the door. "Hang with me, I'll be right back."

He stepped over to the door and knocked lightly on the hatch. It slid across, revealing the Constable.

"Yes?"

"You're gonna need to get him fresh clothes. The ones he's wearing now aren't fit for his injuries."

"What size is he?" she asked bluntly.

"He's a small, but make sure you get a loose outfit."

The hatch slammed shut without another word, and Olsen returned to my side. He unfolded the blanket from the bed and tried to wrap it around me.

"I'm not cold," I said sharply as I pushed my arm out to stop him.

"It's not for the cold, mate."

I gripped at my sleeves and rocked back and forth as he draped the cloth around me. I was grateful that someone even respected my privacy. I guess I was so used to not having any I was overcome with awe when it came back, even if I was still being watched through the camera. Dr Olsen then took his seat back on the tiles and slipped my battered shoes from my feet.

"You really got far. I'm impressed." He looked up at me and smiled.

I couldn't smile back. I hadn't the energy. I was barely able to stay sat up. My head drooped from side to side. My eyes were bloodshot, sunken and grey. As was my skin. All over. My hair was matted and greasy with patches seeming to be missing.

I became fixated on the doctor's actions. After he slipped the jeans from my legs, he found his way to the bandages. He carefully fumbled around each one, searching for the end and unravelling it down to my blood covered skin. The only part that wasn't grey. Olsen reached into the green bag and pulled out a cloth. He then took out a bottle. He dampened the cloth then dabbed it lightly around the gash. It uncovered the true size of the injury – they were actually smaller than they seemed. Dr Olsen then took out another bottle and ushered me to hold onto the blanket.

"This is gonna sting, okay? But it's gonna help you."

I nodded and bit my lip, bracing for the pain. I didn't see what he did, I only felt it. I whimpered loudly and buried my head into the cave of fabric as the burn of the ointment seared across my leg.

"I know, mate. I know." He rubbed my back as he continued with the process.

I then bit at the sheet, tearing several strings of cotton away as Dr Olsen moved to the final step. He reached for a clean bandage and covered up the slice. It was nice to think that was the end of it, but that was only the first cut. There were still two more on my left leg and four more on my right, including that dog bite, and this didn't even count for what was on my arms. By the time Olsen reached my second leg, I collapsed onto my back. I was still conscious, but I couldn't stay up any longer. The cell was spinning, the bricks on the wall were throbbing, and the light was splitting in two.

Then came a pound on the door. I tensed my body and the doctor quickly scrambled over to the opened panel. Through it, they shoved in my new clothes. A light grey tracksuit. Dr Olsen brought them over then forced me to sit straight once again.

"Come on, Noah. You're doing really well here."

My shoulders slumped forwards and my head hung so low it reached my thighs. I felt as the cotton trousers were shuffled over my feet then shimmied up my legs.

Olsen patted my back again. "Good boy. We're nearly done. Here."

He lifted the blanket from me and adjusted its position to allow me to wiggle out of my soaked layers of tops. I slung them into the corner then huddled up in the blanket as Dr Olsen inspected each arm. He performed the routine, did the same to the gashes on my face, then gently lifted my arms above my head and slipped the clean top over me. Then he took out a small comb and spray bottle and lightly unmatted my hair. It took the horrendous itching away and brushed the torn ends back to where they used to hang.

"There." He patted my shoulder as he packed the kit up. "I can see you now."

I nodded and leant my head on his hand, falling into him as I gave in to the painful endeavour.

"It's alright," he said softly. "You're gonna be alright." He edged me towards the bed behind us. "I'm gonna get you there, okay? You need sleep, mate."

I shook my head, my hair flinging what was left of the dirt out. "No... They'll... they'll..." My body flopped against the side of the bed, and I fell on the brink of sleep.

"Come on, mate. I'll be here the whole time."

He scooped me into his arms and strained as he lifted me onto the bed pad. It took effort from the both of us, but we managed. I rolled onto my side, facing the thick bricks on the wall, as Dr Olsen adjusted the sheet around me.

"I'm gonna see if we can get you some medicine, okay?"

I nodded.

"Did you get any withdrawals?"

I nodded.

He sighed and slowly approached the door. "What kinds?"

I took in a shallow breath. "Shakiness... I can't... I can't understand... anything... my head it's..." I sighed. "I don't know..."

He knocked on the door. "It's alright. I'll see what I can find."

Soon after, I fell asleep. Olsen didn't even get a chance to ask me another question, but my guess was that they gave me my meds anyway because when I awoke the next morning there was a needle mark in the fold of my arm. I was in just the position everybody wanted me. Lethargic, immobile, but I was also the largest threat in the building at the time. I was one of four detained in the station. There was nobody left to attend to. That's why there was so much attention on me. I wish there wasn't, but nobody seemed to have a thing to do.

I slept for eighteen hours straight, Olsen by my side the entire time, even though he was probably sleeping too. An hour after I awoke, a knock came from the other side of the door. I kept my back to them as the doctor approached.

"Yeah?"

"Is he ready?" came the voice.

"It'll be useless, y'know? He's in the height of a delusion."

"There's no time. This case is most important at the minute, and all that matters is finding that boy."

Olsen sighed. "Fine. I'll sort him out."

The shutter slid across with a clang after a clatter of chains were pushed into the cell, the doctor picking them up and cautiously stepping back over to me. His figure appeared at my side, and I glanced up at him, seeing the sets of cuffs swinging from his hands.

"You've gotta do it, mate. They really need your help."

My eyes drifted to a close as I gave him a weak nod.

"Good boy. Come on, sit up."

I forced myself up, dragging my body limply into a seated position – my legs hanging loosely over the edge of the bed. Olsen knelt down and began untangling the chains.

"Is she dead?" I muttered.

"What? Who?" he replied sharply.

"River... I pushed her and she... didn't wake up..."

The doctor clasped one of the cuffs around my ankle. "No, mate. She isn't dead. She was just concussed." He looked up and smiled. "She's gonna be okay."

I sighed deeply as he moved to the next leg. "Where's my book?"

The second cuff crunched together. "It's, uh... it's being held in evidence, mate. The investigators wanted it screened to see what you've written in it."

"Are they expecting a confession?"

He began wrapping a chain around my waist. "Confession to what?"

"To Ryan... I know everyone thinks I took him... It makes sense, don't it? I tried to kill him... wouldn't it make sense for me to kidnap him too?"

He locked the chain in position. "But you didn't kidnap him, did you?"

I shrugged. "No..."

312

"Well, then. I think you're in the clear. Wrists, please."

I limply dragged my hands across the sheet and onto my lap. "Nobody believes me... Nobody ever has."

Olsen locked one hand in position and sighed. "Sometimes people can't find a way to believe you." He locked the other hand and edged back.

I stared down at the metal between my wrists before turning to the concrete on the floor.

The doctor carefully hoisted me to my feet. "Come on, mate. It'll be over as soon as possible."

It was almost icy in the interrogation room. The cold clamps of metal around me sending shivers across my body and the frozen-like bricks enclosed the tiny space, the fluorescent light above flickering with every other second. The detectives entered, striding towards me with confidence before sitting across from me. They adjusted themselves and their equipment, mumbled a few phrases then pressed down on a recording machine button.

They looked up at me, sending a shudder down my neck which forced my gaze to the floor. I couldn't bear to look at them, the two of them held such fire in their eyes that one second of contact with them would scorch me.

"Questioning start on interviewee Noah James Coleman, time is 16:32, interviewee is here without legal counselling, interviewee is here with Dr Joel Olsen, trained psychologist. Interview conducted by Detective Whitney Hunt and Detective Robin Pence." The woman turned to me. "Mr Coleman, do you know why you're in this questioning?"

I didn't move.

"Mr Coleman?"

Dr Olsen ran his hand up and down my back in a considerate manner. "Noah?"

I gazed out of the corner of my eye.

"You need to answer the questions."

I peered across the tabletop.

"Do you know why you're being questioned today?" they repeated.

"For breaking into the school..." I muttered quietly.

"Yes. We want to ask you what you know about this boy." They presented me an image. "Ryan Axel."

I stared at it, analysing every inch of his appearance. Pale, freckled, and frizzy raven-haired, his mischievous personality beaming through his bright eyes whilst the hermit side of him hid behind them.

"Mr Coleman," said the second detective, her voice calmer and more caring than her colleague's. "Do you know Ryan Axel?"

I nodded meekly.

"You've got to speak out loud, mate," added Olsen.

I glanced between him and the interviewers. "Sorry… yes."

"Okay." She scribbled in her notes. "Are you aware that he is missing?"

"Yes…"

"Do you know where he is?"

I stuttered, staring hopelessly at the photo of the lost boy, clenching my eyes and turning away from guilt.

"Mr Coleman?"

My head hung low. "I…"

The doctor chimed in again. "Come on, mate. We want to find him."

I refused an answer.

The woman cleared her throat. "Mr Coleman, why did you break into Layset Secondary School?"

I trembled, my voice whining as I let out a breath.

"Noah?"

"To… To…" I shook my head and looked to Olsen with teary eyes. "I can't…"

He wrapped his arms around me and held me close. "It's alright, mate."

I shuddered at the embrace but clung to him as he spoke.

"It's not likely that he's gonna tell you much of the truth. He has severe memory issues—"

"Yes, we know, doctor," the detective interrupted. "We've read his files. Mr Coleman seems to have quite an array of psychiatric problems."

He grumbled under his breath. "You're telling me."

"Listen, doctor. Ryan Axel has been missing for over 4 months and your patient is the only person left that links to his disappearance."

"Well, if you think that he kidnapped him, you've got a lot of faith in him since he was hospitalised at the time."

"We don't think he did it, but he has connections to Axel."

Olsen sighed and I retracted from his containment, wiping my eyes and sniffling.

"I didn't take him…"

Their voice became calmer. "We know you didn't, Noah."

"I—was—only—trying—to help."

"By doing what, Noah?" the woman asked.

"I… I don't know… I was… confused and… I didn't…" I gripped at the chain around my waist.

"Hey." She lightly tapped the table. "It's alright."

I let the chain slump down, the metal rattling as it coiled around itself.

She smiled. "Maybe if we start from the beginning, will that make you feel better?"

I nodded.

"Okay." She adjusted the papers around her and inspected the pages of my file. "Now, when did you first learn about Ryan Axel's disappearance?"

"When I saw it on the TV… in Riptide."

"Riptide?"

The other detective shrugged.

"It's the nickname of the sector he was in back at the hospital," explained the doctor.

"Oh, right," the woman replied in understanding, jotting down some more writing. "So, after you escaped the hospital, Noah, where did you go?"

"I… broke into a house."

The officers glanced at each other then slid an image of the invaded home.

"Is this the house, Noah?"

I nodded shamefully.

They tucked the image away. "Okay." They spoke towards the recorder. "Interviewee is nodding his head."

"I didn't mean to hurt them…" I continued.

"It's okay, Noah," said the woman. "We're not here to talk about that."

"I'm sorry… I was just scared."

"It's fine, Noah. It's okay."

I swallowed the dryness in my throat away.

"What happened after you left the house?"

"I went to the train station. I met with… Aaron."

"Your boyfriend Aaron?"

I nodded.

"I see." She added another note and explained my action out loud.

"And what happened to Aaron? Do you know where he is?"

I frantically shook my head. "No, no. We stayed in this place overnight and we went to the shops, but then the police found me, and we ran, but then he disappeared, and I looked for him and, and—" My breaths sharpened as my cheeks were suddenly swept with tears.

Olsen began to comfort me. "Shh, shh, Noah. It's okay."

"It's not! It's not!" I cried. "He's gone! They got to him!" I yanked at the chains once more, the guard in the corner edging closer.

The woman turned to him with her arm out. "It's alright. Don't touch him. He's fine, leave him." She turned back. "It's alright, Noah. We'll find him."

"Th-they took him! Like they took Ryan! They found him! They got to him – he said he was scared – they found him!"

"Who's 'they' Noah?"

"The people! C-Caleb! He d-drugged me. Him and the people with the ovals."

"What are the ovals?"

"There's three of them. One blue, one red, one grey, and they go over each other. Ryan's seen the same."

Each officer glanced to one another as one shuffled the pictures. They presented the image of my room wall.

"You mean these ovals, Noah?"

I edged closer to the desk. "H-How did you get that?"

"Noah—"

"That's my room! How did you get that? " I reached forwards, Olsen grabbing my handcuffs and holding me down.

"It's fine, mate. I gave the picture to the police after you escaped. I gave them quite a few, but it was all to help bring you home."

I shuffled. "Y-You gave them… Oh…"

The detective exhaled slowly. "So, these people – they had this mark on them? Like a gang symbol?"

I shook my head as I sat back down. "No. It wasn't on them, but it was always there – the USB, the lab – so was the monarch."

The detectives grew more tense with every question.

"What was in the lab?"

"The drug! They gave it to me!"

"Was the drug LSD?"

"No! Otherdoxersiderin!"

"Is this a new drug? Is it being produced?"

With each word, I gradually rose from the chair. "Yes! They're drugging criminals! That's why they're all going! They took Aaron! And they probably took Ryan too! That's why I went to the school! To help River and Tess get their friend back! To protect them!"

Dr Olsen shot up, pushing my chair out of the way, gripping the chain, and yanking me away. "That's it! I don't want this to go any further."

"Let go of me!" I yelled as I writhed back and forth in agitation.

"Doctor, we are trying to solve this case! If there is a new drug on the market then we need to be ready for it!"

He wrapped his arms around my chest as I jolted for freedom. "There is no drug!"

"YES, THERE IS!"

"No! There's not! He's manic! You're feeding his delusions by playing into the idea!"

"I'M NOT DELUSIONAL!"

The others leapt forwards.

"Coleman, please. Calm down."

I twisted my wrists, trying to slip out of the metal as Olsen tightened his grip around me. "No!"

The guard ripped the doctor away and kicked my legs to buckle them. I collapsed to the ground, yelling as my ankle crunched against the leg cuff. As the guard pinned me in place, a buzzer sounded and several other officers charged in, all of them forcing me into a different position. They lifted me up, my legs flailing as my sense of direction was flipped.

"PUT ME DOWN!"

They barged out of the door, dragging me through the dull, paint-peeled corridor, all whilst Dr Olsen chased after us.

"Stop! You can't treat him like this!"

"There's no other choice," replied an officer. "If he wasn't restrained, he could've attacked you."

"I wouldn't!" I cried.

They swung my cell door open, and the group pinned me to the bed. I tensed my body harshly, panting just the same, knowing that fighting would only worsen my situation. The chains were ripped from me as the group retreated into the corridor. I curled up on the bed in tears before hearing a woman shouting from down the hall minutes later.

"No! I'm gonna see him! He's my SON! It's my RIGHT!"

"Mrs Coleman, please, your son is far too unstable for you to make contact with him."

"I've been told that for a year and a half! I'm sick of him thinking that I'm not there for him!"

Footsteps began marching towards the cell corridor before a thunder of others swarmed them as I rushed to my door.

"NOAH!" the woman bellowed. "PLEASE! I LOVE YOU, SWEETIE! IT'S GONNA BE OKAY!" she began to sob as officers backed her away. "Please!"

"Maria?" I called through the gap.

"HE'S THERE! Oh, my God. He's there! Noah, I love you so much! I'm so sorry!"

I collapsed against the cell door. "I love you!"

It wasn't before long that the voices distanced, and it was clear that my mum had been taken far from me, but her faint pleas still echoed.

"What's wrong with him? Please, just tell me what's wrong with my son!"

"Noah's very sick, Maria," said Dr Olsen calmly. "He's been spiralling ever since the New Year. His mania is high, he's delirious and his delusions are extremely dangerous to both himself and everyone around him. I'm sure you've seen the news."

"I have! And I'm fed up with these people disgracing him! Every day I read something about him being a psycho and life-threatening, but not one seems to understand why he's turned to this."

"I know, I don't like what they say either. But the thing is, Noah isn't likely to be able to come home again, Mrs Coleman. Who he was isn't there anymore. His mind is scarred. Both mentally and physically. His brain is literally altered, he can't go back to who he was. I'm sorry."

Maria's cries tortured the corridors. They rang through the pipes and ceiling cracks, looming in the dark cells and ripping my wounds open as I begged for forgiveness. I wasn't sure from who.

A few moments later, a small knocking shook the door. I crawled to the corner and watched fearfully as Olsen edged inside. He allowed the cell to be sealed and he leant against the wall, keeping a respectful distance.

"Noah, there's a lot I've wanted to tell you ever since we've met, but all these rules and policies never allowed me to. I used to believe it was for the good of the patient to never trigger their traumas, and I still do believe that, but when you know more about a patient's life than they do..." He sighed. "Do you remember what it was like living at home, Noah?"

I sniffled. "Barely. I remember... a trip... yeah." I spoke with a smile. "When I was seven, I went camping with everyone. I remember running around the campsite with my brother, collecting shells with my dad..." Tears streamed silently down my skin. "... and stargazing with my mum.

One night, when my dad and brother went to go buy marshmallows for the fire, me and mum settled down on the grass. She laid my head on her stomach and she stroked my hair as we just... stared. We stared up at that black night sky, gazing in awe at those bright, twinkling dots that burned millions of miles away. We barely spoke a word, but instantly, I fell in love with that simple feeling, thinking that if this was what life was about then I wouldn't change it for anything." I let my head sink into my knees.

Olsen sighed. "I'm sorry for all of this, Noah. I really am..." He glanced back at the door. "I was sent to tell you that the transfer arrangements to take you back to Ocean Cliff are happening tomorrow evening. I'll be with you all the way." He tapped on the door and it slowly creaked open. "Bye, Noah."

It was true. Five o'clock on the dot was my eviction time. A massive hoard burst into my cell and fixed me to a wheelchair, where I was taken outside, restrained to a bed, and kept down by a low-acting sedative. I was able to hold on long enough to see what the blurred figures around me were doing. They dragged me out to the empty car park, the streetlights flickering as I listened to the sounds of the unlocking van, of the fading voices, and of the slamming of metal against the concrete. The florescent lights dimmed as I was sealed inside the back of the vehicle. Only one person joined me, however. Dr Olsen. He was the only one with me for the duration of the transfer. Even when I was brought to Ocean Cliff the first time, there were at least two people. Now, only one? I let the thought fade. No point in questioning now.

I watched as Olsen strapped himself into the seat beside me as the engine rumbled.

"Do you believe me?" I asked drowsily.

He exhaled deeply as the van pulled away. "I don't want to get into this, Noah. I don't want—"

"You can just say 'no'." I lopped my head to the other side.

"It's not that, mate, it's just... I want to. I really want to, but..." He looked up and shook his head. "I can't."

"It's okay..." I replied. "It doesn't matter anymore..."

He didn't reply. There wasn't anything to be said. We drove a good five minutes before I spoke again.

"I'm not leaving the hospital again, am I?"

"I don't think so, no," he replied softly. "At least not for a good few years."

I nodded. "Do you hate me?"

"Course not."

"Why not?"

He shrugged. "I can't be bothered to hold a grudge. I find it easier to just accept people as who they are at the time. It takes too much energy to be angry." He smiled down at me.

I gave one back before letting my eyes drift close. We carried on with the journey. The rain outside hammering against the top of the van. It was actually quite peaceful. It was loud – I mean recklessly loud – but it didn't seem to bother me. I couldn't say how much time passed. It felt like we were driving in circles, skidding from one lane to the next. I thought it was just me, but when I opened my eyes again, Dr Olsen seemed just as confused as I was.

"What is it?" I questioned.

He flicked through the map on his phone. "We're going the wrong way."

I jolted as I began to panic. "What? "

He slipped his phone back then unclipped himself from the seat to reach me. "Hey, hey, hey. It's fine. It's alright. It's probably nothing." He laid my head back onto the pillow. "It's fine."

I panted violently and my heart pounded heavily against my chest, provoking a nauseating feeling. Dr Olsen knelt down and stroked my forehead whilst he kept hold of my shaking hand. We took in breaths together as we furthered on the concerning journey. This concern reached its peak as the van slowed and the crunching sound of a metal gate echoed through us.

"W-Where are we?" I stuttered, gripping tightly at the doctor's hand.

"I-I don't know, mate."

The van rumbled forwards again, causing the doctor to stumble before the engine disengaged. There were voices outside. Muffled voices. Voices neither of us could understand. Then the doors were flung open. They crashed against the sides as a group forced their way onto the van.

"NO!" I screamed, hysterically yanking at the restraints as I witnessed them grab Dr Olsen's arms.

"What the hell are you doing?" He yelled as he was dragged out of the vehicle with his arms pinned behind his back.

I continued to rip at the restraints, the sound of slow and sudden tearing following each tug. After each hoist forwards, I grew ever so slightly closer to freedom until I was able to leap off of the bed. Except I didn't get far. After the amount of paranoia the police had, they assured themselves that I wouldn't be going anywhere so they added the chains and handcuffs too. They were clamped onto me tightly, so I was forced to watch helplessly as a black jumper-wearing pack wrenched my last remaining friend into the dark mist.

"Don't touch him!" I shouted as a group came for me. "GET OFF!"

"Calm down, you'll only hurt yourself," said a slim, blonde woman as she and her colleagues released the cuff on the bed.

The instant they unlocked, I swung the chain from the railing around me and lashed it at one of the men. He cowered back as blood drew from his cheek, whilst the others quickly lifted me up and flung me over a figure's shoulder. We stepped off of the van and began walking through what appeared to be the back of a warehouse. It was vast and metallic. The walls towered hundreds of feet into the sky with the only light coming from the slim line of windows across the tips of the walls and the gaping open space behind us that led to an empty blackened car park, large pines shrouding the background, giving little knowledge of what laid beyond them. The clanging from before resulted in being the uprising of the thick steel shutter that gave access to said car park. It had now began lowering again.

To my right were rows of lorries. All of them in pristine white with a single symbol printed on the end and several words just to its left. The symbol. The image flashed in my head. It was *that* symbol. The symbol that had no connections. Just three ovals overlapping. One red. One blue. One grey. The words beside it?

'THE ALTERNATING CRIMINAL CORPORATION'

My chest tightened and my heart pounded faster against it. The combination made me sick to my stomach, which was also wrapping itself up in knots. I flailed my body up and down as I tried to escape from the man carrying me but became distracted as I saw the remainder of the pack drag Dr Olsen through a side door.

"Where the hell are you taking him? Let him go! He's done nothing wrong!"

"I didn't know you cared so much about him," the woman replied as she scanned a key card and typed a code into the keypad below. "You never cared about me like that."

The machine beeped and the woman pushed the heavy door inwards. Behind it was a large staircase that curved back and forth with concrete walls lining the sides to cover any kind of spoilers of what could be below. I twisted in the man's arms to face the woman as she marched down each step, her high-top heels echoing with each one.

"I don't know who you are," I said to her quietly, my voice falling back to its normal pitch as another kick from the sedatives surged in me.

"I didn't think you would," she returned as we reached another door. "Even after everything we did together at Wyegate."

"What?"

She scoffed as she typed in another code. "Charming."

I stared at her as I was carried through to a corridor. The sight of her hair, the way she walked, the way she dressed, it did all seem familiar. She walked with a swing in her hips and the sway of her arms. She knew exactly how to play a situation. She had obviously experienced manipulation herself and had learnt how to play it on others. But it wasn't that that triggered my recall. It was her hands. She was the woman who was with me in that lab. She was the one who held the dart gun. The one who drugged me and ripped my skin off. My eyes flickered back and forth as another factor played in my head.

"Abigail?" I muttered.

"Well done," she replied with a glance over her shoulder. "I should think I deserve remembering after letting you off so many times in that place. You and your mates did a whole lot you shouldn't have."

I stuttered as we furthered down the endless hallway. "W-What did we do?"

She raised her eyebrow. "You really want me to answer that?"

I swallowed and turned away in embarrassment.

322

"I thought so."

We reached another door. Through that was another vast room. It was dim. The artificial lights that shone from above seared into my eyes. They blinded my true sights of the room, but from what I could tell, there were countertops lined either side of the crimson-marked walkway. Both were centred between glass-cased shelves, all were packed with different coloured files. All a different size to another. It wasn't all shelves, however. Fixed high on the end of the left wall was a screen. More of that same artificial lighting beaming from it. I became transfixed on it for several moments before my attention shot to a voice.

"What do you think then?" he said as he approached. "Is this what you imagined when you ran with your delusions?"

I kicked my legs out towards him, but he grabbed my ankle quickly and forced them back down. "I knew it..." I whispered. "I KNEW IT!"

Caleb chuckled maliciously. "It's a shame, really. I was hoping to surprise you, but I did really need you back here so there was no time to take you the way we took the others. We needed to take the slow approach with you. In fact, I even thought about letting you live your life at that hospital, but things got out of hand."

I tensed my body angrily and was finally lowered back to my feet, skidding them back as I tried to run for him. I was held in place by the group and the thick chains that hung off me.

I panted harshly. "I'm gonna kill you..."

Caleb smiled in a gleeful way. "I'm glad you've had time to reform."

I swung my leg, missing the attack again. "You're the whole reason all of this has happened!"

"Too right, it is."

"This is nothing to be proud of!" I bellowed, edging inch by inch away from the grasps behind me.

"I think it's everything to be proud of. I've built this place from the ground up, and everyone here has come together to stop people like you."

"THE INSANE? "

"No. Never. The insane need help not punishment. I never took a single person who fell a little too far from the forest."

"The news said you did."

"The news is *never* right, Noah. Too many stories blur together. I took the malingerers. The fakers. I left the ill to get help."

I gritted my teeth. "Still! You kidnapped hundreds of people! Why? "

"Why? Is that really a question? I'm doing this so that people can actually feel safe living their lives again. Do you know how many people I've met that are too scared to walk alone at night because they fear being robbed, because they fear getting kidnapped? Do you know how many women I've met that have a panic attack every time a man walks down the same street as them? Do you know how many men I've met that feel so lonely because every time they step outside others assume they're only going to cause danger to the lives around them? These are the people who have never done anything wrong in their lives but have to suffer because of what other people do. Do you want people to live in fear?"

"Of course not!" I replied, tugging at the chain.

"I'm sure you don't, but that doesn't mean it doesn't happen. Because of predatory men, trans women can't even use a public toilet. Because of the apparent innocence of every woman, the ones that prey on others are let off easily and the victims are left in fear and embarrassment, feeling like it's their fault. This all happens because criminals like you put the thoughts in our heads that we should fear everything."

I stamped my foot and snapped at him. "I would never want someone to feel like that! Never! The only reason I broke the law is because of you! You made me do it! You made me do it all!"

"Did I now? Was I around when you had that LSD? Was I around when you struck your mother square across the face? Was I around when you forged an identity to work in a place you knew you were banned from? No. That was you. They were your actions."

I loosened my stance, the guard behind me stepping closer.

"Do you know what else you did? You escaped the institution you were ordered to stay in, you broke into a family's house, robbed them, nearly *killed* them, then tried to kidnap a teenage girl. That wasn't me, Noah. That was you. You were one of the many files that we had around here. You'd never have been through any of this if you'd have just kept to yourself and been in control of your actions."

I hung my head shamefully and closed my eyes as I spoke. "What about Ryan? What about Dr Wilks?"

Caleb sighed and took the chain from the man. He began unwrapping it from me, finally allowing the heavy weight to be lifted. "Both Ryan and Dr Wilks were accidents. I didn't make the Other Side to kill people. As

324

you may recall, there was a certain phrase that was said on the TV in the common room."

I looked up at him with intrigue. "Monarch's fly in the rain." I made myself shudder from the sentence, the sense of compliance sending a surge through me.

"That's the one. Of course, if anyone else were to say it you'd be complied, but thankfully for you, it can't be self-triggered."

"What happened? Back at the hospital?"

He removed the chain from me and placed it on the counter. I was confused as to why he did it, but at least I wasn't getting pain from it anymore.

"After the phrase complied you, there was a short window where you did whatever someone told you, and it was proven that anyone could give the command, and anyone could trigger you. So when you passed a patient who was screaming about wanting to kill Wilks, it stuck with you until you carried out the action. A similar thing happened with Ryan. A miscommunication here, a complier there, it all led to you attacking Ryan. That was when you came back from the Other Side. It shocked us and it proved another fault in the drug, but we were thankful that the kid survived. That's what forced us to find a new way to induce compliance and why we've scrapped our original plans. This is why we test things."

"What original plans?"

"We weren't gonna keep criminals compliant all the time. We were gonna use them when necessary, but seeing all the trouble we get from just one person, you can see why we've had to resort to plan B."

Caleb stepped away, his back turned for a few seconds. I glanced over my shoulder and watched as a man approached him.

"Why are you telling him all this?" he asked.

He shrugged. "I think he deserves to know. He's helped us a lot in getting to this point. Plus, he spent months trying to figure it out, we might as well mark his test."

I edged my foot and felt the guard's hand slip from my shoulder. I then glanced at Abigail. She was busy flicking through her phone – probably to distract herself from her obvious boredom. No one was watching me. I took another step. They didn't notice. With this in mind, I quickly darted away. The group shouted and a short burst of footsteps followed, but they didn't pursue. My legs carried me past the counters, but moments after I initiated my escape, a piercing chime sounded from behind. It shattered my eardrums and I collapsed to the floor as the pain seared down my neck to my spine. I writhed around on the tiles, yanking and ripping my clothes to try and block the noise out. My eyes watered and reddened as Caleb slowly stooped over me, the noise growing ever more disorientating as he approached.

His voice was firm and loud, and balancing between his fingers was a long, black cylinder, the centre flashing aqua with the speakers on the end seeming to be the cause of the racket. "Pretty cool, right?" He twiddled the machine in his hand. "You know, I wasn't sure if this thing would work since I can barely hear it, but it seems to be effective."

I continued to cry as the ringing drilled into me. That's why he took the chain off, he wanted an excuse to play with his toys.

"Well, even if it didn't work, you couldn't get anywhere. There's no doors down here."

He pushed the cylinder back together, the noise dissipating and the light switching off. I panted breathlessly and rested my exhausted body.

His voice returned to normal. "The Other Side, it enhances your senses. Tactical advantage in most cases… until it's used against you." He clipped the device onto the belt that I didn't even notice he was wearing. Dangling from it were several pieces. The disabler, handcuffs, sedative, and the dart gun. The O.S. vials were glowing as the light hit them. "Did you never wonder why you could hear things so easily when no one else could? Or how you get around so fast and mostly unnoticed? You've got the Other Side to thank for that." He gripped my collar and hoisted me up. "You gonna behave now?"

The group approached and brought me to my feet, gripping at my limbs tightly. "You can't do this…" I said. "This is illegal."

"Wrong again, buddy."

Caleb stepped over to a panel that was fixed beside the cabinets. He typed across it and a section in the case lit up. There was a whirring as the cover unlocked and pushed a single file forwards. Caleb took it out and laid it on the desk. He gestured for me to approach, so I did – mostly due to the fact I had no choice. He opened to the first page, and I gazed across it.

"This file confirms the whole project's legality by several leaders, governments and court systems. Quite a few countries are in on this now. The US, Canada, Russia, Spain." He flicked through several pages then pointed to a signature. "See? The Prime Minister himself approved the whole project, gave money for research, everything."

I stuttered and shook my head. "H-How? That's not possible."

"You've been away from the outside a long time, Noah," he replied. "Prison then hospitalisation. A lot has happened since 2010."

"2010?" I said breathlessly.

"Thirteen years it's taken. Damn, if patience doesn't win the day."

He dragged me across to the other end of the room and typed across a small monitor that was fixed inside the wall below the larger one above. The screen flickered, and several graphs were displayed across it. The left graph displayed an unsteady line with the words 'rates of crime' across the side, the lines jumping up and down as time progressed.

"You see this?" He pointed at the left graph. "It seems you're not the only one who can't control themselves."

I swallowed anxiously as I read over it. I then turned my attention to the graph beside it and shuddered as the line shot downwards. The label across that one, 'After Project Initiated.'

"See? It works. We don't kill anyone, we don't keep people in cages, we just make them comply. We use their skills in ways to help people instead of using them against them. Surely that's better than what was happening before?"

I looked back to Caleb, malicious intent hinting in his eyes. "But people can change. You just need to give them a chance!"

"I gave you a chance. Did you change?"

"I could have!" I yelled, the guards stepping closer.

"Could you? You could have done anything after you got out of prison, you could have done anything after you escaped the hospital, but what did you do?"

I twitched my head as the scenes of my actions flashed in my mind. "No, that doesn't count! I *can* change. I can!"

"Fine! You *did* change! You went from an innocent, loving child, to this!"

I stuttered and took a step back.

"Changing isn't always for the best."

I lowered my head in shame and Caleb took me by the arm and switched off the screen. He escorted me back out to the corridor, the group following behind as I was slowly shuffled along the tiles.

"Can you explain to me why half the people I took care of never changed?" Caleb continued. "Can you explain to me why even though I treated each person the same no matter their race, gender, or sexuality, and they all had the decency to still call me the bad guy? I was the one who took care of them, I was the one that tried to help them become a better person, but what does that get me? MY FAMILY WERE FUCKING SLAUGHTERED!"

I shied away, barely able to accept this reality, and barely able to set myself in Caleb's. "W-What happened?"

He took his time to reply, possibly fighting off his own tears of anger. "I did my job. That's what happened. I punished the guilty, so the guilty had his gang storm my house. I came home to see my wife sliced open in the kitchen with my son ripped apart across his bedroom floor."

I felt a sickness rise up my throat, swelling it shut as the calmness of his explanation haunted me. "Oh, my God…"

Caleb took in a shuddered breath. "I punished the guilty, so the guilty punished me." We reached the metal doors of a lift and Caleb swiped his card through the reader, a small light beeping as it accepted. "They stole my life, so I'm stealing their minds."

Stiffly and heavily, the two steel doors scraped into the hidden slots beside them and revealed a large elevator, the screeching it made sending shivers of pain through my ears.

"I don't understand," I muttered as we stepped in. I went to turn around to face the doors, but Abigail stopped me as everyone else faced the other direction.

"What bit?" Caleb replied as he pulled a latch on the side for the doors to close.

"How did you fake all of it? Blake Hayes, getting into the hospital?"

"I never faked anything. Blake Hayes was my legal name at the time. I changed it after…" He took a pause in his speech and fiddled with the ring around his neck. "… after things happened. I then changed it back after the project gained traction. I… never really liked my other name. Then I met Dr Hawthorn. He seemed to hold the views I had. He's the one that swindled the system to let you into Ocean Cliff. That way we could keep an eye on you. Then when Jaiden left, I had the perfect opportunity to come."

We all stumbled as the lift began to lower. I stared at the slates on the floor as the lift furthered underground until it thudded into place and came to a stop. I glanced behind and noticed the group zip up their jackets. I then

328

glanced at Caleb as he adjusted the long black coat he was now wearing. I hadn't even noticed him pick it up, let alone put it on. He fastened the disabler on his belt as the doors pried themselves open. As the seal broke, a blizzard of frosty gusts attacked us. Some of the guards behind shivered as we stepped into the initial mist that shrouded the elevator. I did the same as I was directed through it to the clear air.

It appeared as a corridor at first, but as I reached my hand out to what I thought was a wall, my hand pushed through it. I retracted it quickly as I glanced back at Caleb. He smirked at my confusion then fiddled with a control panel on a wall beside the lift. A switch engaged, causing the mountain-high poles above the curtains to retreat effortlessly into the shafts in the wall, the hundreds of feet of fabric clenching together.

As I turned back, the true room was revealed. It extended further than any sane mind could perceive. The system merged into one. The system, it was fixed to the towering black ceiling. The thick, matching pipes rumbling and gushing as its contents were rushed through to the rapid fans and escaping frozen gas that filled the space with its cold chill.

As this drifted down, it cloaked what was most disturbing. Each ending of the pipe was fixed to a metal square that connected to a neon-glowing glass case. There were five main levels, each case lined with a metal walking grate. Inside each one were draping wires and tubes that extracted the liquid from the holding above. The wires were fixed onto a device with several metal plates. The plates, they were tightened to the temples of the person trapped inside. Each one was unconscious with every one of them wearing the same outfit. Crisp white overalls. Across the left side was the same symbol that was printed on the trucks, and underneath, the words 'Property of the A.C.C.'. They weren't their own person anymore. I caught in the reflections of the glass at the large black letters printed across their backs. 'COMPLIER'. Attached to their arms – the tubes. Every single case, every single level, the same.

Except one. The figure inside was a lot smaller than the ones around them and seemed to be the only one without this silky outfit. Their hair was dark, and their skin was bright and freckled. Around the front of their neck was a thin scar, the length of the wire I had once used to strangle him. I placed my palms on the pane of glass and stared at the young boy attached to the machine in regret.

"Why did you take him?"

"He was getting too close to the project. If he found something to set you free then our plans for you would have been destroyed."

I glanced over my shoulder at him. "But he's not a criminal. If this is about saving the innocent then why drug one? "

"We're not drugging him. We're just wiping his memory. Like the drug did to you. He won't remember a single part of this project once he's released. It'll keep him sane. He was falling into a pit. Sound familiar?"

My breath shuddered, the swirls forming from the cold. "How did you do this to me?"

I saw Caleb's reflection in the glass as he shrugged and placed his hands in his pockets. "When the drug had finally dissipated in your mind, a small trace of it was left to linger. It settled into the grooves in your brain and caused your memory loss. The drug never went away. It's why whenever your brain was scanned, the machines couldn't comprehend it. It was read as scarring."

"What about my disorders? You caused them too?"

"Merely side effects. What you were seeing was caused by the tiny traces of lingering LSD. We're honestly not too sure how it stayed there so long, but you learn something new every day. We took this and altered the drug so that the compliancy won't take effect within Ryan. He'll be let go soon."

I stared at Ryan's lifeless form. "How?" I swung my head to face Caleb whilst keeping my hands firmly on the glass. "How did you get so many people?"

Caleb shrugged. "We just gave them a drink and a choice." He stepped over to a table opposite me. "For those like Ryan, we used the dart gun – used sedation needles – they gave a short spout of compliancy on the subject before they collapsed. Then for the ones already in prison…" He typed across a laptop and the screen inside the wall behind me flickered. "… we told each inmate that if they drunk a small vial of the O.S. then they could be out of prison over the next month. The only condition was that if over that time they decided they wanted to stay, then we'd have to transfer them." He smirked. "We didn't tell them where."

"So what happened?" I questioned, my hands slipping from the glass.

"Almost all agreed to the deal," he replied. "Except a few. We had to deal with them in a more forceful manner to get them here." He flashed the dart gun at me slyly as he tapped a series of keys. "As for the ones that took it…"

The video crackled and revealed Caleb sat in an interrogation room with a different inmate sat across from him every few seconds. Between the two, resting on the metal table, was a bright crimson vial. Each inmate acted so normal. But then they took the vial. The screen switched to the main cell block and showed the pixelated image of every one of them in a state of hysterics and bliss.

"… they all decided to stay."

I stuttered and stared at the recording in sorrow.

"The Other Side has been made in many forms," continued Caleb. "But drinking this version was proven to be most addictive. It's the slowest one to result in compliancy, but the side effects were near to instant. Happiness, excitement… hallucinations." The screen switched to another scene caught by the CCTV. It showed the excited inmates all dashing around as they fought for food. "It also causes the munchies, apparently." Caleb chuckled. "Increased metabolism. It's why you're the size of a twig." He stepped back over to me. "It wasn't until they were finally complied that the searing, poisonous pain set in, but by then they were already ours. It wouldn't have been so bad if they hadn't kept begging for more… but that's what addiction gets you, I guess."

"That's because you made them take it!" I yelled. "You drugged them and brainwashed them into wanting to be happy—"

I reached my hands towards him, gripping at his coat until he unclipped the disabler from his belt.

"Now, now," he said teasingly.

I sighed and forced myself to release him, fighting even harder to contain my emotions.

"Good." He slipped the device back onto his belt. "Anyway, I didn't force that lot to do anything. They chose to take the drink, and I followed through on my deal. We transferred them. To here."

He then lowered his other hand and wrapped his fingers around the dart gun. He pulled it out and edged the tip of the needle towards me. He backed me into Ryan's container and grinned. My skin shivered and crawled as I felt the phantom pressure against my neck.

"All it took was patience." He pointed the gun at the screen.

I followed its direction and watched as the video fast-forwarded to show those same inmates dotted around the block streamed head-to-toe in piercing aqua veins. All of them completely numb to their surroundings. Not a shred of emotion within them.

Caleb turned the needle back to me, this time holding it against my skin, and brushing the tip across my scar. "This method was far too risky to use on over 300 inmates at a time. We'd have been easily overthrown." He tapped the gun lightly on the glass. "The case stimulates them enough for the drug to reproduce itself inside the body. The cold numbs the body – compliers deal well in the cold but stick them in the heat and they'll collapse.

Once that stage is complete, the machine keeps them alive until a handler comes for them. If no one comes, they'll still be living their lives – just not a real one. It'll be a simulation in their minds.

And within this simulation? Guilt. The guilt is what torments them to obey the compliancy. It inflicts trauma onto them. They'll have no memory of what came before. Each part of this project is just a puzzle piece. Without the rest, you can't complete the picture." He smiled. "Of course, a year ago we didn't have all this figured out, so we needed to send you somewhere where we knew you'd never be taken seriously if you ever did remember what happened." He gripped at my wrists and dragged me towards the guards. "It was just time before we took you too."

The guards held my arms as Caleb returned the gun to his belt. I had another flash of memories. "So you're the one who brought in that book? You wanted me to read it."

He shrugged. "It was a long shot, but it's pretty easy to divert your attention to something. I at least wanted the thought in your head before I gave you your choice."

"What choice?" I said carelessly.

"I told you that if you ignored this then you would get to live on as normal, but you didn't, did you? You had to press on! Everyone gets a choice, and you just took the wrong one." He began stepping further down the walkway. "So I guess I'll give you another one."

Caleb headed down the empty strip, the group dragging me behind him with my feet getting drifted across the floor. We didn't walk very far, we passed a few tanks but stopped at one I wouldn't have even noticed. It was to the right. It was alone with the machines surrounding it. Inside, slumped against the glass donning the same outfit as the others, was Aaron.

"Oh, my God…" I said shakily, darting for the container as I was released.

Caleb stepped beside me. "Found him lost in the woods. Damn shame it was us that found him instead of the police."

I glanced at him as I kept my body against the glass.

"If you take his place, we'll comply you instead. Aaron will be free to live another day without you."

"And if I don't?"

"Well, you'll be complied anyway. Aaron would just have to go through the same route the others did. Either way, you both broke the law." He gently pulled a magnificent crystal from his pocket and presented it in his palm. "Look familiar?"

The lump in my throat clogged my ability to speak. Only a name slipped out. "Bella?"

Caleb chuckled and passed the ruby away to his colleague, who appeared familiar. "They got caught the same time as Aaron. Bella brought us to her home. Thanks to her, another criminal operation was brought down."

I followed his gaze to one of the upper levels and caught sight of Bella's unruly hair before I turned back to the woman holding the ruby. "You! You were the one at the hospital! You were that investigator!"

"Oh, you remember her then?" said Caleb. "Those two were sent for a catch up with you. We needed to see what state you were in, only those two girls pleaded with the police to join them, which kind of battered the plans."

I sighed and turned back to Aaron's case, ignoring more of my betrayed life. He was helpless. Unless I took his place. Even if I had never met him in Wyegate, he'd have still wound up in that box – only without someone to save him. He has more of a family than I'll ever have. He's got two sisters. Three nephew's. A niece. A mother. All of whom he can remember, and they remember him. I switch with him, and he can go back to that. Or was it all a trick? If I don't switch, I'll end up in a case anyway. We'd both be trapped.

I rested my forehead against the glass. "Can I know one thing?"

He smirked. He must have known exactly what I was thinking. "Sure."

"You'll let him go. You'll let him walk out of here, and you won't touch him?"

"He'll have to be kept a few nights for us to launch this all to the public, but yes. We'll let him go. As long as he doesn't try anything. If he does, he'll have to pay for it."

My breath shook as I reached my hand for the release leaver that was attached to the side of the case. It was the one for the many. I pulled the latch underneath, and the seal was broken. The cold air swarmed out of the cracks, and I crouched down beside Aaron. I lightly shook his shoulders, and he awoke.

His eyes were heavy, and his movements were slow, his head flopping to face me. "Noah…"

I held his neck. "Hey, A." My voice began to break.

He tried to inspect his surroundings, placing his palm against the side pane as he tried to lean forwards. "What's going on?"

I shook my head, my smile teetering on the edge of a cliff. "Don't worry. Just… here." I gripped under his arms and hoisted him up from the ground.

He stumbled back as he tried to get the feeling back into his legs. From what expression he could form, his face told the same story mine did upon facing the glassy sea. "What the hell is going on?"

Two ACC members pulled him from my arms whilst another backed me into the machine. Aaron, trying his best, attempted to pull away, but his body was still too weak from the sedation. I knew that feeling too well.

Caleb stepped towards me, his coat revealing the dart gun as he turned. "I'm glad that you made that decision." He gestured to his team. "Equip him."

As the group approached with their tangles of metal and wires, I heard Aaron become progressively more frantic. His voice grew louder, and he was starting to regain his strength to an extent where he swung one of the members behind him as he angled his body. I watched through the heads around me as Caleb approached him, his hand hovering over the gun.

"Be quiet. Don't move another muscle. Try anything and I'll shoot you. That'll really take the shine away from your boyfriend's beloved deed."

Aaron stuttered. "I don't understand. What are you doing to him? What are you doing?"

I evaded my eyes from the scene as I had a catheter injected into each arm. I had my chest strapped into the thick restraint that was dangling on the wall of the container, along with similar material keeping my hands back, followed by the wired device that was fixed to my head, two silver plates clinging to my temples. I flinched as they fastened them, as I did

334

when they snapped a monitor connector onto my fingertip.

"Complying him," Caleb continued. "He's one of many that will help change the world for the better." He turned as he called. "Isn't that right, Noah?"

I remained silent.

"See? He's learning the ways of the complier already."

The members laughed, but I still refused to fight them. They'd won. They'd won far before all of this. Then with one final action, I had the blood drained from my left arm. It was only a short withdrawal, but it was enough for them to get their fix. My blood was sealed into a container of its own before being enclosed into the data machine that stood to my left outside the compliance tank.

Caleb returned to me. "You see, this is where we'd start the whole monarch transfer – it eats up the whole day – but since we've done this dance before..."

A doctor approached with an orange butterfly in a glass cube. It was stuck to one of the sides. Caleb took the cube and presented the bug to me.

"Do you recognise this guy? He's been with you all the way through your stay at Ocean Cliff. It took you a while to notice him, though." He stepped closer. "Here. Wanna see something cool?" He moved the case away, the butterfly franticly flapping over to the side closest to me. He turned the case again, the same action happening. "See? He's only interested in staying with you. It's how we found him so easily. We have you, we have your monarch." He gave a short glare at one of the younger members. "Although... due to a slight *human error*, several monarchs managed to escape without the process being completed. Hence the fact there's a few butterflies already out there." He then traded the creature for another item. "And one more thing." He presented the cover of my book.

"My journal."

He flicked through the pages. "You really got it all down, didn't you? I'm surprised you've still got your hand attached."

"You learn to write fast when you've had to do four English GCSE papers."

He scoffed. "You know what's faster, though?"

Caleb stepped over to the machine beside me and slotted the book inside. He swiped across different screens until a whirring sounded. The plates around my temples began to buzz as the sensation of sharp pins prickled across my skull. The whirring grew faster, and a familiar sound of printing seemed to jerk from the machine. The buzzing slowly faded as Caleb reached for the printed paper.

He cleared his throat. " *'The buzzing slowly faded as Caleb reached for the printed paper. He cleared his throat. Wait. How? How has he managed to do this? He's literally reading my mind.'"*

The group of ACC members snickered as Caleb turned the sheet to me. "Feeling exposed?"

I whimpered and lowered my head in embarrassment.

"See? We can see exactly what's in your mind once you're in that machine. We can see exactly what you've done. You can't hide from your crimes when they get printed straight from your brain." The gathering snickered more as Caleb slotted the paper in with my journal. "Seriously, though. You're so poetic. Maybe in another life you were a writer... with those four English GCSEs."

Aaron grumbled behind him and kicked his legs towards him. "Stop! It's bad enough you've got him strapped in there like some test subject, you don't have to taunt him!"

Caleb smirked. "Well, that's the thing, int it? He *is* a test subject. Subject E if that paper read correctly." He approached my case and rested on the handle. "I guess all that's left now, is for me to close this door."

I kept my eyes on his. They were no longer caring. They were no longer considerate. They were just cold.

He whispered into my ear. "I guess you weren't crazy after all, huh?"

I bit my lip to contain my anger as he chuckled and swung to the side. "Hey, Wickers."

Aaron looked up at him after fighting to hold his tongue.

He nodded at me. "Say goodbye."

The group let him go and he rushed to me. He ran his hands across each of the devices that hung off me, pulling at them lightly in an attempt to free me, but all it did was cause shooting pains up and down my body.

"Please! Please, just stop," I trembled through teary eyes. "Just go."

He wrapped his arms around me and spoke softly. "I'm so sorry, Noah. I'm so, so sorry. This is my fault. I went to find you after you got lost, but they found me. I'm so sorry."

I closed my eyes as his embrace lingered. "I'm sorry too. I love you."

"I love you too."

We retracted. "Remember that for me. Please."

He swallowed as he nodded. "I will."

Aaron was then yanked backwards by the guards and restrained once again. This time he did not fight them. He understood what had to happen. It's the one for the many. Take the mind of one so that the many can live on without fear.

"How touching," Caleb replied sarcastically. He pushed Aaron away from his path and grabbed the latch on the container door. "All those years ago, if you had just stayed put in your house, you wouldn't have done any of the things you have. Think on that."

And with that, he slid the door across, the metal latches on the side interlocking with each other and cutting all contact with me. The chaotic noise of the O.S. lab ceased to nothing. Every word that was said on the outside was nothing but a muffle, and whatever word I'd say would never reach out of the box, but I could still see. For my last few moments.

I watched as Abigail typed on the keyboard beside me and ignited the Other Side. She flipped a switch and pushed a button, and that was all it took. The vents in the top of the container creaked and shot out the jets of frozen air. I jolted from side to side, but the restraints restricted my upper movements, all I could do was kick my legs about which only led to me falling and getting held up by the chest strap. I felt my nerves start to give in and my hands lost all ability to move, and the drug hadn't even entered my system yet. It wasn't until I could no longer stand that they let the O.S. loose. It sawed through the tubes from the source box and flooded into my arms.

The thing was it didn't hurt. It wasn't in any way like the last time. Well, that's what I thought. My nerves had been so dampened that I couldn't feel what they were really doing. The device on my head started to blink and vibrate and shock volts through to my brain where it met with the Other Side that was slowly working its way through me. I closed my eyes and my head drooped to the side, only for me to shoot up again as I realised what was happening to me. I had phases of complete bliss followed by extreme terror. It felt like a part of me wanted it whilst the other part tried to keep fighting for me to stay in control. In fact, I had spent so long going over what I was doing I hadn't noticed the commotion through the glass.

The ACC members were being pushed up against the different complier containers by Aaron and several other figures. The layers of glass that surrounded me blurred the view of another member casting what seemed to be a young girl to the floor. She skidded across the tiles only to jump back to her feet and try another attempt. She kept returning to the same case with another girl to try and break through to the unconscious boy inside. Like they were on a loop, the scene kept replaying with the violence increasing. Upon further inspection I noticed that one of the men fighting back was Dr Olsen – he'd broken free from his captures and had somehow made it all the way down here.

Caleb seemed to be getting outraged by the swaying of his plans and reached for the dart gun on his belt, cocking it and forcing the full vial into position. He pointed it towards the group as Dr Olsen grabbed him from behind, moving his arms to direct the drug away. I made an attempt to help warn them of the oncoming swarm of coated maniacs that were ready to take them. I shrieked. I shouted. I screamed. But just like a faded memory, not one person could hear me, and I was forced to watch helplessly as Dr Olsen had his arms ripped backwards by the guards and crumple to the floor in pain – I can only imagine the cracking that came with it. I can also only imagine the smash and shattering of the sheets of glass that finally gave in as the girls broke through to Ryan on their last attempt before being hoisted from the ground and dragged flailing across the lab.

Before I could make another cry, I watched as Caleb marched over to my machine and ramp up the rate of the drug. The increased flow caused me to twitch and jolt violently to the point where my entire system was trembling and the shocks from the device on my head came at me harder. They came in short bursts like before, only this time they were too much for me to handle and with the power of the Other Side, it all stopped. I was catatonic. My eyes floated shut and I was left gripping at the very few thoughts I had left, until one by one, they left. I became empty.

As my movements ceased, I heard a voice. It was a child's voice. It was behind me. Suddenly, I had the power to awaken, but as my eyes burst open, I was no longer in the lab. I was in a school. It wasn't Layset, it was another. It was a lot smaller too. I towered over everything. I barely fit through the doorframes.

I felt a strange fuzzing inside me, like I was trapped inside a broken TV, static floating through the air. I faded across the room. It was a classroom. The tables were cramped together, each chair facing the static board on the wall. I ran the tips of my fingers across the front desk, feeling

338

the specks of dust across my skin. I lifted my hands and watched as the specks separated and floated through the colours in the air. I kept sight on it as it merged with pastel streams that circled past me until the young voice came again.

It came from another room. I followed the waves. They led me through the tiny halls and found a little boy sat on a green sofa. He was kicking his short legs over the edge with his hands wedged beneath his thighs. I stepped around the corner of the wall, spotting a woman standing over him. Her black heels morphed back and forth between the simple shoes that they were, and the claws that they became when the growl came from her mouth.

"Why did you do it?" she snarled.

The boy kept his head down.

The woman's voice became deeper, the growl forming. "Why did you do it? "

The boy whimpered and began trembling.

"There's no point in sulking! That won't get you anywhere in life!"

I felt a flash come across my head. I could feel what the kid was feeling. Scared. Embarrassed. Guilty. He wanted to go, he wanted to be anywhere but there, but he couldn't. He had to sit and have his guilt hammered into him. He couldn't leave. He had to be punished. Because that was in the rules.

"Well? Why'd you do it?"

The boy sniffled. "I don't know…"

"You don't know?"

His voice was broken. "No…"

"That's not an answer, Noah!"

I hid behind the wall and scratched my nails at the paint as the little boy's sadness became my own. I ran my fingers through my hair and peeked back around the corner only to shout in distress as the woman appeared inches from me. Her face was melted, and the bones had been stretched outwards, forming a skinless muzzle, the melted fragments of her facing dripping down to the bone claws that ripped up the carpet as she preyed upon me.

"WHY DID YOU DO IT? "

I fell to the floor, backing up frantically to escape the growing beast. "I-I don't know!"

The creature extended its abnormal self towards me as I was trapped

339

by a corner. Its legs snapped and crunched as it enlarged. It jerked and zapped to a new position every second as it screeched.

"WHY DID YOU DO IT? " The beast swung its paw across the bricks, tearing each one apart and sending them flying into the deep mist behind it, its battered wings blackening the room. "WHY? "

I cowered amongst the rubble, hiding my face from the nostrils of the darkened demon. I sobbed loudly. "I DON'T KNOW!"

Then suddenly, a gust of silence. I darted my eyes up from my arms, scanning around to see that I was no longer in the school. It was a large, blank corridor, the walls built up from large bricks. I brought myself to my feet, slowly straightening my body as I stared down the halls at a shining door. I approached it, carefully pulling at the handle. It easily drifted open, and I stepped through to a place I hoped to never see again. The door creaked shut, and I was left staring helplessly at the net above. It dangled from the two grated walkways that connected to the rows of steel doors. It was repeated on several levels. I shook my head and held my hands on my neck as I stumbled back and forth across the abandoned block before freezing as I caught sight of Aaron on the staircase ahead.

"Aaron!" I rushed over to him, but he ignored my calls and headed up to a higher level. "Aaron?"

He quickly dashed across the grate, hiding his face from me as he swung himself into our old cell. I followed him, the walkway rattling as I swiftly bounded after him. I shoved the door outwards as I stumbled in. It slammed shut behind me, but as I looked up, I was alone. Alone in an old house. There was a soft orange glow coming through the curtains that shone over the brown and navy room. I circled the coffee table, dusting my fingers across the dead petals of the lone daffodil that was rested in the slim pot.

I took my hand away as it shrivelled up and heard another string of voices coming from another room. I followed the conversation out past a staircase and into the kitchen with the same amber glow. Sat at a circled table in the centre were a gathering of people. Maria, Richard, my brother, a woman, and me. I jumped back behind the wall as I saw them, listening closely to their conversation.

"Why didn't you tell us?" Maria began.

My other self shrugged and picked at his fingers. "I was scared, okay?"

"You shouldn't have to be scared to talk to us, Noah," she replied. "We would never have judged you for it."

340

"How was I to know that?"

I began to mouth my own words.

Richard waved his hands as he spoke. "You couldn't have, but you should have trusted us, mate. We'll love you for who you are."

"I'm sorry…"

The young woman placed her hand on my shoulder as he teared up. "The main thing is, you've told us now."

I watched as I fell forwards onto the table with my arms to guard my face. "I'm sorry. I'm sorry."

Maria rubbed her hand on my back and pulled me towards her. "Shh, honey, it's okay." I shook in her arms as she lifted my head and stroked my cheek. "I just wish that we knew this before all of this mess happened. Maybe you wouldn't have gone to that place, and you'd have found somebody."

I sat up and wiped my eyes. "I, um… I did find somebody."

Maria swallowed and shuffled in her seat. "Oh? Really?"

"Yeah… and… I met him… at… Wyegate."

The group glanced uncomfortably at each other.

"Oh… um, right," stumbled Maria. "W-What's his name?"

I felt a gush of wind belt past me, causing me to wince and cover my eyes as the sharp specks of dust sliced past my skin and whisk the scene away. As I peered through the gap between my arms, I watched as the bright beams of the kitchen faded to become the greyish-cream tint of a smooth papered wall. I let out a breath as the static specks merged to form the old room.

"You look funny like that," came a voice from behind.

I quickly spun to face him, revealing the navy bed behind me. "Aaron?"

He was stood staring in my direction with a quaint smile across his face, his hands in his trouser pockets and his hair curling over itself in its usual way.

"I can't bloody get it off!" another voice called.

I stepped to the side as I saw myself hanging half out of the wardrobe. I had my head poking out the hole of a very tight jumper, my arms hanging limp at my sides as the sleeves cut their movements.

Aaron chuckled and stepped over to save me. "Dear, oh dear." He grabbed the cotton and tugged it off.

"Ow! My beautiful face!"

Aaron threw the top to the floor and smirked. "Oh, shut up."

My alter chuckled, as did I.

"Maybe I'll just wear a blazer," I replied.

We both smiled as Aaron swayed me back and forth. "Seems like a smart idea."

I reached into the wardrobe and took out a black jacket that matched the rest of my neatly ironed outfit. I swung it over me and closed the doors.

"I feel like a marshmallow," I continued as I waved my arms about, the overly large blazer swinging with me.

"Well, I like marshmallows," Aaron replied as we stepped over to the centre of the room.

"You might like them now, but when a hoard of Year 7s come at you swearing 'til the sun goes down, you'll change your mind." I lifted the backpack from underneath the desk and placed it on the bed.

Aaron followed. "Why are you still working there? You don't need to now, nobody's tracking what you do every hour of the day anymore."

"I know," I returned. "But I don't think I wanna risk trying to find another job – you know how it went before this one."

Aaron wrapped his arms around my back and rested his head on my shoulder. "I know."

"Plus, I like it there. There are a lot of kids that are annoying, but the others are pretty nice. They trust telling me things that they don't even tell the actual teachers. I don't want them to have the same school experience I did. I didn't even get my A-Levels in the end."

Aaron stepped back as I faced him. "Neither." We embraced. "I love you."

"I love you too." I pulled back and swung my bag over my shoulder. "Right, I gotta go. I'll see you later." I darted out of the room before he even replied.

"Bye." He chuckled then tidied up the pile of strewn clothes.

I approached him slowly, holding my hand out to reach for him. I swallowed and felt my fingers faze through his shirt, sending a shiver across me as Aaron's figure shimmered and split into static. The room shifted once more. This time as though on a conveyor belt. The floor trembled as it shot me towards the wall. I fell back and scrambled the best I could to escape, but there was nowhere to go. I was fixed to my side as the wall burst in two, ready to consume what was inside. The belt gave jagged movements back and forth before I was slammed through the blackened opening and smashed to a tiled floor.

I winced and rolled my heavy body to its front. There was a sense of metallic in the air, the sounds of electric whirs swarming the white painted hall around me. I pushed up from the ground and straightened out. I ran my hands across my face as the fuzzing grew louder. I drifted my gaze down and jolted frantically as I noticed my clothes. I sprinted towards the flickering light that was fixed to the ceiling and placed my hands firmly on the metal sign that was fixed below it.

'SECTOR 3'

I slammed back against the wall and began to hyperventilate. My legs twitched violently before giving in and dropping me back on the cloud-coloured tiles. I gripped my nails across them as I buried my head inside my chest. I felt my heart skip and pound as the static thunder started to control my body. I writhed back and forth as I stared down at my hand in horror as from underneath my sleeve came an aqua glow. I pulled it down and scrambled up again as the vibrant beams consumed the veins beneath my skin. I ripped down the other sleeve. The same thing. I quickly scrubbed at the pristine tiles and watched my reflection turn blue. Across my face came the trail. It nestled inside me as it worked its way to my eyes. They became cast over. Glowing strong with the beam of the Other Side.

I let out a stifled cry as from above, a song began to play. It was calm. The voices were from a choir of children.

'When the world calls for us, we should never make a fuss.
Comply. Comply.
When we're told what not to do, we should always listen to you.
Comply. Comply.
If you question, there's no doubt, we'll have no choice but to shout.
Comply. Comply.
We'll tell you when, we'll tell you where, but don't you dare to feel
despair.
Comply. Comply.
Never steal, never lie, don't ever feel, don't ever cry.
Comply. Comply.
If we wish to not be cruel, we must comply to every rule.'

The final line kept on a loop, the words hooking to me and echoing in my head. I rocked back and forth as I tried to block it out, but it proved to be little effect. The song wouldn't stop. It clasped onto my soul and dragged me to my front. I trembled, clawing forwards to escape. It weighed me down. The guilt. The fear. The desperate, uncontrollable urge to do just that. Comply.

As I clenched my eyes shut to fight the painful impulse, I felt a hand touch my shoulder. I shrieked as they turned me to my side, but as I darted my head back and forth, I fixed my gaze on Dr Olsen.

"Hey, hey, mate. It's alright." He spoke with his signature calm tone. "Look at me, mate. Look at me."

I jerked about as I noticed Jaiden to my left. "W-What? No! How? " I backed onto the now cushioned wall and returned my attention to my hands. They were clear, the aqua streams had snapped away.

"Noah?" Jaiden said softly as she crouched to my level. "Try and stay calm, okay? It's really important that you stay calm."

I scrambled away from them, the looks on their faces cast with panic and worry. "No. You're not real. It's not real."

They both stood up, edging in my direction with their hands held up.

"Noah," Dr Olsen began. "Listen, mate. You're not in danger, you're not in trouble, we just want to talk. Alright?"

My elbow buckled as I continued crawling back and collapsed on my side. I let out another cry as the two doctors rushed to me. They cradled me kindly as I whimpered.

"GO AWAY!" I yelled. "YOU'RE NOT REAL, GO AWAY!"

Jaiden stroked her hand across my forehead and held my arm. "Shh, Noah. Try to take a breath. Just listen to us. We're just gonna take you back to your old room."

"NO!" I writhed around more as I tried to pull away from their loose grasps.

Dr Olsen gripped at my collar and pulled me up, locking his eyes with mine. "Noah. Look at me."

I kept my eyes shut, tossing my head side to side as my tears splashed against the tiles. "No…"

"Noah," he repeated. "Look. At. Me."

Hesitantly, I lifted my eyelids to meet with the doctor. He smiled at me and held my hand in his.

"That's it mate. Breathe."

I took in a shattered inhale and trembled it back out as I collapsed onto his lap. "Wh… What h-happened?"

He kept me close as Jaiden joined us. "You had a break, Noah. In the midst of the transfer."

I gripped tightly at his coat. "What?"

"Last night. We sedated you and brought you back to Riptide."

I shuddered as I sat up, still wary of where I was. I placed my hand on the cushion that lined the edges of the Riptide halls then stared down at the other doctors who were edging the other patients away. I patted my hand across the floor rhythmically. It was just as it had always been. The wall – just as it should be. I swung back to face the doctors and reached for Dr Olsen's hand. He presented it willingly as I felt across his skin. I held it in distraught as more staff surrounded us.

"No… They… They attacked you… They… They broke your arm."

Dr Olsen shook his head. "No, I'm fine." He smiled. "Nobody's hurt me."

I raised my knees to my chest and buried my head. "Oh, God. Oh, God."

"Oh, Noah." He reached forwards and took me in his arms. "You're gonna be okay. It's gonna be okay."

I shook my head as my eyes became red and puffy. "No. I'm not."

He sighed and helped me to my feet. "Come on. Let's get you home."

I kept wrapped around him as we shuffled away from the crowd. I couldn't feel who I was. I was empty. With my final tear falling, I became void. I couldn't even feel why I was crying, or even comprehend any form of existence. Everything I had, stripped away.

Dr Olsen took his key card from his belt and scanned it against the reader. It beeped and the door to my old room slid up. We both stepped into the airlock, and I shuddered with the thought of… nothing. I didn't have a thought. I just shuddered. My grip on Olsen released and my arms hung loose at my sides, the doctor turning to me in concern.

"Noah? Are you okay?"

I opened my mouth to reply, but not a single word came out. Just a noise. A stifled noise. I felt across my neck as I gasped to speak, but once again. Silence. My voice had been taken. Just like my thoughts. I couldn't talk, I couldn't think, I could barely move. Then reflecting against the metal surroundings was the neon aqua glow. I stared at it, spotting the wrapping of the drug as it swerved through my body. Then as the door to my room slid up, the drug reached my eyes. The world enhanced around me, the sounds of pounding and escaping gas, the scent of frosty air, the vibrant appearance of the glass case opening.

There was a click in my ear as I felt the equipment get stripped from my body by a duo of doctors. I tilted my head slightly as they unhooked me and had me directed onto the thick concrete. I loosely batted my eyes and cleared my vision of the red and blue haze. Stood inches away from me was Caleb. He had his hands placed in a grey jacket that gripped is figure tightly. His hair was trimmed – the wavy locks that were once on top were now snipped into a short forward flick. He had an accomplished smirk on his face as I stared at him blankly.

"Noah James Coleman," he began. "I, Dr Caleb Hudson, am now your handler. I swear under the Criminal Compliance Act 2023 to care for you, control you, and order your every move. If you wish me to not be cruel, you must comply to every rule."